Mystic Prince

By

M. A. Richter

Dedication:

This book is dedicated to J. R. R. Tolkien, my inspiration for writing fantasy.

Also, to the luminaries of authorship whom I have personally met in my life thus far: R. Buckminster Fuller, Ray Bradbury and more recently, Steven Barnes and J. Michael Straczynski. It is also dedicated to those who have helped me and stood by me all these years in my writing: my son Alex, my partner Patricia, my friend Lenny, and my editor, Diane Davis-White.

Thank You All!

M. A.

1. Cambridge

"True enlightenment arises from self-mastery; thus, kinshuh (temperance) is the primary discipline of the Saiensu." ~ Foundations of the Mystic Order

Khael squinted impatiently toward the head of the motionless gate queue. His hopes for some relief after his strenuous journey so far, perhaps an extended break from the string of assassination attempts, dimmed. In all his travels, only once before had he needed to wait to enter Cambridge. He could have exercised royal privilege and skipped the line, but that implied publicly revealing himself, an action he deeply wanted to avoid.

Molniya, his gnu-horse hybrid steed, shifted under him, hoofing his own vexation on the stone roadway.

Khael reflected that gate guards needed nothing more than to inspect incoming travelers visually for signs of suspicious activity. They might converse with familiar travelers, but that process would be simple and reasonably quick. Suspects could be escorted to the guard shack for more detailed searches.

Unable to see any obvious cause for the delay, Khael closed his eyes to scan the life energies in the area. To his relief, he detected no assassins amongst the travelers on the road. He shifted his focus to the front of the queue. One of the City Patrol rangers at the gate blatantly groped a peasant woman, right beside her husband, while another ranger held out his hand for—a bribe?

Outraged, Khael stiffened out of his relaxed bearing. Had those guards no sense of decency? These people might be commoners, but even peasants deserved more respectful treatment. He prodded Molniya's flanks with his heels. The great gongyangma snorted as he walked around Grant on his gongyangma, Phantom, to pass the line of merchants, tradesmen and herders.

"We're jumping the queue?" Heidi's strawberry blonde head poked up from the other side of Phantom.

3

Mystic Prince

Khael looked at her. At his change in posture, Molniya stopped beside the two friends. Next to Molniya and Phantom, Heidi's full-sized charger resembled a large pony.

Khael strained to keep his fury quiet. "The Patrols extort fees from these travelers and grope the women going in."

"They never learn." Grant's cavernous bass rumble carried only a short distance.

Khael glared up at his best friend. Though Grant slouched down to minimize his bulk, he still towered over everyone in the queue. His dusty cloak and hood hid his polished armor, Legion surcote, and oversized weapons.

A year ago, Khael and Grant had exposed an extortion scheme by a few corrupt guards at the city's northern gate. Those guards had been convicted and imprisoned. These seemed destined for a similar dishonorable fate.

"I'm with you, but is this safe for you?" Heidi asked, her fierce voice quiet.

Khael pursed his lips. A decent question, typical of Heidi's leadership qualities. "I will attempt to remind them of their duties with minimal exposure. We will manage any consequences."

Molniya snorted and shook his unbridled head, eager for action. Khael patted his mane and nodded. Sensing this, the jet-black gongey whinnied and strutted down the center of the road. Grant and Heidi fell in close behind.

Khael noted people in the queue huddled away to the grassy edge of the broad stone highway, grumbling. No one wanted to tangle with the large, fearsome, horned riding beasts. On the other side of the wide road, a steady stream of traffic passed unhindered through the exit arch of the lofty city gates. Of course, no one leaving the city would be stopped, questioned, or harassed beyond a quick check for export permits. Unlike them, the shepherd couple held at the guard shack radiated palpable waves of helpless fear.

A dozen rangers in the black chainmail and crimson tunics of the City Patrol lounged around a wooden shack beside the looming entry arch. They pointedly ignored the abuse right under their noses. At

Khael's approach, two rangers armed with pikes marched out to block his path.

"Halt," the burlier, bearded guard said. "Wait your turn in queue, like everyone else."

Khael wanted to smack this red-shirt blow-hard and berate them all for their incompetence. Or was it ignorance? With minimal effort from extensive training and practice from his upbringing to inhibit such reactions, he adopted a diplomatic tone. "Perhaps you can explain why this queue barely moves at all."

The shorter one, a corporal, stepped forward. "Don't interfere, just get back in line." He brandished his pike much too close to Molniya's nose.

Before Khael could even blink, let alone warn the foolish guard, Molniya lowered his horns and batted the long, heavy weapon to the ground like a mere toothpick. The corporal staggered back in shock, shaking his stinging hands.

More of the Patrols near the shack jumped to the alert and advanced toward them, crossbows cocked and swords unsheathed. Half a dozen guards along the high white wall over the gate brought drawn bows to bear.

Khael squinted at the lethal arsenal bearing down on him. His neck prickled. If the guards ignored all their protocols, would they dare to shoot an unannounced noble in public? Families in the crowd hunkered together to protect their young. Had he endangered them all? Determined to pursue a rational approach and not get anyone injured, or killed, he spread out his empty hands. "I bear no weapons."

A paunchy, older sergeant, an arrogant curl on his lips, swaggered out of the guard shack, one hand firm on his sword hilt. He stopped between the burly guard and the corporal, who nervously retrieved his pike. "What's the problem here?"

Khael flattened his features to mild disdain. "These citizens wish to enter their kingdom's capital."

The sergeant sneered. "We'll process them as they're due. You can wait like everyone else."

5

"Wait for your men to collect bribes and fondle defenseless women? I recall no Cambridge law allowing such abuses for admittance." It came out calm and smooth, even more effective as an insult.

The sergeant bristled as if slapped. "Back off, stranger. We don't answer to you."

"Public servants must answer to everyone, especially their citizens."

Flushing bright red, the raging sergeant jabbed a finger toward Khael. "You're under arrest for disturbing the peace and interfering—"

"Unwise to threaten prince." Grant's voice rumbled like an angry swarm of bees.

Khael's insides constricted. *Fog!* So much for keeping his rank covert.

To his surprise, half the guards laughed. Two more with nocked arrows emerged from the shack, sniggering.

"Prince of what, the wild?" The sergeant harrumphed and waved his hand. "Enough of this dung. Get back in the queue. Or else."

Grant sat up tall and threw back his hood and cloak. Waves of anger rolled off his angry features. "Officer Granton Finnleigh, Royal Legion. You think we guard just anyone?"

The laughter faltered into nervous silence.

His shoulders down, the sergeant rubbed his chin. "We have a royal mandate. I command here, not you, or the Legion."

Grant tightened his grip on his sword.

Khael gestured for him to sit fast. "Easy, Grant." As high as he rode, he now presented a wide-open target for any nearby deep undercover assassins. *Time to end this.* He took a deep breath. "I am mystic Khael Stratton, Prince of Shielin."

That should settle the matter. As much as he despised the inherent inequities in their social caste system, there were occasional uses for it. All the arms would be lowered and the doers of misdeeds would apologize and rectify their behavior. Or so he hoped.

6

The sergeant stared, his eyes narrowing in doubt. None of the guards moved.

Khael stared back. For what were they waiting? Then he realized his travel-worn guise might have made him difficult to recognize though not hard enough to hamper any Chelevkori assassins' efforts to kill him. These guards might never have seen him outside the annual Carnival festivities, if then. Nor so disheveled as now. However, that failed to excuse their belligerence.

"Funny thing." The arrogant sergeant hooked his thumbs in his belt. "The last fraud who claimed to be the 'Prince o' Shielin' at least looked the part—neatly groomed, fancy dress; no peasant garb, scruffy beard or unkempt hair. I say you're no better."

Grant stiffened. "Legion escort? Rode gongey?" He stabbed a finger at the sergeant. "Show prince proper respect." His knuckles cracked as he clenched at his sword hilt.

From behind Khael came the crisp pops of Heidi's battle-axe harness snaps opening.

The sergeant narrowed his eyes and reached for his own sword.

"Stand down." Khael raised his hands. "All of you." Glaring at the sergeant, he fished into a deep pocket for his signet ring.

As if itching for action, the belligerent guards maintained their nervous aim on him. One twitchy hand and blood would spill.

Khael thrashed in his pocket. Where was it? His fingers resisted wearing the signet more than he realized. Every second he took to find it could turn fatal, and he had already lost too many friends. He knew the ring was somewhere in the pocket, but it seemed determined not to be found easily.

With fearful murmurs and mutterings, the crowd herded themselves clear of the conflict zone. Gongies and threatening weapons were more than most of these folks had come prepared to see. The shepherd couple clung together, their faces curious over this turn of events, uncomfortably close to the Patrols who had manhandled the woman.

At last, Khael located the familiar shape. He slipped the ring on and raised his fist.

All the Patrol rings vibrated in response. The bowmen preparing to fire shuddered and quickly lowered their heads and weapons. The sergeant dropped to one knee and saluted, his fist to his chest. A fair-sized sack on his belt jangled against his leg. His eyes bulged with dread.

"I crave pardon, Your Highness," he whined. "How may we help?"

"Show me your purported authorization."

The sergeant raised a shaking hand and waved toward the guards nearest the shack. One ducked inside for a moment and ran out bearing a parchment scroll.

"Here you are, Sire." Sweat beading on his brow, the sergeant stood to hand Khael the scroll.

Khael skimmed the document and snickered. "What a pathetic joke. 'King Ryan Cambridge VII?' My brother is the first king in Meridium's history." He rolled up the blatant forgery. "Who concocted this incompetent chicanery?"

The corporal's jaw dropped. "What?" His eyes flayed his wilting sergeant with angry accusation.

Khael wondered how he knew not already? A quick view revealed most of the guards' surprise. The pair who had abused the shepherd's wife exchanged a worried glance. They cast questioning expressions at the sergeant as if for guidance. Perhaps it was just those corrupt three. Much better than the whole platoon.

A surreptitious twitch from the sergeant caught Khael's peripheral vision. He closed his eyes to scan with his shikah discipline, as he had earlier. Every kih, every life-energy, within two hundred yards lit up in detailed, full-color images in his mind. The sergeant's guard ring still glowed from the royal signet's effects, but now he fingered another ring emanating a different energy pattern.

A fledgling teleportation field. Khael flexed his eikyo discipline to divert the growing effect. Several cobblestones around and under the sergeant's feet disappeared.

8

The sergeant stumbled and gaped in astounded disbelief. In his panic he tried again. Khael tweaked the ring's discharge to teleport itself off the man's finger.

The sergeant yelped.

His heart cold with rising wrath, Khael glowered at the craven fool. "How stupid do you think me?"

Trembling in fear, the hapless sergeant shook his ringless hand as if it burned. "What are you?"

"I am mystic." Khael took the self-reminder and inhaled deeply to withdraw from his righteous tempest and the wild fears around him. He chose a quiet, icy command pitch. "Show me what is in that weighty bag on your belt."

"Sire?" The sergeant's voice shrilled. He stood stiff from head to toe.

"Open. Your. Sack."

The sergeant's bravado deflated like a punctured bladder. He complied, his slow hands shaking. A small glittering fortune bulged inside the sack.

Khael raised his eyebrows in surprise. "You coerce bribes, maul the innocent, corrupt or bully your fellow City Patrols—such meritorious service to Cambridge, Sergeant."

The sack thumped heavily, upright, on the paving stones. The sergeant's jaw went slack, his shoulders slumped, his head low. "I beg pardon for my—our conduct, Your Highness."

"Denied." Khael had no intention of excusing these wretched knaves so easily. Between the criminal activity and their astonishing disrespect for the incoming travelers, he felt no need for mercy here. He raked his piercing gaze over the guards, stopping with the corporal. "You are senior?"

The corporal bowed his head as his fist thudded to his chest. "Corporal Randolph, Sire."

"You cooperated with this thuggery?"

Randolph stepped closer, with his voice hushed. "He's not alone, Your Highness. We've been afraid to act. He has powerful friends."

"So do I." Khael entertained a brief notion to reprimand him but dismissed the idea. "Take charge of this post, Corporal. Arrest your sergeant." He pointed at the men who had taken liberties with the shepherd woman. "And those two as well."

"Yes, Sire." Randolph sounded happy enough to cooperate.

"File a full report with the Patrol on all you know. Be sure to include this one's 'powerful friends,' and the entire gate registry. Henceforth, you shall arrest no one for disturbing the peace without genuine due cause. Give Officer Finnleigh that money bag. He will apprise the Legion. I will inform the king by nightfall."

Randolph puffed up his chest. "By your command, Sire." He turned and pointed. "Arrest those two." Then he set his pike to the sergeant's belly. "You're under arrest, too."

His burly cohort disarmed and manacled their disgraced superior. Randolph picked up the bag as the other Patrol rangers turned their weapons on the two abusers. The cornered pair darted recreant glances around at their fellow guards and the angry crowd.

"What do we do now?" one whispered to the other.

Khael held his breath. Despite his mystic training and his concern about the Chelevkori, he itched for a new challenge. Those two might fight back despite the odds or try to use the shepherds as hostages. Potential exercise for some of his less-frequently used disciplines... provided no one else got hurt.

The two guards exchanged a defeated look. They laid their weapons down and surrendered. Torn between disappointment at the lost opportunity and relief from the swift, peaceful resolution, Khael opted for the latter.

Randolph turned the money bag over to Grant and saluted.

With a low whistle, Heidi re-harnessed her battle-axe. "I wonder what the Collectic knows about this kind of competition from these crooked City Patrols. They might not take it well."

The corporal's men shoved the white-faced sergeant and his two cohorts toward the guard shack.

Khael exhaled. *Fog.* Not that he cared what might happen to the

10

corrupt brutes. They would receive their due soon enough. However, by the time Khael and his friends entered the city, the Collectic would have heard everything, if distorted. Rumors would abound wildly after such happenings, as usual. He might as well wear a target and invite the Chelevkori to take free shots.

Relief? Not today.

2. Thieving Collector

Khael turned to Grant. "You secured the money?"

Grant held up the seized bag of bribes and stowed it in one of Phantom's saddlebags. "May we enter now, Your Highness?"

Khael scowled at his best friend's sarcasm. He had already blurted out the words to spur the encounter with the guards. "We may let these people through." He nudged Molniya toward the side of the road. Safer to wait out the queue.

The crowd burst into cheers. Grant and Heidi followed Khael.

"I'm pleased to count among your friends, Kyle." Heidi beamed at him.

Khael relaxed his face. "The honor is mine."

Inside, he grimaced, neither at her comment nor how she mispronounced his name—even Grant did that. The failure of his plea as an ordinary citizen for Patrol integrity and the blatant forgery irritated him. What so tempted those three men into such criminal behavior? Power? Money? Influence? Every person merited equal treatment under the law, regardless of social position. He had been compelled to pull rank on these guards, which burned at him. Time to push the king for deeper changes. Past time.

Once he delivered Ryan his report, Khael anticipated three serene weeks of study at his favorite kyoshitsu to learn his next discipline, then three more weeks to work the school-farm or assist other mystic students there. Much more satisfying prospects. His breath came easier at the thought.

With the corrupt guards out of the way, the queue rapidly proceeded through the enormous gate. After a few minutes, Khael and his friends merged into the dwindling procession entering the city. Their passage through the fortified wall tunnel reverberated from the loud clacks of gongey hooves and horseshoes. These massive walls had withstood the last Chelevkori attack on the city almost a thousand years ago. His ears rang when they emerged from the racket into the heady tang of street dung.

Many merchant and collector stalls occupied the busy avenue, a motley bazaar of open tents, vending carts, lean-tos and other makeshift sale-shelters. Children playing around the stalls gave all the riders waves and smiles as they rode in. The towering spires of Cambridge College, and beyond them Sorcery Row, stood tall over the mist ahead, high above the market district and many less fanciful houses in between.

Heavy foot traffic near the gate made riding awkward. For any speed, they would have to bully the pedestrians. Khael had no stomach for that. He signaled to dismount and dropped to the street beside Molniya.

They walked through the bustle to a corner of the first major intersection. Pedestrians and carts shuffled past them in an uneven stream. A potpourri of smells from the market stalls surrounding them, some even pleasant, swirled around as the friends paused.

Heidi and Grant had been walking hand in hand. When they stopped, they indulged in a fierce hug. Her bright gray eyes matched the leather armor under her brown travel cloak. Just sixteen palms tall, she had proven to be a promising leader during their journey.

At this refreshing sign of normality, Khael smiled and scratched his beard. They seemed well suited for each other. "You can get drinks at the Bar-Jay." He stuffed his ring into a vest pocket, hoping not to need it until they arrived at the castle. "I will shave off this scruff in my suite, then join you in the pub."

"Mm, best ale in Cambridge." A grin split Grant's beard.

"Best dining room, too." Heidi still clutched her arms around her huge knight.

The image reminded Khael of a bear cub with its mother—for a moment. He smirked. Bear was close enough, but anyone who mistook her for a cub would sorely regret it, and Grant was no mother.

Grant's big hands caressed Heidi's shoulders. "You need a woman, Kyle."

Khael shook his head. The profound spiritual path of the Saiensu

13

required conscious, rigorous focus. The path's next two disciplines were crucial to his development. Any other pursuits could wait. His anger got in his way, and he had expressed too much of that already. "Time to move on."

As they prepared to remount, a small boy burst through the passing crowd. He crashed off Grant's armored knee to the pavement, stunned. Right behind the boy, a larger, hooded figure stumbled headlong into Khael, scrabbling at his clothes as if to avoid falling.

"Hey, kid, watch it." Grant knelt to the fallen boy. "You all right?"

"Whoa." Khael caught a pair of thin, bony shoulders on the falling hooded one.

A husky, child-like voice emerged from his captive. "Pardon me, sir."

"You must exercise greater care with your trajectory, friend."

"I was chasing my little brother."

The frivolous lie triggered one of Khael's deepest peeves. He tightened his grip as his captive twisted to break free. "There is no need to fear the truth. Name yourself."

A pair of round eyes peered up at him from a dirty, girlish face. Her eyes were two swirls of the most incredible kaleidoscopic green. The ragged hood fell back to expose a tangled fiery mop. What a combination! His pulse raced, caught in a new fire. He had never felt so entranced by anyone.

"I have to get home."

This second lie shattered the moment and annoyed Khael. "Save your false innocence, lass. Who are you?"

Her face contorted into a grimace of excruciating pain.

Had he hurt her? That was not part of the plan, nor by his intent. He loosened his grip and projected a telepathic command. *Tell me your name.*

She screamed, as if his thought had exploded in her mind. As she fought to escape, he seized the collar of her dress. Her frantic struggle ripped the flimsy garment from neck to hem.

14

"Pervert!" She scrambled to wrap her ragged cloak around her exposed scrawny nudity. "It's freezing and I'm underage. Let me go!"

Though thin, hers was no child's body, and her kih easily revealed her age of seventeen. Khael scowled at her blatant dishonesty.

"Ah, there you are." A new, cool male voice beside him broke into his concentration.

Khael glanced at the interruption, a City Patrol ranger on foot.

The girl tore out of his hands and launched into the passing throng, headed in the direction of the Enclave, the walled district of the Collectic.

Khael started to raise a hand to stop her, but a tiny impulse held him back. While they might catch her along the way, even unregistered collectors could gain sanctuary there. Yet another detour would waste too much time, and the king awaited him.

Fine. No harm letting this liar go. He faced the man in red.

"I wanted to thank you, Sire, for turning in those bullies at the gate," the Patrolman said. "No one else has dared to interfere." He paused. "Did that troublesome girl bother you?"

Khael shook his head as he patted his pockets. The one that should not have been empty was. Impossible. He froze. *My ring.* "Fog!"

"She steal something?"

Khael's mind raced, but this time discretion overrode all other concerns. "Never mind. I will handle this. Thank you."

"By your command, Sire." The Patrolman saluted and sauntered on his way.

Khael hauled himself back up onto Molniya for a better view. Where was that sly minx?

There, already more than two score yards off. Talented, fast, and most desperate. She hurtled away, plunging through the traffic, struggling to keep her clothes together against the wintry chill.

Wait. But his last command had failed. He groaned. Would this one work any better?

She turned to look back at him.

Oh, she does respo—

The blazing image of her kih erupted into his open eyes. Vivid colors seared his mind, a shimmering collage of exquisite life-energy patterns. Her unrealized capabilities glowed exciting promise far beyond her wildly disparate youthful abilities, alongside her already exceptional talents. Filled with extreme grace and lithe fire, she shone with blazing spirit and intelligence. Interwoven with unresolved pain and severe hunger lurked obscure torments he did not recognize. Above all, she was terrified of him.

Khael's heart pounded a new ache in his chest, bursting with compassion, drawn to her in a way that mystified him.

Her glorious kih muted the rest of the world, as if a dense mist had set in. People, animals, everything in sight, blurred. Normally he closed his eyes to use shikah, but they were wide open. Normally he saw all kih within range, but hers was the only kih visible, the only image in focus. His palms sweated, his whole body hot, stifling.

The vision dissolved when he blinked. The lass methodically barreled her panic-stricken way through the haphazard market swirl.

What to do? *Return my ring and tell no one else of it.*

Her mind faded out of range. His racing heart slowed and sank in despair. How would she comply without knowing when, or where he would be? A sudden chill made him shiver. *Fog.*

An unintelligible rumble from Grant nudged at his dulled awareness.

"Hmm?"

"Took what?" Still in a squat, the child firmly in his grip, Grant glared at a few lingering onlookers, who scurried away.

"My ring."

"Fog." Grant squinted up at him, amazed. "Don't we stop her?"

The fire in Khael's brain finally cooled. If his command failed, the ring had its own subtle influence. That should prevail. Doubt gnawed his stomach. Mystics did not often use 'should.' The ring had returned to him before. He shook his head.

16

"This kid?" Grant pushed the boy forward. "Stole nothing from me."

Khael lowered a warm gaze at the cowering boy. "How know you this girl, child?"

"I d-d-don't, g-great s-sir." The boy's whole being screamed fear.

Underneath his terror Khael read complete, innocent ignorance of the entire setup. "Let him go."

"Say nothing of this, boy." Grant watched as the boy ran off. "How'd she get your—uh, it?"

"She picked my pocket." Whoa. Khael caught his breath. How did she accomplish that? Scores had tried, but he had foiled them all, even master-class pickpockets.

"You let her? You'll need that—back, especially with impostors around."

"You believed that bloated miscreant?" Heidi muttered.

"That much he spoke true." Khael shook his spinning head. "This thief piques my curiosity."

"Curiosity?" Grant stared at him in disbelief and muttered, "That'll get us killed."

"Your confidence underwhelms me. I commanded her to return it, though my focus slipped."

Heidi raised her eyebrows in shock. "Your focus slipped? You? I don't believe it."

Khael finally relaxed his stiff bearing and chuckled. "Even mystics are still human."

"You could've followed her kih." Grant planted his arms akimbo. "What'd your thief look like?"

'My' thief? An intriguing possibility. "Extraordinary, for a starving street urchin."

"How, exactly, does a starving street urchin look extraordinary?" Heidi frowned at him.

Khael fought to recall the thief's physical appearance through the glowing image of her kih. "Tangled red hair, dirty face, and large, fascinating green eyes." His gaze wandered aimlessly through the milling crowd. Such a clever, spirited lass might be worth tracking down, when he had the time. Not just for his signet—anyone with such skilled talents and the potential her kih suggested he wanted on his side. At his side. "We must go."

Grant and Heidi mounted their steeds amid the thinning crowd. Khael led them north toward the Bar-Jay at the city's center, away from the Enclave.

"That's a pretty vague description." Heidi sounded baffled. "How would she look to me?"

Khael peered at Heidi. "About a palm taller. Gaunt, much thinner than you." Too thin.

Grant cleared his throat. "Still thirsty."

"Yes, and I must shave. Then we visit Castle Cambridge to complete our mission."

"What about your thief?" Heidi wondered.

Khael raised and lowered his eyebrows. *Indeed. What about 'my' thief?*

3. Castle Cambridge

The polished, blue-veined marble walls of the castle came into view as Molniya sped Khael down the boulevard. Grant rode with him, though Heidi had turned aside to go home a mile ago. The men slowed to duck through the entry arch of the outer keep, each huddled against his gongey's neck under the gate's threatening portcullises.

They left the gongies at the spacious royal stable and walked across a neatly groomed grass courtyard bordered with a lush flower collection of pansies, roses, orchids, daffodils and more. Two mailed, bored-looking rangers with royal blue Castle Guard tunics took up defensive postures inside a locked, iron-picket fence.

"Your turn, Bethany." The man with chevrons on his sleeves backed away to observe, a hand on his sword hilt.

Bethany stood at ease behind the bars. "This gate is restricted."

When Grant took a moment to look her over, Khael raised an eyebrow. True, her fair face complemented a nice enough figure with distinct feminine curves. Unlike the ring thief, this woman's kih did not blast out to obscure his sight. He withheld comment.

"Officer Granton Finnleigh. This's His Royal Highness, Prince of Shielin."

Bethany peered up at the giant knight. "Identification, sir?"

"You kidding? No other Legionnaires my size."

"Rules, sir."

Khael tightened his lips. His ring would have eliminated that need. Shaving had not helped. Clearly she did not recognize him. He might be able to duplicate the signet's effect, but how?

Grant grumbled as he dug into his belt pouch for his Legion ring. He slipped it on and showed Bethany. "That do?"

"Thank you, sir. My lord?"

"By the king's order, Grant is my bodyguard." Khael shrugged. "I have no other identification." Under normal circumstances, that would have been enough. What had made the security so tight? Was Ryan just being paranoid or... ah, the impostor must have been here.

"Grant." The sergeant came forward. "Didn't recognize you with all that hair. We have recruits from western Metacresta, about your size and, well, similar grooming."

Grant's face brightened. "Alden. Sergeant now, huh? Nice work."

"Thanks. Welcome back." Alden smiled. "Your Highness is welcome here."

Bethany waved back toward the house door. The heavy steel house grate glided up as guards inside wound the lift mechanism.

"Thank you." Khael smiled at their pleasant attitude. "I appreciate your courtesy."

He preceded Grant through brightly lit corridors to the throne room. Its thick oaken double doors hung open. Dozens of staffers hurried about, setting up tables and chairs for a banquet in the enormous chamber. A uniformed knight on either side of the doorway saluted as the pair passed inside.

"Fine looking woman back there," Grant muttered as they threaded their way between tables toward a throne in the center of the rear wall. "Well developed, not scrawny, or thief."

Khael buried his amusement behind a curious expression. "As I recall, Heidi may not appreciate your roving eyes."

"For you, not me. You're single."

"Not seeking a mate." Not before the next two disciplines; after that, perhaps.

They made their way past a number of guards to the hall behind the throne room. On the far side, two more knights guarded a pair of tall, arched doors.

Khael nodded back to their salutes. "Please inform King Ryan that his brother, the Prince of Shielin, requests an audience."

"Go right in, Sire."

Before Khael touched the doorknob, a chill from his chokkan discipline scrambled up his spine. Something inside the office posed a deadly threat to him. He closed his eyes to scan as he opened the door. "You need no weapons with me, Ryan."

As he entered the office, the door slammed. An armor-plated arm pushed him back toward the wall, a dagger rising toward his throat.

Khael swept one hand up to intercept the dagger. His other, open palm, thrust a lethal force blow to Ryan's armored chest.

Disarmed, Ryan staggered two full yards back. He righted himself to charge again.

Khael shut his eyes and levitated his brother enough to deprive him of any footing. He blew out his upset in a slow exhale. "I have thwarted five attempted assassinations since I left Al-myna-alghrby. I expect better treatment from my own family."

"Put me down." Ryan labored to catch his breath. "Five? I only knew of three."

Khael let the king down gently and held the dagger out, hilt first. "May I suggest less violence?"

Ryan retrieved his weapon, sheathed it and raised his voice. "Come in."

Khael stepped aside as Grant walked in, his eyes sweeping the large office. The guards followed, their swords drawn.

"Put up your weapons. Lieutenant, you two may remain outside." Ryan pulled off a gauntlet, his keen brown eyes watching his guests.

"Majesty?" The lieutenant's voice rose in surprise.

"I hereby rescind the security alert. Resume the normal guard and pass the word, especially to all the city gates. Henceforth, no one is to be admitted without proper identification."

The guard saluted stiffly. "By your command, Sire." He and his partner left, closing the door.

Ryan walked the few yards to a splendid, dark wood desk and lowered himself into its well-padded chair. Khael hung his cloak on a fancy stand by the door and introduced Grant.

"Your Majesty." Grant bowed his head, his fist over his heart.

"Officer Finnleigh. I hear you are ready for certification.

Examiners await you at the Legion office. That will give Kyle and me some time alone."

"By your command." Grant gave Khael a startled glance.

Khael nodded his approval, amused at his friend's response. After Grant left, Ryan let out a deep breath. He set his gauntlets on the desk.

"You are fully armed and armored, in chronicon no less, yet alone you attacked an unarmed visitor?" Khael retrieved four scrolls from a cloak pocket and headed for the desk. "You used to be more casual."

"Nice to see you too, brother. I hear you took out a small Chelevkori army, purged another gate crew, manhandled an under-age minx on the street, and blew up your penthouse on your way here."

Khael raised his eyebrows in curiosity. "I found explosives in my bedroom carpet when I went up to shave. I sent the blast up the chimney. Barek's manager will clean up the charred furniture. And that minx might well be the best pickpocket alive. She stole my signet ring."

Ryan's eyebrows shot up in surprise. "What happened to all your vaunted mystic powers?"

Khael snickered. As if mystics had any such thing... "Mystics hold no such airs."

"How foolish of me. You'd better hope it comes back like they're supposed to."

"Here are your treaties and a poorly forged royal mandate." Khael dropped the scrolls on the desk and sank into a luxurious, high-backed velvet chair facing his brother.

"Thanks." Ryan glanced at the forgery. "Sloppy work. I'm disappointed it fooled anyone." He tossed it back on the desk and scanned the treaties. "What's all this added scribble?"

"I changed the crown's inspection interval to five years. The cities perform annual local inspections and file written reports to the crown. If the five-year inspections fail or the reports are insufficient, the crown sends its inspectors to train a new local team at the city's cost."

"Capital idea—that'll save us a fortune. Why didn't I think of that?" Ryan dropped his gauntlets chiming into a large, velvet-lined bin beside the desk. "Thanks for your clean-up at the gate by the way. Brandy did one about five months ago. I don't like how that kind of thuggery keeps happening."

Khael narrowed his eyes. If that had involved the royal mage, he might be able to impress the need for social change on Ryan. "It seems some people think their rank entitles them to dominate those who lack one. Our society's class-structures frequently cause such problems."

"I sympathize, but not too much. It's been this way for centuries. What can I do?"

"You changed your title from High Prince to King last year, Your Majesty."

Ryan raised his hands in a hopeless gesture before he continued to remove his armor. "We need a hierarchy or society breaks down into chaos. Look at what's happening out east."

What? Khael frowned, baffled. "I just returned from the east coast, at your behest."

"I sent you to the southern cities. While you were there, the elected Mayor of Findumonde, up north, declared himself *'Empereur de la Normande.'* He now has troops all along the borders. My mage says his mage is not cooperating with either side because those two are rivals over the leadership of the Sorcery."

"This happens when money, rank and class are treated as ends in and of themselves. The guilds already hold tremendous influence. Yet the so-called lower classes are treated as burdens rather than as valued workers, the providers who help us all survive."

Ryan frowned. "The guilds make sense to me, and our family exemplifies the benefits of royal governance. Has for centuries."

Khael's heart sank. It would take more time than he had now to convince his brother.

Ryan stood and paced. "I think I know who's behind the problems with the gate guards. The same people allowed an assassin posing as you to see me about a week ago."

"You appear unhurt. What happened to the impostor?"

"Fatal drop, over the patio cliff into the gulf. I kept his demise quiet in an effort to flush out his supporters. I told the guards to let in anyone who looks like you. I wanted to judge potential impostors for myself. With the castle's anti-sorcery wards, I reckoned I could handle any would be assassins myself and be safe enough with the real you."

"A drop?"

"I threw him out."

Khael's stomach tightened. Three weeks ago, he had accidentally killed a Chelevkori deacon, in self-defense. He had vowed to himself then never to repeat that violence if any peaceful alternative could be found. There had to be better ways to resolve conflicts.

Ryan unstrapped his cuirass and dropped it into the bin with a jingling crash.

"Is that comfortable?"

"Not enough. Chronicon armor's light, though, and protects me better than steel. Otherwise, your defense might have crushed my ribs."

"Forgive me."

"I should know better." Ryan shrugged. "I'll live. Just do not do that again. You'll be in town for the Carnival?"

"I need to go home to Skemmelsham."

"Fine. Be back in two months. I'm holding a conference the four days before the Carnival to institute some changes in the alliance accords." Free of his armor, Ryan stretched from side to side. "Let's continue this upstairs in my chambers."

"I have urgent business elsewhere." Khael remained seated.

Ryan glared at him. "At the Bar-Jay?" He leaned forward, his hands on the desk. "You like Barek Jayne's pub better than this magnificent family castle?"

"Barek brews the best ale in Cambridge, or anywhere I have been. Also, he told me disturbing rumors about my home, and he has an idea to accelerate my next study."

Ryan set his elbows on the desk, his hands steepled before his mouth. "You let too many things distract you from your royal duties."

Khael dipped his head. "The Saiensu is my primary focus in life. I accepted your errand to enhance my disciplines."

"Your independent mind gets you into trouble. You have too much of your grandfather in you."

Khael smirked. "He would say not enough."

"He would." Ryan rolled his eyes to the ceiling. "He has always been difficult."

"What in the accords needs to change?"

"The eastern slave trade must stop."

Khael raised his eyebrows in pleasant astonishment. "You have my full support. Of course, you know the slavers will never allow the east coast mayors to agree. They grew rich from the legal trade, and this new emperor likely as well."

"Regardless of both of those factors, slavery's my biggest issue in the accords. I'm devising incentives to gain their cooperation."

Khael rubbed his chin. "You could declare modifications by royal fiat, though I prefer your proposed approach."

Ryan shook his head. "Our ancestors incited wars with their fiats. Consensus will make enforcement much easier, so we must negotiate the difficult points."

"People respond favorably when they are involved in such decisions."

"Still pushing that agenda?" Ryan sighed. "I've missed you, brother. You make the best company and conversation, and you don't just kowtow to whatever I say."

"Thank you." The royal compliment warmed Khael's heart.

Ryan reached for a pot of tea on the settee behind him as they chatted. They covered local politics and more personal family issues. He still worked to teach their younger brothers how to govern their own states. Their sister had taken a shine to Brandy and was training with her to become a sorceress like her, rather than a governing princess.

"Have you tried to delegate out responsibilities to lighten your load?"

"That doesn't seem to be working out in Skemmelsham for you."

Khael nodded. "Fair point. Have you any information about that? All Barek knew was that my viceroy has become a despot, possibly from Chelevkori interference."

"I received the same message, and that Skemmelsham is closed. There was a riot two months ago and no news since."

"Fog." A cold lump settled in Khael's chest. "Is my mother all right?"

"I haven't heard. Your grandfather would surely act if she were in peril." Ryan pursed his lips. "Still, if I don't get more and better reports soon, I may send a legion of the cavalry up there to sort things out, or take them myself."

Khael stiffened. Ryan's responses tended more toward aggressive than diplomatic. "Let us pray I have enough time for my business here and to rectify the situation there before you resort to that."

"I'll give you until the Carnival to straighten it out."

"Eight weeks?" Barely enough time for any action at all. Khael stood up, determined to leave. "With your permission, I must go."

"With my permission?" Ryan snorted. He strode around his desk and stood nose to nose with Khael, a thumb taller and broader in the shoulders. "I am burdened with rule of half the known world, but you think you're hard done by. You were the lucky one, raised outside this marble prison by your mother's father, the wisest man in the world. I only had our father and his parade of sycophants."

Khael stepped back to avoid a similar response. "Self-pity from the king? Life is only as hard as we make it."

"Pithy as ever. At least the Chelevkori are focused on the Stratton side of the family."

"My impostor most likely was a Chelevkori minister." Khael frowned. "Perhaps the incident was intended to goad you into a lethal confrontation with me."

Ryan snapped his head back in shock. "I hadn't thought of that. Still, it was only one incident. They've been after your grandfather forever, and you for how many months?"

26

"Like all challenges, theirs only serve to strengthen me." Providing they failed to kill him... Khael held out his arms.

Ryan moved forward and the brothers embraced. They walked together to the door. Khael collected his cloak.

"When Finnleigh passes the Legion evaluation, he'll be commissioned." Ryan squinted into an expression of deep thought. "I'll have to assign him something more suitable for an Ensign of the Royal Legion than mere bodyguard."

Khael froze, horrified at the idea. He seized Ryan's arm. "You jest."

"Me? Jest?" Ryan put on an innocent face.

Khael relaxed with an audible exhale. "Grant is my best friend. I want him with me."

Ryan chuckled. "I did promise he would not be assigned away from you unless one of you so requested." He pointed a finger at Khael. "But I had you for a moment."

They reached the door and Ryan opened it.

Khael clasped his wrist. "I will return."

"Bring your ring."

Khael nodded and headed down the passageway.

Behind him, Ryan told the guards, "Locate Brandy and ask her to join me here. And stand at ease unless there's danger, for fog's sake."

Khael's mother and city remained in danger. Would his attempt to learn zarute, the next mystic discipline, not be better done after he went north? His intuition shivered intense resistance up his spine—somehow, he needed zarute to regain his throne. Barek's idea to shorten that study had better work, or Khael risked losing his mother, his throne, and his city—maybe even his life.

Khael looked around outside the keep. Grant fairly danced his exuberance across the courtyard. He must have enjoyed his new commission. *When might I be so happy?*

27

4. Extraordinary

Saturday evenings at the Bar-Jay had always struck Khael as too lively and raucous for pleasant conversation. Not so much for discreet encounters. Once an L-shaped stable, Barek had converted the enormous building into a well-stocked taproom, restaurant and sleeping quarters for himself upstairs.

From Khael's favorite small table, the stage area at the far end of the bar's long leg looked dark. This might turn out to be a peaceful evening, without the usual suggestive dancers, raunchy singers, and rowdy audience.

Khael slumped back in his chair. He never thought he would miss such frivolities. Barek's idea had succeeded flawlessly. Only two short weeks since he left, not the three he expected, and he had realized his new discipline. On this overnight break, he wanted a drink, a plan to reclaim his throne, and his ring.

A twinge shot through his heart. Would his ring thief reappear tonight? The dazzling image of her kih leapt into his mind, clear as the first time. Her life-energies wove a vibrant tapestry so appealing he smiled, enjoying the beautiful memory. What a find she might turn out to be, if...

A loud slam heralded Grant's arrival through the doors nearest the stage. His eyes glinted under the cavernous bar's evening gas lights as his gaze swept the room.

Khael nodded a disapproving frown to greet his noisy friend.

Grant casually sauntered across the pub. When he glared at the patrons who stared at him, they quickly lost interest. In this bar, such uninvited, prolonged attention could easily escalate to broken body parts. One did not rile such a giant of a man without risk.

Grant folded his coat onto the chair facing Khael, sat next to him and waved imperiously for service. A barmaid hurried over to take his order. When she turned to go, Grant reached out to speed her with a slap on the rump. Khael caught his eye and Grant dropped his hand.

Khael blinked away his judgmental comment. "Fair evening, my friend. Subtle entrance."

"Eh." Grant shrugged. "Didn't mean it that way. Hit doors too hard."

"I noticed. Nice outfit, not your usual style."

Grant nodded. "Heidi likes it." Instead of his armor and uniform, he wore a casual green jersey and heavy tan trousers over brown boots. He passed well as an oversized commoner, not a legionnaire.

"Enlighten me."

"Thought you went to kyoshitsu for enlightenment."

Khael snickered. "You know perfectly well to whom I refer."

"Oh, her." Grant kept a straight face under his beard. "Who or where she is, no one wants to say. I convinced one reluctant bigmouth to spill. Paid him few pence, after threat about my ax, and his skull. Wasn't going to hurt him, but I didn't say."

Khael swallowed the itch to chide his ferocious friend. "And?"

"Most likely girl is novice collector, less than a year's experience. Works transients' slums around here. No name, but nasty, violent reputation. If she has your ring, she'd be crazy to keep it, or sell it. No sane fence will touch one of those."

The barmaid returned with their drinks. She set down a full pitcher of Barek's best house ale and two pint-sized steins filled with the heady, amber liquid. Grant paid her and she sashayed away.

"Few collectors steal anything that seeks out its rightful owner. I want to meet her. No one else has ever successfully stolen from me." Khael raised his stein for a deep swig.

Grant took a quick draught and smacked his mug on the table, sloshing foam over the rim. "Thought she piqued your curiosity."

Surprised, Khael almost choked on his mouthful. "Yes, that too."

"What if she threw it away? May not know what she got. Makes it harder to locate." Grant drained his pint.

"She knew exactly where it was. Must have been watching us when we stopped." Khael shook his head. "Collectors never willingly give up anything made of gold. I commanded her to return it. By now she must burn to do so." *If it worked...*

"Hasn't surfaced all fortnight. Our collector friends had nothing on her, though Zorn thought he saw her race past him into Enclave."

Gingerly, Khael took another swallow of his ale, not sure if his command had any effect at all. The thief seemed too well able to resist him.

Grant raised his napkin to the froth in his whiskers and widened his eyes. He sat bolt upright and his eyebrows shot up in astonishment.

Khael followed his friend's surprised gaze. Inside the nearest entry's double doors stood his thief. Her ragged cloak masked her gaunt figure. She wore the same shabby dress he had torn, over another tatty garment. Much like a hunted animal, she threw quick, furtive looks around the bar.

Her kih flared into Khael's open eyes, as if beckoning to him. Several paralyzed seconds later, he gasped a sharp intake of air. His heart restarted in thudding slow motion. He took still longer to re-assert his self-control with kinshuh, an action that should have been instantaneous. Under its influence, his heart and breath returned to their normal rhythm, but his focus stuck on her kih.

The image shivered, probably from the bitter chill outside. When her skittering glances reached Khael, her kih rippled with fright. The energy flow through her torso faded as her pulse and breath both stopped. A new, intense heat flared up through her abdomen to stop at the fear in her heart. For a moment, her kih churned, as if she battled a powerful urge to fly across the room to him. Her dread expanded to smother both that impulse and the flare.

She gasped and her belly heaved. Her face blazed as she lurched back against the wall.

Would she flee out the door to avoid him? Khael held his breath. No, she drew herself upright and clenched her fists. The ring in her pocket tugged in his direction. He exhaled in relief and waved her over. She stiffened for a moment, then stalked gracefully to their table. With her back perfectly straight, she made a tiny curtsy.

"I may owe you an apology, kind sir."

Her low, silken-honey voice sent a thrill up Khael's spine. His self-control wavered. Having her around might prove more trouble than she would be worth. A flash shot through her kih, not overriding terror, but something... different. Annoyed at his weakness and his fixation on her kih, he flexed his kinshuh. The dazzling image faded into a thin, pretty, quite dirty lass.

"What you owe me is what you stole from me a fortnight ago. Return it."

His words sparked a shiver throughout her torso. Those magnificent green eyes bored into his with a new intensity. She assumed a curious expression of smug superiority, as if she had put one over on him, yet she seemed terrified that she had. Her whole body vibrated with such excess strain he thought she might break from the exertion.

"I might." As she spoke, her jaw barely moved. Her eyes narrowed with annoyance. "What're you gawking at, muscles?" She did not even look at Grant, but she had clearly aimed her words at the hulking knight.

Grant growled like a hungry bear. Khael shot a quick glance at him. His sleeve quivered while he gripped and released the hilt of his dagger, frowning at her.

"Peace, both of you." Khael studied her closely, like a myopic bookkeeper.

She shivered under his scrutiny. Her wild mix of heat, terror, and smug bravado confused him.

The barmaid strolled by to check on their drinks, looked the lass over and sniffed, her nose wrinkled in distaste. The thief rolled her eyes. Grant waved off the barmaid.

"Maybe I have this item, and maybe I don't. What's it worth to you?"

Amused, Khael tilted his head. "You wish to bargain?"

"Whatever it takes to stay out of jail." She flicked a glance at Grant. "A reward for the return, if I have it, which I might not, would be nice."

Grant growled his anger. "Reward?"

The thief jerked her head to stare him down.

Khael raised his hand toward Grant. "Relax, my friend." He kicked the chair beside him back from the table. Despite Grant's appalled grimace, Khael waved to the chair. "Have a seat, lass."

She hesitated, surprise on her face. From her expression. Khael pictured the thoughts whirling around in her head. Could she trust him? Would he punish her, or let the muscle man do it? The heavy table and chair could trap her. How would she escape if she sat in that prison?

He tweaked his lip corners into a quiet smile. "Join us for a drink."

Her shoulders relaxed a fraction. She slid into the offered chair with exceptional feline grace, but she did not move closer to the table. With a deep breath, she sat ramrod straight and glanced at the pitcher. "I could use one."

Khael waved for the barmaid, who skittered over as if she had been desperate for the chance. He made his request. Moments later she returned with another stein. The thief kept her eyes fixed on Khael. After thanking the barmaid in dismissal, he poured his guest half a steinful.

She drained the mug in a single draught, staring at him.

"My property?" Khael held his voice low and nonthreatening, intent to keep her present.

"What do I get out of it?" She burrowed one hand under a fold in her clothes and squinted briefly at both men. With a few quick glances, she scanned the near-empty taproom.

"What'd you have in mind, girl?" Grant glared at her, but his focus followed her hand.

She threw Grant a brief glimpse of utter disdain.

Khael studied her while her eyes flicked between him and Grant. She drummed her fingers on the table. Her long, rough nails clicked on the polished hardwood. A pang of empathy for her plight touched Khael's heart.

"I am mystic Khael Stratton. Most people call me Kyle. This is my friend, Grant."

A shadow flashed across her face as he spoke. Did she react to his name or something about mystics? She blinked and her eyes cleared. His quiet voice and lack of accusation produced the desired effect— she sat back in her chair in a less edgy posture.

"Tell us your name and where you are from."

"I'm Diana Merack from up north near the coast."

Normally, lies upset him, but she delivered hers so smoothly. Khael tried not to smile and failed. "Impressive, but that is not your name."

Under the grime, her skin paled. "How do you...?"

Tell me only the truth! An uneasy chill settled over him. He had intended the statement as a simple warning. Instead, it came out in a telepathic command.

She stiffened. Her hand rose to the base of her skull. From the shock on her face, she realized his words did not come through her ears. Renewed misgiving widened her eyes as she looked around in vain for a potential escape route.

A word stole into his mind. *Vixen.*

Khael froze his face rigid to mask his shock. He had not read her thoughts, at least not on purpose. That would have constituted an attack, a gross invasion of her private thoughts. Still, Vixen was not her real name, though it fit her well enough. The compulsion to know her better raged a storm behind his kinshuh veneer.

5. Vixen

Simultaneous disturbances at the three sets of the Bar-Jay's entry doors distracted Vixen from Khael's piercing, hypnotic, dark blue eyes. A pair of rangers stepped in each entrance. All six wore the black chainmail and crimson tunics of the City Patrol.

Fog. Vixen's heart leapt into her throat. A cold knot formed in the pit of her stomach, souring the ale. She clutched the ring in her pocket. How could she get rid of it before they caught her?

A shift at the table stole her attention as Grant and Khael exchanged a glance. She snapped her focus back to the more sinister threat, those Patrols. As they advanced across the floor, their careful choice of paths blocked any escape for her. Other patrons in the bar slipped away behind them and out the doors. The ache in her gut worsened into a sharp pain.

No choice left—cleanest pick ever and now she had to give it back.

Damn it. She carefully extracted the ring from her pocket and reached under the table to touch Khael's knee. *Take it, please!*

He looked at her, startled, but his hand grazed under hers. She dropped the ring.

The Patrols headed straight for their table. Vixen shuddered, even though she had returned the only evidence of her crime. Her last arrest still terrified her far more than this mystic or his monster.

She caught the fast frown Grant shot at Khael, who nodded back.

What were they up to?

As the Patrols drew closer, their hands near their weapons, Grant rose to his feet. He towered a full three palms over all the Patrols. "Help you folks?"

"Stand down, citizen." The woman with three gold chevrons glared up at him. "We're here for this redhead. She's wanted for multiple counts of vandalism in the north markets at midday."

Where did that come from? Vixen's throat tightened, depriving her of speech. Her hand near her dagger shook. She darted glances between Khael and Grant. To her surprise, neither one responded, though the monster flashed a disgusted frown at Khael.

Grant faced the sergeant with an impassive expression. "Impossible. She's been with us since late morning."

Vixen' hardened her face to hide the confusion that jolted her mind. Why did he do that? And what was that reaction of his all about?

"Do not interfere, citizen," the sergeant said. "We've been tracking this girl since the incident."

Vixen sat up straight at this nonsense. The Patrols grasped their weapon hilts.

Grant raised a fist. His ring twinkled in the flickering light. "Ensign Granton Finnleigh, Royal Legion. You question my word?"

Oh, no. Vixen's whole being shriveled into her core, her bravado vaporized. Which was worse, the Legion or the Patrols? Either way, she was trapped. No matter who prevailed here, she lost. A cold fire in her brain consumed all rational thought.

"I beg your pardon, Ensign." The sergeant raised her fist to her chest in salute. "Sergeant Dorchester, Cambridge City Patrol. This is Corporal Anderson. We heard you were back, but I didn't recognize you with that beard, out of uniform.

"In any case, two of our best trackers have followed this girl's trail since noon. She's been by the Collectic Office in the south marketplace, and at several known gray market stalls along the way here. Our duty is to take her before a tribune."

"I say she's been with us," Grant drawled. "My word against yours, Sergeant. Don't think much of your chances. Your men are mistaken or confused."

"I know my trackers, Ensign," Dorchester insisted. "We can sort this out at the tribune." She and Anderson stepped toward Vixen.

Overwhelmed with fear, Vixen shook from head to foot. Her one trip to jail had been vile, but that was her first offense. This time she knew their treatment would make her mentor's beatings seem tame and respectful. "No, please." Her moan came out cracked and dry. "They'll torture me."

"They will do no such thing." Khael's stern pronouncement made the Patrols freeze, staring at him. "We will resolve this here. State the exact charges, please."

Vixen held her breath, her pulse pounding, incredulous at this amazing turn of events.

Grant glanced at Khael and sat, his face stony. The Patrols snapped to attention. This serene mystic gazed at them with absolute fearlessness. Unexpected heat flared low in Vixen's belly. Something about this cool powerhouse ignited her soul despite her fears. The new blaze thawed the icy dread of tormented imprisonment that gripped her stomach.

"My lord," Dorchester said. "Three merchants in the Norfair Market claim this girl tried to steal some of their wares. Their lookouts spotted her. They allege she slashed some valuable, decorative hangings and led them on a chase between other stalls during her escape."

"Horse dung, that wasn't me," Vixen burst out. "I don't know where that is, my dagger can barely cut mud, and I don't destroy valuables for nothing. I'm a registered collector, not a vandal. Or an idiot."

She set desperate, pleading eyes on Khael. The patrols argued with a legionnaire, but deferred to this mystic as to a nobleman, as if their lives depended on it. Did hers? He had caught her lie earlier, so he must know her denial was true. His face remained impassive. *Fog.*

"Hush, lass." The soft tone Khael used for her hardened when he turned back to Dorchester. "What kind of merchants and what are their putative damages?"

"They're, uh, jewelry resellers." Dorchester cleared her throat and lowered her voice. "Actually, they're three of the more infamous Collectic fences. They claim ten crowns damage."

Grant snorted. "Must've been gem-encrusted Chitayan silk for that price."

Vixen breathed with care. If a nobleman and a Legion officer both supported her, she had hope. Grant had already lied on her behalf. Khael gave her an inquisitive look, but he said nothing to refute the lie. She shook her head. His stare provoked another battle between that unfathomable attraction to him that inflamed her body unbidden, and panic at what he, or they, might yet do.

He nodded once and his gaze reverted to the Patrol sergeant. "Known Collectic gray-marketers allege a starving collector stole nothing, vandalized their stall, ran six miles to the south market and returned four more miles here, with stops. Is that correct?"

Dorchester frowned, uncertain. "We saw the hangings, my lord. They were slashed."

"You heard Ensign Finnleigh. It was not this lass."

Vixen's mouth fell open in shock. Relief loosened the knots in her abdomen.

Dorchester grimaced, obviously unhappy with where this was going. "My lord, I believe you, of course, but those merchants will cause trouble if, having found the alleged vandal, we do nothing."

Khael gave her a stony expression. "Perhaps you can go find your alleged vandal."

Dorchester's brows knit in frustration. "By your command." She nodded at Grant. "Pardon us, Ensign." She gave Vixen one last glare and led her troops to the nearest exit.

As the last Patrol went out the door, other patrons began to slink back into the deserted room. Vixen let out a silent sigh of relief. Khael studied her, his elbows on the table, hands steepled before his mouth. His grim expression transformed into a smile.

Vixen's suspicions evaporated—he was the kindest, most generous man she had ever met. Her senses reeled, then steadied. What was she thinking? The positive vision died as her defenses sprang back into place. She pressed her lips tightly together in a hard, thin line. Gratitude to strangers had its limits, especially nobles who could just take anything they wanted.

Grant scowled at Khael.

"What's your angle?" It came out raw, angrier than she had intended. "What's in it for you? It better not include me." She drew her dagger as she stood up.

Grant snarled and began to rise. Vixen jerked away from him. To her shock, Khael raised a hand toward his friend without breaking eye contact with her. How did he maintain that inviolable, compelling cool?

"This is how you treat your benefactors?"

His tone was so mild.... Had she misjudged him that much?

Grant glared at him and sat again, his fists clenched.

"I preserve your freedom and treat you with dignity. In exchange, you tell me lies and now you threaten me?" Khael leaned back. "Suppose you sheath your weapon and sit down so we can talk."

Vixen blinked. Grant seemed ready to break her in half, but he stayed in his chair, his face pinched with controlled rage. Khael just watched her, too relaxed to be any threat. His approach seemed decent enough. What the hell. She sheathed her dagger and perched on the edge of her chair.

Khael kept his piercing gaze focused on her eyes. "What is in it for me is that you come to work for me."

Dumbfounded, it took a moment for her pent-up frustration to unleash. "As what? Your personal slut?"

"Is that all you believe yourself to be worth?"

"Hell, no! I'm not—" She caught herself and lowered her voice. "I don't do that."

Khael nodded, as if he approved. "I have use for your professional skills, as a collector."

Vixen sucked in a breath. Her rage dissipated against the impenetrable wall of his composure. If he kept his hands to himself, it might be fun, even profitable. Maybe even if he didn't. She was sick of wearing rags, freezing every night, starving, only to get beaten if she went home.

She looked pointedly at Grant and hostility reentered her voice. "How does he fit in?"

38

"Grant is my friend. We three will work together."

Grant rolled his eyes and slouched back, his arms crossed. "Oh, fine."

Vixen set her palm over the pendant she wore under her collar. That miserable fake at her mentor's shop had sworn it would protect her against any charms around. *Liar.* It hadn't worked on that foggy ring's constant nudges. They'd been impossible to escape. Khael's mental mandate had prevented her from getting rid of the stupid thing, no matter how hard she fought. What else about him would she find irresistible? The thought stirred up a whirl of fears and irrational desires.

Her pulse raced and she shuddered. He could have turned her over to the Patrols, but he'd defended her, even knowing she'd stolen his ring. Though a noble with enough clout to tell them off and probably order her around too, he'd negotiated with her. Everything he'd said so far rang true. The risk was worth it.

To her own surprise, she reached a hand across the table to him. She hated physical contact, except to distract from her thefts, or in self-defense. "I can do that."

At his wrist clasp, a shock jolted her skin. She snatched her hand back as if bitten by a snake. His equally surprised expression caught her eyes.

"Still need your name," Grant rumbled in disgust.

A vicious retort rose to her lips, but she bit it back. No point in deliberately offending an oxen hunk like that. Maybe he wasn't really as nasty as he pretended. He had stuck up for her to the Patrols, even if Khael had somehow arranged that.

My name is— The thought ended in confusion, as always. *Fog.* He knew when she lied.

She took a deep breath. "I go by Vixen."

6. Impressions

An unfamiliar mental shudder shook Khael at her moniker. She clearly knew not her real name. Her response to his seemed odd, and the shock at their contact—what was that? Regardless, his inquiries would have to wait. They yet had no solid foundation for such pursuits.

"Well met, Vixen. I travel, and I minstrel on occasion. Your talents will prove useful."

She sat back, her face less pinched with concern. "I'm just a tyro."

"No worries. Just follow my directions to the best of your ability. Unless a threat intervenes, I shall respect your person and privacy."

Vixen narrowed her eyes as she absorbed his words. "What if I don't like those terms?"

"What is to dislike?"

"I'm thinking." She frowned. "What about wages for me?"

Grant snorted. His peeved expression broadcast that they should just send her to jail. Even when Khael first met him and they were both starting out, Khael could not remember a time when Grant had liked having novices along on any of their travels.

Khael's heart warmed to her despite her tenacious, combative attitude. Or perhaps because of it? Her extraordinary potential urged him to give more. Kinshuh helped him keep his balance.

"I will supply whatever you need for projects we pursue. Food, shelter, equipment, new clothes, any training you may require. That should cover at least... six months. Unless I release you sooner. If we happen across any enrichment, I decide who merits shares."

Grant made a retching sound.

She groaned and pointed. "Do I have to work with that?"

"Rather not," Grant grumbled.

"Likewise. Just keep your hands to yourself—"

"I like clean hands, urchin."

"Enough." Khael stared at Grant. "We work together as a team." He faced Vixen. "All of us."

Vixen looked impressed at his firm approach. Her stomach rumbled. "If I say no?"

"You agreed to work for me. I have no use for anyone who lacks integrity."

She shook her head. "I suppose that's fair enough."

"No, Vixen. For this, you must make an oath."

Vixen took a deep breath. "I so swear on my honor as a Registered Member of the Collectic."

"I accept." Khael smiled. "What would you like first, food, clean up, or rest?"

* * *

Vixen followed Khael up the sloping, rock-solid spiral stairs to his sixth-floor suite. Thankfully, the Grant monster had stayed in the pub after their snack. Her stomach quieted around the delicious, cheesy, garlic bread sticks this singular gentleman had shared with her. They went well with her second, full pint of that fabulous ale.

She glanced back down when they reached the top. "That's quite a climb."

To her puzzled surprise, he closed his eyes for a moment before he opened the heavy door and waved her in. She shuffled slowly into the fancy paneled entry, staring wide-eyed at the variety of decorations and open, vaulted space of his enormous sitting room.

Vixen recovered from her awe enough to look for another way out, from picture window to arched hall to entry niche. None in sight. Her eyes reached his beautiful dark blues again, which crinkled with amusement. Had he read her mind?

He hung his cloak on one of the entry wall hooks. "If you remove your boots and wipe your feet, I will show you where you may enjoy a hot bath."

Did she really want to undress this close to so powerful a strange man, in his abode, no matter what he said? "I'm still a little hungry."

"I will have a dinner brought up while you bathe." When she still

41

hesitated, he added, "The washroom locks from inside."

If that were true, she would be safe with him. Not that being naked around him bothered her. He was a noble of some kind and could do with her what he pleased. There were many advantages to such a liaison. She could do much worse.

His open face heated her far more than she expected or wanted. Her whole body tensed, like a tightly wound spring. He looked so comfortable she didn't know what to make of it. If he were lying, he hid it better than anyone she'd ever seen. Tingles scrambled around in her lower abdomen.

She gritted her teeth to clamp down another abrupt, involuntary flare of desire for him. Where did that come from? It felt distant, detached, like someone else's feeling that invaded hers. With a few grunts, she pulled off the tattered boots and wiped her feet on the rough door mat. Her soles were so tough she barely felt the coarse bristles.

He led her around an opulent couch against the wall into the corridor to the left end of the suite. They passed a fancy kitchen and a huge, sumptuous bed chamber across from a cozier bedroom on the way to a spotless washroom.

She had never been this close to so many elaborate artworks or elegant tapestries. Wares as fine as these never showed up for sale in the public markets. Even the small crystal carvings on his shelves looked expensive. Twisted pieces of other materials that surrounded them struck her as trash. Easy to discard. One sweep through this place and she wouldn't need to steal for the rest of her life.

He'd never let her do that. The monster either. And she had agreed. Her shoulders slumped. A ferocious yawn wracked her.

Khael stopped at the washroom door and waved her in. She entered slowly, still on guard.

He pointed. "If you leave your clothes in that hamper, we can have them washed later."

"It's a little chilly to run around naked in here."

Khael shook his head through a mild smile. "There are clean robes by the towels. I will locate something suitable for you to wear."

He closed the door, leaving her alone.

Her shoulders slowly unknotted, sore from the cold, the streets and her frazzled nerves. She unfolded stiff arms to run her hand over the cool ceramic of the clean-scented commode. Beside it stood a shell-like washbasin with golden faucets. Around the half wall behind them, plush towels and fluffy green robes hung on the back wall across the room. Just as he'd said.

She opened the door to make sure it worked, closed it and slid the bolt through its hasp. Probably not needed, but still she checked for peepholes in the walls. None.

That done, she dropped her ragged cloak and torn dresses into the hamper. Her nose wrinkled at their stink. He was wrong about washing them. They should be incinerated and replaced—they were trash when she stole them anyway. She proceeded to the rear holding her dagger belts.

The tremendous bathtub resembled a small, empty indoor pool, inlaid with beautiful blue tile. Three could easily lounge in it and never touch, or maybe just the Grant giant.

Mystic Khael Stratton. His name hinted at a vague memory, too elusive to grasp. She shook her head at the mysterious annoyance.

The faucets released only cold water. It took several seconds before the promised hot flow came through. She sniffed at the smoked-glass bottle beside the soap—shampoo, something she hadn't used in... how long?

She set the daggers on the floor and lowered herself slowly into the steamy tub. Her quick scour left so much gunk in the water she switched to the shower. Two more scrubs and three hair washes later she felt clean.

The moist heat revived all her soreness from weeks of sleeping on frigid, snowy streets. Her muscles cheered from relief. She drew another hot bath and lay back in it for a moment to soak. It seemed safe enough in here, and her eyelids drooped.

* * *

A loud drumming noise in her nightmare startled her awake. She jerked up, crouching in the tepid water. One wrinkled hand thrashed to keep her steady as she grabbed the nearest dagger.

A gentle tapping came from the door.

"Plan you to emerge soon?" came Khael's muffled voice.

She waited, dagger ready, silent, her eyes wide open.

"Vixen? Are you all right?"

Her ears twitched. Right, it was Khael. "I'm fine."

"You have been in there for over half an hour."

"I'll be a few more minutes."

"As you wish. Dinner is cooling."

Vixen lowered the dagger. Her muscles had loosened during her nap, but this new tension wound her right back up. Why did she feel so unnerved? He gave her no reason for that at all. She recovered her breath and rinsed herself through another soothing hot shower. Water-logged and all, clean felt much better.

The green robe cuddled her skin in soft, warm fluff, all the way to her ankles. One dagger went back on her thigh. The other she carried in her hand.

She crept back down the deserted hall to the main room, eyes darting everywhere. He sat on the couch around the corner toward the entry, watching her return. His outfit was different. The dark green vest and long trousers showed off his strong, sculpted arms and chest.

Her hungry stomach squirmed at the sensuous fire burning inside her. Enough. She clenched her jaw.

Khael stood up. "Please have a seat."

"You said something about clothes?"

"I found some night-shirts that ought to serve."

She squinted disappointment at him. "That's all?"

"I have never had a female overnight guest here. My clothes would neither suit nor fit you. I arranged for the inn tailor to come up after dinner to measure you for new apparel. The bedroom you just passed is yours. The shirts in its wardrobe are for you."

Her stomach churned. More food would be nice, and a long enough night-shirt would be fine. For now. Better than what she'd had at home. She wandered back to the bedroom. The bath had been fantastic, and private. He hadn't ogled or touched her, or even tried. Come to think of it, he'd freely given her more respect than any man—or woman—she'd ever met, and he bore no trace of weapons. What did all that mean?

* * *

Khael watched her walk to her room. Her robe swished from side to side. His whole body tingled. Since his mystic initiation into learning to see the real person behind the physical form, the mere sight of a female, regardless of looks, had meant nothing to him.

This one was different, special. Dangerous. He needed firm self-control more than ever.

When she came back down the hall five minutes later, he had not moved. Still staring at her. She wore a dark green, knee-length nightshirt. It complemented the robe and offset her flame-red hair. His heart raced at her unexpected beauty until he forced himself to calm down.

"What?" She sounded less challenging, possibly even pleased at his attention.

"That outfit suits you well. The green complements your eyes."

"Thanks."

He nodded. "You are welcome. You may stay here for the next fortnight."

She crossed her arms and narrowed her eyes, puzzled and annoyed. "I assumed your shelter offer meant my own place, not just a room in your apartment."

He locked eyes with her. Six months of keeping their roles straight irrespective of her clear femininity and oppositional nature might be the greatest challenge of his life. She shuddered. Did she just have the same thought, about him?

"You will be safer here, and I leave tomorrow for two weeks."

"What?" Her mouth flew open. "You'd just let me live here, in this—palace, by myself?"

"Yes."

"I'm a collector. I collect... things, like all this."

"You gave me your word."

Eyes still wide, she nodded. "I'll keep it." She waved around the room. "The art I can see, but why do you keep all this junk?"

"What junk?"

"It's everywhere. Lots of cheap stuff, with only a few works that look valuable. Like that collection of twigs and wood chips next to the carved wooden bull on that shelf."

"The child of a struggling artist I know made that to sell as a toy farm. They needed support."

"Looks like trash, except the bull. What about those glass blobs around the unicorn?"

Khael smiled. "Scraps from a glass-blower's tyro experiments. They reflect interesting colors in the right light. The unicorn was a gift she gave me a few years later when she had mastered the craft."

Her stomach rumbled, loud enough to reach his ears.

"Dinner is over here." He waved toward a cart next to a dining set by the kitchen.

Vixen skittered over to the table but hesitated. "Smells great, but I don't know what it is."

"Half a coney and steamed vegetables." He pulled a frosty pitcher and mugs up from the cart's lower shelf.

She sat down and tore into the food. "Mm. Delicious."

Khael nursed his ale while she speedily devoured the small meal. His hunger for food paled under his fascination with her. When her plate was empty, she sopped up the last drops of gravy with the last dab of bread. She drained her mug and covered a huge burp. A yawn later, her eyes returned to his smile.

"If you find yourself hungry during the night, there is a bowl of fresh fruit and a bread box in the kitchen."

"Thanks, but that was plenty for now."

"Formal dinners and public feasts require the most refined, practiced manners."

"Formal dinners?"

"Part of my routine. I will provide enough food to preempt any need to rush through our meals. In some circles, appearances matter, and we will be more impressive if you look well-fed." He paused. "Can you read Arcana?"

"Never heard of it." She yawned.

Khael stared at her, baffled. A collector who had never heard of the Ancients' language? He filed that unexpected nuance for later reference. "Fascinating. Can you read Meridian?"

She shook her head.

"That we must correct." He stood up. "The tailor is late."

"Some real clothes would be nice." Another yawn.

"I will check." Khael went to the entry to speak into a horn-shaped tube. A few minutes later he turned back to her. "Olivia fell asleep...." His voice trailed off at Vixen's absence.

He closed his eyes to scan. During his brief tube conversation with Barek, she had slipped into the bedroom and curled up on her new bed. Even resting, her kih flared clever, lithe, and exceptionally skilled, though quite feral. A smile grew on his face.

He released his kinshuh and a dammed-up firestorm of passions inundated him. His blood pulsed fiercely. Parts of him awoke for the first time since his initial kinshuh training. The air fought his efforts to breathe.

Deep inside, his chokkan itched. Such blazing fervor for her might well pose a lethal threat to him.

Khael frowned, deeply puzzled. The warning chilled his walk to his own bed. His chokkan had always been perfectly accurate. He would have to control his feelings, with kinshuh if necessary. That he might need to do so all the time sent shivers up his spine.

He expected the Saiensu to guide him to the right choices.

Expected? He shuddered. The mystic way discouraged expectations.

7. Comfort Zone

Persistent knocks on the bedroom door startled Vixen awake. She slid out from under the warm comforter and grabbed her dagger. The toasty fire from last night had burned out and she shivered in the chill. A large mirror standing in the far corner to her left, beside the small hearth, reflected wide green-eyed caution surrounded by a tangled scatter of fiery hair. After a moment, she realized the knocks were probably her host waking her up without breaking in.

"Just a moment. Please." She began to stand up.

"Dinna take too long, lassie," a woman's voice called out.

Vixen froze. This was Khael's suite. Who was this stranger? In wary silence, she pulled on her robe—it too had chilled overnight. Another woman might be safe, but... "Who are you?"

"Olivia. Inn tailor. Yer laird wants ye to have a wardrobe afore the night, so we'd better get started on it."

Vixen twitched at the woman's unfamiliar term for Khael. She hitched the dagger belt around her waist, her hand on the hilt as she opened the door. "What's a laird?"

"The dear man ye work for, as we affectionately call him." A short, rotund woman bustled in and set a small basket on the floor by the bed. "Ye'll no' be needin' daggers, dearie, nobody's gonna harm ye. Shuck the robe."

"It's cold."

"I need to measure ye so yer clothes an' armor 'll fit right, lassie."

Vixen gave her another quick once-over before she took off the robe. She held onto her dagger belt. "Is he here?"

"Dinna ye fret, he'll be back, an' I'll be quick. Have to."

The cheerful tailor fussed around her with a measuring tape and a feather touch. She fished some slinky wisps of cloth out of her basket and tossed them on the bed.

"Here's some decent undergarments for ye. They ought to fit ye well enough, tho' ye're awful scrawny. Eat hearty. Ye need more meat on yer bones. I'll be back later wi' something no' too ragged." With that, the speedy tailor trundled out.

Vixen closed her door and breathed a sigh of relief as her heart slowed from its rapid pace. She looked over the new articles, picked one to add under her thick night shirt and pulled the robe back on. The slinky bloomers thrilled her skin.

The hardwood floor cooled her bare feet as she stalked out into the hall, armed against any other potential intruders. Bright morning sunshine lit up the whole suite through the enormous sitting room picture windows. Peaceful silence reigned. Too quiet. She poked her head into the master bedroom. No Khael, but what a huge room. Its fireplace still glowed.

Some fancy dresses lay across the armrest of the nearest couch. Those weren't there last night. An appreciative glow warmed her chest as she studied them. This mystic gentleman had kept his word with her to the letter. So far. He hadn't hurt her, not since that first, horrid time, when she stole his ring.

She couldn't really blame him for that one.

The hearth's glowing embers still emitted heat and an occasional pop. The heat drew her nigh. She sat on the stone and hugged her knees to her chin, comfortably bored. Soon enough the warmth on her back enticed her into a daydream.

Only a tiny girl, she ran around in the tall, cool grass of an enormous field under a bright, cloudless sky. Other, bigger children nearby, three boys and a girl, chased around in a random pattern, laughing with glee. They playfully bumped into each other with carefree abandon.

A tall, enraged woman stomped up, yelling incomprehensible words. The other children ran away in terror, but Vixen couldn't move her feet. The glare of the sun hid the woman's face as she towered over Vixen and raised an immensely long sword. Vixen fell back on the ground, mute in fear, unable to breathe, her eyes riveted on the huge, gleaming blade of death.

A strong, bearded man stepped between them. The livid woman

viciously smashed the sword hilt hard across his face. He swayed but stood fast. They argued in muddled words, not Meridian. Still furious, the woman stormed off. The man turned back to Vixen, his beard bloodied, but with a kindly smile for her.

Fully grown, she smiled back and reached for his hands.

The suite door opened to jar her out of the recurring daydream. She jumped to a defensive crouch, her dagger out before she recognized Khael.

He peered around the corner from the entry nook. When he saw the dagger, he stepped out with his hands raised. "Breakfast is dead and cooked, but you are welcome to kill it again."

She felt abashed at her overreaction and sheathed the weapon. "Sorry. I just had another one of those daydreams that—well, never mind."

He pulled a small cart from the entry to the table by the kitchen.

Her stomach rumbled. She followed him to examine the plates of food on the cart beside a kettle steaming with a sweet, spicy odor. "Smells delicious."

Khael's unruffled friendly regard fanned more of those foreign flames in her core. She shoved down the strange urge to do more than sit and partake of the tasty sandwich. His pleasant small talk helped her relax and enjoy the food and the conversation. He seemed less interested in his food than her, but he relaxed in his chair across the table from her, a safe distance away. The scene reminded her of when she was younger and felt safe with her uncle and her soon-to-be mentor.

"Where is your home?"

She stiffened away from him, surprised at the question. "Why do you care?"

"I like to know the friends with whom I work."

Friends? That sounded fair enough, even comforting. "I've been living on the streets."

"The streets are no home."

"They may be bitter cold this time of year, but at our flat my mentor beats me if I talk back or can't bring in enough." She bit her lip and shrugged. "I haven't been there since I took your ring."

"Is that what made you steal my ring?"

She narrowed her eyes, suspicious with where this might be headed. As much as she'd grown to hate her mentor, his arrest wasn't part of her deal with Khael. "Does it matter?"

"I presume you acted neither on impulse nor alone. Names matter not."

Not much of a threat. An answer without names should be safe enough. "This... person came by last week and offered us five hundred marks to steal a gold ring off a man of your exact description. You showed up right when he was due in town. They gave us a hundred marks up front, of which I got nothing, and described you down to that thing you rode and the heavy beard and mustache."

* * *

Khael squinted at her, not quite sure what to make of her fabrications. "That seems a substantial reward for so small a task."

Vixen nodded. "Five crowns is a fortune. It'd feed us for years." She waved around the room. Her voice fell. "I guess it's not so much to you."

Khael shrugged. "Please continue."

"I tracked you from the gate to where you stopped. When that little brat put his hand up my leg, I caught him and kicked his butt. He ran right at your mons—Grant, and I saw my chance. I wasn't expecting your voice in my head to split my skull."

"You sacrificed the front of your dress rather than tell me your name."

"I was caught stealing, once, a hellish nightmare. What you did promised another one, or worse." She shuddered hard enough to shake her chair. "The dress was stolen trash anyway. What's so important about that ring?"

Astonished, he forgot his intended response. "Know you not who I am?"

"You are mystic Khael Stratton, but most people call you Kyle.

51

Mystic Prince

You travel and minstrel on occasion."

He blinked, startled at the precision of her words and that she pronounced his name correctly. "Impressive. You nearly quoted me verbatim."

"I have near total recall." She fiddled with her fork, avoiding his eyes.

Khael kept his mouth shut. That explained one of the many unusual contours in her kih. His curiosity itched to know more about the others, though he held it firmly in check.

"But I'm only a novice, so I may botch up at times."

He nodded. That statement rang true despite many anomalies in her kih that suggested otherwise. So many questions... A mental sigh escaped into the silent whirl of his thoughts. Questions would have to wait until she knew him well enough to trust him.

Vixen demolished the last of her food. "What do I do while you're gone?"

"Grant will train you to enhance your dagger skills. My friend, mystic Barek Jayne, who owns this inn and the Bar-Jay, can start teaching you to read and write Meridian."

She groaned. "I can't stay cooped up in here with Grant for two weeks. I need time to myself, fresh air, and exercise that won't encourage me to kill him."

Khael smiled his sympathy. "There is a covered terrace right outside the kitchen. However, you will be safer and warmer inside, away from the edges."

"I can't just go out for a walk or a drink?"

"Some persistent folks out there want to kill me and anyone around me. If they find out about you, they may try to kill you too, or just ransom you for me." His warning had no obvious effect on her. Did she not care about her safety, or was she that confident? He pushed his half-finished plate toward her. "Would you like some more?"

She started to shake her head. Her nose wrinkled at the enticing aroma and she took the plate. "Why would anyone want to kill you?" she asked after a mouthful, then dug in.

52

"They have a misguided vendetta against my grandfather and his entire family."

"I can fend for myself."

"No doubt, but you should be safe here. I will feel better with that assurance."

Her grim expression of thoughtful deliberation lightened after a few seconds. Khael enjoyed a growing warmth in his chest at her show as he sipped his tea.

She finished the plate and peered back at his stare. "Studying me again?"

"You intrigue me."

"I'd rather not."

"Fair enough." He sat back and glanced toward the entry. "What thought you of the dresses Olivia left this morning?"

"They're beautiful, but they're huge. I'll bet they're expensive."

"You may have the one you like best."

Her eyes narrowed with suspicion. "Why?"

"You deserve respectable clothing." He rose and headed toward the couch with her not far behind. "Olivia can finish the one you choose so it will fit."

"I like this one." She picked up the royal blue silk dress with paisley sleeves.

Khael nodded his approval. An unexpected wave of passion surged in his heart. Fortunately, it crashed into his kinshuh and dissipated. "When Olivia fits it to you, it will be perfect."

She shivered and set the dress back across the arm of the couch. His pulse sped up at the easy poise in her moves. Someone knocked on the door. Khael breathed a silent sigh of relief. He scanned through the door before opening it. Olivia bustled in and ushered Vixen to her bedroom.

Khael waited for them to clear the room before he moved. Watching Vixen head out made his lips dry. His head fell. Too many issues to settle before considering any kind of liaison. The Saiensu always came first. Deep inside, part of him laughed hysterically at such claims.

Shaking this off, he went to his desk to study his map of Meridium. He needed a stealthy route home through Shielin that the Chelevkori, and his viceroy, would not suspect. Without that, they would most likely not survive the journey. None of the scenarios he had dreamed up so far held enough promise to satisfy his fervent wish for a peaceful victory.

A long while later, Grant and Heidi interrupted his ruminations.

"Where's urchin?" Grant said.

Khael took a deep breath. "Her name is Vixen, not urchin. She is with Olivia, hopefully dressed by now."

"This is really nice." Vixen's husky voice came from the hall. She paced in wearing a dressy green leather outfit. "I never thought armor would..."

She noticed Grant and Heidi and stopped cold. The couple both whistled low while Khael blinked, his head spinning.

"This lovely young woman is your ring thief?" Heidi said, shocked.

"Vixen?" Grant managed.

Their quick responses gave Khael the seconds he needed to regain some refuge in kinshuh. He dismissed his wild emotions, along with his irritation at the unruly feelings.

After he introduced Heidi and Vixen, a silence fell. Khael struggled for a topic to renew the conversation. "Olivia trimmed your hair."

Vixen watched him look her over, warming at his cool gaze. "She said it looked frizzled."

"We have plans to make."

"I want to try on the dress."

He smiled at her. "We will wait, but please make haste."

She clasped her hands briefly and marched out to the other room. His palms felt sweaty at her lithe, graceful movements.

"Don't like casual way she talks to you." Grant knit his eyebrows together, his eyes dark with stern, guardian-like disapproval. "How many clothes you giving one destitute collector?"

"I mind not, and enough, thank you." Khael took a breath and wiped his hands on his vest. "You could act more casual with me."

Grant shrugged through his return glare.

"Does she know anything about your court protocols?" Heidi said.

Until he reclaimed his throne, Khael preferred casual, but she was right. "We can work on it."

"Work on what?" Vixen said from the hall arch.

Olivia had added pleats around the waist of the silk dress to flatter Vixen's slim figure. Her belted dagger hung low enough not to ruin the image.

Khael fought to keep himself steady. "Work on protocol."

"Ye'll have to feed this li'l slip better, milaird," Olivia said, behind her. "She's too skinny."

Khael chuckled as Vixen trotted across the room. "Nice outfit. Thank you, Olivia. This will do well for casual occasions."

Vixen's eyebrows peaked. "Casual? It's the most expensive, beautiful thing I've ever worn."

"You are welcome." Khael gestured to Grant and Heidi. "Come here, please."

Olivia gathered up her basket and sack. "I'll be off. Shall I send ye the bill?"

Khael strode over to duck his head near hers. "I thought we had agreed on the price."

She pouted at him before she nodded, her face mildly flushed. "Aye, we did."

Khael chuckled and handed her some coins. "Thank you for your excellent work. I count on your future services."

"Fine reward for me hard work." But her eyes twinkled and the corners of her lips turned up. "Fare you all well."

Khael returned to his desk as Olivia left. "Vixen, Grant can give you advanced dagger lessons during the day. In the evenings, Barek will start your Meridian lessons."

"Whoa. I have to spend two weeks, all day, every day, with him?" She sneered at Grant. "He'll break me in half."

Grant flipped his eyebrows up and down, but he seemed more amused than threatening.

Heidi rolled her eyes and elbowed his chest.

Khael glanced between all three. "I prefer you both cooperate. Vixen, you must learn much and quickly. Grant is a polite, expert instructor." He paused. "Know you how to ride?"

"A horse?" At his nod, she shook her head. "Never wanted to."

Khael stifled his instant comment. Even the poorest children in the Enclave enjoyed any opportunity to ride the ponies and horses that came through. He added that to her growing list of oddities. "Grant and Heidi can also teach you the basics, somewhere our foes will not expect you."

Vixen frowned in curiosity. "Where are we going?"

"Skemmelsham, the capital of Shielin and my home city, five hundred miles north of here."

"Skemmel sum?"

"It is the Shielin word for fish-market town. We depart a week from Saturday."

On his way to the door a shuffling noise from behind caught his attention. He turned toward the commotion as Vixen skittered up. It almost looked like she wanted to hug him, but she pulled up short and reached her hands toward him, then just one. With tempered calm he returned the wrist clasp.

"Thank you, Khael."

"You are welcome."

She let her arm fall. "You know, I only just met you, but you've been more decent to me in one day than most people I've known my whole life. Take care of yourself. You have to come back safely and

56

rescue me from your monster."

8. No More Vacation

Vixen jerked upright. Her nightmare faded under the distant knocks at the suite's front door. Only Grant and Barek had come by while she had been in. Last Saturday and Sunday she had spent with Grant and Heidi at his family's ranch, learning to ride. She slipped on her robe, drew her dagger and stalked out to answer the door.

The terrified maid clearly did not expect an armed woman in the suite. She nearly threw her linens all over the sitting room floor in fright at Vixen's threatening pose. After a violent shudder, she rushed through her duties and hurried out in complete silence. Vixen stood immobile the whole time, not at all sure what, if anything, she should do. The idea of a maid seemed familiar, but she recalled no such personal experience.

She wandered back to her room to freshen up and dress. By the time Grant and Heidi arrived, she sat tucked in her favorite chair across the sitting room from the door, reading a book from Barek about early Cambridge history.

"When's Khael getting back?"

The couple faced her from a crowded loveseat beside the hearth. Grant caressed Heidi's shoulder while she toyed with his leg.

He shrugged at Vixen's question. "Dunno. Should get ready. He'll want to leave."

Vixen stared at him. Get ready?

"You'll travel in armor," Heidi said. "I can help."

"I do know how to dress." Vixen stood, irritated at the patronizing offer.

"Have you ever packed a knapsack for long-distance riding?"

Vixen shook her head with an abashed lump in her throat. Heidi gave her an expectant look and Vixen led the way to her room. They packed everything she planned to take and not wear. As Vixen started to unhitch her belt the suite entry door slammed. Muffled voices drifted through for a second, then all went quiet.

Vixen drew her dagger, wary again. "What was that?"

"No worry, Grant's here." But Heidi gripped her own dagger hilt as they headed out.

Grant stood alone by the hearth with a puzzled frown.

"Was that Kyle? Is everything all right?"

"Yes, but not sure. He said rest. We leave this evening." Grant wobbled his head side to side. "Not himself."

Annoyed at his lax manner, Vixen sheathed her dagger and planted her arms akimbo. "Won't you talk to him?"

Grant paused and shook his head. "He'll come out of it."

Heidi glanced at him and held up her hands in doubt to Vixen. "You could try."

Vixen raised her eyebrows in surprise. It wasn't her job, but the idea appealed to her, so she set off to Khael's room. When she came in, he didn't respond. He sat upright on his huge bed in a strange, interleaved cross-legged position, his eyes shut. Her heart leapt into her throat. Something was different about him. She crept over and stood close by, hoping he'd notice her.

"I need some time alone," he whispered at last.

His response chilled her to the bone. He'd been gone for two weeks and now he wanted to be alone? She slumped across the hall and threw herself on the bed, her stomach jumping with unease. If that was the way he appreciated her, she should just leave.

No, she'd given her word. *Fog.* It had to be something else, but what?

As her disquiet began to settle, a quiet melody from plucked strings filtered through the closed door. Curious, she picked her head up to listen. The minor tune wrenched at her heart. He must have been devastated to play something so achingly sad. No wonder he'd been so short with her. A hurt she didn't understand swelled in her chest. Her eyes dripped.

* * *

Khael's unexpected, violent confrontation at the kyoshitsu played out in his mind, over and over. His assailant strikingly resembled Vixen, yet her face twisted from a pain he neither knew how he had caused nor to undo. The woman's bloody flight still jarred him. Playing his grief out on his mandola helped soothe his concerns, but they refused to let him go.

Hoping to overcome the distress, he immersed himself in another kinshuh. Twin drops fell from his eyes. He felt certain he had failed somewhere.

After a long meditation, he checked Vixen's sleeping kih, glad she found rest. Her hunger glared at him, so he went down to the inn kitchen. Barek met with him for an astonishing update about Vixen's skill mastery and a first-class set of high-quality lock-picks for her. Khael puzzled over Barek's revelations on his way back. He left the meal tray on the dining table and went to collect Vixen.

She lay asleep on the bed, still in her new dress. The frowning twitches on her face made him wonder what kind of nightmare she suffered. Her figure had smoothed out since he saw her two weeks ago, which fanned his inner fire, but he held fast. This was not the time. He set the picks on her nightstand and gently shook her shoulder.

Vixen sat up in a jerk. A sigh, like a quiet scream, whooshed out of her. She seized his arms hard before her wandering eyes focused on him. Startled, he drew back, but she gripped him so tight he pulled her right off the bed. With a whimper, she clutched at him for support, a surprise embrace he instinctively returned.

Khael stood still as passionate waves thrashed his insides. Her firm softness fit in his arms so well he ached to free her from their contract right away. He flexed every muscle in his body to keep control. Neither of them was ready for that yet. Reluctantly, he let her go and drew back a short step. "May I help?"

Vixen crossed her arms and shook her head. "I'm fine."

An odd heat radiated from her across the gap between them. Was that anger or something else, something better?

"You may want to change into your armor and weapons." His tense control hung wafer-thin over the churning emotions inside. He cleared his throat. "Please pack up what you want to bring along quickly."

"I'm packed. I'll just be a few minutes."

Khael walked stiffly to his desk in the sitting room. The sight of his knapsack by the entry renewed his disturbing memories, but they lacked the harshness from earlier. Vixen's embrace had somehow enabled his settling to complete. Though uneasy about the kyoshitsu attack, he needed to tell Vixen and Grant about it... somewhere along the way. This did not bother him at all, far less than he expected. His inner peace prevailed—he had forgiven himself, and Vixen had been the catalyst.

He smiled as she emerged from the corridor, dressed in her new leather armor. She looked ready to burst with relief, though she tried to hide it.

"Where did the pick set come from?"

"Barek, and I, thought you might find it useful."

"Thanks. It looks expensive." She watched him look her over. "You prepared well."

"I promised my best." She peered at him. "Where are your weapons?"

"I am all the weaponry I need."

She looked nonplussed. "Well, I'm hungry." Her eyes drifted to the food and she sauntered over to examine the light meal. "This is all we get?"

"It is unwise to ride on too full a stomach."

Khael's chest tightened as she slid into the chair with sublime, cat-like grace. A quick dive into kinshuh quelled his inner turmoil.

While they ate, she winced whenever she reached across the table for a napkin or bent her left arm to adjust her hair. He waited to bring it up, hoping she would.

When she finished, she looked up at him. "What now?"

"Your left elbow seems to bother you." Even her frown intrigued him.

61

"Your ton of Grant fell on me and twisted it last week in training. It still hurts. Of course, he never apologized."

Khael closed his eyes, his curiosity unsatisfied. He tightened his focus to her elbow. "That was not the original injury."

"How do you know that?"

"My disciplines include one with which I can read life-energy and its subtleties." He reached for her wrist, but she drew back. "Another stimulates healing. May I?"

Her apprehensive reaction faded into a slow nod. He gently slid his hands up her arm to her elbow. She sighed. Excited flares rippled through her kih up her arm, across her chest and down her torso, until he pressed her sore spots.

She squeaked. "Ouch. That hurts. Let go!"

He let go. "The more you tell me, the more effective I can be."

"I—oh, fog," she muttered. "My mentor hit me there about a month before you arrived."

Khael checked back his outrage while he carefully expanded his survey to her entire kih. His chokkan prickled as he studied her. Strange—how did she pose a threat to him? He compared this sensation to the one he had when Zorn had entered the room they shared in Finnipal a few weeks ago, wearing a booby-trapped cloak-frog. There, Khael had immediately recognized its lethal threat. This was different—more subtle and harder to discern.

"Your mentor struck you?"

"He, I, it's complicated."

"I specialize in complicated." He found no other distinctive anomalies in her kih.

"He... beat me... with a stick," she stammered. "When I tried to block it, he smashed my elbow. I think he broke it."

"He did." Khael frowned, inflamed at such abusive behavior. He set that aside for future reference, puzzled and curious at the healing challenge. "I have never treated an injury that healed so poorly. This may take more time."

"What?" Vixen raised her eyebrows in confusion.

"The shuri discipline induces accelerated physical healing. I gauge the time required from my past experience. In this case I have none."

* * *

A chill shot up Vixen's spine. Her stomach convulsed. "Sounds like magic."

"Mystics do not practice magic. It lacks sufficient reliability."

She drew back with squinted eyes. "Your voice in my head isn't magic?"

"Our disciplines are well-defined."

"I've seen what clerics can do and I won't have any of that."

His eyes twitched when she said 'cleric.' He shook his head. "That would also be magic."

Her stomach eased up a fraction, her face less tense. "How does it work?"

"I influence the flow of energy in your body. It will heal your elbow, but it will hurt. Briefly."

Vixen narrowed her eyes. She hated pain, and magic terrified her, but her elbow constantly ached. If this not-magic healed her... "All right, I suppose."

He closed his eyes. His hands warmed up around her elbow. Her arm responded with a heat that burst into a fire all around the joint. At first it burnt like a torch held too close for comfort, but bearable. A sudden scorching agony seared her eyes shut, as if the bone broke again.

"Ow!" She tried to break free, but he kept his grip firm.

"Hold still, or you may make it worse."

Vixen gritted her teeth to suppress a scream and the blaze slowly mellowed, becoming more like the painful relief of massaging out a wicked cramp. After what had to be an hour in the torment, he let go and the blaze cooled. Unable to move, she opened her eyes to his kindly half smile.

"That really hurt."

He reached out a gentle hand to brush away wet tracks on her cheeks. "How feels it now?"

Vixen bent her elbow a few times. Flawless. She hesitated, then tried positions that used to hurt worse. When there was no pain, she smiled, laughing as she went further. "That's great!"

Khael nodded. "Undoing the improper healing made it take fifteen minutes, not my usual ten."

"It felt like hours." Her eyes grew round. "Wait. You can heal a broken bone in only ten minutes?"

"In this case, fifteen. Once the ache fades away, you should have no further discomfort."

"Fantastic!" She twisted her face with intense curiosity. "That wasn't magic?"

"Some of our disciplines enable us to manipulate natural life-energy, or kih. Magic consumes energy emitted by kih—what we call zhukih—but magic shapes it to force new, unnatural effects that tend to be less permanent. Most magic is also less beneficial, and there are often unpleasant side effects."

"Thanks." She blinked. "That's a great trick. Can you teach me?"

"We only train mystics in our disciplines."

"Is that why you close your eyes so much when you say you're looking at something?"

* * *

Khael smiled. "Shikah lets me perceive kih with my eyes closed. I have learned to read in detail its patterns and flows—fundamental attributes, abilities, injuries, strengths, and so on. Kih is the energy source for all our exertions."

"Oh," she muttered with a new frown. "This... shikah... is mystic too?"

"Please, tell me about your last fortnight."

She hesitated a split second, then told him how she rearranged their schedule to put Barek's lesson between Grant's two torment sessions, about her progress, her arguments with Grant, their trip to the Finnleigh estate, and other trivia. Her detailed description of the ranch marveled him. He could remember everything about his own experiences if he used kinshuh, but her memories just flowed, and her tale revealed an uncanny familiarity with ranching...

"When were you on a ranch before the Finnleighs'?"

She sat back. "I don't know that I was. It just seemed so familiar. Maybe from my nightmares."

Someone boomed on the door. Vixen shuddered and crossed her arms and legs.

Grant came in and shut the door. "Nightfall soon."

Khael sighed. "Thank you, Grant." So much for this chance to enhance his new closeness to Vixen, learn more. The paradox about the ranch bothered him. "No Heidi?"

"Skipped second farewell." Grant glanced at the love seat to his right, but he opted for the couch farther along the same wall instead. "Wait ten, fifteen minutes. Should be dark enough."

Khael faced Vixen. She seemed deep in thought, but she shook her head.

"I can't remember anything on a farm or a ranch."

"Might get your pack," Grant muttered.

She looked unhappy at his suggestion, but Khael nodded. With her lips pressed shut, she shook off an impulse to react and left the room.

"She is dangerous," Grant said quietly.

"How so?"

"She's better than me with daggers, and her Collector's martial skills are way past expert level."

"Manshao?"

"Whatever they call it. She also moves with lightning precision. You said she's a master-class pickpocket. No tyro can do that."

Khael frowned. Her kih bore indications of expert mastery in several skills, yet her tyro claims rang true. That made no sense.

65

"Barek told me she is a notorious street fighter. He also said she is fluent in Meridian, though she seems to think not."

"She's lousy at riding."

"She rides with me."

"That's safe?"

Khael pursed his lips. "We need the speed, and gongyangmas are rarely sold. I will risk it, until we stop at Strattonmoor."

Vixen returned and set her knapsack in the entry. "What's Strattonmoor?"

"My family haven, five miles southeast of Skemmelsham." Khael beckoned them both to his desk and unrolled a map. "The forest road is best. It is not charted, but it runs through here and has no inns. We will camp out a few days."

"Camp out?" Vixen looked curious.

"You and I will share a tent."

"Hold on." She held up her hand. Her throat pulsed. "What if I don't want to share your tent?"

He chose a cool tone, gazing deep into her eyes. "Our main goal in this ride is speed. To minimize our load, we only bring two tents. Neither of us will fit with Grant. If you can continue to trust me, you will remain safe, dry and warm in my tent."

She crossed her arms with a pout and slumped onto an easy chair. "You don't seem to trust me."

"I left you here alone for two weeks."

"Under his and Barek's close watch isn't alone. I took an oath to you, and I'm trusting you not to betray me."

"Then our mutual trust will grow. Trust now that you will be safest in my tent."

She stared at him. Khael took a quiet breath and held her eyes. He struggled not to notice every single detail about her all the time.

A few moments later, she nodded. "What do I ride? I'm not too comfortable with horses yet."

"We will load our steeds in the stable," Khael said. "You may feed Molniya a snack to gain his favor. He will let you ride while I walk him. Grant rides his Phantom. At the street, I will mount and ride with you. We can take a moderate pace to the north gate."

"How do I feed or ride lightning?" Vixen asked.

Khael stared at her, astonished that she understood Yazyk. Grant's eyes widened.

She glanced at Grant. "And I thought phantoms were some kind of horrible spirit."

Grant turned his lip corners down and shook his head.

"Chernaya Molniya is my gongyangma, Phantom is Grant's." Khael gave her a puzzled frown. "You speak Yazyk?"

"No, why?" Vixen seemed quite puzzled at the idea.

"*Chernaya Molniya* is—"

"Black lightning," Vixen's eyebrows shot up in astonishment. "That's Yazyk?"

Khael nodded, wondering what more surprises the long ride ahead held in store.

9. Rain on the Road

When they rode through the city's northern gate without the slightest delay, Vixen felt awed. No one got through the gate near the Collectic, where she had met Khael, that easily. Yet he was a noble, and nobles had it made in life. Having to ride with him in the same saddle gave her the willies, but she'd already decided to tough it out. He also gave her a waterproof poncho to wear, right before the present angry thunderstorm began its freezing deluge. The cover helped keep her somewhat dry.

She held him tightly as they rode through the downpour. Molniya was tall enough that riding this high, coupled with her minimal experience in such circumstances, wore on her grit. The longer they rode, the more she worried she'd crash to her death on the brick road racing by so far down if she let go. Her grip tightened despite the cold, or maybe because of it. His solid warmth kept the chill at bay. This ride was the first time in years she'd allowed anyone so close.

Sopping hours droned by as they drummed the slick surface of the paved highway. At one point they passed an inn. Its heat called to Vixen as they rode past. Her pelvis and legs waxed sorer from the interminable ride, while the heavy rain and bone-chilling cold wore on her. The great animals they rode galloped on, seemingly unaware of her plight. All her other feelings shrank as her misery swelled.

"When can we stop?" she mumbled through frosty wet lips that barely worked.

Khael took a few seconds to respond. "I would rather not. For what purpose?"

"I need to empty out."

"There is a shelter close by we can use."

Khael slowed Molniya to a canter. Phantom somehow sensed this from in front of them and slowed to match speeds.

"Why're we slowing?" Grant called back. "Already behind schedule."

68

"Rest break."

Vixen groaned and sat up, aching. Her muscles creaked in protest and she flopped forward against Khael's warmer back.

"Are you all right?" He sounded as if the weather didn't faze him at all.

"I'll never be warm again." She moaned. "My legs are sore from all this strain."

"I can assist with your pain, for which I apologize. The shelter is right ahead."

"Oh, thank the stars."

Vixen twitched her insensible fingers and barely felt any movement. Her hips ached at another painful change in Molniya's gait. She peered around. In the darkness, she recognized nothing and hoped they weren't lost. Grant led them down into the wet, needle-covered, uneven dirt of the murky forest that surrounded the road, along a faint path into the tall pines.

She groaned. Everything not yet numb hurt. "Where are we?"

"About one hundred fifty miles north-northeast of Cambridge," Khael said. "Shielin's border is a few miles farther. We progress much slower than I planned, so we may ride into the day."

"You mean we'll get some light?"

"Only if the lightning returns or the storm lets up."

Vixen rolled her eyes. Great. More wet, black gloom ahead.

"I had meant to ride full speed, not this slow gallop. The storm interfered."

"Slow gallop? Ooh, I bet I'll hate a fast one. What about this shelter? I can't wait much longer."

"Hang on." Grant sounded irritated. He always seemed grumpy around her.

Molniya's slower, bouncier gait made every step hurt worse, straining Vixen's abdomen. She dragged her head up, over Khael's shoulder. The path wound around up onto a dry area under a large wooden canopy that sheltered a modest fire pit and a tethering rail, with three small cabins next to it.

"Wow. How did you know this was here?"

"Been here before," Grant said. "Take break, eat something hot."

A man in a long coat crept out of the middle cabin and yawned. "I can take your, uh, steeds, gentlemen, missy."

"No need, we will manage," Khael said. "Get your rest, friend."

"Thank you, kind sir." The man bowed and went back inside."

"Permit me to dismount first," Khael told Vixen.

"I hope I can." She grimaced.

Grant dismounted with surprising grace, his touchdown quiet. Khael carefully swung his leg up over Molniya's neck as the bullish gongey bowed his head. The mystic slid to a noiseless landing.

"My legs don't feel right. Would you help?"

Khael reached up to pull her down gently, sideways from the saddle. A strange heat flowed from his hands through her armpits down to her sorest muscles. She clung to his arms, thankful for his strong, graceful support until her legs unkinked and her feet touched the ground.

"Move your legs."

She twitched them. Sharp prickles rose up her legs. "Ouch."

He held her up until she could stand steady. She took a few careful steps, fighting to keep from spilling and upright. By the time she could shuffle in a small circle, Grant invited them to the fire. He had some pots and was throwing stuff into one already filled with water, resting on the flames.

"Where?" She squeezed tight.

"The nearest cabin is the loo," Khael said.

When she shuffled back minutes later, Khael disappeared inside. Something around her smelled delicious. She wasn't sure if it was desperation, her numbed nose, or a genuinely pleasant aroma from whatever Grant was boiling.

"What's that scent?"

"Barek's honey-spice tea. That, few dried meat chews, warm you

70

up, feel better."

She rubbed her sore abdomen. "Ow. Is this how you always travel?"

"Better."

Her jaw fell. "You're joking."

"Yeah." He smiled at her for the first time. "Riding in torrent's not my first choice either. But we're rushed, so personal comfort must wait until we reach a certain moor."

"Are you both always this cryptic?"

"We must be cautious," Khael said from behind her. "The less said for now, the better."

Vixen nodded, but the caution seemed extreme. Her legs felt better and she hobbled over to the fire. She squatted slowly on her second, less painful attempt, rubbing her bum with both hands. The leather armor made this difficult. Grant was gone, probably in the loo. Khael tended the tea.

"This may not be a penthouse, but I expected something more like that than this."

"We are pressed for time. We can relax in a few days."

"Rich people have it so easy." She pouted. "Hope I get that someday."

Khael's face went blank. "What rich people?"

"I saw how easily you got us through the gate. I know you nobles get privileges, but those guards didn't ask a single question or even slow us down. That means money. Lots of money."

Khael shook his head. "Money is uninvolved."

"Privilege then, but come on, Khael, I've seen your suite. You said you had it built a few years ago. How many people who aren't rich can do that on top of a busy tavern like the Wayward?"

"My suite is Shielin state property."

Vixen raised her eyebrows in surprise and frowned, baffled. "What kind of state property?"

"Forget who I am?" Grant murmured, back from the loo.

"Hardly. You're an Ensign in the Royal Legion of Honor." She stopped and faced Khael. "But you're not. They're all knights."

"Yes."

"Then he... you—" Her heart missed a beat as her stomach rumbled a nervous earthquake. She raised a hand to her mouth, her eyes rounded in angst. "Oh fog. You're not just rich, you're royalty."

Khael shrugged. "Yes. So?"

"You should have told me."

"For what purpose? So, you can abandon your self-respect around me the way most people do? I prefer the company of my friends as equals. If I wanted otherwise, I would have said so."

Vixen held her breath, bewildered. That made no sense. Nobles were the cream of society, and royalty was the icing of the nobility. They were her targets, to be hit and escaped, or avoided, or shown respect if distance was impossible. Even the most minor noble could dispose of her on a whim if he wanted, without consequences. Any of his fellow nobles...

"If I may ask, my lord, how royal are you?"

"Please, I am just Khael. Prince, of Shielin."

Vixen blinked.

Un-ho-ly fog.

She'd treated him like one of her street acquaintances—casual, simple, no concerns about what she said or how she said it. Her stomach hardened with dread. A cold lump settled in her chest. Maybe if she kept her mouth shut, she'd be better off.

Khael raised his eyebrows. "What is it?"

"Nothing, Your Highness," she whispered.

He closed his eyes. "Please do not do that."

"My lord?"

"No. Khael. I am a whole human being, just like you, equal to any other. Nobles are just people with titles, often attitudes."

"Please forgive my audacity, Sire, but I've seen what nobles can do to commoners. No one can just use you or throw you away with

72

impunity."

Khael smirked. "If only. You might be surprised at how many have tried."

"Other nobles have tried to throw you away?"

"I would not call them noble."

Vixen raised her hands. "But how am I supposed to act around you? Do I bow to you, kiss your hand or anything like that? I was raised to respect the higher classes, even if I steal from them."

"Have I asked you for any kind of special treatment?" Khael shook his head. "I like your casual approach, and I despise our class system. It demeans everyone." He took a raspy, deep breath. "If a situation requires formal behavior, a nod will do, but otherwise, and especially while we are operating undercover as now, never."

She widened her eyes and blinked. "Well, I'm just a common tyro collector, Your—uh, what do I call you?"

"Khael. I like that you pronounce it correctly."

"Oh." She smiled. "Thanks, Khael. I guess."

"You are welcome and thank you."

"Need to ride," Grant said. "At least another six hours full speed."

"I'm afraid to ask." Vixen closed her eyes to brace herself. "What's full speed?"

"Near double what we've done so far. About forty miles an hour."

She groaned and buried her face in her hands.

"Fastest gallop's smoother. We'll walk five or ten minutes every couple hours."

"I'm sure it sounds better to you, Sir Finnleigh." She crossed her arms and opened her eyes. "It's all too new to me. I hope I share your opinion after the ride."

Grant wobbled his head, amused.

"The tea is ready," Khael said. "Let us drink and be off."

By the time they finished the snack, their wraps were dry enough. The rainy hiss from outside had softened. After they dressed, the men mounted. Khael reached down for Vixen's hand and swung her up

73

behind him. Knowing his title, she didn't feel comfortable hugging close the way she had before. Instead, she reached down to grip the sides of the saddle.

She frowned and closed her eyes. *Fog.* If he'd meant that bit about equals...

Khael reached back to take hold of her hands and gently pulled them together around his waist. "You will be warmer and more stable if you hold onto me."

Vixen snuggled against him. His body felt strong and sturdy, a most welcome heat source to comfort her. How many tyro maiden collectors got to ride with a Prince, and as his equal?

They rode out of the shelter into the muted forest drizzle. As soon as they were back on the road, the gongies launched into full gallop. The ride felt both smoother and more dangerous. Now that she'd warmed up and she could still hold this prince close to her, she didn't mind so much.

The stop after two hours made the ride less painful. She could walk around and stretch out some of her pain between the bouts of saddle drubbing. By the time they left the road, she almost regretted they'd have to stop for rest.

Almost.

10. Dark Surprise

Vixen sat up when Khael woke her before sunset. To her delight, no part of her felt sore at all. At her request, Khael had used his shuri last night to heal her aching pelvis and legs. Though he'd held her elbow when he healed that, he hadn't touched her this time. She finished dressing with a smile.

A faint aroma from outside the tent smelled appetizing enough that she hurried to find out what it was. Khael made them pack up the tents before he presented his soup concoction for their breakfast. She enjoyed the taste, though it lacked the zest of the food to which she had become accustomed over the past two weeks living in his flat. After her second mug, and Grant's third, she finished the final quarter-mug on the excuse of cleaning the pot.

Grant cleared his throat. "After we stop at moor, what?"

"Depends on what our host can tell us," Khael said.

"Need troops, support from people, strategy?"

"I thought you were just going home," Vixen said. "Doesn't a prince have all that and more?"

"It seems my viceroy has usurped my throne, but that is all I know at the moment."

"Won't you need your army to take back your city?"

"I have no army as such. Ideally, along the way we will find a hidden force of loyal troops, awaiting my return. With the right help, we can retake my throne shortly after we reach the city."

Vixen squinted. "How many loyal forces do you have?"

"I would hope my reign earned the support of enough of those whom I trusted."

"Didn't you trust this viceroy?"

Khael pursed his lips. "Fair point."

"Paladins wouldn't fail you. Finding any'd be great start." Grant shook his head. "You said city's closed. Viceroy must have naval support we need to cut off. Impossible without troops."

"Nothing is impossible. Much depends on what we glean from our stop at the moor."

Vixen shrugged. "I don't know anything about Paladins, so I'm counting on you. Otherwise, I'll just be a well-dressed pauper."

"Assuming you survive," Grant muttered.

"Paladins are the knights of my city." Khael raised an eyebrow at her. "You will help."

She delivered a deep curtsy. "I live to serve."

When she straightened up, Khael had his eyes closed under a puzzled frown. Looking for something, probably with his shikah. But why?

"What is that pendant?"

Vixen swallowed the lump that rose in her throat. She had never shown him or told him about that rotten thing. "It's supposed to be an anti-magic charm, but I don't even know if it works. A shop vendor in the Enclave cheated me into it, at my mentor's urging."

"May I see it?" His voice remained level, his eyes closed.

Vixen shivered as a chill chased away the warmth he normally evoked in her. Her stomach fluttered. She didn't really like the foggy pendant, but his reaction unnerved her. "You can have it."

She undid the clasp behind her neck and held it out.

Just before it touched his palm, Khael recoiled, as if it would burn him. Vixen widened her eyes, frightened now. He grabbed the pendant. His eyebrows shot up and he clutched the thing in his fist like it was alive and trying to escape.

"Get down!" He thrust Vixen behind him with his free hand.

Grant dropped into a protective crouch over her. She squirmed around under him until she could see Khael. Every muscle in her body tensed. Her full stomach churned around its contents.

Khael raised the hand he'd used on her arm to clasp his other hand. A glow leaked out between his fingers. He opened his fists but held one hand between himself and the growing blaze in his other.

The flare in his hands erupted into a blinding, thunderous blast. Vixen's vision went blank. She thought she said something, but a ringing in her ears drowned out all sound.

Her mind in a fog, she blinked. How long before she'd be able to see again? Or hear? Was she all right? Was he? The cloud over her eyes began to dissolve into the fading light of evening. The warmth of Grant's presence blew away as a cool breeze washed over her. She squinted around to see something, anything. A huge, swirling, dark form mounted something black that raced off.

Maybe she should try to run away too. A tug on her arm prompted a slow turn to look up. Khael's mouth moved, but whatever he said failed to penetrate the ringing in her ears. He seemed undamaged, but upset, almost afraid.

With a short, gracious bow, he reached out and picked her up. She tried to move, but her body refused to cooperate. He gently loaded her onto Molniya and leapt into the saddle behind her. Adding to the never-ending stream of surprises, she didn't feel his movements until his strong arms wrapped firmly around her waist.

She gasped when Molniya charged into the trees. He took off in the opposite direction from where the shadowy form, Grant of course, had gone. As she struggled to make sense of this, she had to close her eyes to keep out the icy wind whipping into them.

They pounded along, dodging through the thick pine trunks at death-defying speed. It felt like they raced along in a panic, but the fog in her mind interfered with her comprehension.

Her pendant. The flash and thunder must have been an explosion.

Did he destroy it? The pendant was her only defense against magic, though it hadn't interfered with his healing her elbow... Unless that really was not magic, like he said.

Vixen forced her head down and squinted at his hands. His gloves showed no sign of scorch marks and they held her close and snug. Her street sense awoke and began to itch. He rubbed all over her back, his grip too tight, too personal.

"Khael, you're holding too tight," she mumbled.

"I will not have you fall."

"I don't like this."

"That blast would have been visible for miles. We need distance. Bear with me."

The rough, jerky terrain abruptly stabilized. They were back on some sort of road. Molniya accelerated even faster and the freezing wind tore at her face. Her mind still fought through the fog of confusion. At least her ears finally stopped ringing.

Grant pounded up on Phantom a while later. They rode in relative silence for a long time into the blackening darkness before they slowed and turned off the road. A few minutes later, they stopped in a small gap in the trees.

"Can I get down now?" Vixen grated out through a dry throat.

Khael let go immediately. "I meant no offense."

She started to turn and almost fell off the saddle. Khael caught her arm in his strong grasp. Even so, she struggled loose and clambered down to an unsteady landing. A hand on her elbow kept her upright. Khael's. Somehow he slid down from the high saddle without a sound.

When he let go, she almost fell over. "You destroyed my pendant back there, my only defense against magic."

Khael started. "I saved your life."

"Your spell blinded and deafened me."

"What spell?"

"Whatever." She waved her arms. "The flash was deafening. Everything went foggy, silent."

"I did my best to send the blast straight up. Vixen, how think you I knew you had the pendant?"

Vixen squinted away the last of the mind-clouds as reason battled its way through. "Your shikah. But you blew up my pendant."

"I assure you I did not. Without my intervention, your remains would be scattered over the forest floor."

"I don't understand."

Khael took a breath.

78

Before he could say a word, Grant started, but not on her. "Made false trail. You two all right?"

Khael looked sad but relieved. "Yes, but the blast destroyed the flier that must have been tracking us."

"Better that way. What kind?"

"Unknown. It must have been unnatural."

Vixen broke in. "Wait. Why did you shikah me?"

"My intuition. Your pendant suddenly began to emit a dangerous energy."

"What does that have to do with a flier?"

"A flying creature was soaring above us. I saw a trace of an energy signal that immediately preceded the detonation. It may have caused the reaction. I tried to alter the energy of the explosion, but it was too strong for me. I could only channel the blast up, away from us and right into the flier."

"So, there's no trace of who'd want me dead."

Khael shrugged. "Who gave you the pendant?"

"That foggy scum in the Enclave, but... my mentor made me get it." *But why would he even do that? Unless...* "That rotten bastard wanted me dead. Just not by his own hand." A wave of rage flooded through her. She frowned and tipped her head, confused again. "How did you save me?"

"With eikyo, I can influence the shape or form of most energies."

"It looked like magic to me."

"We have had this discussion."

Vixen nodded, still shaky. "But why would anyone do something like that, to me?"

"I believe I was the actual target, not you. It fits the Chelevkori pattern."

Vixen snapped her head back. "Them again?"

"Pretty obvious, no?" Grant sneered. "Saddled you with explosive pendant. Paid your mentor so you'd steal Khael's ring and get close enough to die killing him."

"Maybe it's obvious to you." She glared at Grant. "How could I have known?"

"Exactly," Khael murmured. "Had you known, you might not have performed so well."

Vixen breathed easier, but her thoughts still raced. "How do you know it was those people?"

"They have used devices with that particular energy against me before. The only question is why they waited so long to trigger the device."

"I thought they wanted to conquer the world. Why kill me? I have no influence on anything."

"You are with me, possibly by their design. My family is their primary target."

"So, they want to kill you even if it kills me too?"

"In the last three months, they have tried five times to assassinate me, now six."

She shook her spinning head. "How could they know I'd do their work? That you'd take me in, or I'd be with you today, or ever. How does anyone plan something like that?"

"All fair questions. I know not."

Vixen quivered. Khael stepped forward and gently grasped her shoulders. His solid warmth reeked of support and she craved more. The comfort of his strength reignited the heat in her loins.

Huh? Where the hell did that come from? It wasn't her heart, although she liked him well enough, but it kept flaring bright hot at the most inopportune moments. She fought off the compulsion to respond.

"I don't understand." She held onto his arms. "I barely know who or what they are, but I run into their schemes every time I turn around. They've invaded my life and used me to do their work, as if I belong to them."

"You belong to yourself, always."

Vixen's nervous flurry faded along with the horrifying death threat. He really had saved her life. She soared through another red-hot fantasy of intense, passionate intimacy with him. *Not again.* Her temples throbbed. The vision faded. It took fierce concentration to slow her breath.

He let her go as soon as her pulse and breath normalized.

She stepped back with both fists clenched. "But I have to do everything you say for at least six months. I know I agreed to, but that just means I gave you control of my life."

"You made that choice of your own free will. I want you to flourish and fulfill your potential." Khael smirked. "Fortunately, this twisted Chelevkori scheme failed much like the others."

"You may find it amusing, but I don't. I hate them, for all this. I'll get them back."

Khael sighed. "Anger and hatred have blinded me when I needed most to see."

"Fine. I'll keep my cool while I kill them."

"How will you know whom to kill?"

Vixen opened her mouth and shut it. Nothing came to mind. "Teach me."

"You have their most common traits," Grant said. "Flame red hair, hazel eyes. Left-handed but right-footed. Your eyes are green, but otherwise—"

"I'm not right-footed. I don't know what you call it, but I use both feet equally." She glanced at Khael, who nodded. Thinking back over the experience, another thought popped into her mind. "So, the explosion almost killed me, all of us, and you were worried about some dead bird?"

Khael nodded. "Mystics shun harm to most natural life forms. For now, we must go."

He mounted Molniya and reached for her hand. Once she was back in the saddle behind him, Vixen made her choice. She snuggled up to him and laid her head on his shoulder. His closeness and strength made her feel better, though her whole body itched for vengeance.

11. First Catch of the Day

An hour after dawn, Khael pointed at a distant light, like a large campfire, flickering between the trees southeast of the road. His curiosity itched to investigate, but his urgent mission weighed heavily against the risk that might entail. A few miles later, they reached another gap in the trunks on the northwest side. Khael led them through this to another hidden shelter a short trot from the road. No one appeared to greet them and the cabins looked deserted.

"How do you find these things?" Vixen wondered.

"The Forest Rovers maintain them all over Shielin." Khael waved to the lack of firewood and empty horse troughs. "This one seems to have fallen into disrepair."

"What was that light?"

"No concern." Grant dismounted. "Forget it."

Khael helped Vixen down from Molniya's high back and slid down to join her. The fire they passed might represent people who could help. Perhaps the Rovers here had moved over there. He scanned the area for threats and found nothing obvious. His chokkan lay silent.

"I'll water gongies," Grant said. "Wait here, be right back." He led the two steeds off between the large trunks.

"We just wait here?"

"We are alone and fairly safe." Khael slid down to sit cross-legged beside one of the tall pines. "Relax, take a breath. Feel free to stretch."

He closed his eyes and her stretching kih flared into his open mind. The vision never ceased to enliven him, all the more as she stretched out her kinks.

A shock broke through his focus on her. More kih appeared within his range. Nine knights slipped among the trees, five approaching them from the road, and four more headed toward Grant.

Khael put a finger on his lips and rose. Vixen's kih washed from relieved appreciation to tense concern under defensive readiness. She backed up to a tree with her hand near her waist.

Fog. He swallowed his alarm. These were centurions and archons who moved with amazing, quick stealth, incompatible with plate armor. Their tactics indicated expertise in trapping prey. They could be deserters or bandits or... what?

Three men and two women moved in on them in a pattern through which Khael saw no path for escape. All five carried enchanted swords, four with charmed daggers, and three held magic crossbows. A year ago, he knew all the centurions in Shielin, but he recognized neither of the two among these five, nor the one with the three archons stalking Grant.

Vixen opened and closed the hand near her waist. It must have been on the hilt of her dagger. She strained to hear something, anything.

Khael focused on the five closing in on them. The female nearest the road headed straight toward them. The other four maneuvered closer, hiding among the trees. The male without an enchanted crossbow made slow, quiet cocking motions, as if he had a mundane one. Vixen's kih twitched at the muted sounds.

Remain alert but fear not. Five disguised knights approach us. I would learn who they are in case they may assist us. Grant can respond if we need him.

Her kih reflected surprise, but he nodded. Grant had passed out of his shikah range on his way to the stream, but he kept that to himself. Alerting Grant at such a distance was beyond his abilities. However, so informing her would only cause her more anxiety and possibly encourage a more aggressive response than what her kih already indicated.

Khael opened his eyes. A few seconds later, steel rasped against steel. The female centurion stepped out from behind a tree. Her long black cloak hung back over her shoulders and strands of her dark hair peeked out from under her hood. Her blotchy brown-and-black leather appeared washed and well maintained. This conflicted with Khael's past experiences with seamy brigands. Most of them had been more ragged, less clean and considerably less well-armed. She pointed her gleaming sword at them.

Vixen squinted at this woman, sizing her up. He gave Vixen a wary look, but she seemed not to notice.

"What have we here?" the centurion said.

"Travelers passing through."

"I see." The woman looked them up and down and lowered her sword. "I be Lynn. Some friends an' I were hunting hereabouts. I reckon we got a little carried away with our first catch."

Khael sifted through her words while he spun his response. Though some of what she said rang true, her name and attitude buzzed in his head. She and her friends were hunting, but not for game. Their 'first catch' could mean him and Vixen, who finally glanced at him, her curiosity evident.

"I go by Aelrich, troubadour from Fiorenzi." Would Vixen catch on? "The lady and I travel with our caravan to the Aistdrum road for a pending betrothal."

"This be no' the safest road for travel, 'specially for a caravan o' two. Bandits 're about, what wi' the prince missing and the viceroy gone mad." Lynn looked square at Vixen. "Yer name, lass?"

"Forgive my poor manners. My sister, Felicia, can be shy with strangers."

Lynn's four associates still hid in the trees, like brigands ready to pounce. He suppressed a concerned frown. They might not be as safe as he had predicted.

Vixen lowered her eyes and coughed into her glove, still alert and tensed to act.

"Pleased to meet ye," Lynn said. "Ye seem better attired for travel than yer brother."

"My brother?" Vixen's puzzled eyes lit up and she shrugged. "He's a minstrel."

Her quick recovery quelled Khael's original concern. The four hidden knights held back, as if waiting for some cue to swoop in on them.

84

"Yer profession?" Lynn said.

"I, uh, well—"

"Tyro collector." Khael forced a smile. "She is shy about announcing it. And you?"

"Centurion. Lost me attachment to the crown since the viceroy went balmy last summer."

"Pray tell. I might make a song of it, spread the tale."

Lynn cocked her head with a suspicious frown. "That could take a while, an' yer caravan might no' wait."

"They will return soon enough. Will you impart a brief version?"

"In brief?" Lynn snickered. "The earl our prince left in charge when he took off last April grew deathly ill during the rains. Mid-July he got better an' made everything else worse. Supplies got scarce an' e'en poor folk need to eat. Mayhap you've some you could share."

That sounded like deserters from his own forces, probably more dangerous than ordinary bandits. Khael kept a straight face against the renewed twist in his gut.

"We couldn't." Vixen wrung her hands, her head down. "All our money went to our guards for this journey and barely enough supplies to get there. My betrothed will reimburse us and pay for my brother's return, but that'll take days. It's getting light out, Aelrich. Shouldn't we get back to our caravan? My betrothal won't wait forever."

Khael nodded, stroking his cheek. "You are so right, sister. We must rejoin our friends. Far to go, not much time. Farewell then, Lynn."

"Not so fast." Lynn raised her sword toward them. "You'll come wi' me."

"Oh really?" Despite her soft voice, Vixen glared at Lynn, her fist tight around her dagger hilt. "You and who else?"

Four knights stepped out of the trees, their loaded crossbows aimed at the pair.

"Us," the gruff bearded man said. "Walk, or do we leave your remains here?"

Khael and Vixen exchanged a glance. She seemed eager to engage in a fight, the last thing he wanted. Would she stick to their agreement and follow his lead, or risk a violent confrontation? These people were far too skilled, well-equipped, and well-dressed to be ordinary bandits. Honest Shielin folk would recognize their own prince, or at least not threaten to murder two strangers.

He sighed. "A song no longer appears to comprise sufficient payment."

"Never was," Lynn confirmed.

"You seem certain we travel this route alone."

"Get movin'." The beard sneered. "We'll explain it to you."

"No tricks or we'll bind an' drag you," the shorter, stouter woman added.

Khael coaxed Vixen's hand off her dagger with his hand and nodded to her. He emanated soothing energy through his hold, though he had no idea yet what their situation truly was. Her narrowed eyes shot suspicion at him, but she did not resist. The knights marched them through the trees toward the road.

"No caravans 've come through here," the beard said. "Only two heavy chargers went by afore we found you. Your future's lookin' pretty dim."

"We'll just take 'em to the demon for judgment an' see what he decides," Lynn said. "Lead on, Sir Fred."

A demon in Shielin? Khael swallowed any visible expression of his shock.

"What's a demon?" Vixen wore a curious frown.

"Powerful creature." Fred's beard split into a wicked grin. "Likes to eat intruders, 'cept he prefers to have fun wi' pretty girls first."

"I never heard of such a thing." Khael shook his head and squeezed Vixen's hand to reassure her against the rising outrage he sensed from her. The flood of anomalies made his thoughts spin. He no longer felt so confident, which may have leaked out to her. Her tense grip worried him. "Sounds more like an excuse for bandits to terrorize and rob."

"Watch yer mouth." Fred swiped his crossbow stock at Khael's ear.

Khael stumbled to evade the impact without being too obvious. He loosed Vixen's hand in the process in case they needed to act.

"We'll just let Bleckston decide," Lynn said. "He might accept a weregild for your release, in addition to yer song, troubadour."

"Bleckston?" Khael raised his eyebrows, baffled at the strange name.

"Ye'll see." Fred chuckled coarsely.

They arrived at the clearing where the fire burned. The wide circle of thatched cabins around the large fire pit resembled a kind of camp Khael knew the Rovers used. But these were advanced knights, not rangers, and the shiny black stone block behind the large bonfire pit looked like an altar.

Should he read their minds? Given the lack of an overt threat or attack from these knights, he had concerns about such an intrusive act. Twenty-one horses munched in the open stable behind the altar. A sizable force to confront. Also, Vixen remained armed. Neither of them had been searched, or even touched.

None of this made sense.

Khael suppressed a snicker—no doubt Grant would curse his curiosity. Yet part of him insisted he resolve this conundrum without violence. This many advanced knights in the camp, with or without a real demon, would overwhelm them, even with Grant's help.

The escort took them around the circle to the cabin closest to the stone block and latched the door once he and Vixen were inside. Cots and trunks took up most of the space in the small room.

Fred's voice filtered through the door. "Any tricks or escape attempts will be punished."

Khael sat down to puzzle this one out. Vixen glared at him. She began scoping out the walls, apparently seeking a peephole or a way out.

"It might be best to relax," he murmured.

"Go ahead," she whispered back. "I hate being confined."

"We can wait for this demon Bleckston to appear." Khael blinked his eyes open wide. He choked back a laugh. "Demon Bleckston?" *Could it be...?*

"You think that's funny?" she hissed through an icy glare before she continued her hunt. After several minutes, she snarled her frustration and flounced down on the cot next to his, her arms and legs crossed tightly.

Disjointed conversations began to filter in from outside.

"... no' even travel gear. We've our own horses an' weapons."

"An' we left 'em theirs. Why'd we do that?"

"They ain't those misogynist viceroy's rangers," came a woman's voice.

"We need every resource we can get. These two might help us scout."

"Trust a troubadour an' a thief? They could be spies or just useless civvies in..."

The conversation drifted away as another came near.

"... if we join wi' others, that'll reduce our spread an' coverage."

"An' the city has less supply than ever. Their supplies might help."

"No."

"Unless the Rovers return to their stations—"

"We're no' thieves...."

A rustling shuffle of several people struggling with some kind of heavy load drowned out the conversations. A thump shook the ground and a slam rattled their door.

"Keep yer mouth shut or else," someone outside growled.

A more distant voice called out, "Muster up!"

The sounds outside dwindled to nothing. Vixen shivered again.

Khael closed his eyes and shuddered from shock. Grant lay on the floor of the next cabin, trussed up and chronicon-free. The gongies appeared nowhere in shikah range. They could be dead or have run away to avoid capture. He buried his head in his hands.

"What now?"

"Grant lies restrained and weaponless in another shack. Molniya and Phantom are nowhere I can see. I may have underestimated our danger, but... these knights are far too refined and well-equipped to be mere bandits."

"They talked about seizing our property and ransoming us. Who's going to pay that? They could kill us, or... 'have fun' with me." She shuddered with a grimace. "I'd rather..."

Khael shook his head. "I remain certain things are not what they seem."

"I'll say. You said mystics were honest, but you told that woman a string of lies a mile long."

"Did I?" He frowned at her unflattering assessment.

"Aelrich? And Fiorenzi? Me being your sister Felicia, engaged to somebody from Aistdrum, wherever that is. And a caravan? What about the truth?"

"Nothing I said was false."

She glared at him with slitted eyes. He put a hand on her shoulder, but she shrugged it off and turned away from him.

"Fiorenzi's village troubadour, who taught me to play when I stopped there some years ago, called me Aelrich because I resemble his estranged son. I never said you were my sister Felicia, nor that you, or she, was engaged. There are always pending betrothals. Aistdrum is the easternmost shire in Shielin, the road to which lies ahead. Our caravan numbers three, one of whom is officially my bodyguard, though he lies captive nearby."

Vixen made a sour face. "Humph. I wish I could spin a yarn like that. Not that it was any help."

"Sadly, she also lied. Honest knights do not hide out in the forest, or take over Rover camps, and much of their gear is enchanted." He frowned. "Yet I recognize none of them."

"So much for your assurances." Vixen dropped her head into her hands and shivered.

"I will do what I must. Keep your guard up and follow my lead."

89

Vixen's new glare at him could have withered a whole field of flowers.

Khael closed his eyes again. The knights stood in an arc facing the altar, within clear sight of their cabin. Two of them marched up to the door. He forced his hands open, in fervent prayer he would not have to use them.

The knights opened the door. They brandished their spears. "Outside. Move it."

12. Bleckston

Vixen shuddered at the deafening noise from an animal horn Fred blew, not more than a yard away from her ear. She glared at him. An even louder, ear-splitting screech made her cringe and cover her ears. For people who used to serve Khael, they seemed awfully ignorant and rude.

"Who dares ta intrude on me domain?" a discordant chorus roared out across the camp. The horrendous squall had three different pitches, all not quite a whole octave apart. Echoes bounced off the cabins and the surrounding trees. "Who dares?"

Vixen stood close to Khael, away from the dissonant racket. He stood tall and strong, as if he had figured something out about their captors. She hoped so.

"Great Bleckston, mighty Demon of the Rock." Fred lowered the horn. "These two trespassers intruded. We present them for your judgment."

He waved at Khael and Vixen, then bowed low toward the altar. Vixen slowly turned her head and looked up at the humanoid thing that stood on the block. Long fur ran down the center of its chest and abdomen from an oversized goat's head. She averted her eyes around its oversized male genitals. The thing's furry legs descended into bovine tarsals and hooves. Random paint splattered its arms, chest and thighs.

The creature lowered its bizarre gaze toward her and Khael. Its wild eyes rolled side to side non-stop, as if it had trouble focusing. Smoke rose from its nostrils as it gnashed its teeth. Vixen pressed closer to Khael and peered up at his face. He seemed engrossed with the monster on the stone block. His eyes sparkled in the firelight.

A shiver jolted down her spine. He was enjoying this! She straightened up away from him, not too far, but he said nothing, not even in her head.

"Ah see food! Trespassers 're eaten, an' Ah hunger! Ooh. A lass for me pleasures!"

Khael smiled. "Marvelous," he murmured.

"What if I get eaten, or raped?" she whispered.

"It is all show. Enjoy it." He reached for her hand and grasped it gently.

Her stomach tightened anyway. He never told her enough. Revolting show.

"Wheesht! Identify yourselves for the Demon Bleckston, mortals!"

Khael sniggered into full laughter.

Vixen stared, torn between amazement at his laughter and disappointment over his reticence. His eyes met hers and his laugh became infectious. She couldn't help herself anymore and chuckled.

The baffled knights stared at them, muttering unintelligible commentary. The two nearest pointed spears at them.

"Get serious, you clown," one growled at Khael.

Instantly sober, Khael seized the knight's spear and tossed the weapon to the ground off to the side. Following his lead, Vixen snatched the other knight's spear and threw it behind them past their shack. She reached for her dagger, but Khael placed a calming hand on her wrist.

"This is priceless, Damon." He snickered as the whole clearing fell silent. "Whence obtained you that get-up?"

"Infidels," the goat creature said, its screech subdued. "Ah 'll eat you half-burnt."

"I doubt that." Khael grinned.

One knight brandished his sword. "Show some respect, you gruntling!"

"Of course." Khael applauded.

Vixen started to play along when her eyes widened in amazement. The monster pulled up on its horns. The goat-head, shoulders and upper torso came off in one piece to reveal the grizzly bearded face and chest of a middle-aged man.

"Who are ye?" came his bewildered, raspy voice. He jumped down from the altar. Within two steps, his eyes flew wide and he dropped to one knee, his fist over his heart. "Yer Highness."

All the knights immediately snapped to attention.

"Rise," Khael said. "No honorifics, please. Trees have ears and our enemies have spies."

Vixen slitted her eyes at Khael. "Would you kindly fill me in on the joke now?"

"Forgive me, dear lass." Khael took her closer to the rising costumed man. "Meet Margrave Damon Mackintosh, Baron of Obsidian Hall and Captain of my Paladins. Damon, this is Vixen, my personal collector. Your men have Grant in the hutch next to where we were. Please free him before he breaks something, or someone."

"Lynn, loose Grant immediately," Damon said. "Forgive me no' recognizing ye, milord. The view from inside the mask is poor." He gave Khael an abashed look. "How'd ye ken?"

"This particular camp is unfamiliar, but your demon's name sounded familiar. Your kih resolved the rest."

"Obsidian, of course." Vixen nodded. "Damon black stone."

"Ye found the show funny, Sire?" Damon asked.

Khael chuckled. "Indeed. Randy costume."

"'Twas supposed to scare ye," Damon grumbled, but he cheered right away. "Had it a long time. Souvenir from me first expedition as a knight. Works better wi' non-mystics. Ah, well. Tis excellent to see ye here, Sire. We've much to discuss."

"This baron is the captain of your palace guard." Vixen waved around at the camp. "Isn't this your ideal scenario?"

"This scenario's no' ideal." Damon sounded like her grumpy mentor.

Vixen's eyes wandered down his costume as Lynn led an angry Grant over from his cabin.

Damon grinned and bumped his hips. "Ye fancy that, lassie?"

She recoiled. "No."

He chuckled coarsely. "Fred, breakfast for our guests whilst I change into something more presentable." With that, he grabbed the costume feature prominently waving before him and sauntered off to a hut on the far side of the block.

"You had me seized and bound?" Glowering, Grant held out his hand. "Where're my weapons?"

"I beg your pardon." Lynn bowed to him as Fred returned Grant's gear. "We guard this area against all intruders, an' we've only heard o' ye by rumor."

"We've had to be more aggressive out here," Fred said. "The captain 'll explain."

"Please follow me to our dining shelter." Lynn led them to a large building by the stable.

"Might I know who you are?" Khael said.

"Senior Commander Jaclyn Lochbuie, chief o' the captain's temp staff. I go by Lynn. This's Commander Fred Greggson. But, Sire, ye introduced the young lady as yer sister Felicia."

"Not quite." Vixen stood up straighter, pulsing confidence. "He said Felicia can be shy with strangers, not that I was her."

Lynn nodded after a moment of thought. "Ye're right. I should'a paid closer attention. I've seen the princess once an' she looks, well, different from ye."

Khael turned to Grant. "Where are our gongyangmas?"

"Shooed 'em away when I heard stealth noises. They should be nearby." Grant emitted a piercing whistle.

A few minutes later, both gongies trotted in, nickering as if they had enjoyed the break.

Those at Khael's table remained seated after the hearty, hot breakfast. The other knights cleared away the fixings and set about the routine chores of the camp.

"Situation report?" Khael said.

"Ye heard o' John's illness?" Damon said.

"John?" Vixen wondered before Khael could answer.

"John Masterson, Earl of Wastpynt, is my viceroy, or was."

Damon shook his head. "We're no' sure. He was ill for so long, then one day he just got up, but he'd changed. He dispersed half the Paladins to harbor posts, or along the city walls. Then he shipped in new battalions to displace ours. By September, his rangers and knights outnumbered the house guard."

"How many men are in a battalion?" Vixen wondered.

Damon glanced at her. "Ten companies o' twenty men, plus around thirty staff."

"Are you certain this is John, not an impostor?" Khael asked.

Damon shook his head. "More likely John's dead."

Khael let out a long sigh and bowed his head. Vixen fidgeted between him and Grant. In spite of the implications of this information, her heart warmed toward him.

Finally, Khael raised his head, deep sorrow etched into his face. "I will find a sorcerer to prevent this in the future. You may hire anyone else you need." He sighed. "John was Mother's viceroy for fifteen years before I took the throne. I trusted him, but I failed to leave him adequate support."

"'Twas no yer fault, Sire," Lynn said softly.

"I left him without resources that could have prevented this."

Damon raised a hand. "We were careless. At any rate, John, or who e'er this fellow is, concentrated on the city, no' really the rest o' Shielin. He cut us back so much I deployed the Paladins wi' out his ken. One battalion's along the road to Cambridge, one's on the Metacresta road, an' one's scattered throughout the forest. I set up here in case ye came this way."

"Well enough, but who defends the city?"

"Mostly his troops. More sailed in to take over, an' stuff began to disappear from the palace. He also raised taxes an' fees monthly, an' issued new regulations making commerce harder."

"What stuff?" Khael narrowed his eyes.

"Paintings, jewelry, sculptures an' other valuables, e'en the carpets. I had folk checked on their way out the door, and methinks naught actually left the palace. When John found out, he ordered me an' me knights out o' Skemmelsham. I took five companies as if they were me only remaining ones, an' he bought it. The real John knew better than that."

Vixen did a quick mental calculation. "That's only four battalions?"

"Mine's spread out coordinating an' gathering the others."

"That explains the new faces here," Khael said.

"These here're new since ye left. Things've worsened. Rovers an' Watchmen deserted. Fees an' restrictions increased. John arrested hundreds on phony charges an' jailed 'em."

Khael took this in with a flat expression. "How is my mother?"

"I wish I ken for sure. She hasna interfered wi' John's tyranny yet, but he probably threatened her wi' some kind o' retaliation, mayhap arrest."

A warmth in Damon's tone made Vixen frown. Something went unspoken about Khael's mother and this captain. Her mind itched to find out what.

Khael pursed his lips. "The jail only holds a dozen or so."

"Two months ago, he seized one o' the harbor warehouses for confinement. The dockmasters staged a protest. When his patrols moved in, a riot ensued. After that, the mariners put all ships out to sea an' blockaded the harbor. Nothing gets in or out by water anymore."

Grant clapped his hands. "Excellent. Forces them to open roads."

"Excellent?" Khael shook his head. "No, my friend, without the harbor business, many shops and inns will be ruined, along with the dockworkers, and the families. Their whole support system will shut down. Winter is no time for such foolhardiness."

"There's a kind o' market along the Cambridge road outside the main gate," Damon said. "But John's so paranoid about yer return or outright rebellion tis difficult to ship anything in or out. Shall I gather the troops an' storm the city?"

"Certainly not. Our people will get caught in the middle."

96

Vixen touched Khael's arm. "Isn't this your ideal scenario?"

Damon squinted at her. "What's this 'ideal scenario,' lass?"

"He said, ideally somewhere along the way we find a hidden force of his loyals, awaiting his return. With the right help he could retake his throne by surprise within a day or two of reaching the city. If we could sneak enough of your forces into the city—"

"I will visit a certain moor, for advice, and I wish to look around, incognito." Khael paused. "Gather as many as you can in the next week and infiltrate the city."

Damon rubbed his beard. "I can get a fair number, but no' everyone wi' out alerting his men."

"How certain are we the rest of the house guard is still in the palace?"

"I've na reports otherwise, so far."

Vixen shook her head. "That's the first group I'd replace. I'd want loyal people around me in my house, especially if it's not really my house. This usurper must be some kind of idiot."

Damon shrugged. "He moved slowly at first, so's not to arouse suspicion. But he ne'er trusted the women an' dinna much care for our men. Wi' the harbor shut down, he canna get more imports and has to use everyone who's left that's no' fomenting revolt."

"If conditions are that foul, why is everyone so cooperative and not rebelling?" Vixen muttered.

"Violence is the last refuge of the inept," Khael said. "People are known to endure much unwarranted suffering before they respond assertively. Perhaps too much. What about the Watch?"

"About half an' half, last I heard," Damon said.

"His add-ons will make trouble," Grant said.

"Aye." Damon nodded. "At least Trevor'll side wi' us, e'en if he ain't the commandant no more. He'll have his own loyal contingent, too. Mayhap we can round up some o' the Rovers on the way in."

Khael rubbed his chin. "We must meet again once I know more. Use the network."

"Network?" Vixen murmured to Grant.

"Spies," he muttered back.

Khael glanced around. "Your company appears short of full."

Damon nodded. "When we set up here, two o' me junior knights had heard the legends o' the shrine treasure an' went below to investigate. They ne'er returned."

Vixen opened her eyes wide. Shrine? Treasure? At last, a chance for profit! "What legends?"

"The shrine under the altar was built here by a small, wealthy sect last century," Damon said. "They were massacred or died out, dependin' on which legend ye believe. The shrine fell into ruin an' was buried in the flood o' 2674. All that's left above ground's the altar. I kept the stairs inside an' the room below clean to support me act. The rest is strictly off-limits."

"Maybe we could take a look around inside." Vixen's eyes danced.

"Tis haunted, or worse," Damon said. "Cost me two fine men."

"Forgo this time." Grant gave her a stony face.

Vixen stifled the shudder that threatened her intrepid hope. She returned him a calm, level gaze until he looked away. No cooperation there. *Fog.*

Khael yawned. "We can rest here until nightfall."

"As ye wish, Sire. We must leave. If yer plans change, inform yer mother."

There it was again. Vixen squinted at them. Khael nodded. Damon, Lynn and Fred rose and headed off.

Vixen whispered, "Grant, what's with this captain and Khael's mother?"

"Ask him," Grant muttered back.

Vixen looked at Khael. He looked so tired, or sad. Probably grieving again.

After a quiet moment, Khael stood up. "We need to rest. Would you like to share a cabin?"

Vixen felt another wash of warm tingles. He could have shut her down flat out about the shrine, but he said nothing. With the closeness they now shared, she might get some leeway to forge ahead on that. She adopted a breezy tone. "Fine with me."

A lull descended on the camp after the knights rode out. Grant settled in one of the cabins alone, well before the normal sounds of nature returned. Khael and Vixen used one whose door latched from the inside. He sat in his usual position on a floor mat, facing away from her chosen cot.

Vixen yawned, hoping she could sleep in this place. The chance of treasure still energized her, as well as more privacy with Khael. Unlike all her former sleeping companions, his presence made her feel cared for, more secure. Maybe if he weren't so sad, he'd pay more attention to her. No, their rotten contract would interfere. A twinge of regret over her initial aloofness tugged at her heart.

She removed only her armor. More would be too blatant and she wasn't ready yet for the passions that bizarre, hidden part of her craved. He acted respectful enough most of the time, but he displayed little personal interest and limited affection. This close would have to do.

The cool hut was warm enough under her cloak and a blanket. The bitter, late autumn cold outside didn't penetrate the forest so much, the huts less.

There had to be a way to get them into that shrine, and she was going to find it.

13.   Adventure Beckons

Khael stopped short before awakening Vixen. She lay on her side, facing him, her flame-red hair strewn over her face and the pillow. He gently smoothed her silken tresses back and gazed at her. A shiver chased its way down his spine. Her presence still excited him in ways he dared not explore or even show.

He caressed her shoulder. She stirred and opened her eyes. When she saw him, she yawned.

"What time is it?" She rolled onto her back and stretched her limbs off both ends of the cot.

"Mid-afternoon. Still determined to endanger us in the shrine?"

"That's not fair." She stood up beside him and pouted.

"Is it not?" Her impudent proximity and graceful movements stirred his blood. He tip-toed a delicate path through his emotional gauntlet, without kinshuh, and emerged unscathed. At least he did not collapse.

"I just want to look around," she grumbled. "Finding treasure is what collectors do. This is my chance to be useful, maybe find some money to pay back you and Sir Finnleigh."

"Doesn't justify risking lives." Grant's rumble filtered through the door.

"You're eavesdropping on us?" Vixen clenched her fists.

"Warrants open discussion."

Vixen raised her eyebrows toward Khael.

"Arm up and join us outside. We will decide together."

The plea in her eyes morphed into a glare. He returned her a cool expression.

Her face went slack. "Fine. Is there a loo?"

"On the far side of the altar. We can eat when you are ready."

Grant followed Khael to a table by the fire pit.

"You're not really letting her take us down there," Grant said.

Khael sat down. He had not seriously considered the idea. Rescuing his people came first. Still, the possibility of finding something useful to his quest tickled his fancy.

No. Grant was right about the danger. "Unlikely, though I admit curiosity about what lured two archons to their deaths."

"Your curiosity's almost gotten us killed." Grant shook his head.

"You discount our many rewarding travels, your chronicon ax and sword, Phantom, Molniya, a fair income for us both, and recovery of my ring and heritage?"

"Most of those came when you took my advice."

Khael raised his eyebrows. "I listen to everyone. Then I follow my instincts."

"Your privilege." Grant scratched his beard. "Long as we survive to reclaim your throne."

A light breeze whispered through the trees. Khael closed his eyes and enjoyed the sounds and scents of the forest, the crisp pine aroma and the rustle of the branches overhead. When he opened his eyes, Grant seemed lost in thought.

"You have other concerns?"

"Just wondering about you and that little minx."

Khael chuckled. "No worries. She slept in our hut while I exercised."

Grant's eyebrows shot up. "Out here?"

"We have no audience."

"Your evening kinshuh?"

"After, inside our hut. Now who is curious?"

Grant cleared his throat. "Just passing time." A smile cracked through his pursed lips. He seemed ready to relax when new lines creased his face. His eyes wandered toward the cabin Khael had shared with Vixen. "She coming out tonight?"

Khael scanned around for her. The cabin held no kih. She should have been in the loo, or on her way back, but no humans appeared in the vicinity.

"I see not her kih." His breath caught.

Grant sat up straight, alarm on his face. "No. You think she—"

A faint screech of metal on metal rose through the altar.

Khael stood, a hollow in the pit of his stomach. "So it seems."

"She can take care of herself." Grant hunched down.

Khael headed toward the altar. "Did you not point out the deaths of two archons? I want her safe and whole."

Vixen's knapsack leaned against the black rock, a bag of torches beside it. The top slab of the altar lay turned to the side, revealing a staircase. Despite her exceptional fighting skills, she could die down there. Filled with concern, Khael stepped over the lip to head down.

"Wait." Grant pulled two sticks out of the bag and tucked the drawstring into his belt. He lit both torches. "Here. Me first."

Khael took the torch Grant held out and let him go ahead. The stairs took them down to a square stone room with a heavy wooden door on either side. The door on the right refused to budge.

Grant growled. "When we find her..."

He opened the door on the left against the creaky resistance of its hinges. The dark, stone corridor beyond was littered with torn and burnt cobwebs, a gritty stone floor and a dank, musty smell. Grant torched away the webs and ducked through the door. The hall looked tall and wide enough for two, with a door on either side half a yard in. In the dim light, there was no sign of Vixen.

Khael pointed at a ring on the wall by each door. Grant inserted his torch into one and pulled another torch from the bag. The new light revealed the corridor's end, more than five yards off, at an arched double door with a single door in the walls to either side.

Khael closed his eyes. "Fog, these walls must be thick. I read no kih here."

"No footprints either. Guess we check every room."

The door on their left stood part way open into a dirty closet with something on the floor that stunk of moldy sewage. Khael peered into the room across the hall. Its rotted bedroom furniture had dust in and around multiple slashes. The window in the wall held out solid dirt, but no light.

Still no Vixen, or any life other than mold.

They hurried to the other end of the corridor. The open room on the right looked like the mirror image of its predecessor. This one's window had a large hole in the middle that led into a dark black tunnel. Vixen crouched with her torch in the far-left corner of the room, just beyond two fractured skeletons, examining something on the floor.

"Death wish?" Grant snapped.

Vixen whipped around and fell on her rump with a squeak. Something squished underneath her. "Fog. You trying to scare me to death?"

"Would've served you right."

She stood. "I knew you wouldn't approve, and I wanted to look around. It's deserted."

"Something killed those two." Grant pointed at the skeletons.

"Nothing in here."

Khael frowned at the altercation. His chest tightened. The relief at finding her flew away. Something close but out of reach felt wrong.

Grant frowned at Vixen. "No guarantee it, or they, won't return for us."

That seemed to get her attention. She shivered.

Khael scrutinized the room, seeking any threat that might justify his unease. He bolstered his calm with kinshuh against a growing urge to flee as the danger invisibly drew nearer. His shikah revealed nothing, increasing his edginess.

"Lucky you're alive, urchin, and you've endangered us all."

A chill of the nearing danger reached to Khael from the black hole in the window—the tunnel. Even there the stone and dirt were too thick for his shikah to penetrate. "Grant."

"Need to finish." Grant fumed. "Ought to tie you up and carry you as baggage."

103

"You want to try that?" Vixen raised her torch and dagger and marched up to the towering fury.

"Grant."

Two large insect-like antennae twitched in the tunnel opening. Khael backed toward the door. Every muscle in his body clenched tight. Mystics went out of their way to avoid harming natural animals, even dangerous giant arachnids. With their lives at stake, he would have to defend his friends first. He clenched his teeth.

"Kyle, this's important," Grant insisted over his shoulder.

"So is that gargantula."

Vixen spun around as Grant finally looked past her. A huge, furry, brown and black spider crawled out of the hole. It's two-yard-long legs set it gently on the floor near the corner.

"What's that?" Her voice an octave higher, Vixen backed into Khael.

"Most likely the mother whose eggs you were examining." Khael grimaced. He left out that her fall had damaged some of them. Mothers usually attacked those who harmed their potential offspring. Large, poisonous mothers presented a mortal peril.

Vixen squirmed to hide behind Khael. "Let's get out of here."

"It can outrun us," Khael murmured.

Grant beckoned her off to the side. "Spread out. Better odds."

"It's too big, a real monster." Her face screwed up in panic. She raised her trembling dagger and the shaky torch, her knuckles white.

The gargantula finished checking its eggs and turned toward them. It charged straight at Khael, clacking its mandibles.

Vixen dodged away to the side and tripped. Khael stepped over and reached for her arm.

"Fog." Grant lunged at the giant spider and jammed his shield into the thing's beak. Frustrated noises emerged behind the steel disc as Grant yanked his ax from its harness.

Khael helped Vixen to her feet, but she was too petrified to do more than shake. He closed his eyes to keep shikah watch, his breath held. Telepathy was no use against non-sapient life forms, and his zarute was too new and weak to help. Despite the risk of poison, he clenched his fists.

Grant charged in with a forehand swipe that sliced the gargantula's left front leg in half. He spun through the blow, swinging his ax up and down in a spiral arc. With a soft, squishy crunch, the large blade neatly severed half of the human-sized head from the rest. A quiet gurgle oozed out of the creature's jammed beak. Its legs flailed and collapsed, its kih fading to lifeless oblivion.

"Was expecting some help, urchin." Grant snorted.

Khael opened his eyes. Vixen cringed and looked away. Grant wiped his ax on the furniture remains. He yanked his shield free of the dead mandibles, wiped it too and slung it back over his arm, glaring at her the whole time.

"I am sure Vixen appreciates the rescue, as do I."

"Uh-huh." Grant snarled at her. "If my ax wasn't chronicon, we'd be skeletons, like those."

Khael opened his mouth to tone down the argument.

"You don't have to make it so hard for me to thank you, Sir Finnleigh." Vixen sniffed. "Maybe you were right about coming here. Want to leave?"

"Want to smack you, but I don't hit girls, and it's Sir Grant."

Vixen narrowed her eyes. "There's still one more room." She pointed. "Across the hall."

Both men stared at her.

"The double door wouldn't open. I think it's jammed."

Khael widened his eyes. "You are serious?"

"There's treasure down here somewhere. It's not in this room. All the other rooms were empty and trashed."

Grant shook his fist at her. "Almost got killed. Almost got us all killed."

"We're alive, and you handled the spider like a hero. Would there be another in a closed room?"

"Maybe another tunnel."

"Wait." Khael's sense of danger had abated, though not all the way. His throne was still at stake, his people in danger. But they were already here. The two skeletons could be the dead archons, in which case Grant had slain the worst threat—so far.

On the other hand, if there was a treasure, it might have a guardian worse than a gargantula. No kih showed through the door in the last room, but stone and packed dirt had hidden the gargantula until it crawled out of its tunnel.

Grant shoved the torch bag into Vixen's arms none too gently. "Yours," he grumbled.

She slipped her arms through the tie strings, like a loose backpack, but scowled. "Thanks."

Khael exhaled slowly. This close to finding out what might be worth the risk, his curiosity seized the moment. "As long as we are this far, and I see no immediate threat, we can look."

Vixen grinned. Khael nodded toward the closed door. Grant rolled his eyes and moaned his displeasure. He gripped the door handle and pushed to no effect. Pulling also failed, so he hauled sideways. The door slid into the wall in smooth silence.

Khael scanned the room, entered and looked around. The hairs on his neck rose. This floor was somewhat cleaner than the hall or the other rooms, and cobweb-free. Rusty torch rings hung on all four walls and a few scattered bone fragments lay strewn about the stone floor. Against the wall to their left stood an antique leather couch behind a shiny, low, empty coffee table. An old wooden chest with a fancy, ancient lock sat in the corner straight across from the door.

Where is the trap? Khael checked the ring a yard along the front wall from the door. It looked clear of triggers, so he slowly set his torch into it. Nothing to justify his new tension appeared. His heart sank. *What am I missing?*

Grant stalked along the near wall to slide his torch into a ring there. Khael beckoned Vixen inside and took her to the far wall. She set her torch in the ring after he inspected it and squatted to study the lock on the chest.

"Nice, but I've practiced on better. Fishy though. Why waste a decent lock on a shabby old trunk like this?"

"Shabby can hide value. I sense danger."

"Maybe you're right." Vixen started to rise. "We should get out of here."

Khael caught her arm in a firm grasp before she made it up.

"Some collector." Grant snorted. "Your idea, remember?"

"We have come this far, in part for you, lass. Do your job."

Vixen stared at Khael. Her pulse pounded hard on her temple and in her neck. He sent soothing energy into her arm to help calm her.

With a deep breath, she squatted back down and pulled out some picks. She opened the lock in a few quick moves, stowed the picks, and gingerly pulled the lock out of the hasp. The tongue swung down slowly on its rusty hinge to hang near the front of the wooden trunk. The lid resisted her best efforts to open it, so she checked for extra latches.

Not finding any, she turned to Khael. "I can't lift this lid."

"It may be too heavy for you."

"Kyle?" Grant oozed worry.

Khael squatted beside Vixen to seek for anything that might trigger a trap. With kanjuh, he sensed what seemed like ordinary internal latch mechanisms. He concentrated his strength to lift the heavy lid, slowly. The lid creaked all the way up until it rested against the wall. Vixen gasped beside him as he peered into the chest.

Five neatly packed sacks sat beside a small nondescript oaken box, a lacquered jewelry case, and about a dozen weapons. He closed his eyes and smiled. His heart swelled in response to the box's tantalizing kih.

"What?" Grant's rumble intruded on his reverie. "Can't stay all foggy night."

"Patience."

"Yeah, hold your gongey," Vixen muttered.

Khael scanned the trunk and carefully reached one hand in. He

107

picked up the box, a mere two and a half palms long, one wide and a thumb thick, etched on the top. Opening it, he nodded.

Yes!

"What's so great about a flat wooden box?" Vixen said.

"Let us see." He lifted out one of the coin sacks and inserted a flap into the box's mouth.

Vixen's eyes grew wide as the box sucked the bag in, its bulges and fullness warped to fit. She grinned as Khael stowed the other four bags. Her face glowed. "What is that?"

"A perfect find," Khael murmured.

The lacquered case and the armaments also had kih, but he had a hunch there was more in the trunk he could not sense. He stored the jewelry case and held the box next to the trunk.

"Can we get those weapons?" she asked.

"Better not to touch until we can examine them." Khael levitated the weapons out of the trunk and into the box, one at a time.

Vixen's kih shone amazement. When only three were left, all daggers, she gasped in delight.

"Can you do that a little faster?" she said. "Those look nice."

"Haste kills."

"I want to get out while we still can."

"You brought us here." Grant leaned over her from opposite Khael. He had come in closer to see for himself. "Rather survive the effort, no?"

Khael dropped the last dagger into the box and stashed it in a pocket. A chill rose along his spine and he looked back toward the door. It finished rolling its silent way shut with a faint click. Something about its motion and markings sent icy chills through his brain.

Seals.

Fog!

"Thanasynfo," he whispered.

Grant shuddered. Vixen rose at Khael's urging and they all turned to leave. A thick, greasy looking, dark red cloud poured out of the wall next to the doorway. The stench of rotting flowers reached their nostrils.

"What. Is. That?" Vixen whispered, her eyes bulging.

"A real monster," Grant whispered back, shivering.

"Do not let it touch you." Khael's voice shook, his calm shattered.

14. A Real Monster

Khael sucked in a sharp breath. A thanasynfo made the gargantula look like a charming friend. He flexed his kinshuh to reclaim his waning self-control.

"What happens if it touches me?" Vixen asked.

"If the vapor wraps around any part of you, it will drain your kih, a slow, excruciating death."

Vixen shrank back in horror between the men. Her heels thumped against the trunk. "What do we do?" she hissed.

"Stay calm."

"Get torch." Grant edged over to the nearest, the one he had hung on the side wall. "And pray to your gods for mercy."

Khael reached with zarute for the one on the wall behind the trunk. The tiny mental claw leapt out and clasped the torch handle in a feeble grip. He wrestled the incredibly heavy burning stick up out of its ring. In his hand it would have been a simple act, but the new discipline felt more like a baby's weak first clutch. Panting, he reeled it back to him with all his might. The torch dipped toward the floor several times in its slow, vague bobble in his direction. His arms beaded up with sweat. The weight fell into his outstretched hand.

Vixen stood immobile, her eyes stuck on the last torch, which hung on the entry wall—behind the hovering death-cloud.

Before Khael could hand her his, the cloud swooped across the room. He turned to pull her by his side. She had frozen rigid and his hand slipped off. The cloud lanced out straight toward him.

Vixen shrieked and fell backward into the trunk with a crunch. Khael leaned away from the creature's advance, but the wall behind the wooden box gave him no retreat.

The stormy red cloud shooting toward him stopped dead and splayed out a few thumbs short, as if it had slammed into a barrier.

Amazed, Khael stared at the maroon murk boiling against the

invisible wall. A realization flashed into his mind. "Vixen. There is a ward in the trunk. Find it."

She just blinked up at the blood-red vapor, too terrified to move.

Khael's chokkan tickled as he recalled her fears of imprisonment. He reached a gentle hand to turn her face toward him. If he kept her busy, she would focus on that rather than the source of her panic. "Our lives depend on that ward. It is our way out of this trap."

Trembling all over, she clasped his hand and hauled herself up behind him. "Ow."

Khael faced back to the looming threat. The crimson fog churned in waves that thinned out and expanded sideways, toward Grant. The knight waved his torch and the cloud recoiled from it, sparking where the flame touched it.

Another crunch made Khael look back. Vixen held up a ring and a thin gold pendant with a black gemstone. He nodded. She stepped out of the smashed false bottom in the trunk and huddled close to him.

Ripples shuddered across the murky cloud that now filled most of the room. The red lightened as the vapor coalesced into a solid, moldy-gray giant with three arms and two tree-trunk legs. When it stood upright, its twin heads banged the thick ceiling beams. One drooling mouth growled at them, the other snarled.

The creature swung a three-clawed hand out toward each of them. They swept right past where the ward had stopped the cloud. Vixen ducked. Grant blocked the triple talons aimed at him with his shield. The impact slammed him back against the wall with a grunt.

Khael dodged the claws and threw his torch. When it struck, his eikyo fingers amplified the flame. The resulting explosion left an angry, black burn spot on the thing's barrel-like chest. An ear-splitting, discordant stereo bellow reverberated in the darkened gloom.

Vixen rose toward the exit across the room. She tripped over a scaly root-like foot and crashed to the floor. The monster swung at her. Its razor-sharp talons raked the air mere thumbs above her collapsed form.

The other two claws reached for Khael. He slipped inside the curve of one arm and drummed his fists along the other. Resounding crunches of broken bone vibrated up his arms with each punch.

The giant roared out in pain. Its damaged arm dangled low in a twisted, limp curve.

Grant leapt up and cut off one head with a mighty swing of his ax. Scarlet blood fountained into the air. The head snarled as it dropped to the floor. The bellowing monster turned to deal with the knight. Its pulverized arm swung loose.

Khael slid around the creature's massive leg to Vixen. His stomach clenched at her limp form. She lay sprawled on the floor as if dead.

He grasped her arm. "Vixen, get up."

Vixen bobbled a disoriented nod. Her attempt to rise failed, but she clutched the pendant. Khael wound his arm under her shoulders and hoisted her.

"G'way," she mumbled, barely coherent. "I c'n fen' f'r m'se'f." She sounded drunk and hung limp on his arm.

Alarmed, Khael looked her over. Aside from the dirt on her armor she looked fine. He shifted his grip and checked her back. Three bent darts stuck out of her bum.

Her fall into the trunk must have set off a secondary trap. Those darts might well be poisoned. He had to get his friends out of this room. How? His pulse raced. *Fog!*

"Here, boy." This time Grant's reddened ax swung clean through the creature as the ugly gray dissolved back into the red vapor. Grant slipped on the bloody floor and fell hard. He grunted in pain but hauled himself back to his feet.

"Grant," Khael called. "Ward."

Surprised, Grant hesitated. The cloud swooped all over him. He screamed.

"No!" Khael seized the pendant and hoisted Vixen over his shoulder. He strode into the bloody murk toward Grant. If this didn't work, they were all dead.

The red vapor parted violently away from the ward and swirled

112

off the howling knight.

"Out now," Khael barked in Grant's ear. He gripped Grant's arm and scanned his kih. In their last encounter with a thanasynfo, even brief contact had inflicted severe damage. Here, too. That kind of damage Khael could not undo. *Fog.*

Grant shook his head and wobbled, still in shock. He raised his shield and winced. His yanks on the door met with no success. "Locked. Fog."

Khael looked around the room for anything that might help. Too much shadowy murk blocked most of the dim light from the remaining torches. The churning cloud swirled a storm of hateful fury. There had to be something....

A new oddity in the wall beside the door caught his roving eyes— a small, open niche. Inside it, a shiny thumb-switch flickered in the torchlight. Khael tightly focused his zarute and ham-handed the switch. The door slid open.

Grant shambled out into the dark hall, his shield arm slack, his ax dangling in his right hand.

Khael lowered Vixen to the floor outside the room. She slurred again about being fine. Gritting his teeth, he took a deep breath and slipped back into the room. The vapor boiled toward him, piling its threat tall and wide. It stopped cold a yard away. He took another zarute stab at the switch and darted out. The door quietly latched shut behind him.

"Whew." He slid his tired bones down the wall beside the door.

"Need more light." Grant's wobbly voice echoed in the hall's silent near blackness.

Still catching his breath, Khael pulled a fresh torch out of Vixen's sack. He touched Grant's hand with it.

With only the dim flame at the far end of the hall by which to see, the knight set his ax down. He fumbled to light the new one. With a grimace, he raised the burning stick and picked up his bloodied weapon.

Khael crouched beside Vixen. Was she still alive? His concern smothered his relief as he closed his eyes. Her kih glowed from three small angry spots around the darts. He plucked them free. She still slumped, though the points lacked any kih or visual evidence of poison.

Why was she so lethargic? He scanned her punctures. No obvious indication of spreading injury, but not all poisons left immediate traces in their victims. His compulsion to be polite wrestled with his care for her well-being. Her healthy recovery trumped his issues.

"Vixen, permit me to check your bum for poison traces."

She waved a hand.

He frowned. Did she mean yes or no? "You need not undress, but I must feel the injuries."

"Mm hm." Her mumble was barely audible.

Closing his eyes, he slid his hand under her waistband. His gentle palpations found three firm lumps on her otherwise smooth skin. Poisoned. He retracted his hand and shuried her without further contact. By the time he finished, her system shone a healthy clean.

Unfortunately, he could not do the same for Grant. He would have to recover over time.

Vixen stirred a few seconds later. She rolled over and sat up with an annoyed expression.

Khael drew a kerchief to wipe the creature's blood-spatter from his face.

Grant looked down at them. "You recovered now?"

"The stench and splatter made me nauseous, and I hate enclosed spaces." She straightened her clothes and stood up, one fist on her dagger. "Hope you enjoyed the show." Her focus switched to Khael. "And you your free grope."

"Didn't see a thing." Grant shook his head.

"I asked for your consent." Khael rose to his feet and dusted off his trousers. He gazed into her narrowed eyes and held up the pendant. "I believe this is yours."

Her eyes widened with wonder. He reached over her head and

gently clasped the ward pendant around her neck.

She blinked. "I can keep it?"

"You found it."

"Thank you." She gazed at him, a mix of curious and delighted. "May I?"

Vixen squinted, instantly more suspicious. He held out the kerchief. Her expression softened to a smile and a nod. She held firm as he wiped red sprinkles from her face.

As they emerged from the altar stairs, Khael fingered the oak box in his pocket. Grant rubbed his left arm. His outfit dripped browning blood. He looked exhausted.

Vixen bounced with an excited prance. "What did we get?"

"Dirty," Grant said. "Wash up before anything else."

"You certainly should, Sir Finn-mess."

He rolled his eyes. "Really?"

"We're richer."

Khael threw Grant a look of caution.

Grant took a breath. "Maybe. Sacks could hold sawdust or sand."

"There's a jewelry case."

"Probably empty."

Her enthusiasm faded.

"We're alive. You're undamaged. Creatures defeated, treasure, exhilarating. Feels great to breathe, new toys, maybe some coin. I hurt, could've died. Lucky we survived."

"Because of this pendant." She clutched it.

Grant nodded.

"What was that thing anyway?"

"Thanasynfo."

"Never heard of it."

Khael stared at her, amazed. Did not everyone know about the infamous creatures? Infuriated parents frightened their children into behaving with stories about the wicked killer clouds. He mentally

115

ticked another entry onto the growing long list of her unusual characteristics.

Grant's eyebrows tried to crawl under his hair. "You sure?"

"She said no." Khael faced Vixen. "The thanasynfo has three forms. The blood vapor is the fastest, most flexible. It can slip through any opening, even the slightest crack. I failed to notice the seals on the room door until after the trap fired. The niche had one too. Had I seen them, I would have insisted we leave. The solid form is immune to the ward. It can switch forms in twelve seconds, as often as every twenty-four."

"Someone timed it?" Vixen stared at him in awe.

"Taxonomy is a science. Thanasynfos are created by special, powerful sorcery. They serve their creators forever."

"What if the creator dies or the thing is killed?"

"If the creator dies, the thanasynfo is free. The vapor cannot be damaged, though it avoids fire. If its solid form sustains lethal damage, it dissolves into a thin mist for hours before it can reform."

"Can't be killed," Grant added.

She fingered the pendant absently. "I thought anything alive could be killed."

Khael rubbed his chin. "A potent enough fire spell might destroy one. Or a kih drain if such is possible. Its only saving grace is it never harbors grudges. It attacks all life forms indiscriminately."

"That's a saving grace?" Vixen shook her head at Khael's nod. "Maybe it's hungry, or in pain."

Khael gazed at her. His experience and previous studies had not suggested that.

"Going to wash." Grant marched off toward the loo.

"What about us?" Vixen said.

"Showers open," Grant called back. "Baths private."

"Interesting idea," Khael mused.

"About the showers?" Vixen's eyes widened at the thought. She finally let go of the amulet.

116

"The thanasynfo. What you suggested may be useful." Khael shook his head. "We should join Grant in the bath house."

Vixen's eyes went round. "You want me to shower with you and—him?"

"You are welcome to bathe in private, but you must resist any further urge to explore alone."

"Fine," she muttered.

"Thank you."

From the slump of her shoulders, he could not tell if she was more relieved or disappointed.

15. Healing the Damage

"Well? What did we find in there?" Vixen's voice brimmed over with excitement.

Khael tilted his head, amused at her boundless energy. "We must leave."

"Excuse me?" Grant's eyebrows bristled. "I got hammered down there. Shoulder still sore. You took pocket vault, gave her pendant."

"Fair enough." Khael pulled out the box and reached inside.

Vixen gasped and waved her arms. "Careful! Won't that swallow you too?"

"It only stores inanimate objects." Khael fished around. "But I am pleased you care." The jewelry box was not Grant's style, nor the inferior, extra shield, sword or mailed boots. Not the bow, either. The money could wait. The three daggers held the most promise. He set them on the table.

"What about the other stuff?" Vixen's hand wandered to her amulet.

"Grant gets his choice now. We can divide the rest later."

Grant squinted at each of the daggers. "Enchanted. These two match. Mine."

"You could tell that just by looking at them?"

He peered at Vixen from under his bushy eyebrows. "Enchantment leaves traces. Knights learn to read 'em."

She took a closer look at the tiny glyphs.

Grant held up the third one. "This one's easier to use than yours, and better edge than my two. Take it." He pulled the daggers off his belt to replace them. "Want two more? I don't need four."

Her mouth widened into an astonished grin. "Sure. Thanks."

He set them onto her outstretched hands. She stood up and gave the bewhiskered knight a quick peck on the cheek. Grant double checked his belt.

They had not ridden far when a mental itch prompted Khael to slow down. A short way into the trees, a starving, injured kih shivered on the ground. He turned Molniya off the path. Vixen sat up from her cozy snuggle against his back.

"What now?" Grant sounded wary.

"Someone lies wounded among the trees."

Khael stopped them a few trunks away from the kih and crept nearer. Around one last stout redwood, a woman lay huddled in the fetal position. Her clothing hung in tattered shreds, exposing much flesh riddled with scratches, bruises and scrapes. She could have been Vixen's twin, almost as gaunt as Vixen had been when he first met her. Hazel slits in a haggard face gave him a bleary look. He closed his eyes.

Grant snorted. "Chelevkori witch."

"A dying deacon." Khael took a step toward her.

Grant caught his arm. "She's dangerous. Let her die."

"No."

"Why not?" Vixen blurted, surprising Khael. In response to his look, she shrugged. "They tried to kill me once, and you? How many times?"

"She is harmless to us."

"Maybe, now. Not so much later." Grant's caution blared through the beard.

"This I will not abide. Allow me."

Grant stared at him like he was out of his mind, but he backed away near Vixen.

Khael knelt beside the wretch. "How may I help?"

The woman closed her eyes, cutting off a blank stare.

"We need heat and something warm for this woman to ingest." Khael scanned her.

"This would be better." Grant half-drew his sword.

Khael stood and glared at him. "A fire and soup. Now."

Even Vixen frowned back.

119

Not now. Khael walked back to Phantom, fished out the cloak he had stowed in their only saddlebag, and covered the woman with it. Grant and Vixen had not moved.

"What is your delay?" Khael raised his eyebrows, expecting cooperation.

Vixen crossed her arms and stepped back against a tree. Grant exhaled frustration and slammed his sword back into its sheath. He strode off into the woods, muttering all the way.

Khael turned his attention back to the deacon. She lacked any trace of sentient thoughts, only thirst, hunger, exhausted fears, and rage, too weak to move. He raised a water-skin to her lips and gave her sips. The rage subsided. On a closer look at her face, he shuddered.

He knew her, and Vixen had unknowingly provided, no, been the missing clue. This was the same deacon who had tried to kill him at the kyoshitsu. Should he heal her? Risk another inflamed attack? Grant said they should let her die. Perhaps he was right.

However, in her current, weakened state, she was no enemy, just a helpless animal, devoid of intelligent thought, thirsty and starving. If he treated her, that might help bridge the gap to peace with the Chelevkori. The worst result? Another attack, possibly later, after she betrayed them, or together with a horde of comrades. If she had any nearby...

No. The vendetta had to end, or it would kill them all.

Her teeth chattered.

Enough.

Khael activated shuri to heal her, but his view of her kih made him stop. She was so weakened his healing might easily burn out what little energy she had left. Shuri could restore his kih, but only physical health of others. Using his own zhukih might help reduce her damage, but the amount required for all her injuries would consume more than he could safely give up.

She shivered again.

Khael gritted his teeth and plunged ahead with the most serious injuries. He might not be able to heal everything, but he could at least

120

give her some relief. It took longer with her system so weakened. His arms and face beaded up with sweat at the strain. After tending to only the most serious gashes and welts, he had to stop.

Still no indication of intelligence.

Fog. What was he doing wrong? The cloak helped warm her, and Grant's fire shed some heat in their direction. Her mind seemed gone, so kinseh was no use.

A shadow in her kih caught his attention. Something in the center of her brain blocked her ability to function. A tiny thing, barely a fingernail's width, right in the worst possible location. Shuri had not affected it at all, so it was more than just an injury. He used kanjuh to feel the minuscule object. Hard, but not entirely inflexible. A blood clot? How did it get there?

A chill shot up Khael's spine. His final defensive blow with zarute, directly into her brain, did this. Nothing else made sense. He could probably dislodge the clot, also with zarute, but how without doing even more damage? Especially with so little experience and no practical finesse. More likely he would kill her this time for sure.

Khael took a deep breath. She would die without his help, and he had thoughtlessly caused the injury himself. He frowned hard and concentrated on the clot. Tiny, ultra-fine nudges ought to work. If they did not kill her. Or him from the tight control he needed to learn on the fly.

This was not like dragging a torch or flipping a switch, more like carving a bone fragment from a fish dinner, except this fish was supposed to live, and with undamaged brain tissue. He nudged at the clot. The tissue flexed but loosened only a speck. Fog. This process could take even longer than her scratches. His focus blurred with each excruciatingly fine, mind-numbing touch.

With a groan, he plodded on. It took forever. Sparkly colors invaded her kih. Wait. No, that was just his exhaustion creeping in. He cleared his mind and poked again. Barely any effect. Fog! Another clumsy one almost tore a new gash in the delicate structures surrounding the clot. The claw vanished.

Sweat burned his eyes. He dragged his sleeve to clear them.

121

Fatigue wore on his concentration. Could he finish this? Too close to quit, and nothing else would do the job. Without rational thought, she would be at the mercy of the wild, and it had not been too kind thus far. As he had said, he would not abide this. Holding his breath, he reactivated zarute and made one more push.

Ah, progress—the clot slipped, just a fraction. Another and another...

At last the stubborn nugget popped free of the web. His lungs screamed for relief.

Soldier-like kih images swooped in and engulfed the clot as if desperate for the chance. It must have been her internal health system, energized from his shuri, coming to finish the job. Amazing—it still worked.

New thoughts arose, sentient thoughts. Who was this man? Why was she here? It was cold.

Khael breathed and placed a gentle hand on her forehead. Icy. He raised her up to a more seated position and wrapped his arms around her. A slow crawl of her shaking arms crept out for his warmth.

He opened his eyes.

Grant glared stony incredulity at him. Vixen had her arms crossed with a curious frown.

"Is there any food for this woman?" The croak blazed pain in his throat.

"Usually takes longer." Grant held out a mug of something that looked warm, his stare dark and unchanging. "Cost us hour."

Khael nodded. Seemed like four, but one?... Fair enough. They still had two or three days to go. His neck and shoulders ached, but he held the shivering woman until she finally smoothed out. He took a swig from the mug for his throat, then brought the woman's hands to it.

"Drink this. It will warm you up and give you sustenance." Still raspy, but not as painful.

She took the mug in both hands and gulped at the contents. *"Spasibo,"* she whispered.

Khael dragged himself to his feet and beckoned his companions closer. "Please give me one of your tunics," he whispered to Vixen, too wasted to speak louder.

"For her?" Vixen sounded incredulous, but her face softened as she stared at him. She glanced at the woman and went to Phantom. Her knapsack was strapped behind the saddle and too high for her, but Phantom sank to his knees. She fished out the tunic. "Here. Get her dressed."

Khael nodded a silent thanks. The woman shrugged off his cloak. He guided her head and arms into the tunic. Grant looked on with a hard, pinched expression.

The tunic settled into place as Khael helped her stand. He picked up his cloak and wrapped it around her shoulders. She raised her head to face him and handed him the empty mug.

"Are you well?" Khael wanted to read her mind to catch any potential threat, but he was too worn out. If she attacked now...

She nodded dreamily. Her fuzzy hazel eyes were puzzled. "Where am I?"

"Five hundred forty miles northeast of Cambridge. Have you no memory of what happened?"

She squinted as if the recall attempt hurt. "I go to Cambridge— no, *mystic* farm, north of city." Her melodious voice started out weak, but she spat the word 'mystic' like a curse. "I aim to rid Family of dangerous enemy. When I arrive, witch take me inside. She leave. Man arrive. Then... I recall nothing else, just fragments."

"Know you who I am?"

For a long moment, she studied him. "You are he." She frowned. "I try to kill you, yet you save my life. Why?"

"I seek only peace."

She nodded. "Thank you, yes. We have peace. I must return home. I not know how from here."

"This road leads to the Cambridge highway." He pointed back the way they had come. "A few miles from here is a path on the right to a camp with shelter, food and clothing. Take what you need. You have a long walk ahead."

She shivered and hugged herself. "I am unarmed and without supplies."

"Unarmed?" No Chelevkori deacon qualified as unarmed.

She bowed her head.

Khael took a deep breath. Giving her a weapon could invite disaster, but perhaps as a gift not so much. "Wait here." He walked out of her view between the gongies.

Grant cleared his throat in disapproval. His knuckles whitened around his sword hilt.

"Who are you?" Vixen sounded remarkably sweet.

"Iulianna Silnyikrov, Deacon of Manticore Family. You?"

Khael closed his eyes and held his breath.

"Felicia Finnleigh," Vixen said between her teeth. "I'll be sure to remember you."

Khael exhaled his relief. He drew the oak box out of his coat and reached inside.

"Not weapons," Grant protested quietly from behind him.

"She needs something." Khael retrieved the boots, the shield, and the long sword with its belted scabbard. "Generosity to a foe in your debt sows future rewards." He stowed the box and came back to Iulianna. "I regret this is all I can give you."

Shivering, she adjusted the scabbard to hang on the right side of the belt, buckled it on, and drew and examined the blade. Her eyes sparkled as she re-sheathed it, stripped off her tattered boots and struggled on the new ones. She looked the shield over before slinging it onto her arm, then pulled the cloak back over her shivers.

"These noble gifts, *moy knyaz*." She gave him a grateful, unsteady curtsy. "Enchanted. Sorcery taboo, but—no mind. I use for now. I owe you."

"Let us renounce our enmity."

Iulianna gazed at him, deep in thought. Finally, she nodded. "Agreed. You are not monster they tell me to expect. I remember this generosity." She reached out her arm to clasp wrists with him. "Fare

124

you well."

"And you."

She disengaged and marched unsteadily back up the road the way they had come. When she passed out of sight, Khael faced his companions.

"What in hell?" Grant's frown carved deep chasms in his forehead.

"Are you all right?" Vixen's concern touched Khael's heart.

Khael nodded, blinking back tears of gratitude. He stretched high his tired frame. "We lose time and I must recover. Let us talk when we stop."

16. Pause

Khael led their ride on at full speed, with Grant close behind. Having expended so much energy in healing Iulianna, Khael needed time for his own recovery as they rode. Vixen seemed somewhat detached, not snuggled up quite as close behind him as before. The cold chilled his back,

Light from the short moon filtered its way through thin patches in the canopy overhead. The long moon was either down or hidden by the clouds. When the next path appeared, he led them off the road to a clearing where they dismounted for a lunch snack.

Neither of his friends spoke to him while they ate. Their silence enhanced the chill around him.

"How are you two?"

Grant blew out a breath. "You gave that Chelevkori... witch... clothes, weapons, told her about camp. She'll clean it out, betray Damon, Paladins, all of us."

Khael raised his eyebrows in surprise. "I healed Iulianna and we parted on amicable terms. The camps are for any travelers and I owed her."

"But she could wreck everything." Grant's face pinched. "She could break her word. Turn us in or ambush us later. You don't know." He shook his fists, muttering vague, incomprehensible fragments. "She's the enemy, damn it. Doesn't that matter to you?"

"We renounced our enmity. How do you not see that?"

"So you instantly trust sworn enemies who make nice?"

"Even if you are correct, what can she harm out here?"

"You tell me. Oh, wait, your disciplines have limits. Do they have to kill one of us, or you, to get through to you? Or is that part of your plan now too?"

Khael wanted to smack his friend. That would not work even if it did not violate his integrity. He needed to remain calm, and a different approach might work better anyway. "Thank you for your first such blunt honesty with me since I took my throne four years ago. Finally."

Grant stared at him. "I'm always honest with you."

"But rarely so forthright."

"Doesn't change what I said." Grant's scowl returned.

They stood rock still; chess pieces waiting to be moved. "Would you truly harm a helpless, injured being if you could heal them?"

"Chelevkori yes, others maybe. Depends."

"Mystics discourage vengeance—yours and theirs."

Grant growled. "You're an idiot."

"Fine." Khael turned away. He was not the idiot or blinded by prejudice.

Khael looked around for Vixen. She had moved from where he last saw her. At the edge of the clearing, staring up at the moon. He walked over to her. An odd wave of comfortable unrest flowed from her. "You seem disturbed."

"I don't understand why you risked yourself to help an enemy." Her big green eyes radiated puzzled curiosity. "She would have killed us if she could."

"She more resembled an injured child to me."

Vixen snorted. "That woman was no child."

"Surely you have mercy in your soul."

"They tried to blow us up, remember? That doesn't deserve mercy."

He raised his hands. "So, the only answer is to kill them whenever we can?"

"I thought you hated the Chelevkori as much as I do."

"We cannot overcome fear or rage with hatred and hostility." He shrugged his shoulders. "The risk was mild and she needed my help."

Vixen stared at him like he was from another world or a different species. Nothing came out for almost a whole minute, though her tight lips twitched more than once. "I won't agree with your friend, but you are crazy."

Khael smirked. "Perhaps."

"Why bother with her at all? It would've been simpler just to let her die, and any threat she might prove to be in the future with her. Or was she too pretty to resist?"

"What has that to do with anything? Her beauty is irrelevant." He shook his head at Vixen's widened eyes. "Mystics hold every sentient being as unique and worth individual treatment, and this incident may help resolve the Chelevkori vendetta."

"You weren't impressed?"

"With Iulianna's appearance? You seem to be stuck on that."

"Most men are."

Grant snorted from his crouch by the fire. "I'll agree with her. You are crazy."

Khael frowned his frustration at the knight. "Every group has dissidents, Grant, an old mystic saying Grandfather always liked. In this case, I repaid a debt." He turned back to Vixen. "Physical beauty is too ephemeral to have any lasting value. Only spirit matters."

"Never seen one of them dissent." Grant stoked the fire higher.

A true knight, stubborn as always. Khael kept his focus on Vixen.

Her stare gave way to another frown. "What debt?"

"When I returned to the kyoshitsu, this deacon came to call. Musoka, the sensei, let her in, ostensibly for me to evaluate as a candidate, really a test for me. I began evaluation when she conjured her poisonous claws and attacked.

"I seized control of her mind and tried to erase her memories of our meeting. I still believe that is possible, but what I did failed. I had to choose to kill her or let her go, and I hesitated."

"Didn't hesitate with Nechetnayas we met coming back to Cambridge," Grant muttered.

Khael was about to respond, but Vixen paled at the Nechetnaya name. Her eyes glazed. She almost fell over.

He caught her arm and steadied her. "Vixen?"

"I'm fine." She recovered her balance, frowning her own

confusion. "I just felt dizzy. Maybe from standing still so long after riding. You hesitated and then what?"

Khael let her go, but the inaccuracy stuck. She recognized that name. How? Was there no end to the mysteries surrounding this lass? "In my defense, I injured her severely. My attempt to heal her also failed. She came to, leapt up snarling like a wild animal, and fled into the darkness."

"She tried to kill you twice, and you spared her life?" Vixen's jaw dropped.

Grant shook his head in disgust.

"Mystics strike only as a last, desperate resort, and we never kill the defenseless. Also, on first sight, she reminded me of you. You could be sisters."

"When I was cold, you didn't hug me, or put your cloak around me."

Oh fog. As much as he wanted to respond, that was just not possible yet. "You work for me and we have a contract. I have—"

"What about after that?" she blurted too soon. She bit her lip.

No point in thinking about it, as if he could stop. "Let us survive that long." He swallowed, hoping it did not show too much, and smiled.

Once they began riding again, Vixen snuggled close against Khael's back. Her warmth inflamed his senses. He itched to turn around and kiss her, pull her body to him and explore it in intimate detail. His mind spun.

No, no, no...

With a determined effort, he stowed that image away for future reference. Maybe, just maybe, after he achieved his next, crucial discipline. And their agreement ended. If she still felt the same...

Within an hour they came to a place where the hard-packed dirt roadway simply ended. The forest and grass alongside now rose in front of them.

"Hold tight. This part of the ride is rough and can disorient the novice."

Vixen's head rose off his shoulder and she stiffened. Her horrified gasp choked off as Molniya took them right into the wall of trees. She dropped her head and seized Khael's waist in a frantic, painful vice-grip. Molniya moved quickly, though much slower than his full speed gallop, through gaps barely wide enough for them.

Khael clasped her wrists. "We are about to descend a sharp hill. Hang on."

The ground disappeared.

Molniya plunged down a virtual cliff beyond the trees. Although he had dropped his speed, the hill was too steep for a mild, safe descent. Shocks and bumps jolted them both all the way down. Vixen grunted. Khael's stomach floated behind him. At the bottom, the ground leveled out. His weight returned, but her grip slackened. He tightened his to ensure her safety.

They shot across a paved highway, perpendicular to their path, up a matching exposed slope. The ascent slowed them until they reached the top and headed into more dense trees. Vixen's breath became more unsteady and she fell back from him.

He drew her as close as he could. "We are almost there. Stay with me."

A short distance along the higher, flatter ground, the trunks widened out. The gongies picked back up to full speed on the next length of the hidden road.

Vixen swayed, as if she had passed out.

"Are you all right?" She seemed ill or faint. Khael shifted around to elicit a response.

She groaned. "Stop," she whispered. "Please, let me down."

Khael urged Molniya to a halt. Vixen struggled out from behind him. She fumbled through an unsteady dismount and nearly fell over. He slipped from the saddle and stood facing her.

"You are crazy," she moaned. Her eyes rolled up and she began to collapse.

Khael plunged in and caught her by the waist before she fell. "Vixen?"

130

She reached her weakened hands to his arms and groped at him to drag herself upright. Her head hung limp against his chest.

"Forgive me," he murmured. "I did not think how rough that can be the first time."

Vixen raised her head and gave him a bleary look. She slid her hands up his arms and wrapped them around his neck. He set aside his concerns and folded her closer in his arms.

"Mm. You're forgiven," she whispered. "For now."

A heat arose in Khael's belly that felt improper. She worked for him, and he refused to take advantage of their situation, as he had promised. With an effort, he pulled back, but she held him tight. The dizzy swamp in her eyes cleared.

He narrowed his. What was she up to this time?

Without warning, she clinched her arms and planted her lips on his.

The soft, gentle touch sizzled lightning in his brain. His kinshuh dissolved. He wrapped her in his arms and clung fast, the best sensation he had ever felt, as if they were the last two people in the world. Her demanding mouth tasted irresistible, unbearably sweet, the most fantastic dessert ever. Feverishly he returned the savory marvel, enjoying every gliding, fiery contact. Their bodies melted into each other.

Sometime later, the world decelerated to its normal rotation. He drew back, panting.

"Don't... do... that," he rasped, shaky. Her delicious hot press still inflamed his whole body though they stood a few thumbs apart. His head blazed as never before, torn between an urgent need to recover his alertness and the inferno erupting in his loins, ravenous for an encore and more.

"I'm sorry." Her voice husked deeper than ever. She drew in a ragged breath. "I shouldn't have done that. My lord."

"No, it's—no worries." He closed his eyes. What he would not give to do that again... Impossible.

A reluctant kinshuh finally wiped away his ache from their

separation. He gazed at her. Her eyes widened. They stood immobile, their stares locked on each other.

Phantom snorted.

Grant cleared his throat. "You finished? Can't stay here all night."

"Right." Khael nodded slowly.

He remounted Molniya, who softly echoed Phantom. Vixen cuddled up close and warm behind him, heating his back, her arms firmly around his waist. Did she thrive on their new coziness as much as he could not? It sure felt like it.

The delight of their kiss faded on his lips, slower in his mind. He had thought anything like that might never occur. Why did she have to do it now? His heart sank.

This is going to be the longest six months of my... ever.

17. Wild Night

It seemed like forever to Vixen before they stopped again. Her legs ached too much for such a ride. Khael took them to another Rover shelter. He did his shuri thing to soothe her pains before they had a quick lunch.

"What was that road we crossed?" she asked after they had eaten.

"Metacresta highway." Grant doused the fire.

"So, we're close."

"By morning we should overlook the mirror cliffs." Khael's eyes bore a brief, wistful haze. "After that, one or two days of ride remain through the trees."

Vixen groaned. "Do we have to go through the trees?"

Khael flipped his eyebrows up and down. "We could ride faster in the open along the cliffs. If it rains, we may risk it."

"I'm not sure that sounds better." Vixen stowed away the last of her gear.

"Depends on how you see it, urchin." Grant finished lashing down his saddlebag. "No spies in rain. Faster but no road."

"I figured that, Sir Finnleigh." She kept her voice cool, though she seethed at his rudeness.

"Must you call me that?" he grumbled with a pained frown.

"I'm using your name."

Shortly before dawn, the road ended at another dense cluster of trunks. They slowed to pick their careful way through the maze to the edge of the forest. The sky was still overcast and a slight drizzle wet the open air.

"Have you ever seen the mirror cliffs, Vixen?"

She shook her head. "I've never left Cambridge."

"Come look." He slipped down from the saddle after her and took her hand.

Her heart raced like mad, and she had trouble breathing. He seemed to like her more since she'd kissed him. Wild passions clouded her mind for a moment, different from those hot flashes she'd had before. Maybe her own feelings coming to life...

They left the forest through the falling mist across a stretch of short grass to a rocky expanse. Vixen balked at the hundred fifty yards of slippery rocks and gravel, but his comforting hand kept her quite steady and she cleaved tightly to stay with him. Where the ground ended, she crept to and peered over the edge.

The moons shone bright enough through the clouds to see hundreds of yards out over the dark water. Not too far to the north, the cliffs sloped their steep, craggy way down a quarter of a mile to the waves on the ocean surface. Right here and to the south, it looked like the ocean washed right under a ledge where they stood.

Vixen gasped and jumped back. "Holy mother! How thick is this shelf we're standing on?"

Khael smiled and crouched down, beckoning her forward. He held his hand over the edge. When she stuck her head out and peeked, a reflection of his hand gazed back at her.

"The cliff is glazed to a near-perfect mirror. It is quite solid."

That explained why the waves appeared to crash against each other down at the surface. They must have been hitting the cliff face. She took several moments to enjoy the spectacular reflections of the ocean in the walls. "Is that natural or...?"

"No. I could sing you a lay of the story if we had time, or our soon-to-be-host can tell you his version when you meet him."

"Is there a short version?"

He chuckled and tugged her up beside him. She clung to his hand as they trudged back toward Grant and the gongies.

"The short version? We are near this end of a semicircular cliff that is one hundred miles straight across. Fifty miles out, where the center of the complete circle would be, is where the city of Monistarnie once stood."

"Never heard of it."

He frowned. "Are you certain?"

"I'd recognize a name like that."

Khael paused, then nodded. "Three millennia ago, a huge explosion destroyed the city. In an instant, everything within fifty miles disappeared in a miniature star."

"Oh!" Vixen clasped her hands over a fierce tightness in her chest.

"So began the Great Darkness, during which most records of what happened were lost. Were there no ocean, you could see the crater. It is the deepest part of the ocean."

"How awful. All those people."

"That is the reason the technology of the ancients is shunned in our society. Flying vehicles, devastating weapons, even miraculous healing devices all became taboo. People feared the same thing could happen again." He paused. "At least, that is our theory."

"Theory? Without records, how could you know?"

"My grandfather investigated all the places where any records survived the darkness. The crater has been studied and the cliffs have not eroded since."

Vixen shook her head. "How does that matter?"

"Ocean water corrodes almost anything, given long enough. The blast that forged these cliffs rendered them impervious to such decay for three thousand years."

"Maybe I'll ask our host to tell the long version," she muttered, deep in thought.

"I sing it better, but he does have a way with these stories. A history lesson may benefit you." He glanced around. "It looks like rain. Let us make shelter for the day."

* * *

Khael kept shikah watch and meditated while his friends slept. Vixen's reaction to Monistarnie threw him. Virtually all the children in Cambridge, even in the poorest families he had encountered, knew the legends and of the language of the ancients, Arcana. Many such tales abounded in Cambridge, especially in public performances, from amateurs to classic actors. She said she grew up in the city, had never left, but there were other anomalies too – her reaction to various names, her natural fluency in Yazyk, her exceptional skill mastery for a genuine tyro.

That seemed strange, too. She had picked his pocket, whereas master thieves had failed. Her expertise in combat skills would be expected of... an assassin? But no tyro collector could do more than aspire to become an assassin, and only after years of training and experience. Unless the Chelevkori had flaunted all guild laws and done just that with her.

A chill settled on him. How was that even possible? His chokkan would have warned him if she represented a lethal danger to him. Or had it already? How could she hide this so thoroughly that even her kih showed no such indications. Or did it?

He scanned her sleeping form. Only her deep rage stood out, and that she seemed to feel toward the Chelevkori, not him. Her kiss had been completely sincere, affectionate, and intensely enjoyable. No answers came up.

Near sunset Vixen woke up screaming. Khael spun over to her and held the shaking, terrified maiden close. With a vague, jingling rustle, Grant scrambled out of his tent. A shrill wind whipped the air around outside, promising a wicked, cold storm for the night.

"You all right?" The wind almost buried Grant's voice.

We are fine. Prepare to ride. Khael caressed Vixen's shoulder. "What nightmare had you?"

"I killed you." She sounded weak and anguished.

"Tell me." Khael stroked her hair, willing his touch to calm her. Her fiery silk thrilled his palm and she clutched his other hand.

"It was horrible. We were in some opulent place with a huge bed covered in rich linens. There was a gigantic bathtub outside in the middle of a fancy, polished stone floor, and a rail overlooking a garden, or maybe a field. We were in bed together, naked, me on top of you. I guess we were... I felt a surge of incredible pleasure wash over me, but it was twisted, wrong.

"Something tore me apart from the inside. It was so agonizing, I dug into my body, ripped out a hideous rusty knife and plunged it into you, many times. The pain merged into a fiery rapture. I laughed hysterically and shattered into a million stars while our blood flooded the bed and the tub."

He took a breath to stifle a shudder. Would she really kill him to end her own pain, even if imagined? "It was just a dream."

"But what if it comes true? Maybe not like that, but somehow."

"From what I know of dreams, they rarely do. Most are highly symbolic rather than real predictions. Dream death usually implies some other kind of transformation. However, we can make every effort to ensure its literal implications remain a dismissed fantasy."

She blinked and nodded, her eyebrows more relaxed.

"Is there some reason you would want to kill me?"

Vixen gazed up at him. She seemed so sweet and innocent he just wanted to hold her in his arms for hours, kiss her fears away. He flinched. Neither of them was ready for that kind of response.

"I don't know," she said in a small voice. "The compulsion was so overpowering I couldn't think. It was like you were the source of all my ills and I had no choice, no control."

"You are awake now and have choices. We should go. The storm will hide our passage."

She made a frustrated twist of her face at him. Did she expect more from him?

Khael crawled outside the tent to let her dress in private. He needed the distance to puzzle over the pieces of her dream and help Grant pack up everything else. What he had said about dreams was true, but her talk of an irresistible, uncontrollable urge to kill him unsettled him.

If she had been indoctrinated by the Chelevkori to assassinate him, his chokkan would warn him, as always... unless it already had. He sucked in a deep breath. Her expressions of hatred for them rang true, so why would she kill anyone for them? The matter required serious consideration, when he could make the time. If he had his way, they would both live, for a long time, together.

When he straightened up from dousing the fire, a pretty blue flower at the grassy edge caught his eye. He picked it and rose as she emerged from the tent. She looked glorious in the waning daylight with the wind whipping her fiery hair around her sweet face.

His pulse raced, but he kept his feelings and his concerns in check. Any change had to wait until he knew more if they survived.

She noticed his gaze. "Hi."

Khael handed her the flower. She accepted it with a tiny, almost shy smile. His heart raced for a few beats. He pulled on his coat.

Dark angry clouds of the impending storm coalesced overhead. The rough wind blew a salty ocean smell through their small campsite.

"Better eat fast and ride." Grant spoke just loud enough over the wind.

Khael tore his distracted eyes from Vixen toward Grant. "Trees or grass?"

"Grass 'ed be slippery and wind's strongest I've seen here, but inland and cold. Your call."

"Vixen, please get the blankets so we can fold up the tent."

She nodded and scrambled back inside to get their blankets. Together they packed everything in Phantom's saddlebag. The great gongies both stamped and snorted, fiery determination in their eyes.

"You want to see the castle, too?" Khael ducked inside Molniya's vigorous, sharp-horned nods and stroked his head anyway. "Grant, what is our breakfast this evening?"

Grant silently handed each of them a warm mug of Barek's tea and a napkin holding some dried fruit and carrots. Vixen made a resigned face, but she devoured the fruit while the wind howled mournfully outside the tree line.

She seized the moment to get closer to Molniya with her carrots. Charmed by her efforts, Khael gave her a few of his. Soon enough Molniya's huge eyes seemed softer in the fading light when he looked at her.

138

"He has no bridle." She petted the shaggy creature's nose.

"Gongyangmas bond with their riders," Khael said. "We need no reins."

"He uses them." She jerked her head toward Grant.

"Not mystic," Grant muttered. "I work better with 'em."

Phantom nickered.

"Yeah, yeah." Grant kissed his gongey's furry head and rubbed his neck. "Laugh it up, fuzz-gong."

They threaded their way through the trunks to the grassy strip between the forest and the rocks. The harsh wind rang in their ears, but its force seemed muted nearest the trees. The riders exchanged glances, then headed out.

Khael faced sideways. "Want to ride in front?"

"No, thanks. I may be crazy to be here with you, but not that crazy."

Khael chuckled. She wrapped her arms around him and laid her head on his shoulder. The heat from her contact felt so nice he itched for more, battling his concerns about her lethality. Probably best to enjoy these moments with her as they came, but let them go, too. He nudged Molniya with his heels. The great steed leapt to a full gallop.

18.   How Natural Need It Be?

The wild wind chilled Khael to the bone as they sped along outside the woods. Icy salt air stung their faces from the northeast across the gulf into the forest. Angry clouds continued to puff themselves up, the new ones darker and more sinister than ever. He took them a fair way into the trees to light a fire for their second break.

"Are we close?" Vixen asked over the toasty flames.

"This stretch has no landmarks." Khael frowned in his uncertainty. "Perhaps a hundred fifty miles? But we cannot ride full speed in that wind."

After they had warmed up, he and Vixen mounted Molniya while Grant doused the fire. A blinding flash of lightning forked overhead as they pulled out of the trees. The deafening thunder blast a split second later made the gongies' fearsome brays sound tame.

They rode at a mild gallop while a few cold sprinkles fell, not the cloudburst Khael expected.

Not yet.

Another lightning bolt struck in the trees to their left. Its thunder drowned out the squeals of a small herd of young wild pigs. They tumbled out of the trees directly in front of Molniya, who crashed headlong into the hapless animals. He tripped on two of them and thudded to the ground with a less thunderous ear-splitting bray.

Khael leapt clear. A mid-air kanjuh landed him safely a few yards away, but that discipline only affected one target and his zarute was yet too feeble to help anyone. Vixen hurtled a shorter distance through the air and crashed heavily on her side on the rocks with a grunt, then a moan of pain. Grant successfully guided Phantom clear, away from the rocks and the squealing piglets. The little noisemakers raced around and disappeared among the trunks, all but two who lay still.

Khael hugged his ribs. Vixen's pain from the rocks stabbed at him, too, but Molniya lay on his side on the ground. With a gasp, Khael rushed over to kneel by Vixen and take her hand. He caressed her cheek with his other. A quick scan showed that she sustained only minor injuries, but Molniya had splintered his left foreleg.

"Great, you're here." She groaned.

Khael cleared his tight throat. "Molniya shattered his leg. I must heal him first, if I can, or we may not complete our journey. I have never healed so serious an injury in a non-human."

Vixen opened her eyes and looked up at him. He searched for approval in her eyes, torn between his urgent desire to assist her and Molniya's more dire need. Even without her permission he could simply do the right thing, but he had to be sure she understood.

With her teeth gritted, she nodded. "Go ahead with him. I'll be fine."

"Thank you," he whispered. As he kissed her hand and blinked, his tears dripped on it. Profound gratitude warmed the gaze from her eyes. He rose as quickly as he had come.

"Grant, protect Vixen," he yelled over the fierce wind. He fought his way to Molniya, who was trying to stand. "Molniya, stay down."

The huge steed obeyed, his large black eyes filled with absolute trust for his bond-mate. Khael knelt beside him to position his legs so he could reach the broken one. He looked into Molniya's eye as his own stomach lurched with doubt.

"I know not how well this will work, dear friend. I have never done this."

Molniya nickered gently, as if laughing at the possibility of failure. He looked at Khael and blinked a silent 'go ahead.' Then he laid his head down and shut his eyes.

Hoping his faithful steed was right, Khael closed his. Failure would cripple them all. He took a deep breath and offered a silent prayer.

* * *

Vixen shivered in the light drizzle as Grant guided Phantom to her.

He dismounted unsteadily in the gale and made his jerky way to her side. "You all right?"

"It hurts like hell. I think I'm bleeding and maybe cracked a rib or two. Molniya comes first."

"May take while. Never seen Kyle heal animal. Guessing it takes longer, if at all. Need to dress your injuries at least."

"What, you're a medic too? Is that also part of being a knight?"

His big teeth flashed in his nod through the long hair blowing about his face. "Need you out of gale. Treat you on other side of rock."

He spread a blanket out on the ground beside a larger pile of rock. When the blanket threatened to blow away, he weighted it down with a few heavy stones. Then he knelt behind her.

"No, that'll hurt." Her voice came out weak, but he'd already slipped an arm under her shoulders, another under her legs. "Careful, please?"

He lifted her slowly. Whenever she gasped or moaned, he paused. Her heart warmed at the great care he took to keep gentle while he carried her to the blanket as smoothly as the raging wind allowed him. The light drizzle assailed her eyes in the gusts.

"Let me, ugh, see him."

He set her down where she could watch Khael between the rocks. She blinked wide. Khael sat low beside his gongey, unmoving.

"Need to see your side."

"Try not to drool in my injury." She closed her eyes in pain. A tear worked out.

Grant snickered and unlaced her leather hauberk. He gently opened the soft, tough armor jacket and rolled up her blouse. Vixen had to look. Blood had oozed onto the material he gingerly pulled free. She whimpered a couple of times, but his gentle touch amazed her and did not add much to her pain. Slowly he rolled the blouse up to her armpit.

"Mean bruise, grazed open. Bandage should help—"

"Do what you can. You have a fair touch. When you're not bullying me."

Grant retrieved a pouch from his saddlebag and unrolled it beside

142

her on his knees. He selected some cloth strips, holding tight to keep them from whipping around in the wind. Under her glance, he applied a salve from a small jar to the strips before he laid them over her angry wound. She flinched at the sting, but their cool helped dull the fiery pain. As he wrapped the strips down with a longer bandage, she looked back at Khael.

"What in the fog is he doing?" She failed an effort to sit up. "Oof. Oh fog, that hurts."

"Stay down." Grant turned to see.

Khael stood over something on the ground near Molniya's bulk. Two vague lumps lay still on the ground at his feet. He shook his head and sank to his knees. His behavior baffled her.

"Don't know," Grant said. "Boarlets look dead from here."

"Why does he care about a stupid dead pig?"

Grant shrugged his shoulders. "Maybe it's alive."

"It'll be food for some wolf soon enough. I won't."

"You hope." He straightened out her blouse over the bandage.

She meant her feeble wave to indicate it wasn't important, but he re-dressed her and covered her with her poncho. Once he'd packed away his first aid supplies, he stood swaying in the gale to watch Khael. Her chill began to ebb away.

Something stirred near the trees. Vixen cried out. Khael stood slowly to face the enraged animal that ran at him.

"Kyle!" Grant took off, alarmed. "Phantom, guard her!"

He drew his sword as he struggled toward Khael. It seemed to Vixen an inadequate weapon to deal with a full-sized wild sow protecting her young. His ax would have been better. Khael weaved in the gale, but he stood fast. Vixen gritted her teeth as the sow charged.

Get out of that thing's way. Please!

At the last possible instant Khael leapt away. As fast as he dodged, the sow wheeled and charged again. For a moment, he posed to strike the creature, but he evaded instead.

Grant tripped on the rocks and fell hard. He stood up slowly and closed with more care.

Vixen ground her teeth in frustration. Far too soon, Khael seemed to tire. He caught a foot on a large rock and slammed to the ground. The sow charged into him and threw him into the air.

"No!" Vixen cried out, an awful stabbing in her belly.

Khael flew backward and fell flat on the rocky surface. Vixen screamed, shrill through her anguish and the wind's howl. The sow wheeled and looked at Khael's crumpled form. Molniya's horned head weaved up from the ground but fell away.

The sow paused for a moment and charged again. One yard closer and Khael would be gored, this time probably to death.

Get up. Do something. Anything!

A huge black shape rose between her and the angry mother. Molniya brayed his rage and butted the sow three full yards away from his master. The two animals faced off, roaring at each other. One of the boarlets arose and ran squealing to the trees.

The sow turned toward Khael, but Molniya stood over his master, growling, his horns lowered for the kill. Grant arrived within sword's reach, ready to attack. The moment he stepped close enough, Molniya roared louder and charged the angry mother. She ran off to chase her little one.

Grant stopped. He slowly sheathed his sword and squatted down to pick up Khael. Molniya followed him toward Vixen. Khael hung limp in Grant's arms.

"Is he all right?" she called as soon as she thought Grant could hear. *Oh fog.* She couldn't tell if Khael was breathing. Her own breath caught and new water leaked from her weary eyes.

"No, gored bloody and thrown, like idiot," Grant grumbled.

"Don't you talk about him like that. He's your prince."

"Can't treat this. Not trained for serious injury."

Grant looked worried for the first time since she met him. Even the thanasynfo had not provoked this reaction. Fear, yes, but not worry. He knelt again to lay Khael beside her on the blanket. She couldn't stand his injuries. Blood stained his torn-open abdomen and his breath

144

came too shallow and far between. Her ribs hurt, but the worry knot in her stomach rivaled that simple pain.

"Damn stupid mistake," Grant said, raspy with vexation. He went to Phantom.

"What're you doing?"

"Can't stay here. Too cold and wet. Need him warm, dry, now, or—"

With a deep scowl, Grant hastily wrapped Khael in tight dressings, pulled the gongies together and tied two blankets between them. He carefully hoisted Vixen into one makeshift hammock, Khael into the other. With Phantom's reins and one hand on Molniya's neck, Grant took them under the trees to find a quiet shelter.

The wind's howl penetrated less and the drizzle had yet to break through the towering canopy. Despite her pain and jostling around, Vixen was amazed at how swiftly he found a large space between the massive trunks to set up a crude camp.

He built a quick fire from debris and branches lying nearby. Ever so gently, he lifted first Khael, then her, to set them on the ground near the fire's heat, still in the blankets. Water glistened on the big knight's beard. Was that rain, or tears?

Khael's ragged breathing tightened Vixen's uneasy gut. *Ow.*

After staring from a silent worried face, Grant broke out his cooking gear and food supplies.

With the excruciating transport over and Khael's life at stake, Vixen glowered at Grant. "What, you're hungry, now, too?"

His beard dripped as he shook his head. "Nah. You'll be if he lives to heal you. Last time he did me, was ravenous for an hour." He wiped his face on his sleeve.

"Oh right. Me too." She lowered her head, moved at his nonchalant response.

Khael looked so pale, his skin slack as he lay in the blanket. She couldn't move, or think, just stared at him, waiting for something to change, hoping…

What seemed like hours dragged by until Khael groaned and

145

opened his eyes. He looked around for a moment and closed them.

"Hey, are you healed?" Vixen blinked her dripping lids.

"No," he whispered. "My belly is gashed open."

Vixen had to put a hand over her mouth to stop any noise from escaping. Her worried stomach clenched tighter. That just made her side hurt more. She wouldn't distract him, or even let him know she was crying. More than anything, she wanted to hug him and hold him together in one piece until...

What if he couldn't heal himself in that state? What then? Silent sobs shook her more painfully.

Grant glanced at each of them, but he didn't stop stirring and adding to his stew.

Vixen glared at him. Didn't he care about anything but the food? Fog.

She looked back at Khael. His breathing had slowed so much. Was he still alive? Anxiety clenched her muscles into more pain in her ribs.

After another eternally long wait, Khael opened his eyes. He coughed up blood and spit it away from him. Her heart convulsed in a fist of fear. Was he dying now?

She widened her burning eyes as he sat up. With less than his usual grace, he fought through a slow climb to his feet and shook as he shed the blanket, his coat and his boots. He stumbled to the fire and threw up into it. For a while he stood, hands on his knees, his trunk expanding and contracting with deep heaves. Grant set a hand on his shoulder briefly and went back to his stew.

Khael straightened and wrestled off his shirt. Vixen's eyebrows crawled up her forehead when he dropped the shirt into the fire. Though she searched for his ghastly wound, she saw no trace on his finely chiseled trunk, just his smooth, unblemished lean form. Her mouth watered until the pain in her chest lanced into her.

Khael threw Grant's wound dressings into the flames, then stripped off and burned his trousers. She groaned from the ache as he made his way to Molniya. He fished out a fresh outfit from his knapsack and put it on. On his way to her, he picked up his boots.

"Your turn." He forced a smile as he sat down and pulled them on.

She dragged in a deep breath. The accompanying pain made her gasp.

Khael caressed her cheek. "None of that, lass. Time to heal."

"Aren't... you... hungry?"

"Starved, but healing you comes first. I will manage."

Grant disappeared into the trees while Khael tended Vixen's wound. It felt hot, but bearable, nothing like before. His recovery eased her discomfort.

When Grant returned, he had the dead boarlet in his hands. He skinned and dressed the pig for roasting. It looked large enough for a few days' worth of meat.

As her healing wound down, Vixen sighed. Her injury still burned, but she didn't care. She reached up and hugged Khael fiercely, glad he was still around. Then she drew back and glared at him.

"Yes?" He didn't seem the least bit upset.

"What did you think you were doing with that stupid pig? And how come you didn't flatten the sow? Or let Grant kill it?"

"Change your clothes and burn the bloodied ones."

"You're avoiding my questions." She squinted at him.

Unflinching, he watched her with his mesmerizing dark blue eyes.

She shook her head. "Well?"

"Blood is best not left around outside the body. Fire helps the incongruity pass."

Vixen gave him a blank stare. Gaining no response, she groaned. She stood up, shed her slicker and hauberk and went to the fire. Nothing hurt. Facing Khael, she took off her bloodied blouse and chemise and threw them into the fire, baring her torso. He looked away before she got that far.

Despite her upset with his unresponsive conversation, she smirked. For all his reticence, he had considerable charm.

Her bandages went into the blaze next. She looked and felt around to verify her wound was actually healed. Then she went to Molniya to get another blouse. All she found in her pack was one last chemise. *Fog.* Once she put it on, she checked for blood inside her hauberk. Not finding any, she pulled that on with a smile.

"Excellent." His eyes were back on her.

"What's that mean?"

"Your composure in the circumstances held well."

"Thanks for your chivalry." She crossed her arms over her chilled chest. "You scared the hell out of me, and I still want an explanation."

M. A. Richter

19. Home on the Way

Vixen stared at Khael, waiting for a response.

"The injured boarlet needed minimal assistance, so I healed her."

She groaned. Sometimes he could be so thick. "But you just stood there while that crazy sow attacked you."

"Nothing would have prevented her attack. I have calmed enraged animals before. I had hoped for similar results this time."

"You looked like you were going to hit her at one point." She frowned.

"A feint. Mystics revere nature and we protect animals wherever we can. Had I not tripped I would have fared better."

She flattened her expression. "Still think pigs are friendly?"

Khael chuckled. Grant turned the skinned boarlet on a makeshift spit.

The aroma of roast pork tugged at Vixen's nostrils. Her mouth watered, but... "Won't the clothes, blood and bandages in the fire wreck the flavor?"

"New seasoning," Grant said. "Cloth burns, dressings from herbs and plants. Tasty."

Mulling it over, she sauntered over to the two men at the fire.

Khael took one look at the spit and shook his head. "I cannot eat that. Have you made something else?"

"This is fresh pork." Grant raised his eyebrows, surprised. "We've had worse before."

"I cannot eat this meat." Khael raised his hands.

This time Grant rolled his eyes. "Picky. Porridge was for the side. Will that do?"

At Khael's nod, Grant glared at him, but he handed over the pot.

After they'd eaten and the last of the pig was cooked, Grant trimmed the remains off the bones and packed the meat. They finished

149

cleaning and mounted the gongies.

"Back into the storm." Khael smiled when the others moaned. "We cannot ride full speed through the trees without a road. Out in the rain, we may arrive today if we can avoid any further trip hazards."

Four long, wet hours later, the wall of trees curved away from the rocks and grass around a wide meadow of lush wild growth. Under the moonlit clouds, a darker part of the storm sloped up and away from them in a smooth pattern.

Vixen's stomach lurched and rumbled, not from hunger. "What is that?" It looked like a glass dome, but dangerous, somehow foreboding.

"A magic barrier. Observe."

Khael held out his hand and a small rock rose from the ground. Before it reached his hand, it shot forward. When it struck the dark glassy surface, the stone shattered across the shield. Its fragments slid to the ground with a clatter.

Fog! She swallowed against the nerves tingling in her belly. Magic was deadly, worse than jail, absolutely taboo. How would she get out of this one? "What happens if we try doing that?"

"Nothing. The shield is for strangers."

At Khael's urging, Molniya moved forward right into the solid-looking barrier. Vixen's instincts told her to get away from this murderous thing. She twisted from side to side, seeking an escape. "I am a stranger here, Khael."

"You are with me. There is no need for concern." Khael put a hand on her arm around his waist.

Her panic leaked out of her. She took a deep breath to quell her tense muscles, but they passed in without the slightest impediment. The air felt heavier. The noise of the storm faded, though it looked the same.

Several yards in, the pressure faded. The rain returned, much lighter than before. She gasped for air. Her stomach settled though her skin still prickled up and down her arms and legs.

"Always does that," Grant said in a grunt.

Vixen nodded and looked back at the dome. Only a slight discontinuity in the rainfall made it visible from this side. "How much farther is this castle? And what was that heaviness in the air?"

"Half a mile, the barrier," Khael said.

"That whole thing was the barrier? That must have been ten yards thick."

Khael nodded. "Close enough. He occasionally adds to it." He closed his eyes for a moment. "Its kih now exceeds ten times that of the average guild master."

She shook her head, mystified. "Who adds to it?"

"Grandfather."

Vixen gasped. "He's a sorcerer?"

"The best." Khael patted her arm again. "Relax. We are his family."

Her stomach fluttered regardless of his soothing touch. Sorcerers were worse than clerics, or mystics. She looked up. That did not help. The drizzle wet her eyes. "How high is it?"

"One half mile in radius."

"Where is radius?"

Khael gave her a puzzled look over his shoulder. "It is like half of a perfectly round ball, or sphere. The radius is the distance from the center to every point on the surface, here that is one thousand yards. Since it covers part of the cliff side, it is more like a three-quarter sphere."

"You couldn't just call it a ball?"

They rode at a brisk canter through the wide-open grassy field. Vixen glanced at the barren rocky strip along the cliff's edge. Every other space on the grounds flourished with vegetation. Distant lights twinkled, rising higher into the air in a pattern resembling castle windows.

As they neared, Vixen made out the east end of an island under the castle, surrounded by a small lake. A river flowed into the lake from mountains to the west. The water dropped over the cliff right below the castle's easternmost tower.

Khael waved his hand. "This is Strattonmoor,"

"What's that lake?" Vixen pointed.

"A lake."

She snickered, amused at his first show of humor, and nudged his shoulder with her chin.

He chuckled. "It was a moat, now a mere relic. Nothing enters the barrier unless he allows it."

Vixen swallowed. She wanted to say she'd like to meet this sorcerer, but she couldn't.

They rode up to the moat and to their right along the edge. Vixen looked around for a bridge or other means of crossing. Molniya turned toward the water without stopping. Her surprised protest died in silence as he climbed up a bridge that became visible under his hooves.

Was this what sorcery was like?

Across the moat, the bridge let down into more high grasses on their way toward a blank stone wall. Shivers rocked her. The apparent lack of an entrance was probably another illusion.

At the wall, Molniya turned sideways. Khael reached out and knocked. The sound of wooden barriers boomed out. Molniya sidled away. The stone image rippled into two enormous, steel-bound wooden doors. The echoes died away and one of the doors opened out without a sound.

Vixen nodded. So far it seemed safe, as long as she stayed with him.

They passed into a flatter bailey. The castle stood nestled in the outer wall's east corner, along the cliff where the wall bridged over the moat.

When they reached the castle's dark wooden gate, the men dismounted. Vixen followed their lead, her eyes fixed on the structure. She shuddered. Every instinct warned her to flee this magical place. Khael seemed to sense her upset, and his soothing touch did help.

He tapped the gate, which rose straight up in eerie silence. Vixen flinched as wicked, steel-tipped spikes along the gate's lower edge cleared the ground to stop a dozen hands above their heads. They walked several yards through the entry tunnel into a well-lit courtyard, leaving the gongies outside. A vibrant metallic voice spoke in a language Vixen didn't recognize.

"Thank you." Khael turned to her. "We are bid welcome."

Vixen finished her visual sweep around the yard at a gigantic, stocky humanoid form of shiny metal that towered over them all, at least three hands taller than Grant. It looked like someone in a suit of fine, smooth meshmail, without seams or joints, and mere slits for eyes and mouth. Its mirror-like surface reflected the three of them, the buildings, walls, and many glowing orbs that hung thereon, distorted by its bodily curves. Her hand let go of Khael's and slid up his arm to grip it with both hands.

"What is that thing?" she whispered. She swallowed, and he touched her hands.

"One moment, please. Where is he?" Khael asked, then translated its answer for her. "Within."

It came toward them with a graceful, stately walk. Vixen huddled up against Khael's sturdy form. The thing went right past them through the entry and disappeared around the corner outside with both gongies in tow.

"They are called rompots. Grandfather built two from plans of the ancients he uncovered."

Vixen swallowed. She decided to trust Khael against the danger and magic that lurked here.

Khael led them around a low shack inside the gate, up to the house on the left side of the courtyard. He opened its center double doors into a vast, two-story entry.

Vixen stared in awe at a wide, ornate staircase ahead that ascended from left to right to a sturdy wooden banister along the upstairs hall. Intricate carvings decorated the dark, aromatic wood walls. Their various patterns were partly covered with glorious tapestries and ornate paintings. A sumptuous crystal chandelier hung overhead with scores of small glowing orbs.

Tingles settled all over Vixen as she came through the door. Her arm hairs rose. An enormous presence, of such overwhelming power that she felt it, moved around inside. Khael stopped in the massive foyer and she shivered. She forced herself to wait beside him against her instinct to run.

Eyes wide, she took in the whole panorama. Her tingling sensation heightened as the presence approached. An invisible cloud descended into the cavernous vestibule, toward her, not at random. She clung to Khael's arm and shuddered.

A woman walked out of a door to their right, underneath the stairs. She was stark naked, with striking black hair, flawless fair skin and a well-developed, fit figure. Her hand cradled a morsel she bit with closed eyes, missing their presence momentarily.

Vixen jerked at this sudden apparition of sensuous beauty. The nude made it halfway to the foot of the stairs before she saw them. She started, which shook her raven hair.

"Oh, it's you." She headed up the stairs, unconcerned about her nudity.

"What brings you here, Jolie?"

The sudden chill in Khael's voice made Vixen wonder even more about this woman. His icy tone had never been colder, not even with the City Patrols he had fended off for her in the Bar-Jay.

Jolie stopped on the third step up and faced them. She beamed a bright smile at Khael, which Vixen noticed had no effect on him.

"I am a guest here." Her expression faded at his lack of response and she proceeded up the stairs. "I'd have been dressed, but I thought it would take you a little longer to get here."

"No, really?" Vixen muttered, her teeth quaking. *Fog.* She hoped Jolie didn't hear that.

Jolie reached the top without a backward glance. She turned right and passed behind the wall beside the stairs. Grant muttered an incomprehensible curse.

"Who was that?" Vixen huddled close against Khael's arm. "Why do you hate her so much?"

"Jolianne Corbois." Khael gave her a fond gaze. "Difference of beliefs, no hate."

"I don't recognize the name."

"Mage of Findumonde, sometime thief," Grant grumbled.

"Mage is not a collector's title." Vixen frowned, puzzled.

Grant's eyebrows leaped toward his hairline. "No, Expert Sorceress."

"Oh." Vixen wondered why this brazen woman hadn't conjured up something to wear. Then again, how much sorcery would she have to tolerate in this accursed place of magic? "What's she doing here? Findumonde is a long way off. Isn't it?"

"Most likely entertaining Grandfather. Findumonde is around 2700 miles away." Khael smiled at her. "She and I have crossed paths. No worries."

Her terror finally shrank. His warm expression melted the earlier ice. Unexpectedly, she craved more. "What is that pressure, or tingling sensation?" She shivered a third time.

The men frowned at her, then each other. They shook their heads.

Khael brightened. "You sense Grandfather. He has that effect on newcomers."

They looked back up the stairs. Vixen's skin crackled as though she'd crossed many carpets too fast. Was this another, mobile barrier?

An elderly, fully robed man drifted into the upstairs hall from where Jolie had gone. He glided smoothly to the balustrade. His serenity flooded the whole hall and prickled in Vixen's gut. Built similarly to Khael, he had a close-cut beard and mustache the same white as his arm's length hair, shot through with many red strands. Hazel eyes nothing like Khael's piercing dark blue shone at her.

Each seamless, noiseless footstep vibrated through her as he descended the long, carpeted staircase. Her knees felt watery.

"Welcome home, Mykhael."

The old man's deep voice resonated through the impression overwhelming Vixen. He sounded like Khael, but coarser and gruffer.

His arms went out to the young man beside her. She sagged toward Grant as Khael stepped into the old man's embrace. They kissed each other briefly on both cheeks. Khael turned to Grant and Vixen.

"Grant you know. This is my new collector, Vixen."

"Greetings." A frown flickered across the old man's face when he took her hand.

Vixen bowed and sank to one knee. She touched his hand with her forehead, unwilling to kiss it, but not knowing what else to do.

"Vixen, stand up." Khael rubbed her shoulders. "Meet my grandfather, Loren Stratton."

Something tugged her hand. An invisible cloud of warm fuzz cuddled her to her feet. That name meant something to her, but her thoughts blurred too much for her to think straight.

"Hello, your lord—ship," she stammered.

"Relax." Loren's fine teeth flashed in the chandelier light. "I hunger not, nor do I eat flesh."

Grant snickered. Vixen struggled out a cautious smile.

Khael chuckled. "Incorrigible."

"We have much to discuss, son."

Khael stepped closer to Vixen. She slid her hands back around his arm. Loren blinked at their yawns. Unlike most people Vixen had seen, he failed to respond in kind.

"Methinks you require rest first."

Grant and Vixen both broke their yawns into light laughs. His joke warmed against her tension, which slowly began to loosen.

"You noticed," Khael said. "Have we rooms?"

"Sir Granton, yours awaits if you remember it."

"Of course, lord."

"Congratulations on your promotion." Loren faced Khael. "Your room I removed."

"Wonderful." Khael smiled, though his tone sounded serious. "How do I thank you?"

156

"Appreciate the one I recreated atop the new tower. It retains the style and content of your original. You can see Skemmelsham from the balcony, so the climb is more exercise." He turned to Vixen. "Dear maid, whither would you stay?"

Vixen gulped. "Any warm floor is fine by me, your lordship."

"I possess neither lordship nor realm," he said gently. "You ought to address me by name as I shall you, Vixen."

Vixen's mind shuddered. This man saw right through her. Somehow he knew more about her than she did. The way he said her name practically screamed he knew it wasn't her real name. If so, did he also know who she was? Could he tell her? He was a great sorcerer. His ways must be magic, the worst enemy of all, even if he was Khael's grandfather. She dared not ask. *Fog.*

"You may have a room of your own," Khael said. "Or would you rather stay with me?"

"Yes, with you." Vixen had shared his tent in perfect safety, and he kept his word. To be alone in this place... unthinkable.

"Indeed?" Loren raised his eyebrows. "For certain?"

"Always." Khael held her hand in gentle clasp.

Vixen found Loren's reaction offensive. She deserved better, even from strangers, but this sorcerer was beyond dangerous. Khael's quick answer preempted her response.

Loren nodded. "As you wish. The day is too young for further business. Fair night."

The men said their 'fair nights.' Vixen opened her mouth, but nothing came out.

Loren turned back toward Jolie, three steps up covered in a deep blue dress. Grant waited while Khael took Vixen's hand to lead her up the stairs behind them. Khael yawned.

Vixen stretched her sore jaw through another yawn, a gnawing in her belly. Her survival in this house of insidious magic rested solely with Khael. She broke into a cold sweat.

20.   Loren Stratton

Khael stopped beside Vixen in the door to the dining hall on their way to a wake-up brunch. He enjoyed a study of her face with a smile. Her spectacular green eyes shone amazement as she perused the chairs around the elliptical ring table.

"This table is enormous." She raised her eyebrows. "Does your grandfather often entertain two dozen people at a time?"

"He has."

"If I were still as you met me, this lovely silverware and the goblets would be gone."

Khael chuckled. "I doubt you could take them outside."

Unfazed, she pointed across the table to a fancy, throne-like chair on the other side. It blocked part of the outdoor panorama visible through a wall of metal-framed glass doors behind it. "I'd love to sit in that fancy chair."

"The chair might not let you. It is his. Mine is beside it. I would like you to sit next to me."

On their way around the table, she paused to study the paintings on the wall. She waved at the one where an array of knights and centaurs defended a walled city against an infantry army. "Isn't that the Battle of the Abominations?"

Khael's breath caught. Only the Chelevkori referred to centaurs, and many other hybrid species, as abominations. Another distinct Chelevkori twist despite her professed hatred for them. "Most people call it the Second Defense of Cambridge."

"I suppose. The artwork is excellent. Realistic."

Khael led her past the magnificent seat and sat with her in the next two chairs. While she continued her gaze around the room, he relished the curve of her jaw, the gentle sweep of her neck muscles arcing from her ear to her collarbone. A smile tugged at his lips. "You like art?"

"If it has value." She brought her eyes back to his. "The view through this wall is fantastic, too."

"The view is accurate, but the wall is solid stone." Khael smirked at her stunned look. "It is one of Grandfather's best permanent illusions."

Vixen opened her mouth wide and shut it with a shudder. "I'm starving. Where's lunch?"

The floor inside the table ring spiraled open. Vixen started as a silent rompot rose in from the center. It delivered a tray of sandwich fixings and a pitcher, then dropped back down as the floor returned to a solid level.

"I'll have to get used to these sudden, er, rompots to survive this visit."

Khael offered her a soothing hand, which she grasped. His healing touch seeped out through his fingers and she relaxed. She gave him a tiny smile and proceeded to assemble a huge sandwich.

He watched her while making his own. "Would that not be easier to eat if packed smaller?"

Having failed to fit the monster into her mouth, she sliced it into chunks. Khael savored the show while he consumed his more modest meal. When they finished, both sat back, contented.

"Where's Grant?" Vixen rubbed her full tummy.

Khael enjoyed the provocative images this induced, and he released them. Though enticing, his mystic advancement, and their contract, precluded any such pursuits for at least another five months. "Amusing himself, perhaps out riding, as must we today. Before that, let us meet with Loren in the sitting room."

He escorted her back to a pair of doors they had passed coming around the table. These opened into a large room deeper than the dining hall, but not as wide. Its wooden shelves lined the two-story high walls, crammed from floor to ceiling with a vast array of writings and yet more artwork. Vixen displayed a similar response to this room as the last. Her wide-eyed survey ended at the square sunken couch in the middle of the floor.

"Sitting room? This is more like a library museum, complete with a night sky."

Khael glanced at the ceiling. The patterns in the exquisite painting looked familiar so he paused to peruse it. It took a moment before recognition set in. His chin dropped in surprise. "I do not believe it."

"What?" Vixen snickered. "I thought you knew this place."

"Me too."

She frowned at him. "So?"

"That was the view from the roof thirty-some seconds after midnight, 2766 July 15."

"How can you tell?"

"It was my first sight after birth. Mother later said it was too hot to deliver me indoors."

"Well done." Loren's voice rolled across the room from behind them. "I was uncertain the painting would spark your memory, though I did my best."

Vixen flinched, surprised at his sudden appearance. She swallowed, but she seemed determined to be polite. "You painted that? It's beautiful."

"Thank you. All the artwork in my castle is original."

Khael caught her clutching hand as her face went slack. "Perhaps you would like to be seated."

He waved toward the sunken couch. At her quick nod, he guided her around the pit to the stairs and joined her on the couch. She held his hand tightly, which seemed to reduce her nervous discomfort.

Loren glided smoothly down as if the stairs formed a ramp instead of individual steps. He sat opposite them. "What can I do for you, son?"

"Grant ought to be here for this."

Loren muttered something. "Done. I presume you have less interest in Jolie's involvement."

"None." The less that woman was involved...

Vixen shivered at Khael's frigid tone. She seemed so out of sorts

160

he had to do something. He put a comforting arm around her shoulders and she burrowed in under it. Her cuddle stoked his heart fires more than he expected, yet he chose to enjoy it.

Grant sauntered in and squashed down on the unoccupied side of the couch. "Planning now?"

"Yes, thank you." Khael hauled his focus off Vixen. "I want to scout the city for a few days before we act. When I know more, I can define our approach."

"Risky," Grant said. "Don't want to be exposed too soon."

"You could disguise yourself as a blind abbot from the hermitage," Loren said. "As your guide, Vixen can avert inroads on your honesty."

Khael deliberated for a moment. "That might work. Grant, you can rejoin Damon to forestall any obvious traces of our presence. I considered making you a wheelchair cripple, with us as your care-givers, but we three together are much too easily recognizable."

Grant grumbled and shook his head, but he said nothing.

"I don't understand this hermitage thing." Vixen still seemed overwhelmed by Loren's presence.

"One existed for centuries up the river on the Michtie Loch plateau," Loren said. "The monks always kept it private, though it has been abandoned for at least a century."

Khael nodded. "It will be difficult to challenge, unless John has people up there."

"We'll have to change our appearance," Vixen said.

"I can help with that," Loren offered.

Vixen stiffened. "You mean sorcery?"

He nodded, but Khael shook his head.

"We must use natural methods to deter suspicion." Khael cast a firm glance at Loren.

After a moment, the ancient wizard closed his eyes in resigned consent.

"What does your guide do?" Vixen asked.

"She leads me around the city, at my direction. She engages in any necessary conversation and keeps alert to avoid dangers or risks of exposure."

"So, I tell all the lies to maintain our cover because you can't?"

"You have done so quite well before." Khael smiled.

"You could always tell."

"I am mystic." He grinned at Loren. "Is she not special?"

"She is most unusual." Loren faced Vixen. "*Vy kogda-nibud' byli na Ostrova?*"

"What islands? I've spent my whole life in Cambridge, mostly in the Enclave."

Khael nodded. He caught Grant's stunned face across the couch as the knight spun his head to stare at her.

Vixen looked around at each of them. "What did I say?"

Khael withdrew his arm and took her hand. "*Gde ty vyuchit' Yazyk?*"

"I didn't." She looked baffled. "Why would you ask me that?"

"Loren just asked if you had ever been to the islands."

"Yes, I know."

"He spoke in Yazyk." At her blank look, Khael continued. "I asked where you learned the language, also in Yazyk. You responded to both questions without a trace of hesitation, in Meridian."

Vixen's chin dropped. "Huh?"

"Your native language is Yazyk," Loren said. "Your Meridian lacks any trace of accent, so your education must have been early, exceptional and quite thorough."

She shook her head. "That's not possible. I'd know, wouldn't I?"

"You told me your total recall excludes your first five years," Khael reminded her.

"Yes, but—" She broke off into silence.

"*Thou must beware of this one,*" Loren told Khael in Arcana. "*Know thee who she is?*"

"Not entirely," Khael replied in the same tongue. *"I will not have her privacy invaded."*

"As thou wishest but she is a danger to thee. I know not why she is with thee, nor in such strange semblance."

"Hello?" Vixen glared at them both. "I'm right here, and I don't speak that... whatever it is."

"My apologies. Grandfather has concerns about your presence with me."

"You brought me along. Would you rather I leave?"

"No. We have a contract, and you are safer with me than alone."

"All right then." Vixen nodded. "I'm getting to like, um, you, I mean being with you, and your, ah, quest intrigues me."

Khael steadied his thoughts. "We have much to discuss."

"I could assist," Loren suggested.

Vixen blanched. "You're most kind, but I'd rather we did this ourselves."

Khael joined both of his hands over hers. Any direct confrontation or intrusive magic might damage her, and their friendship. *Not on my watch.* He fixed his eyes on Loren's. "I will attend to this."

* * *

Vixen shivered. She hadn't noticed the differences in the languages when Loren and Khael had spoken. Thinking back, she realized they were right. A chill settled in the pit of her stomach. A totally different question burned to take her mind off the discomfort. "Loren, may I ask you something?"

Loren shrugged and his frown relaxed. "Ask freely."

"Your name is famous, though I know there have been many Loren Strattons. Which one are you, the twentieth or something?"

Loren's surprise returned. "You know not who I am?" he said in a slow, measured pace.

"Khael says you're the best... sorcerer, and you have the same name as the original sorcerer. But you couldn't be him. He'd be over two thousand years old, if he were still alive."

"2,303 this year," Khael murmured.

Loren took a breath. "I am the 'original sorcerer,' as you say."

Unholy fog! She gasped as her thoughts raced. There was no way he could be the Traitor who founded the Sorcery. He was nice... too nice... and Khael's grandfather. He couldn't be! "You're... the... Wizard Supreme?"

Loren nodded slowly. Vixen froze in horror.

"Indeed and thank you for reminding me of my age. I completed the self-portrait over yon hearth a little over thirteen centuries ago."

Her face felt cold and she crumpled back into the couch. *I'm cursed.*

Loren snorted toward Khael. "You told not your own staffer who I am? What were you thinking?"

"Who you are is irrelevant to those in my life. The Chelevkori already target me in addition to you." Khael looked much too relaxed.

"Ignore them, as do I."

"Their repeated assassination attempts make that difficult."

What the hell was she doing here, in this—wizard's home? A cold knot formed in the pit of her stomach. Confusion thickened her mind on top of the horror.

Jolie appeared in the door from the dining room. "Loren? It's getting late."

Loren reached out a hand to her. "I expect you to outlive us all, Mykhael. Make sure you attend to this, or I shall."

"You may recall our last conversation about such things." Khael's icy tone cut into her fog.

"And we concluded that conversation amicably. Should that change now?"

"You're not going to fight, are you?" Vixen cringed beside Khael.

He gave her a warm smile. "No, lass. Loren is right."

She sighed. The knot in her stomach tightened.

Loren stretched from side to side. "Methinks I require food, and exercise."

"I'd love to help, if I may," Jolie purred.

Loren glided up from the couch pit and kissed her hands. "I would enjoy it."

A coruscating light enshrouded them. It quickly grew too bright to watch. Vixen shut her eyes as the blaze peaked. When she could see again, the light and the couple had vanished.

"Dramatic exit." Grant flicked his eyebrows up and down.

Vixen blinked. "Where'd they go?"

"Exercise." Khael said. "Likely more romantic than fitness."

Vixen nodded. At least he was gone. Her insides still jumped and clenched.

"What now?" Grant said.

"Do as you like. We will see you at dinner." Khael smiled to Vixen. "Walk with me, fair maid?"

She swallowed, nodded and stood beside him. His offer lightened her concerns, but she felt more alone than ever. Loren was the ultimate enemy, to be feared and avoided, or killed. As if that were even possible.

Her confusion expanded. Loren had been nothing but nice to her since she came in the door. He was Khael's grandfather after all. Was he faking all that, waiting to pounce at the first opportunity? She had no idea what to do, even with Khael's help. Was she still safe, or would she ever be?

Grant shook his head and headed for the dining room.

Khael led Vixen to a different double door, on the wall behind them. She followed in a whirl of conflicting thoughts. The doors let out into the same courtyard where they had come in before dawn. They headed across the yard and out the back gate, down a slope toward the orchard.

The day shone bright around the beautiful grounds. Various animals meandered through the bailey, ignoring them on their walk. At one point a unicorn bounded up to nuzzle Vixen's sleeve shyly. That made her feel a little better. It seemed friendly enough, though not quite a real horse. She reached for something to feed it, but it leapt off at a gallop.

"I don't understand, Khael, and—I'm scared," she said at last.

"There are many anomalies. What you called the painting, your fluent Yazyk versus an Enclave upbringing, your lack of certain elements of common knowledge. There is a long, growing list. I have yet to connect all the inconsistencies, but we must resolve them, together."

"What about what Loren said?"

"Loren will never harm a friend of mine."

A friend. That was something if it were enough. If she only knew more.... "Can you tell me more about him."

Khael breathed quietly for a moment, as if she strained his patience. His words came out with the same calm as usual. "Anything in particular?"

"Where did he come from? How did he get to be so powerful? Why did he establish the Sorcery? Why is he called the Traitor?"

21.   Khael and Vixen

Khael stopped cold. *The Traitor?* "Where heard you this?"

"That's what everyone calls him."

Khael narrowed his eyes. "Everyone?"

"The person who hired my mentor to steal your ring, but I remember hearing it a lot in my youth."

She sounded innocent and her answer rang true, but too much was missing. The only people who ever called Loren 'Traitor' were adherents of the Family of the Manticore, the cult whose clerics and leaders comprised the Chelevkori. They had been trying to kill Loren for centuries and they never gave up.

Obviously, they had set her up to steal his ring, but their delicately woven complex approach implied a more extensive and sinister plan. He had just survived five Chelevkori assassination attempts in the last three months, six if he included Iulianna's original attack at the kyoshitsu. Vixen's pendant fit right into that mix as the seventh. "Please elaborate."

"He called Loren 'accursed Traitor who founded damned Sorcery.' I've heard it before. I can't believe your grandfather is the same person, even though he admitted it."

"Would you like to know all the details?"

She nodded.

Khael studied her open face for a few moments. She gazed back at him. Her eyes betrayed a plea for help he found perilous, but exciting. He cleared his throat. Answering her question properly would take more time than he could spare until after he had rescued his people. "When we go to Skemmelsham tomorrow, you will need your own ride. Aliotru will do for you."

"What's a lee-oh-true?"

"Aliotru is an older mare with a sweet temper. She has not seen Skemmelsham in years."

167

Vixen nodded. "So, she'll be as unrecognized as we want to be."

He guided her back to the stable. "Show me how well you learned from Grant's riding lessons."

"You're avoiding my question."

"That will take some time. We can talk as we ride."

In the stable, he introduced her to Aliotru, then watched her saddle the mare exactly as he would have. He mounted Molniya bareback and they rode out of the stable.

"Loren grew up near the west coast of Rossiya. At thirteen, he trained as a ranger and progressed rapidly into the knighthood and the clergy. By twenty-five, he was the youngest certified deacon-archon ever."

Her eyebrows rose in surprise. "I didn't know anyone could be both."

"After magic was discovered and the clerics devised their own subdivision of the Knighthood, it was prohibited."

Vixen made a silent "oh."

Khael headed toward the orchard, a short ride out from the castle. "That year Loren and his father came to Cambridge as trade emissaries. They arrived right before the strangers from Kyoshima. Those visitors possessed many special abilities, crude precursors of today's Saiensu disciplines. Loren persuaded a few of them to come to Rossiya to help the Chelevkori enhance their power."

Vixen's jaw dropped. "What? No, the Chelevkori taught the mystics their powers."

"There were no mystics yet. The strangers were just... seekers." Khael frowned at this latest discrepancy of hers. "Only the Chelevkori claim they discovered the powers or consider the centaurs and other non-human sapients abominations. Their native language is Yazyk. Many are trained to be fluent in Meridian, like you." He nodded. "It all fits. They must have educated you... and set you up to get involved with me." To kill him...

She shook her head, her face twisted in bewilderment. "They may have educated me, but they left out the rest, like how Loren betrayed

168

them."

"Once the Chelevkori had developed their particular collection of spells, they stopped. They decided they had found the totality of all magic and declared any further research or development taboo. Mystics believe the Chelevkori are innately predisposed to those abilities, which are not any kind of magic, and they simply reached their limits."

"They're not magic?"

"Sorcery and clerical spells operate in certain, known ways. Their abilities differ."

She frowned. "That doesn't answer my question about Loren."

"Loren wanted to learn more, so he left the Chelevkori to escape the prohibition. He engaged others with similar inclinations in joint studies. The Chelevkori claimed he stole their spells and they labeled him the Great Traitor of the Manticore Family. For two thousand years they have tried to assassinate him, hundreds of times. You have some connection to them, which is hidden from you, and thus from me."

Vixen balked. "They tried to kill me. I... I hate them. How could I be connected to them?"

"A mystery we shall solve. Together."

They reached the orchard and rode along its edge.

He stopped. "Would you like an apple?"

"You're changing the subject."

Khael plucked a large, bright yellow fruit. He brushed it against his vest and handed it to her. The way her face lit up when she bit into it made him smile.

She licked the dripping juice from her lips. "Delicious."

His pulse sped up. He took a slow, deep breath and urged Molniya back into their walk. "I used to sneak out here at night when I was a boy and stuff myself. Best apples I ever tasted."

* * *

Vixen quietly munched her apple. As unsettling as his stories struck her, his comforting voice calmed her jangled nerves. He seemed more friendly since they had arrived here. His story made more sense than the rote history she'd been taught growing up. Would her burning desire to know more put him off?

More than anything, she desperately wanted to believe what he'd just told her. He had proven himself worthy of her trust. Loren's greeting had been loving, downright fatherly, and he clearly loved Khael as his own son. Maybe he wasn't all that evil.

Her thanasynfo ward, a product of sorcery, had saved their lives. How was that wicked?

She glanced at him occasionally as she enjoyed the bounce and tumble of the ride, surveying the fabulous scenery. His scrutiny with those stunning dark blue eyes fanned her inner fires despite her growing doubts and confusion. He presented as much a mystery to her as he said she did to him. Like...

"What was that about your father's memories?"

A shadow passed over Khael's face. When he spoke, his sad tone touched her heart.

"My father left Mother when I was four. Loren helped her raise me. When I found out who Prince William Cambridge VII was to me, I had just returned from Findumonde where I recovered a ring he had intended for me but had been waylaid. I went to his grave to meditate on his permanent absence in my life. His shade arose before me. I asked what was so wrong with his life that he cut me out of it. He merged spirits with me and shared all of his memories."

Her heart pounded. His own father's memories? Vixen shuddered. "All of them?"

Khael nodded, once. "They are as my own, but distant, behind a veil, within reach at my need, though difficult for me. Loren and I argued long and hard over some details. I prefer neither to dwell on nor discuss it."

Her eyes wide, she nodded, lost in a whirl. That he would so openly share such a profoundly personal experience with her, as distant as he had seemed so far, amazed her.

They rode up a low rise toward a high shock of tall grass.

170

A mischievous thought punched through her ruminations. "Race you around those grasses."

She dug her heels into Aliotru's flanks and the mare sped up.

A sharp, loud whistle pierced her ears. "Whoa!"

Aliotru thudded to a halt.

Vixen twisted in her saddle to glare at him. "What was that for?"

"There is a loose gravel bed behind the tall grass. Your riding skill is impressive for a novice, but I prefer you not injure your backside in a fall."

Despite her annoyance, she smirked. "You like my bum?"

Khael chuckled. "Head into the fields if you wish to unleash all restraint."

She led him on a hard, fast ride to the outer wall before turning back. Molniya seemed amused, not the least bit taxed as he trotted lightly alongside. Aliotru panted heavily. Khael guided them to a stream and dismounted. He rinsed his hand in the water and cupped out a drink. Vixen slid down after him through a sweaty dismount and splashed herself cooler.

After they remounted, they rode more slowly back toward the stable.

Her self-doubts returned in full force. "Do you think I'll ever stop saying the wrong thing?"

"When said you anything wrong?"

"Like inside, when I finally figured out your grandfather really is the original Loren Stratton."

"I have heard nothing wrong."

He was just being nice, and Loren too. She glanced down. "Is he really your grandfather, not a great-great-great something?"

"Mother was his last daughter, forty-two years ago."

"He must have hundreds."

"Surprisingly, no."

She paused for a moment, steeped in puzzlement. "I still don't understand something. Why did you bring me along on this quest of yours?"

"What else was I to do with you?"

"You're a prince, you could've done anything—had me jailed, or beaten, or killed. You could've just let me go once I'd returned your ring or taken a fine. Probably other options, too. Instead, you convinced me to work for you."

"Punishment never accomplishes any benefit. To execute anyone is unthinkable. Your release, with or without a fine, would have resulted in your arrest, or even harsher discipline than you have already described. I recognized your talent, so I made an offer, and you agreed."

She ticked those off in her head. "That only counters the options I gave you."

Khael turned Molniya around so he could face her along Aliotru's flank. Her vision blurred under his intense gaze, and sparks shot through her body. She almost fell out of her saddle.

* * *

Khael caught her arm to steady her. Smitten as he was, clearly she had trained as an assassin with the Chelevkori. He needed her permission to perform the invasive telepathic inquiry that would reveal her mysteries. Should he not gain her permission the consequences might kill him or them both. Only caution, respect, and loving support would earn him that level of trust. His own advancement through the next, critical discipline in his path also came first. An impetuous flare of passion or foolishness would only ruin everything, even if no one got killed.

They still had a contract....

"I see a potential, in you, that remains largely untapped. I want to see it unleashed."

"Is that all?" She ran a hand up his arm to the limit of her reach.

His head spun from a flood of emotions. "I defer to elaborate later," he whispered.

Rather than fight his feelings or give in to their onslaught, he retreated into kinshuh. His inner storm whirled around and subsided.

Her eyes regained focus. She understood, even if disappointed.

Their arms dropped at the same time. They picked up their ride back to the keep. Her sweat glistened in the warm sun, her breath shorter. Dark spots plastered her dress to her skin. The cooler shade of the stable provided a welcome relief.

Vixen sighed and looked back, wiping her brow on her sleeve. "This is beautiful. If I had family with a place this nice, I'd be here all the time."

"I chose not to return until our disagreement four years ago was settled. I had other business as well."

"That's when you recovered your ring, and met... er, took your throne?"

Khael nodded and dismounted. He helped her brush down and re-stable Aliotru.

Once back in his room, she plopped down on the bed, panting. "Those stairs are exhausting."

"You will find it less effort with more exercise."

"I'd like a nap." She rolled onto her back and stretched.

His internal burn reignited, but he breathed carefully through that flame. How did she provoke that response in him so easily? He shook his head. "We must pack."

"Do we have to? I mean, can't we wait until after dinner?"

"We can rest after dinner. Come on. Pack."

* * *

Vixen groaned, pushed up to her feet and plodded over to join him at the closet. She leafed through the items hanging on her side. Some of them looked plain while others gave her chills at their opulent elegance. Too much so. Dismissing them, she chose three long, dull winter dresses. They needed to look like ordinary folk, indistinguishable from the crowds.

"Fine choices." He'd selected his own loose fitting dun pants and shirts.

"I figure a hermit's guide won't have much fancy stuff." She pulled some slinky undergarments from a drawer. "Even this is nicer than anything I've ever had."

Khael shook his head. "I would avoid those. Hermits' apprentices are unlikely to wear such sensual materials."

"Who's going to check my undergarments?"

"We know not how irrational the usurper's supporters may be. With pretty maidens, uncouth guards might attempt unwarranted liberties I would be hard pressed not to stop. There may also be spyholes in loo walls. What better place to surveil a person than in their least guarded moments?"

Vixen stared at him. Pretty maidens? Another wave of warm tingles swept through her. Did he just throw that in as flattery? He continued to pack without a break. So, he must have been serious. And he'd protect her. She smiled and put the slinky items away in favor of less elegant, practical alternatives.

"I'll cut the hands off anyone who tries anything with me."

"No peaceful hermit would..."

When he didn't finish, she stopped and looked at him. "Would what?"

He straightened toward her. "Such behavior strikes me as abnormal for a hermit's guide, but an inexperienced one? Perhaps some ferocity is entirely appropriate."

Khael smiled and her heart soared. He crossed to her, his arms open. When he reached her, he drew her into a passionate crush, his lips sweet on hers. She closed her eyes and drowned in his loving embrace, the fever in his kiss....

"Finished?"

"What?" The brief, tantalizing daydream succumbed to reality, leaving a sticky feeling. He hadn't moved one step. She shuddered. "Oh. I suppose so. Do we need anything else?"

"Only the towels, which will return this evening."

* * *

They sat in their same chairs, across Loren from Jolie and Grant. Both rompots delivered large trays loaded with food and drinks.

Before anyone reached for the food Loren spoke. "Let us sanctify this food and give thanks to the source whence it comes." He smiled when Vixen stared at him with such surprised curiosity. "It never pains one to express thanks to the source of one's sustenance."

"So, I should thank the rabbit I've just roasted for coming my way so I could eat it?" She meant it only half facetiously.

"If you are truly thankful and of a mind to do so, certainly." He reached in and heaped a huge pile of steaming vegetables on his plate.

He acted so calm and composed, nothing like the horror stories she'd heard. How could he possibly be as evil as they said? Try as she might, she couldn't detect any such traces.

Grant and Jolie helped themselves liberally to a large roasted fowl. Khael chose from the same foods as Loren. Vixen wondered if this meant anything. She leaned over to nudge Khael's shoulder.

Secret question? His thought popped into her mind.

Should I avoid the meat?

Eat whatever you wish in comfort.

He didn't even stop chewing. She took a breath and dug into her food. No one else seemed to notice.

"Are you prepared for your undertaking?" Loren asked after the rompots cleared the table.

"We still require disguises," Khael said. "More information would help."

Vixen nodded, wishing she shared his confidence...

"Guess so." Grant shook his head. "Still don't like you off on your own."

Khael looked amused. "Of course not."

"Do you require any magical assistance?" Jolie asked.

"No."

"You may trust me, you know. I would never harm Loren's kin."

"Thank you, Jolie." Khael's tone softened. "When the occasion arises, I will remember."

She nodded with a satisfied smile.

Loren also smiled. "It pleases an old man's heart to see you two get along."

"Old man's heart?" Khael's eyes sparkled. "Where hides that?"

"How cruel and unfeeling." Loren assumed a face of mock anguish.

Khael smiled and shook his head. "Always the actor."

Loren's eyes twinkled. He glanced at Vixen and his expression smoothed out.

"I have an idea." He reached toward the doors to the sitting room. They opened and a large, beautiful book in blue and gold floated out of the library into his hand. The doors closed as he rose to present the book to Vixen. "May I offer you some light bedtime reading?"

"It's... huge." Vixen took the heavy volume in both hands, unsure at this offer. "What is it?"

"You may decide after you finish it. It covers much, but in ways anyone can appreciate."

She blanched. "Please tell me this isn't more sorcery." Anything but that.

Loren smiled and gently patted her shoulder. "It is harmless. Just a tale for entertainment."

Vixen gulped. What did a 2300-year-old sorcerer find entertaining?

22. Unraveling

Khael walked softly up the last few stairs to his room. Vixen lay on the bed, watching the flickering images in the book Loren had given her. Having seen the show many times while growing up, Khael knew the book well.

The smile on her face dimmed his concerns over what Loren had shown him for the past few hours. Bird's eye views of Skemmelsham's empty harbor, deserted buildings on the north slopes, the repressive edicts and phony laws, the usurper's troops guarding the harbor warehouses or constantly patrolling the city. Loren had also conjured up a perplexing new image, a string of lines and bulges around the ceiling of his throne room. What it was they could not tell, but it looked ominous.

Vixen closed the book. She sat up and yawned before she saw him. Her expression faded into a curious look.

Khael set his concerns aside. "Questions?"

She nodded, her eyes wide.

"Let us go outside. It is warm in here and I feel a need for fresh air."

She followed him out. At the rail, she twirled a fiery red lock around her fingers. This simple gesture kindled a warmth throughout his whole chest. "I'm guessing you've seen that story before."

He took a cooling breath and nodded. "Many times. He occasionally performs it in grand illusion for guests. Once he narrated it in Arcana after I learned the language. It sounds richer."

"It's quite a fairy tale. Is any of it true?"

"The part about the Ancients fits what we know from centuries of research, not just Loren's own. His memory is what it is. He updates the book as new information surfaces." Her distraught expression tugged at his heartstrings. "What disturbs you so?"

She looked out at the ocean. "The tale has a ring of truth I can't deny, but it conflicts with everything I know. Those—magicians, from Kyoshima, were mystics, like you. They warped the Chelevkori teachings into your powers. Loren was a vile coward who stole the Chelevkori spells and perverted them into sorcery. The Cambridge holy pretenders twisted them into clerical magic."

"Thus, the Chelevkori invented everything, and those they hold the most against are all thieves who stole and perverted their creations."

"Is it so different if the magicians invented everything and the others stole from them?"

"The magicians merely presented immature concepts, developed out of their struggles with survival on Kyoshima, an intensely hostile environment.

"When their leader, Sasha, was killed, they retreated from the world. Eighteen centuries of deep study later, they re-emerged with the Saiensu, a functional set of highly refined disciplines.

"Sorcerers, clerics and the Chelevkori each derived their own separate takes. For example, there are no Chelevkori fire spells. They focus on form control. There is no exclusive concentration on misdirection in sorcery or clerical spells.

"Is there harm in crediting the correct source of ideas?"

Vixen gripped the rail to steady herself. "My whole life feels like a lie."

That sounded extreme. "Only your historical perspective. Who taught you this?"

She started to answer and stopped short. Under a confused frown, her eyes searched. "I'm not sure. My instant response was my mentor, but I also see images of my mother telling us the story."

Khael blinked, his thoughts blown into disarray. "Us?"

"My... friends, and I, I think." She grimaced and swayed. "I don't understand. I have vivid memories of my mentor teaching me, but there were two older redheads. One I see as my mother."

"You said you knew not your parents."

"I don't." She shook all over. "How can that be? My mentor and

178

Uncle Nick raised me since I was five, but there's this mother redhead, and a woman who looks just like me but older."

None of this made sense to Khael, unless... "Do you remember their eyes?" At her shaky nod, he added, "What color were they?"

Vixen stared at him. "Hazel. They both had hazel eyes." She swayed.

He caught her before her legs gave out. "I have you."

She groaned and clutched at him.

"Vixen?" He held her gently until she stood firm again. "Are you all right?"

"I feel numb." She let go and stepped back from him. "I don't know what to think or feel. I thought I knew who I was, but now I'm not sure of anything, It's as though all my moorings have been cast loose."

Khael raised an eyebrow at this new surprise. "Where did you hear that expression?"

"I went on a ship ride with... my family? No, it was—I remember other children, and that other woman, the one who looks like me." Her expression cleared. "It was in the gulf when I was seven. It was stormy, all overcast and windy, with huge, nasty waves, bigger than our ship. One sailor asked me how I felt with nothing solid under my feet and I said I felt lost. He used that expression."

Khael stared at her, unable to find speech.

She looked back at him. "What now?"

"You said you had never left Cambridge. And the gulf never has such storms. The continental cliffs shield it from the wind-stream and it is too narrow to suffer such fits, except at the southern end where it meets the sea. It is the calmest large body of water on this side of the world."

"Maybe that's what it was. We were out for a couple of days, but it was stormy the whole time. That I remember clearly."

"The fastest ship ever built would take four days from Cambridge to the southern end of the gulf." But there had to be something to it. Memories like that almost always had some basis in fact. He shook his head. "Two days in stormy weather more resembles a trip from Ostrova to Abreise, Frantsiya's northernmost port."

Vixen shook her head. "I can't be from Ostrova, that's where the Chelevkori live. I hate them."

Khael took a deep breath. Perhaps now was the time... "I believe this is all part of a larger scheme. The Chelevkori have dedicated their lives to killing Loren for centuries, possibly his whole family. More recently, they have included me. From what you say, and your unusual abilities, you may have been trained as an agent of theirs."

"That's impossible. They tried to kill me. If it hadn't been for you... I don't feel like an agent, I feel used, and cheated. Except you haven't used me at all yet.... Why did you bring me? It wasn't for my collector skills."

"We covered this. You have begun to earn your way."

Another gloomy look shadowed her face.

"You have other mysterious inconsistencies."

Vixen scowled at him. "What does that mean?"

"You say you are a tyro, and that rings true, yet your expertise in Manshao and dagger rivals or exceeds that of most expert assassins. I have foiled even master pickpockets, yet you succeeded." He frowned at a new thought. "When began your initiation?"

"I started a few months after my thirteenth birthday."

Khael shook his head. "That cannot be. A true novice with your innate abilities would require no more than eight months for the basic collector's training."

"I've been practicing for almost a whole year, since Storm."

"You waited four years to begin practicing?"

"I was ill, a lot...." Her voice faltered, face pinched. "My mentor said I was stubborn." She shook, her knuckles white as she gripped the railing. Wild, painful emotions rage a storm in her kih. "But four years? How can anyone just train that long? The guilds don't allow that."

"Have you ever attempted to reconcile this memory disparity?"

"No, I... I never thought about it. I never had this... it's too much. I can't...."

Khael studied her contorted face. His heart leapt to go out to her, and there was a way to help, if she would accept it. "I may be able to resolve your quandary."

She knit her eyebrows in a fierce, desperate frown. "How?"

"With a much deeper, more personal kinseh, we can examine your memories in detail tog—"

"No! Stay out of my memories!"

The shout struck like a fist. He stepped back in shock. Vixen's face washed a bloodless pale. Her body jerked upright, twisting in the grip of her frenzied, internal torment. She clutched the rail so tight her knuckles cracked.

"As you wish," he murmured.

"I don't," she whispered. Tears trickled down her face. "But I... I just can't. When you said that, my brain caught fire. It hurts so much I can't think."

Khael wanted nothing more than to hold her, to reassure her that he cared about her. In her present state, she seemed too fragile for anything he might do. His heart plummeted, a stone of grief. The stress of the whole situation fatigued him. "We can wait until you are ready. Tomorrow is a big day, with more to come. You need your rest, and I a shower. There is a dark shampoo in the washroom to color your hair. Use it tonight on your head and eyebrows... any hair that might be exposed."

He headed inside. Their lives depended on a solution to Vixen's contradictory state. If she were to be his assassin and they failed to resolve the matter, one or both would be killed.

* * *

Vixen waited on the balcony to move until the washroom door closed. When his shower began to hiss, her shoulders finally unkinked. Something deep inside had reacted violently to his offer. Her head still throbbed. She gingerly poked around, seeking to identify what part of her had lashed out with such painful force. Whatever it was lay silent, hidden, like that foreign craving for his passionate intimacies.

He liked her and he protected her. She'd only been around him for four days, but she trusted him with her life and her honor. Why couldn't she let him help her sort this out, even if it involved his weird telepathic skills?

She groaned and shivered as a cold north breeze tickled her hair.

"Rest well, Vixen," came his voice a while later.

She nodded and tried to let go of the rail. Her hands hurt from the death grip she'd held for too long. The excruciating release twisted her whole body and she rubbed her hands to ease the soreness. Closing the doors behind her, she headed for her own shower.

In passing, she noted that Khael lay on his blankets again. He looked like he was already asleep.

I wish I felt that safe. She undressed inside the washroom. Maybe the shower would help her feel clean.

23. Gearing Up

When Vixen awoke the next morning, Khael was not in the room. She sat up, yawned and stretched. Where was he? What did all that mean in the story she watched? How could she trust Loren's magic version of history? How could she trust anyone she'd known all her life only as "the Traitor?"

Whatever she believed about Loren, Khael had been more kind to her than anyone—her mentor, Uncle Nick, especially those red-haired women. He'd stood by her steadfastly. His touch, even his presence, aroused an unbidden craving that made her knees weak and her insides hot and mushy. Even when that lay dormant, her heart yearned for his affection and touch. The cloud of racing thoughts still disturbed her, but she had to put it all out of her mind until later. Today she had to be clear or they might end up dead, or worse.

Vixen swung her legs off the bed, stood up and stretched again. On her way into the washroom, she glimpsed a shadow on the balcony. In the mirror, she studied her reflection. Every filament in sight gleamed hideous in dark brown. Even the thin, fine hairs on her legs were tinted visible, and ugly. She hated it. He probably would too.

"Yuck," she muttered. "I look terrible with dark hair."

A few minutes later she opened the door. She expected him to be right there, but no, not even on the balcony. He was acting the perfect gentleman, as usual, giving her respectful privacy in which to get dressed.

Vixen went to the closet for some clothes. His knapsack, boots and the dun cloak were gone. He must have gone downstairs. Her camisole went flying as she hastily donned a fresh outfit. Since she wouldn't wear any armor soon, a plain, long winter dress had to do. The daggers she arranged so only one was visible. She hurried into her boots and dashed downstairs with her knapsack and cloak.

A strange, old man sat beside Loren in Khael's chair, with gray hair down to his waist and parched, leathery skin. He looked older than

Loren, as if that were possible.

"Fair morrow all." She frowned through her mystified cheer. "Where's Khael?"

The old man rose and delivered a polite half-bow. "Right here."

She stared half a minute before his dark blue eyes registered. He looked so peculiar.

"Would you like some breakfast?" He smiled.

She tore her eyes from his. The table bore an impressive array of fruits on a platter arranged around a strange yellow fluff. Various breads occupied a second platter.

"Yeah, now. What's that?" She indicated the yellow.

"Try it and see," Jolie said. "You look nice in dark hair." A fork-pile of the yellow disappeared between her teeth.

Vixen mumbled her thanks and served herself a small portion of the fluff with a few fruits. She tried the new food first. Her tongue sent encouraging signals and she quickly devoured the rest.

"Delicious." She helped herself to more.

"Careful," old Khael said. "Too much cheese omelet can make one sleepy."

"What's in it?" she asked between bites.

"Half a dozen various cheeses, beaten eggs and some light cream, spinach, a few spices and vegetables," Loren said. "My own recipe."

"I thought eggs were oval and firm when cooked."

"You dislike them like this?" Khael said.

Vixen shrugged. "The only way I cook eggs is boil them for ten to fifteen minutes."

Grant arrived, dressed in full battle armor with a simple, dark red surcote. He clanked over to sit beside Jolie.

"Cheese omelet." He dished up a large portion with a big smile.

"Not too much, it'll make you sleepy." Vixen waved a finger at him.

His face lit up with mild surprise. "You knew?"

184

"See? You don't know me as well as you think." With a tiny smile, she started on her fruit.

The others chuckled.

Loren smiled. "Your lass is a delight in action."

"I miss something?" Grant scowled.

Khael smirked. "Just eat, Grant. We must leave soon."

Grant wasted no time on it. He plowed through the piles on his plate.

Vixen studied Khael's new look. "What happened to your hair?"

"You like it? I used a different shampoo from yours last night."

"No, er, yes. I meant the length, and your skin. I didn't recognize you. How did you do that?"

Khael pulled a lock from up around his waist and sifted it through his fingers. "I thought you knew by now."

"You're mystic. Of course."

Grant wiped the last traces of breakfast from his beard. "How long'm I stuck with this hairy annoyance? Itches, and traps food."

"A few more days," Khael said.

"My falcons scouted the city last night," Loren said. "They report a gathering of forces a mile to the south and increased traffic along the main road." He peered closely at Khael. "Your patchwork scheme may yet coalesce."

"Let us hope so. I yet know far too little for any discrete plan. I will don the blindfold closer to the gate when we part from Grant." Khael gave Vixen his own piercing stare. "After that, lass, you and I will be alone."

Knots threatened to lock up her torso. Alone with him, they'd have no allies around, like Grant. As much as she didn't care for the big knight, he was a great fighter and pretty skilled in areas she was not. More to mask her concerns than out of real pleasure, she smiled. Maybe she should further appreciate Khael's trust in her. She had no idea what challenges they might encounter. Her discoveries last night still jangled her nerves.

"What are our names this trip?" Maybe a little distraction would help settle her nerves.

"Mykhael is the Abbot of the Michtie Loch Hermitage," Loren said. "What shall he call you?"

"Why not Caroline?" Jolie suggested after a moment of silence. "It means freeholder."

"I guess it'll do for now," Vixen muttered. Free would be nice...

"Alpha has your cart ready in the yard." Loren remained seated with Jolie while the others rose. "Vixen, your eyes are too recognizable and I know no natural way to change that. I can make them brown until you wish them green again, with no other effect."

Vixen stifled a groan. "Sorcery?" Still, if this trick saved her life... A deep breath helped settle that tremor. "All right."

"Trust me." Loren smiled. His next word sounded like a short gargle.

Vixen twitched, but she felt nothing. If he just cast a spell, it had no ill effect she could feel. Not yet.

Loren nodded to her and Khael. "Your fortune is in your hands. Use it well and in best health."

* * *

Khael stood up and stretched his arms. He liked the way this visit had turned out, though he would have preferred much more information on the usurper and his city. What he now knew helped not at all. Nonetheless, the rest had been highly beneficial. With a silent sigh, he kissed the old wizard on both cheeks. Loren returned the gesture without rising.

"Come to town next week, Grandfather. You can witness my remains or my victory. Mother would like that."

"Watch yourself." Loren grasped Khael's arm, pulled him close and murmured in Arcana into his ear, "*Remember my caution about this girl.*"

Khael pulled back. This was not the time, even after last night. He nodded curtly.

In the courtyard, Aliotru had already been bridled to a cart. Alpha waited patiently beside them. Khael climbed into the cart and beckoned Vixen to join him. Grant walked back to Phantom behind them and mounted. Molniya was nowhere to be seen.

Vixen stared at Khael. "I'm not riding her?"

"Loren suggested the cart would be less conspicuous for a blind hermit," Khael said.

"Farewell and return soon, young master," Alpha said in Arcana, a ringing metallic bass.

"I shall, fate willing," Khael replied in Meridian.

"What did it say?" Vixen whispered.

Khael translated and eased Aliotru forward. The cart lurched after.

"It sounded fancier."

They rolled steadily down a packed dirt path toward the north side of the outer wall. Vixen seemed more tense than usual this morning.

"Nervous?"

"I could jump right out of my skin." She paused, her face thoughtful. "I should check in with the Collectic when we arrive."

"That would expose us immediately."

"A delay could cost me a fine."

"Our lives are worth the risk. If all works out, the throne has some influence with the locals. Watch how I guide Aliotru. You must take over soon enough."

About halfway to the city, a cold, uncomfortable sensation invaded Khael. It resembled the scratchiness of a new, unwashed burlap blanket of ice all over his body. As they came closer to the city, the prickliness grew sharper, more dangerous, more like the spike of warning his chokkan raised when a lethal threat to him drew near.

In less than an hour they reached a point where the trees thinned. The city wall became visible between the trunks ahead through the morning mist. His prickles sharpened into the icy warning he half expected. From where they stopped, the itch was clear—his life was in

187

danger, right here.

Khael reined in Aliotru. He stopped so sharply Vixen almost tumbled out of her seat.

"What was that?"

"Pardon." A quick scan showed him nothing, but the feeling persisted. "A lethal danger to me exists ahead, one that can kill me right here."

"A lethal danger exists..." Vixen's voice trailed off. An alarmed look took over her face.

Grant rode up beside the cart. The glare he shot Khael would have frozen any other man's blood. Khael returned the calmest gaze he could muster. No sure safety lay ahead for any of them.

Vixen's eye grew round. "You mean, like Monistarnie?"

Khael took this in with a dry swallow. "Uncertain." At the fear in her eyes, a lump rose in his chest. "I can go in alone—"

"Like hell you will." Grant sounded like an angry gongey.

"No." Vixen swallowed hard. "I will not desert you now. I promised."

The lump warmed and expanded, threatening to bring tears to Khael's eyes. He inhaled and, with an effort, set his pride in his friends aside. "As you wish and thank you. We must be cautious at all times."

He shook down the feeling and wrapped a roll of gauze around his head to cover his eyes. If only it were that simple.... When he finished, he tied the ends together behind his head, then pulled his hood up and over his face. "I am ready. Caroline, please take the reins. Be careful."

"Is there a Shielin word for forest?"

Khael shook his head. "Forest, or woods."

Vixen sucked in a deep breath. "All right, then I'm Caroline O'Woods, and you're the Abbot of the Michtie Loch Hermitage."

Grant leaned down toward her from Phantom. "Mess this up and we all die."

"You too, Sir Blame-leigh. I'll take care of myself and his

abbotship here just fine without you. You make sure the troops get there on time."

Grant nodded and clapped her on the shoulder. "That urchin I know. I'll watch 'til you're inside. See you in few days." His face grew serious. "Best luck, Caroline, Abbot."

"You, too." She rubbed her shoulder. "Hope your ham hand didn't cripple my arm."

24. Skemmelsham

Vixen stopped the cart at the blocked city gate. She took a slow breath to steady her nerves as two uniformed guards drew nearer.

"State your identities an' business in Skemmelsham," the tall guard ordered. He and his pudgy cohort both wore full chain mail with green tunics and held a spear. A small crossbow hung from each of their belts.

"I'm Caroline O'Woods." Vixen hoped their false identities would hold up. "The Abbot of the Michtie Loch Hermitage wishes to see the viceroy on a matter of grave urgency, and I'm honored to serve as his guide."

"Pretty fancy dagger for blind hermit's guide, little lady," Pudgy sneered. "I just take look." He advanced, his spear raised.

Just like Enclave gangsters. Vixen set her hand on her dagger hilt and smiled sweetly into the guard's face. "Are searches new since my visit last month, or just you? I'd love to show it to you, but my grandmother gave it to me on her deathbed. She said any time I drew it, I had to blood it before re-sheathing. I'd hate to see you lose a hand."

Pudgy stopped cold in his tracks, his face white. The tall one behind him snickered. At least Tall seemed decent. Maybe they'd get through.

Pudgy cleared his throat and brandished the spear. His eyebrows knit in a fierce frown and his rough voice rose. "Maybe we take you inside and search for other toys, find something to play with."

Vixen's pulse raced hot. She'd rather gut the miserable gangster... but she couldn't allow them to harass her or Khael. Throttling back her fury, she composed a puzzled frown. "I doubt I could return the compliment," she muttered. "I'd have to cut off parts, and they'd be too small for toys or worth playing with. I suppose I could use the exercise...."

"Why you little—" Pudgy stammered, his mouth wide. "I ought to—"

Vixen froze. "I beg your pardon, kind sir. Was I thinking out loud? Whatever did I say?"

"Enough." Tall chuckled. "Leave the lass go. She's belike too young to ken better or be worth the effort."

"But she—"

"Enough, trooper. 'S no' our job, an' we dinna harass children. Old man, let's see yer eyes."

Vixen held in a sigh. Khael was right about these lunatics.

"Just having some fun, Corporal." Pudgy shambled back.

Khael pulled back his hood and slowly unwound the gauze. Vixen watched, fascinated. He finished but left his eyes closed.

"I said let's see yer eyes."

When Khael opened his eyes, Tall gagged. Vixen choked back her own cry of surprise. Khael's eyes were pure white.

"Ugh," Tall choked out. "Close 'em, an' move on."

Pudgy had already retreated into a shack on one side of the gate, retching. Tall raised the gate bar for them, his strained face set. Khael calmly rewound the gauze over his eyes as Vixen guided Aliotru into the city.

The street widened into an empty, divided avenue designed for heavy traffic, with a line of tall, leafless trees down the center. A yard's width of brown grass under more of the barren trees along the sides hinted at greener summer glory.

Once they were beyond earshot of the gate, Khael spoke in a soft tone. "Refer to the court, not the viceroy. Also, tone down the ferocious urgency."

"That fat little creep acted like the street punks who used to threaten me."

"Even so, there is no need for such rage."

"As you wish, master." Vixen felt silly. Maybe she had overreacted.

"Brother."

"Thanks, brother. Does it mean anything that fatso's armor was rustier than the tall one?"

Khael didn't answer for a minute. "Paladins used to guard the gates, but the one who harassed you was a ranger, and he spoke with a certain northern accent. We must remain observant."

A hundred yards inside the city wall, the street curved to their right along a gentle downward slope. Vixen breathed deep to enjoy the familiar tang of salt ocean spray in the air. It softened the mild, perpetual stink of dung. To her surprise, Khael sat stiff, his face set.

"Where to, brother?" She kept her voice down.

"Take care, we have company," he murmured back, then raised his voice. "Turn left at the first major thoroughfare and seek the Crossed Eye Inn." He sounded strained, his head down.

She lowered her voice to whisper, "How did you do that with your eyes?"

"Not now."

His tension, worse than she had ever seen in him, raked her nerves. She looked behind them as if checking the rear cart wheels. The ploy let her scan the street for followers without being too obvious, or so she hoped. When she faced forward, she'd seen no one.

"Are you sure?"

He said nothing. What was he hiding from her?

Vixen found the inn with no trouble, a pair of three-story brick buildings on the left side of the wide avenue. Each tower was shaped like an L, with the short leg a narrow gap from the end of the other's long leg. She braked the cart in the courtyard under a short overhang and climbed down to look around. Khael rose slowly, as if he were in pain. He lightly brushed her shoulder with his staff.

Vixen jumped, then realized he meant she should help him down. Once he stood on the ground she hauled their knapsacks out of the cart. She took his free arm to walk him inside. Her heart sank. Something bothered him, maybe even more than his hunch outside the city, but what?

A quick glance around the courtyard revealed only patchy brown, weedy grass and a few short, barren trees. Otherwise, it was empty except for Aliotru, the cart and a few domestic fowl that chased each other around, clucking. The streets had also been deserted, except for numerous rats.

They walked into the main door. She shivered. No one seemed to be around in the dusty foyer. The worn varnish on the blackened wood counter had cracked, with parts that peeled away. A sign over the desk hung sideways from a single chain, its mate broken in half.

Vixen frowned at a frayed rope within reach that looked like a bell pull. She set their packs down and yanked the rope. A bell rang once. The rope fell out of its slot, a rotted mess that thumped onto the counter.

"Great," she muttered. "The bell-pull broke and the place looks burnt and filthy, like it's been abandoned for years. Is this the right place?"

"Call for assistance."

"Hello, is anyone here?" Her loud volume made him twitch and she snickered. "Sorry, brother."

A grizzled, elderly woman, chubby and hunched over, stepped out from a shadowy doorway behind the desk. She wore several layers of ragged scarves over what looked like a blanket or cloak riddled with holes, her crossbow aimed right at Vixen's face.

Vixen gasped and backed into Khael, who didn't move.

"Whit d'ye want?" the woman snarled. Her eyes darted around the room but focused on them.

"Angela?" Khael said, his voice rough. "What has become of you and this place?"

Angela lowered the crossbow to peer suspiciously at them. "Who's askin'?"

"Whom think you?"

The weapon stayed down. Vixen exhaled slowly.

"None so old an' blind." Angela's whole demeanor softened. "It doesna matter. Ownerships have changed, for the worse. I barely doused the fire a gang o' vandals set last week. There's naught much left here save firewood, 'less the wharves reopen soon. Ye're better off anywhere else."

Khael sighed. "Understood. Come, sister, we must seek shelter elsewhere."

Vixen scrambled to grab their packs as he shuffled out. She tugged his arm before he bumped into the wall and guided him out the door to help him into the cart.

A furtive movement behind it caught her eye. As soon as Khael stepped onto the cart she flitted around the back, her hand on her dagger. There was no one around, but she checked the cart. Nothing appeared amiss. She hopped up beside Khael, still wary.

"Someone was back there," she whispered. "I didn't see who and the cart seems untouched."

"Stray cat. You scared it away."

"Oh. Are you all right?"

Khael jerked his head.

Her stomach twitched. Was that yes or no? "What did she mean about ownerships and firewood?"

"Her place is compromised, and all former safe havens. Proceed to the palace. We may use an inn nearby."

Vixen frowned. He had never sounded so constricted. An image of the sheer cliffs popped into her mind. She shuddered and guided Aliotru out the way they came in, but she stopped at the street.

"How do I get there?" she said, then whispered, "And why do we want to?"

He gave terse directions. "Seek Paladins or City Watchmen to inquire for the best inns."

"I don't know the difference, brother."

"The City Watch rangers wear forest green tunics over their mail, with gold badge emblems. Paladins have green surcotes over their armor and a gold sash opposite a badge."

"Should any have rusty mail?"

"No." Khael sat up straighter. "They must not be locals, like the impolite gate guard."

The rust would be easy to spot. Vixen turned the cart onto the street, a bumpy cobblestone affair as wide as any she'd seen so far. They passed layered rows of houses, inns and other shops, surrounded by withered gardens, leafless trees and brown grass, as she drove up the hill. The land behind them sloped down to the wharves.

By this time, the sun had burnt away enough of the mist to see the ocean clearly. The details of the harbor remained vague, but its utter lack of ships, masts, even boats screamed oppression and abandonment. The few people out between them and the water hurried along the empty streets as if frightened to be there.

Vixen swallowed to manage her tension. Groups of two or three men in gray tunics marched through the deserted streets along the slope. None of the patrols wore any green.

She had to slow down at the top of the hill. Traffic crowded these streets. Two and a half miles along the way, the avenue split around a garden-like park with a low wall around it. A huge white mansion stood tall in the middle of this long, eye-shaped block. Many small streets led up to the block and ended. No other buildings showed above the trees.

"What's going on?" Vixen spoke quietly through the buzz and bustle.

"These people suffer," he muttered. "Speak softly with indirect references."

She nodded, hoping she understood what he meant.

"I know not which places are safe. Many businesses used to thrive on the slopes. Instead, people hide in the empty buildings, shivering and hungry." Khael took a deep breath. "You must ascertain from Paladins or the Watch which establishments they prefer or dislike. Solicit at least three opinions and connect the uniforms with each. Who says what and how they dress could be key."

"Huh?" He lost her on that one. She reined up to avoid a collision.

A terrible suffering happens here, like I have never seen. Angie Millan was one of my key harbor contacts. Only I call her Angela. He paused. *What in—*

His communication cut off, his bearing stiff again. A new chill invaded Vixen's chest.

A dozen or so armed troops marched down the street toward them. Many of them, including the leader, wore gray tunics with a stylized blue wave emblem on the left breast. The people on the street parted grudgingly for them as the troops shoved their way through. Their mail sported numerous dingy spots. The leader watched something in his hand intently, stopped, and cast about, as if lost.

"*Fignya!*" he swore. "Almost had something."

"Na worries." The knight beside him wore the green surcote and sash Khael had described, over clean, polished plate armor. "If he's here, we'll find him sooner or later."

"Pardon me, officers." Vixen gave them a weak smile. "Might I trouble you for information?"

"What, girl?" The leader marched toward them, still petulant. His troops followed.

"My teacher and I seek quality, inexpensive lodgings. Maybe you know of such nearby."

"Your identities and business in Skemmelsham, lass?" The Paladin's demand seemed polite enough. To her surprise, his voice sounded familiar.

"I'm Caroline O'Woods. This is the Abbot of the Michtie Loch Hermitage. We seek an audience with the court on a matter of taxation."

"You'll find his excellency quite strict in that regard," the Paladin said. "There are few inns both decent and inexpensive hereabouts. The Discreet Gossip on Fourth Way is fair."

"You serious?" The leader snorted. "Place is rat-and-roach infested sewer. Try Coach-and-Half, straight ahead, halfway along palace block. Is more, but clean, and secure."

"I'm honored, kind sirs," she said.

"Don't mention it." The Paladin nodded, his face grave after the leader's interjection.

"Move out," the leader called.

196

The company passed them by without another glance.

Vixen flicked the reins and Aliotru moved forward at a modest walk. When the armed men had passed well beyond hearing range, she looked around for another authority to consult while steering through people and debris on the street. "Where's Fourth Way?"

"Past the palace. Three streets beyond where this avenue merges with the other arc, turn right." He paused and his face softened. "How knew you?"

"The first fellow had rust-spotted mail and a gray tunic. The second knight wore clean armor and green. I didn't trust number one, but number two was more likely."

"His appearance?"

"Young man, almost your height." She paused as a realization struck. "He looked like a certain older knight we met recently."

"Most observant," Khael murmured. "That was Damon's eldest son, Desmond."

"Nice." Maybe this wouldn't be so difficult.

At the intersection Khael indicated, Vixen halted Aliotru. She signaled her turn through the intersection, but pedestrians crowding the street vendors blocked her path. Finally, she stood up.

"Make way, make way for a turn!"

Some of the pedestrians stepped aside, but most ignored her. A ranger with the gray tunic stepped out from a storefront awning. He plunged into the street and raised his hands to spread out the pedestrians, who parted for him with frightened looks or glares. As soon as she had room to squeeze the cart through, she turned as fast as Aliotru would move. Her progress slowed right away, and the ranger barreled his way over to seize the reins.

"Where you go, miss?"

"I heard there was an inexpensive quality inn down this way."

"Better ones east of palace. You and grandfather go there."

"Your pardon, please," Khael said in a frail old man's voice. "We seek solitude and peace at the Discreet Gossip."

"Terrible place." The ranger shook his head. "Quiet you find, but many six-legged visitors, or thousand-legged eaters of flesh. I show you better place."

"I wouldn't dream of troubling you, officer." Vixen forced another smile, batting her eyes. "Surely you must have more urgent business than us."

The ranger looked her over, twice. "Not at all."

A leer flashed through his eyes. Vixen struggled not to roll hers.

The ranger guided Aliotru through the crowds half a block down Fourth Way, then right into a cul-de-sac. He led them into the yard of the second building.

"This is Tap-n-Stot Tavern. Excellent repute." He tethered Aliotru to a hitching rail near the front door. "Manager is friend, Gavran Jenney. I go in and tell him to expect you."

"As you say, sir." So much for having a choice.

Lavry bowed slightly and headed inside. Vixen sighed as they climbed out of the cart. She pulled their packs out and took Khael's arm to lead him inside.

"What a tyrannical creep."

"Your Lavry thinks poorly of our choice."

"He's not mine, the leering jerk. His mail was rusty and his tunic gray."

Khael nodded. "This place is unsafe."

"And now we have to stay here." She groaned.

25. Popular Sentiment

Khael let Vixen sign them in for a two-bed room with a private washroom. The exorbitant price seemed worth the privacy, but other muffled voices filtered through the heating vents and thin walls nonetheless. They would have to exercise caution to avoid eavesdropping.

He made his way to one of the beds and sank onto it as Vixen set down their packs. His chokkan warning spikes persisted. It had lessened along the slope toward the harbor, then grown stronger than ever near the palace.

His shoulders had stiffened from the intense strain. The miserable kih of those devastated families in hiding along their way up the slope pummeled right through his active kinshuh. Starving children huddled in the crumbling, deserted buildings. Their parents shivered even as they tried to keep their beloved offspring warm and safe.

All this was his responsibility. He clenched his nauseated stomach, arms tight around his waist.

Vixen showed no sign of understanding, only the same heightened anxiety from his declaration outside the city.

His chest hurt so much he had trouble breathing. He struggled to his feet and said he needed to clean up. She led him to the washroom and he tugged her inside.

"What are we doing in here?" Vixen whispered.

"Is there a shower?" He heard water running. "Aim the flow at the curtain."

The noise level rose. He nodded.

"That's clever," she said, quiet but still audible. "Can't we just whisper?"

"This is better." He dragged in a breath.

"Are you crying?" Her voice echoed the shock in her kih.

"My viceroy is acting like a monster who starves and imprisons

199

my people." He related to her what his shikah scans showed him. "I allowed all this. In addition, those men for whom you stopped had a device that reacted to my kinseh."

"That's terrible." The flickers in her kih expanded from outrage to include frightened curiosity. "The leader of those guards had something in his hand. I couldn't see it, but it looked like he was following it toward us until your thoughts cut off."

"We must go to the palace to arrange a hearing. If the device is not unique, more troops may have them. I need one to analyze."

"How do we get one?"

He kept his face turned toward her, fighting not to choke.

Her head rose. "I steal it?"

"We must also glean more information, perhaps at local taprooms."

She nodded, but she seemed at a loss. "What's a stot?"

"Shielin slang for bullock."

She burst into smothered giggles. "Tap-n-Stot, as in Cock-n-Bull?"

Khael forced a smile through a wobbled nod. At least she had not lost her sense of humor.

"That's funny." She sobered. "Sorry. Do hermits frequent taprooms?"

He shrugged his aching shoulders. "Hermits need nutrition too. However, I cannot see with this on nor may I remove it yet."

"What about your shikah?"

"Most inanimate objects lack distinct kih, but I know not if those devices can detect shikah. I must not use any disciplines until I know more." He sniggered out of morbid cheer. "Actually, that may help. What I see hurts."

The shower's supply tank emptied and the cover noise stopped. Khael waved her back into the bedroom. Vixen tip-toed out and stood still, waiting.

"Caroline? I require your aid."

"Yes, brother." She hurried back to him.

"We must go to the palace."

"A moment, brother. Let me freshen my face."

Clever lass. She picked up the act beautifully. While she was busy, he felt his way to the packs on the beds. John would never betray his trust, or his mother's, with such cruel tyranny. He must be dead. That meant an impostor had taken his place. Chelevkori, no doubt. Khael's momentary cheer about Vixen flew away, leaving behind only the hollow ache over the misery he had seen.

He found his pack by its familiar feel and sat beside it on the bed. If John was dead, what about his mother? Concern for her added to the twisting in his gut.

The sound of running water made him wince. Their earlier use of the shower may have caused her discomfort, but he had not noticed any strain in her kih. He sighed. The desolation of his people weighed heavily on his tired shoulders.

"Ready, brother. Here is your walking staff."

The stately palace stood tall in the middle of the eye-shaped block. Trees and shrubs glowed their dim kih, but the paths flourished with weeds. Long grass, now dry, had grown unkempt all over what used to be picnic areas and children's play areas. At least the river west of the palace teemed with normal kih.

Khael inhaled deeply, wishing he could enjoy the spectacular panorama of a thriving harbor down the hill. Memories of what he had seen there still stung.

Before and during his reign, the palace had always been open to visitors and guests, not a fortress to fend off enemies, like Strattonmoor or Castle Cambridge. A cordon of rangers surrounded it when he and Vixen arrived. A chill went up his spine at the many detectors among the troops. To his relief, his shikah had not provoked any response. He suppressed a puzzled smile.

A fair number of common folks waited in a queue outside the eastern doors, their conversations hushed but audible. Khael and Vixen soon had company as more people joined behind them. The line wormed toward the doors at a crawl. Two clusters of three rangers alternated escorting visitors at the head of the queue inside, then out toward the gates in the garden wall.

Khael's cold itch sharpened as they drew nearer to the palace. The threat lay inside, somewhere, yet its reach extended well past the city walls. It had to be enormous. What shape would it take? How big, and where?

The bustle around him disrupted his train of thought. He adopted his elderly hermit voice. "We seem to be well attended."

"There's a queue," Vixen said.

"Among them, fair dissatisfaction with the current regime."

"Tis a miracle we're allowed to say so," the bulky kih in front of them grumbled. He turned around and looked them over.

"Why's that, kind sir?"

"Seems to think so long as he lets people complain, he doesna really need do anything about it." The man snorted. "But that's just us petitioners. The ones he drags in are treated no' so well."

Khael tipped his puzzled head. "Please explain."

"Some come like us, wi' a gripe. Usually tis taxes, an' he ayeh says they're to keep the city working." The man snorted again. "Like it's been worth a halfpenny since July. The majority get dragged here for petty crimes."

"Of what sort?"

"Taxes, theft, sometimes dissent. At the harbor riot, he jailed hundreds an' shut down the few shops still open on the slopes. Last week there was a big protest down on Seventh Circle an' his troops broke it up wi' na mercy. They arrested about fifty."

"The jail must be pretty big." Vixen seemed more jittery at the concept.

"Na, they hold the prisoners in seized harbor warehouses." The man radiated curiosity. "Me name's Chattan, Gabe Chattan, Master Smith, from Ninth Way. I'd retire if the blackguard'd let us be."

Khael recognized the name despite a haze of rising nausea.

202

Though he had not met the smith personally, Khael knew his reputation as one of Skemmelsham's loyal, prompt taxpayers. He went by Gabriel when he had been on the Artistry's managing council early in Khael's reign.

"Well met." Vixen took his offered wrist-clasp and introduced them. "We're here about his new tax on places of worship."

"You ain't alone. The priests o' the Temples o' Luxea, Ventus, an' Flamma're in jail for protestin' that one."

"Did not their members object?" Khael said.

"No' yet. When the priests wouldna pay, his troops closed the temples. They ringed 'em a week back an' winna let anyone in or out till the taxes're paid." Gabe chuckled. "Tis ironic. Temples've ne'er paid like the rest of us. Wi' na collections, they canna, unless they're hoardin' the gold."

Khael cleared his constricted throat. "What brings you here?"

"Another license restriction," Gabe grumbled. "More limited business hours without yet another foggin' permit. This place's so foggin' petty since the prince left, but ye canna complain about that. If any phrase'll land ye in jail quickly, it's talk o' the prince's return."

"You just said it," Vixen observed.

Gabe harrumphed. "Out here they're a wee bit lenient, so long as it ain't the only conversation an' dinna turn dangerous. Mayhap 'cause they can see us here, an' they listen everywhere they can. A fortnight ago, the crowd got rowdy. His gray-shirts dispersed 'em an' shot three people. Killed one."

Khael swallowed his outrage. "On the grounds?"

"Anythin's fair game to them, but na, twas in the street." Gabe shook his head and lowered his voice. "Ye can ayeh tell, too. Only the new men're so violent. The blackguard already booted most o' the Paladins, so he needs every last man that's left for all the patrols an' prison guards."

"Sounds like a creep," Vixen muttered.

"Wasn't ayeh like that. When he was viceroy for the princess, afore her son took the throne, he was well-liked for fifteen years, e'en this year afore the rains, but now this." His voice rose. "Still, for a lunatic he's pretty decent about this protest an' petition business."

Whoever this viceroy was, he was not Khael's loyal earl. Khael gritted his teeth. "He may be doing his best under the circumstances."

Gabe snorted. "Shoddy best. Ye maun be new syne he took over, abbot."

"Yes." New—and betrayed. Khael fingered his pursed lips. "What about the princess?"

"She's well hemmed in, so sticks to her own business to run, as ayeh, but it's watched too."

"Maybe he's just keeping a list," Vixen said. "The most frequent complainers are probably monitored, or jailed."

Gabe stared at her. He crossed his arms. "I hadna thought o' that. Too busy for this grummel. Sometimes takes an hour to get in, then all they do's take yer name an' yer complaint, an' give ye a time to come back. That's why we're goin' in the east entrance, instead o' the front doors to the main court."

"Thank you kindly, Sir Gabe. Clearly it's wise to keep current."

"'S nothin', lass. I like to chat, an' this new permit waste is rubbish. Ye'd think he wants to hoard all the money in Shielin."

"That seems pointless." Vixen sounded confused.

"Trade's hard. We've na seen more'n a handful o' merchant caravans syne July, an' most o' them left, wi' nasty words about our once fair city."

"That's changing, Gabe," said a woman behind Khael and Vixen.

"Hail, Pilar. What's the word?"

"I heard this morn a whole raft o' folk showed up outside the main gate, some merchants, wi' desperately needed supplies. Sorry to intrude on your conversation, lass, sir."

Khael nodded. "No intrusion, welcome. You are?"

"Pilar Greggson." She curtsied. "I hear ye be an abbot an' this filly's Caroline. Pretty name for a pretty lass."

"Thanks," Vixen said. "It's nice more people and supplies are

204

coming."

"Aye, tis all a pitiful shame," Pilar said. "'Twas the harbor made this city prosper. Ye canna blame the mariners 'cause it goes back t'the viceroy's madness. Condemn that fool t'the fog of eternity. May he rot in whate'er hell's most painful, an' our lord return the sooner to see to it."

"Watch yer lip, Pilar." The bulky smith shuddered. Fright rose in his kih. "That's exactly the sort o' talk to get a person jailed."

"Ah, let 'em," she sneered. "I ain't na threat. Used t'be a fine jeweler, but me eyes ain't so keen na more. Me son-in-law, bless his widowed heart, takes care o' me as he can."

"Dame Pilar, what brings you here?" Khael said.

"Just Pilar, please, yer worship. The rabid mutt wants us wi' na income at all to pay another fee t'get healer services an' potions to ease the ache of age," she spat out. "There, I dinna say his name or title, Gaby boy-o. Ye happy?"

"Just watch yer words. There ain't na healers worth mention in the jails."

"How d'ye ken? There's been more put in since last I saw ye. Prob'ly a whole lot more."

"Prob'ly need 'em. If they don't beat 'em to a pulp too. So, what else's new?"

With that, the older pair began trading stories about their neighbors' failing health, pride in their children and on.

Khael kept silent. The impostor had to have a plan to suppress a popular revolt in Khael's absence. Otherwise, he would already have been overthrown or assassinated. What could it be? The icy lethal threat kept scratching at Khael's brain, interfering with his ability to think clearly. Those detectors did not help. He needed to get his hands on one...

26. Detector Detective

By the time Khael reached the front of the line, the prickle stung. His head swam with that, everything he had never needed to know about Gabe and Pilar's residential neighborhood, and nothing of significant value. The conversation merely calmed his concerns—neither of their line neighbors was involved with the viceroy nor had they recognized him.

Why did this viceroy-impostor impose such mean-spirited subjugation as to make opposition so widespread and revolt inevitable? Unless he had enough troops to put down any popular uprising, or maybe the prisoners were his hostages. Did he think this the only way to lure Khael into his grasp?

That kind of desperation gave Khael more advantage than his own incognito approach. An ambush along the roads would have been smarter. A chill went up Khael's spine. There had been one, with Vixen's explosive pendant. Any report of its detonation would have eliminated the problem here. Thus, they did not know. Unless there was more...

He suppressed a snort. If the oppression continued unabated, he could simply return to Cambridge and the situation here would resolve without him. Ryan would send a legion after the Carnival, with none of Khael's qualms about violence or bloodshed. However, whatever had sparked his chokkan might kill them all—the impostor, his men, Ryan, his legion, everyone in the city... and Khael's mother.

No. Khael exhaled sadly. He had to end this disaster himself, with a workable plan, and soon.

"The people leaving look as unhappy as they came," Vixen said in a low voice.

"I empathize," Khael murmured. "How many remain before us?" He wanted to keep her mind occupied.

"Only a few, five if they're all singles."

"Our patience is due a reward."

An unusual kih appeared that made his muscles tighten.

Vixen started at his change and grasped her belt near her dagger. "What is it, brother?"

"A centurion just exited the door," Khael whispered.

"I see a knight in a gray surcote."

"What we seek is beside his dagger. Who is he?"

She remained silent for a moment. "One of the ushers for the people going inside. I only see a belt pouch."

"Exactly. While I speak to the clerk, ascertain his time of departure."

"How?"

"Be yourself. Act sweet."

"Your friend would say that was impossible."

He stifled the frown that flashed through his mind. "Stay focused, please."

When Gabe came out the door, his escort ushered him onto the exit path. The centurion with the device marched over to the queue, two rangers in tow.

Khael held his shikah active, ready to dismiss it at the slightest indication of detection. At such close range, this risked everything. Any response could expose him. He held his breath.

"Fair morning, citizens. I'm Lieutenant Jack Majestic, Viceroy's Guard. Follow me to the appointment desk and we'll try to make this as pleasant as possible." He turned on his heel and strode toward the palace door.

The detector lay silent. Khael let out his sigh as a feeble cough. "You are not a Paladin?"

"Another time, citizen," Jack said. "Have your request ready when the clerk asks. We'll escort you back out when you're done."

"Thank you, kind sir." Vixen glanced at Jack and quickly lowered her head.

Jack took a closer, long look at her. His pulse and energy levels spiked with interest.

The two rangers behind them waited outside when they entered the palace. The hall sounded wrong, constricted, with muted sounds and soft echoes. They must have set up barriers to block entry to the once-popular royal museum farther in.

The sting in Khael's mind grew into a burn. An unfamiliar line of dead kih made ripples around the edges of the throne room ceiling, just a few yards to his left. He bumped into something a yard in front of a seated man, a table from the scrapes and shuffle of papers when it shifted.

Vixen pulled his arm, distracting him from the odd energy pattern. They waited for the cross, older man behind the table to acknowledge them. Khael recognized his kih—his official court clerk, Eugene MacGray.

"Name?" Eugene finally spoke in a sour tone.

Vixen looked down at something on the table. "Sir MacGray, this is the Abbot of the Michtie Loch Hermitage."

Eugene's kih shook waves of disdain at her. "Lord. MacGray."

"I most humbly beg your pardon, my lord." Vixen gave him a deep curtsy. "I'm but a new student, Caroline O'Woods, honored to serve as the abbot's guide."

"Hmm." Eugene wrote something down. "What's your business with the court?"

Khael had to stop examining the odd kih next door to make intelligent conversation. "The tax status of the hermitage."

"Hermitage taxation." Eugene wrote as he spoke. "You'll find his excellency quite adamant on the matter. He insists on a fair, uniform application of his regulations to all strata of society." He sounded coached and bitter. His response echoed that of Desmond's speech earlier, in the streets.

"The brethren appreciate the concern. I must respond on their behalf."

"Fifteen minutes at three hours after midday on Tuesday." Eugene waited to write.

They had to wait three days? Too risky. "Is there no earlier time available?"

"That's the next appointment for petitioners." Eugene spread his hands as if helpless.

"The court hears petitions all day every day until then?"

Eugene took a deep breath, irritated at having to explain as if to children. "Morning court is for criminals. Petitions are heard between two and four hours after midday. Nothing Wednesday, Saturday or Sunday. Unless you like jail time, be here Tuesday. Or pay the taxes and go home."

Vixen stiffened at the mention of jail, making Khael frown. "Tuesday is fine."

"Wise choice." Eugene relaxed, scribbled something and looked up. "If you don't reach a settlement, you may be fined or imprisoned or both. Where can we contact you?"

Khael stifled a groan. More surveillance throughout their wait. "The Tap-n-Stot."

Disgust rippled Eugene's kih. "Be on time. The viceroy has no patience with late-comers."

"We'll be here," Vixen said. "The abbot never lies."

"Wonderful. Next?"

Jack waved to the door. "This way, please."

The two rangers outside fell in behind as Jack walked Khael and Vixen toward the street. At the grounds wall, Jack dismissed the rangers. Vixen gazed at him with a warm glow around her head. He looked her over carefully, his kih flaring lustful interest despite her unflattering outfit.

Khael feigned blind ignorance. "Is there aught else, Lieutenant?"

"Eh? Oh. Not really, sir. I was taken aback by your ward's beauty. One wonders why such a lovely young woman would devote her life to solitude in a hermitage."

Vixen hung her head, swishing a coy foot in the dirt. "I have my reasons." She faced him.

Jack coughed at her gaze and looked away, heat flaring from his chest to his hair. Khael said nothing. Vixen slid her arms around the surprised knight's waist. He hesitated, startled by her hug. When he began to reciprocate, she stepped away, his device in her hand.

"Thank you, sir knight." She thrust her hands down into her cloak. "Maybe we can meet, after your watch. You know where we're staying."

"Caroline," Khael said sternly. "The Lieutenant explained his motives. Better not to muddy them with temptation for what cannot be."

Jack roiled with envy, even some anger.

"A thousand pardons, Sir Knight." She curtsied. "I apologize if I misled you."

"Accepted." Jack had trouble breathing as he struggled to regain some measure of control. "We'll meet again." He turned on his heel and strode back toward the line.

Another guard had taken over when he failed to return right away. He stood back for a while, his attention split between the petitioner line and the departing pair.

"Nice work," Khael muttered as they headed onto the street.

"Thank you, brother." Vixen radiated appreciative warmth at his compliment.

In their room, Vixen set the pouch she had filched from Jack on Khael's bed. He untied his blindfold and wound it off. The pouch held a small, sealed metal box.

Khael scanned around for others but found none nearby. He sat and checked the one before him for traces of power. It radiated a small amount of kih, as from a spell, but concentrated as if it were contained in a partially untapped power source.

Vixen looked on as he picked up the box to study it. A little over a thumb thick, three wide and four long, it had watch-like crystal covering a flat face with a single needle.

When he activated his zarute claw to pick up the thing, a dead kih surged inside it, the face lit up and the device vibrated. Its needle popped half-way up from the lit-up face and swung around until the longer point aimed straight at him. He lowered the device to the bed and released zarute. The needle swung back to its rest position and the vibration halted.

This is strange. The mechanics of this device are distinctly Chelevkori, but the needle is enchanted from magic.

It reacted to his kinseh with her, just as it had to his zarute. When he stopped, the device went silent. He activated his eikyo fingers, but this provoked no response until he reached into the device.

Fascinating. It detects active use of energy, not specifically my disciplines.

As an experiment, he diverted the light energy into the part that vibrated. The dead kih resisted, stiffer than zhukih. He closed his eikyo fist to merge the two power flows.

The light flashed off with a tiny burst of smoke under the crystal, the needle fell back into the face and the vibration ceased. He probed it but detected nothing, not even the crinkled power outline that had caught his attention.

It is dead.

She grinned. *So, you can defeat them.*

One at a time, with effort. I must ascertain their range, and you must dispose of this one. He paused. *I scanned the throne room.*

What's there?

Some kind of low power dead kih circuit. It felt like the source of the danger I detected outside the city. I could not focus on it clearly, so I must study it more closely before Tuesday.

Khael closed his contact with her and picked up his blindfold. Her grin had faded into a sadder expression. He patted her hand, then wound the gauze back on.

"Is our meditation complete?" she whispered. At his nod, she continued in a normal voice. "Where do we go now?"

"A walk along the shore may refresh us. You can describe the sights to me."

"I am gratified to be of service, brother." She bowed

211

obsequiously.

"Bury not yourself in the masquerade," he murmured into her ear. "Caution is key."

The cold wind drifting up the slope brought a bitter chill with its briny scent. As if to emphasize the cold, the scarce patterns of kih activity made the four watchers tailing them stand out. Other forces scoured the area farther away, but the nearest buildings stood empty, devoid of life. At least no starving families huddled together for warmth in this vicinity.

Vixen peered around. She shuddered when her gaze passed the visible watchers and she squeezed his hand.

"You noticed," he murmured. "Tell me what you see."

They wandered down the hill. Vixen's descriptions depicted the same depressing, abandoned region he saw, including occasional rats and cockroaches. Most of the buildings had been boarded up or just stood empty, their windows smashed in.

The path she took him on had many turns rather than the simple straight line he expected.

After their third turn-around, Khael had to ask. "Dear sister, I sympathize that the view must be dismal, but dislike you a straight path?"

"It would be easier if these blocked and dead-end streets were marked," Vixen grumbled

"Dead-end? The main avenues and radial streets all connect at both ends or used to."

"Did you think I planned all these switchbacks?" She sounded miffed.

He frowned. "This city is as mangled as its new laws."

"Isn't that kind of subversive?" Vixen asked in a subdued voice.

"Truth is, sister. We cannot shrink from it. Our words need only be chosen with care."

"I'd like to survive the trip. Aren't subversives usually executed?"

"The crown never executes anyone."

"The crown has been usurped."

Khael thought this over as they walked. "Someone is in a difficult position if his rival should return with enough support. Even left alone, the problem will go away by itself once word gets out. A response is coming."

"Won't the land trade restrictions make that harder?"

"There are always lines of communication. Any mariners could sail from the blockade to other ports." Khael frowned, baffled. "This makes no sense. What could succeed in so short a... never mind. We can discuss this later in better surroundings, though it complicates things." He pursed his lips. "Lord MacGray seemed stressed, unusual for him."

"The clerk?" Vixen groaned. "You know him."

Khael nodded. "He has been the court clerk every time I have been in the city."

"His face was cross the whole time we were there."

The slope flattened to a mild decline roughly half a mile above the harbor. The streets bore no signs of life, completely deserted other than roving patrols, unlike the busy ones up above.

Vixen looked around. Her kih flickered with mild jitters. "Fair place for an ambush."

27.   Clash of Wills

Vixen's skin crawled. In this run-down area she expected an assault at any moment.

"Who would attack an old man and his guide?" Khael sounded so innocent.

"Outside the hermitage, some would do it for sport, brother."

"Perhaps my background is less jaded than yours, lass."

Vixen liked the sound of that, and her insides unwound a little. Sometimes he said exactly the right words. Common sense and her abiding fear of discovery held her back from throwing her arms around him. Instead, she clasped his hand tightly in both of hers for a moment.

Minutes later, two mailed men in green and two in gray, all with badges on their chests marched around a corner ahead directly toward them. Vixen's throat constricted as her already heightened arrest phobia numbed her brief respite into oblivion.

"What you doing here?" demanded one of the men in gray.

"Must we do this anon, Pete?" the shorter man in green said. "Cooperation's best achieved wi' the polite approach." He turned to Vixen. "This area's off limits to the public, lassie. Ye an' yer grandfather canna go this way."

Vixen closed her mouth. The man's words seemed to rescind the threat of arrest, and her breath returned. She held back on the whoosh of relief that rose in her chest.

"Pardon us, officer," Khael said. "For what purpose is this restricted?"

"We've had a few problems wi' escaped prisoners, an' there's gang activity run rampant. Tis no' safe for the likes o' you. Best head back up the hill, where there's nicer folk an' less risk."

Vixen bobbed her head and took Khael's arm. They turned back up the hill.

"There's a bonnie lass," one of the men behind said. "Kinda

young for such advent..."

Puzzled by the way his voice cut off, she slowed to look back.

"Keep walking." Khael tugged her arm to keep her facing forward.

"I just wondered—"

"They remember only a little girl and her grandfather."

That took her aback before she realized the implication. "You figured it out."

"I devised a method. This looming threat disrupts my focus. I have trouble with what used to be trivial, and that was not. We must be cautious."

Vixen squeezed his arm and hooked her free thumb on her belt near her dagger. "Thanks." As her mind settled down, something he said earlier made her frown. "What complicates things?"

"What would make an administrator oppress a populace so heavily short-term when he must know change will come soon?"

"Maybe he doesn't know."

"He cannot fail to expect it. Some higher authority is due to respond."

She worked her way through this new puzzle. "To get his rival's attention."

"I suspect as much. He has no chance of lasting success; hence he must entice someone to face a direct confrontation or an assassination attempt."

"That fits." She glanced around cautiously. The area seemed deserted. "What do we do?"

"We proceed with our task. After this walk, we eat, and elicit information."

"I guess. But we can't just sit around and do nothing for three days. I'll go crazy."

"There are always new lessons to absorb."

Vixen groaned. Enough lessons surrounded them already. Would they ever end? She looked up the hill for a more pleasant distraction.

Along the crest overlooking the harbor, one mansion stood out. Even from this far away, it had a warm, welcoming look, with lavish gardens in full bloom all around it. It seemed like a friendly place that warmed her heart, maybe even a potential haven.

"There's a beautiful house up there, looks like about three blocks west of the palace."

Khael nodded. "That would be the Gregory Therapy Center. We must go by for a visit."

Vixen shuddered. A therapy center? The warmth in her heart disappeared, but an icy chill invaded her thoughts. "Why?"

"The owner would like you. There is none finer in Shielin, perhaps the whole world."

She snorted. "The only ones I know are disgusting shacks with fancy names."

Khael jerked his head back. "Where is this?"

"The Enclave. Therapy centers are just torture chambers for desperate whores or slaves. I always stayed as far away from them as I could."

"Then how could you know what they are like?"

"My mentor took me to a few during my guild initiation." Pictures flashed through her mind. Her hand strayed to her dagger hilt. She would never go anywhere near one of... those.

Khael stopped. He seemed genuinely puzzled. "For what purpose?"

"I don't know. I just wanted to get away from the screams and the stink."

He didn't respond or move. She pulled him along to continue their climb.

"Perhaps the intent was to keep you away from therapy centers, or specifically this one."

She shot a suspicious glare at him. "So what? Are you planning for me to get training there?"

He shook his head. "The thought had not occurred to me."

216

"That's nice." She stiffened. Why would he go to such a place, or take her? The ones in the Enclave were the most sickening, filthy hovels she knew. Drunks and leering boors who couldn't attract companionship any other way crowded them, with no apologies. And those screams... "I have no interest in whoring. It's sick."

"Most therapy centers are nothing like that. Therapist skills do not include tormented coupling for little or no money. They encompass a wide range of healing arts."

"Really. Like what?"

"Lower your voice, sister." His soothing tone annoyed her. "They work to repair diseased or injured bodies and those with unstable minds. Healing without our disciplines, or magic, is quite an art. The range of services therapists provide differs more than an untrained desperate who steals to survive compared to a certified master collector."

She scowled. "They rent their bodies to whoever will pay to degrade them. It's horrid."

His voice dropped so low she had to strain to hear him. "Ask the owner when you meet her. She always explained it better than me."

Vixen felt the blood drain out of her face. Was he going to take her there anyway? She fought to get words out quietly. "You... know... this... woman?"

"Quite well. Where healing is needed, we serve too."

The chill in her head spread down into her chest. Wild thoughts sprang up about his contact with such filth. Her stomach clenched in cold fury. Uncomfortable with asking for any details here, she pulled her hand from his arm. "I'm not going anywhere near that place."

"There is no need for upset, sister."

"I thought I knew you, brother. You left out about consorting with harlots."

Khael's hood shifted. "Therapists are healers who treat the injured."

"Yes, I know a little about that sort of treatment."

"It seems not enough. However, I still require your guidance."

Vixen started to snap back, but his comment diffused her response. She took his hand but jerked it away when a soothing energy started to come from his.

"Don't do that." She refused to let him placate her and took his sleeve to avoid direct contact.

Her mind swirled with confused anger. She had no idea what he was talking about, and she couldn't ask in an area where spies tracked them, itching for an excuse to pounce. None had appeared yet, but for all she knew they could be right around a corner. How far sound carried in this empty neighborhood, away from the harbor noises, she couldn't tell.

He'd promised her honesty, but his attitude seemed much too familiar with such women for what he'd said about his experience. There was no way he just 'healed' with them unless healing had connotations she didn't care to consider. What he might heal in such a place made her nauseous.

As she turned a corner to get away from one of the barricades, three men emerged from between two of the shabby buildings ahead. They wore the gray tunics of the viceroy's men with no visible armor, but they looked too young to be official. The tall one in the middle had a short sword on his belt. The other two had hilts of smaller weapons on theirs, the sheaths hidden under their wraps.

"What have we here?" the scruffiest one fairly crowed.

"Trespassers in the restricted area," the short sword chimed in.

Between her anger at Khael and suspicion at their rude attitude, Vixen's terror of jail billowed to cloud any rational thought. The three stopped a yard away, blocking her path. Silence hung in the air.

The stout, belligerent one on the left finally spoke. "You really not belong here, old man. We take you for questioning."

"The abbot and I need to eat." Vixen's pulse rose with every passing second. The words she eked out scratched her dry throat.

"We feed you." The short sword leered at her with a toothy grin. "For price. Food in station, warm bedding. We search you there, maybe in private. Maybe you like, be nice to us."

Vixen clenched her teeth, her temples pounding. "I'll ask one more time. Let us pass."

"Or what?" Belligerent sneered, his hand on the hilt on his belt. "You hurt us, little lady? Maybe we hurt you, if you not nice enough."

Scruffy reached toward Khael, a pair of manacles in his hand. "You under arrest. Maybe we not hold you too long after we search pretty girl, find value."

"You think me a threat?" Khael's feeble tone echoed shock and disbelief.

Belligerent moved closer to Vixen. He reached for her.

She slapped his hand away. "Keep your filthy hands off."

He grabbed her other arm. To her surprise, Vixen's cloudy thoughts crystallized into perfect clarity. She'd done an exercise like this in one of her early training sessions. Easy. The hand grabbing hers let her pull him in close. Her dagger slipped out and opened his belly as she shoved him away, right into the short sword's weapon arm. Spinning around behind the pair, she swung her dagger up, around and right into the swordsman's neck at the base of his skull. As he fell, she followed him down, using his dying body for a shield against any possible response.

Vixen crouched between two twitching bodies on the ground. Belligerent's guts spewed onto the ground as his shallow breathing slowed to a stop. She yanked her dagger free and looked over at Scruffy, ready to dispatch him as best she could. No need. He lay still on the ground, asleep or dead, she didn't care which.

"Come. Quickly." Khael gently raised her by the arm and propelled her around the bodies.

"Let go," she mumbled, her throat dry. "My blade's bloodied."

"Here." He handed her a kerchief from his pocket. "Those watchers will be missed."

She took the cloth and mechanically wiped her daggers clean as they hurried along. Once she sheathed them, she took his arm again. Her grip tightened now that the immediate danger was gone and her only remaining upset was with Khael. Or so she thought.

Several blocks and turns later, Vixen stopped. Her guts had twisted up into such a hard knot she sagged to lean on a nearby wall. She bent over to catch her breath and threw up. It took a while between many painful gasps. When her stomach had clenched to the bone, she spat to clear her mouth. Khael's hand on her shoulder gave her brief comfort until she shrugged it off.

"Come on," she rasped. "I need a drink."

28. The Bawdy Babe

By the time they reached the top, her chest hurt so much she had trouble seeing. Each painful heartbeat pounded like a brick against the tender wall of her ribs. Cool air burned her throat and lungs. The snake-march up the hill took a fair while. She took the time to mull over her conundrum about therapists versus whores versus Khael with them, many times, to no end.

At the top, she stopped. Khael waited beside her, silent, unhelpful. A burning desire to shove him down the hill flashed through her.

No, no, no. That'd be crazy and solve nothing. They'd grown close enough she was certain he cared about her. He'd better explain, once they were alone. Damn his secrets! If she didn't already love him, she'd... what?

She groaned and tugged him west, away from the east gate where they'd come into the city. That direction reminded her of the wonderful time they'd shared in Strattonmoor, a fading dream that churned in the pit of her stomach.

"What's the big secret you won't tell me?" she murmured.

"Tact requires secure privacy." He sounded distant.

Are we in some new danger he won't say?

The press of people left her numb as they passed many eateries across the avenue. Three-quarters of a mile west of the palace, she spotted a moderately run-down tavern with a name that tickled through her upset.

"The Bawdy Babe..." She snickered. "Sounds great, smells decent. Let's go here."

The bowed timbers on the ceiling inside looked unstable and the worn, splintered floor creaked beneath their feet. Vixen looked around and spotted an empty table in the far-right corner from the door. It stood close to the bar, a fair listening place and enough to the side for privacy. One step inside the door, Khael stopped, pulling against her hand on his sleeve.

"This may not be the best choice, sister." His face seemed paler.

"I like it." Her icy tone blared defiance. "Nice and crowded, with people I can see."

She dragged him to her chosen table, next to one with a couple of men hunched over their drinks. They looked harmless enough, and she could sit on the other side of her table from them. Unfortunately, she couldn't think up a ruse to put a table between herself and Khael. He got the seat facing the door, closer to the men than her, like it or not.

She tossed her cloak onto the chair between them and pushed her seat out from the table. Leaning back, she extended her legs and stretched. Several appreciative whistles and remarks broke through the buzz. That felt better, and no one would dare to assault her in here.

"What are you doing?" he muttered.

"Nothing. I sat down. Am I permitted that much?"

The leers from the dozen or so men who craned their necks for a better look only improved her mood. At least someone liked her being there and in view. Maybe Khael would come around. But no, he shook his head.

"Listen and observe," he murmured. "Stay alert. Watch who makes the most and least fuss."

"Fine." Her dull tone oozed as much apathy as she could summon. She drew her hand away from him and crossed her arms.

The chatter around them confirmed what they had already heard. The few Paladins still in place received praise, but the hundreds of imported rangers drew only sneers and curses. Four of the largest warehouses on the harbor now substituted for the jail. Most of the new troops kept busy as jail-warehouse guards, stretching their forces thin. That fit in with what had happened down below.

A tall, older waiter delivered a relatively decent meal. At first, Vixen couldn't eat, though her stomach had settled. She almost threw up again, from the worst ale she'd ever tasted. Despite her thirst, she devoured her modest dinner with mannerly gusto. Unlike her, Khael ate little. When he stopped, he asked her to signal their waiter to come back.

"Yes, miss?"

"This ghastly stout is your best?" Khael asked.

"No new shipment in months." The waiter hunched down and lowered his voice. "You try viceroy's latest brew."

"What's that?"

"Modest brew, really. Unassuming, rather ordinary bouquet, but it has special flavor. Most people cannot get enough."

"Aye, 'cause it's drugged," one of the men at the nearest table grumbled loudly.

Vixen shuddered violently at the new voice. She glanced at the table, finally taking a close look at who sat there.

"Two men," she whispered to Khael. "One's slim, with shoulder-length brown hair, beard and mustache, in brown leather and a stained cloak."

Khael didn't even twitch.

She struggled to keep her nerves steady, not sure what to make of his lack of response. "The other's clean-shaven, hair cut square at the neck, brown eyes, wearing tan with dark green cloak and boots, no visible weapons or armor."

"Fine appraisal, lass," the second man said. "I'm mystic Ram Lichtman, no great fan o' the pathetic, ruinous vice-rat. Me friend's John Duffie, professional collector. Mind if we join you?"

A mystic? *Fog.* Vixen's hand scrabbled across the table to grip Khael's, but she couldn't feel it. Her eyes widened as she noticed his crossed arms. She had to come up with an answer to this other mystic. *I can't dispose of these two in here, but how can I say no?*

29.   Risking Trust

Vixen swallowed her nerves. "Fair enough. I'm Caroline O'Woods. This is the Abbot of the Michtie Loch Hermitage."

Ram pinched his eyebrows briefly and shook his head.

Vixen suppressed a flinch. If he knew she was lying, that would ruin everything. Still, Loren had called Khael that, and Jolie had named her—was that truly a lie? Her heart sped up again. She didn't like the idea of killing two more people, especially not in public. Why hadn't she listened to Khael at the door?

"Will there be anything else, sir, miss?" The waiter sounded bored.

"Bring us some mint tea," Khael said.

The waiter spun on his heel and left. Vixen froze as the newcomers brought their mugs and pitcher over. She forced herself to relax enough to share a quick wrist-clasp and a sipped toast.

Grimacing at the drink, she struggled to keep her voice even. "The ale's drugged?"

"No' this slop, lass." John had a gruff tenor. "A bunch o' me friends began pourin' the tainted drink down their gullets a month ago. Methought it strange, so I checked. Something special was in their ale."

"What kind of something, sir?" Khael sounded perfectly calm.

Vixen gritted her teeth. Were they safe or what?

"I ain't no certified 'sir,' Monk, just John." He continued in a hushed voice, eyeing the taproom. "Tain't alcohol. Belike some narcotic. Makes drinkers crave more 'til they pass out."

"I was about to indulge when John warned me," Ram said. "That's lowdown mean e'en for a rat like his dubiousness."

Vixen relaxed a fraction at their words. Maybe they weren't so big a threat. Still, this mystic might be playing her, or he might be stupid, or a spy, or something else she didn't know.

"Are you certain the viceroy is behind this?" Khael asked.

"We ain't seen it, if that's what ye mean," Ram said. "But pubs serve it as the 'viceroy's brew.' Our imports 're dead wi' out the harbor. About halfway since, the drugged ale appeared."

"That an' his announcement the ale supply 'd been replenished for trusted establishments." John raised and lowered his eyebrows twice. "Methinks tis the same ale, altered."

"Aren't there any local breweries?"

"We had five on the north slopes, lass," Ram said. "They're closed, some think from sabotage. Only the stout brewery's left, an' it canna keep up wi' the demand, or mayhap tis his pawn now too."

Khael shook his head. "How disappointing."

"What's that supposed to mean?" John's hand strayed under the tabletop.

Vixen narrowed her eyes, watching him closely. She casually lowered her own hand near her dagger. If he wanted to start something...

"No harm, friend," Khael said. "Drugged stout seems a clumsy ploy."

John grunted, but he relaxed.

Relieved yet still wary, Vixen left her hand in her lap. The haughty waiter delivered the requested tea and absented himself.

Ram waited until the server was out of hearing range. "We ain't so dumb as his rat-ship maun think. Once word got out, an' it didna take lang, most stopped or got help. The rest're only a handful. I hear two died from it."

"The whole thing's sick."

"Agreed, sister. Politics often works this way. Be thankful the hermitage has none."

Ram suddenly raised his head and frowned at Khael. "Forgive me, abbot, but isn't the hermitage abandoned?"

"We prefer to maintain a low profile." Khael fell silent.

Vixen's mind raced. Khael wouldn't lie, but she might be able to stretch the truth enough. "Many years ago, the brethren locked the gates and restricted admission to members only. If I weren't already a student, I'd have had to wait more than a year to apply."

"Oh." Ram seemed mollified, yet still suspicious.

"Our recruiting has been limited for quite some time," Khael said.

Yeah, centuries. Vixen suppressed a grim snicker.

Ram stared at Khael for a moment, flicked his eyebrows and sat back.

John yawned. "'Tis getting late, an' I'm for home. There's work tomorrow, an' curfew comin'."

"Curfew?" Vixen echoed. As if they didn't have enough to worry about.

"Aye." John nodded. "Get caught out after eight, an' it's the warehouse filth wi' na trial. His goons roam the city all night."

"I should leave, too." Ram stood. "I hope we'll meet anon, abbot. I'd like to learn about yer abbey in more pleasant circumstances."

"We welcome discussion," Khael said. "Our philosophies may be quite compatible."

"An intriguing possibility." Ram touched his brow. "Until then."

After they left, Vixen turned toward Khael, but she straightened up to keep some distance. "Did that Ram fellow, uh, know anything?"

"No. Fortunately, he is a novice." Khael interlaced his fingers.

Vixen sighed her relief. She slumped back in her chair. "What did all that mean? They seemed nice enough, and John's information can be useful, if it's true."

"Yet he had one of those things."

Vixen blinked, puzzled. "He sounded fair set against the viceroy."

Khael took a moment before he answered. "He may just be an uninformed tool of some less scrupulous person."

After they overheard the same rumors many times, Khael cleared his throat. "Come with me."

Suspicious, Vixen narrowed her eyes at him. The pub attendance thinned as more people trickled out, probably to avoid the curfew. She

226

liked that idea better than whatever he had in mind. He pulled her closer as they mingled with those headed between the buildings rather than along the main streets. Despite her anger with him, his close presence comforted her against the growing risks they flaunted.

"I expect the gas lights will be extinguished shortly," he murmured. "If we use the alleys, our chances of interception may be lower."

"I've spent enough time on the streets of the Enclave," she whispered back. "No curfew, but I learned to elude most hazards." A few minutes later, she felt lost, "Where are we going?"

"Patience, my dear."

To her surprise, Khael seemed to know exactly where they were going. His sure bearing took them across two full streets before the streetlamps began to fade. Part way through the next block, empty now that the other lurkers had slunk away, the street ahead went black. Khael stopped and she bumped into his arm, held out in front of her. She strained to see his face. He held a finger on his lips. To her surprise, he unwound the blindfold and stuffed it into his pocket.

"Stay close," he whispered into her ear.

His hot breath almost doused her burning concerns. He led her along the side of the alley. Her eyes adjusted to the dark enough to see him checking something at each door they passed. The noise of boots marching along the street not ten yards behind them forced them to flatten against the nearest building. Vixen held her breath.

The boots stopped. Some rustling noises made Vixen cringe. She dared not move. Would the marchers follow them? Had they seen anything suspicious? How many of them could she take before...? Her heart pounded the whole time, making her push even harder into the unyielding brick wall. *Get on with it already.*

"Clear," one voice finally grumbled and the group moved off along the street.

A rat scrabbled across Vixen's boot. She kicked once the shock wore off, but the rat was long gone. Khael tugged her hand and they crept farther along the unlit dirt path. He stopped after a few steps and stooped down, his hand brushing the ground. Why was he cleaning the

227

alley floor? Her eyes widened when he pulled up a trap door.

He waved her over. She took a quick, cautious look in the black hole before she took a hesitant step down stairs she couldn't see. Crowding close behind her, he urged her on. As they descended, he lowered the hatch until it shut. Pitch black.

"I hate this kind of dark."

On the other hand, he stood close behind, warming her whole back. He obviously still felt something for her, but of course he said nothing of it. Her breast swelled in hope of a sign.

"It is safe. Walk." He nudged her shoulder.

She reached out to feel the walls before she moved. This succeeded on one side, so she crept ahead at a snail's pace until he hissed at her to accelerate. They soon came to a corner around which a soft light emanated from a few bricks in the walls. A single globe glowed down the tortuous tunnel, attached to the end wall beside another closed door.

Khael tried the handle, but the door didn't budge. He stood back.

Vixen frowned at him as if he were crazy and raised her hand to knock. He shook his head and pointed at the lock in the handle. It took her three attempts to pick the lock before she succeeded. By then she was sweating and ready to scream. She stood up, glared at him, and smiled her triumph.

"Excellent. That is one of the most secure locks around." His quiet expression sounded eerie.

"Thanks." Her voice cracked through a dry throat. "I noticed." She put her picks away with a smirk. "Now can you please tell me what you wouldn't say outside?"

Khael pressed his lips together. He led her through the door and closed it. At first the other side looked like just another tunnel. This one had its own dim light bricks and a clean paved floor.

"I suppose this is safe enough. We are going to the Gregory Center to ensure my mother is all right, among other things."

A pulse of rage swept through Vixen. "You had to keep that a secret?"

"If I spoke and our watchers had any kind of listening device, we would be dead or in prison."

Her rage blew off like a puff of smoke. She hadn't even considered such a possibility.

"We may expect fallout from your explosion earlier."

"That's what happens when unscrupulous scumbags threaten to rape me."

"I stopped the one. The other two would not have been difficult."

"Thanks, but I protect myself."

Khael shrugged. "Patience and control work better in most cases, but you did well. For now, I thought you might enjoy a pleasant surprise, perhaps unwind some."

She scowled, clenching her fists.

"This is the kind of secure facility we need to restore our natural appearance. We will meet with my most loyal supporters and learn more about the situation."

"At a therapy center?"

"Mother was the head of the crown's intelligence network in Shielin. She may have information that will help us rescue my people and restore the throne. With this threat I cannot shake, any help I can trust is most welcome."

Vixen stiffened, not sure what to make of all that. Was it a compliment, or something else? The passage ended at another door only twelve yards from the last one.

Khael knocked twice, three times, then once. Several seconds passed before the door opened. On the other side stood a dark-skinned woman with coal black hair piled up on her head. Her hard muscled figure, constrained in a tight, short black tunic, loomed not quite two hands over Khael.

"Identity?" came the deepest voice Vixen had ever heard from a woman.

"Lyla," Khael admonished her. "Tell me you recognize me."

Surprised delight blossomed on Lyla's stern face.

"Welcome home, Sire, do come in." Her warm words husked more than Vixen thought decent. "We were hoping it was you in the tunnel. Her ladyship awaits. I hear she has some nice snacks laid out for you."

Vixen held her breath. She rolled her eyes toward Khael.

He smiled. "Yes, she would. How are you? It has been a while."

"I'm fine, given the circumstances, and yes, it has." Lyla closed the door with a wicked grin. "In some ways, it's been forever." At his look of disapproval, she pouted. "No welcome back kiss?"

Though Khael shook his head, Vixen glared at the dark amazon. She was in love with him too, and she could easily be one of those... women.

Khael introduced Vixen to Master Assassin Lyla Kincaid, head of house security. "Shall we go upstairs?"

Vixen caught the abashed look on Lyla's face before she smoothed it away. That confirmed Vixen's suspicions. He must have known. Annoyed, she wondered what else he hadn't shared with her.

Lyla looked her over with fierce, dark brown eyes. "You'd look ravishing with lighter hair, Vixen. This way, please." She turned and led them into the passage.

They passed several people along their way, all dressed in conservatively cut trousers and a matching short-sleeved or sleeveless blouse. Vixen liked their fashionable wear, and the halls were clean and nicely decorated, wide enough for four. Maybe this place wasn't as horrid as she'd feared, though the last few people who went by wore only shorts or just towels.

The residents all ignored the new arrivals, yet they acted friendly enough with each other. A cluster of five flawless naked men and women with wet hair and towels emerged from one doorway.

Vixen tried hard not to stare. "Is it always this, ah, casual?"

"The residential and recreational facilities are on this level," Khael said. "That was the pool."

The men were hunks, and the women gorgeous, all cheery, even the less-fit ones. Nothing like the pathetic wretches Vixen had seen, and heard, in the Enclave. Was that why he barely looked at her? Her heart plummeted. "They're all so... striking."

"We hire only the best," Lyla said with pride.

They arrived at a staircase with a vaulted ceiling high above. Lyla stood aside to wave them up. When they reached the third floor, Khael took Vixen's hand and tugged her faster. Halfway down the last hall, he closed his eyes and set his face. A pair of doors at the end opened by themselves just in time. Vixen nodded—he did that. She took one step past the threshold and stopped to gawk.

Elegant tapestries and colorful paintings adorned the gilded walls, like in his Cambridge suite but much richer. The enormous bed's mirrored canopy rested on four thick corner posts several palms taller than Grant. The rich silks adorning the bed crinkled under a seated beautiful woman. Her wavy brown hair fell to her elbows over a long royal blue silk dress. Vixen lowered her eyes to a stunning, expertly woven, wall-to-wall carpet of a vibrant seascape.

The Enclave hovels she'd seen had nothing on this exotic mansion.

The new woman's shimmering outfit clung and fluttered in the air currents when she came over to them. Her blue eyes shone bright with unshed tears. "Darling."

It was the warmest greeting Vixen had ever heard one person extend to another. If this were another wish-lover of his, Vixen didn't know what she'd do. She prayed she was wrong and held her breath as Khael let go of her hand. He embraced the strange, far too young woman in a long, tender hug. By the time he finally spoke, Vixen wanted to shrink into the floor.

"Mother."

30. Lady Sinaeg Gregory

Khael clung to his mother. Knowing she was safe and free, he released his sore, rigid control on his worries and let his face relax in spite of the ongoing, icy itch.

"I've missed ye, sweetheart," she muttered, indulging his long cling.

Khael finally drew back. They traded kisses to both cheeks. She wiped his face dry and gazed at him, her hands on his shoulders. He ignored the tears he had not even felt and smiled. Her eyes glittered with similar worry and relief.

"Nice gray there, son. Worried about me? Or's this lass affected ye more 'n I thought?"

He laughed, surprised and delighted he could. "It is false, and yes, I worried about you. It is a great relief knowing you are safe and well." After another, shorter hug, he introduced Vixen.

Sinaeg slipped her arms around the surprised maiden for a warm hug. "Pleased to meet ye, Vixen. Any friend o' me son's a friend o' mine, too. Wrist-clasps 're for strangers."

"Thank you." Vixen swayed as Sinaeg released her. "I never expected a therapist."

Khael held his breath.

Sinaeg's gentle tone belied her abrupt stiffness. "'S that a problem, lassie?"

"I've had—unpleasant experiences with, ah, therapy centers."

Sinaeg returned her long stare. "Fair enough. I was a therapist when I met Khael's father. He insisted we be married an' me his princess. I never enjoyed the status, which is why I have a regent. Or so I thought."

She linked arms with them and towed them to an elegant velvet couch. A mouth-watering tray of a few snacks lay on a low table before the couch.

"Sit, enjoy some real food. Now, son, tell me everything ye've done since ye left."

With a courteous nod, Vixen slowly helped herself to a few of the snacks.

Khael gave her a fond smile. "Grant and I fulfilled Ryan's mission to the mayors on the east coast. We survived five Chelevkori attempts to kill me. Vixen stole my signet ring and returned it. She agreed to work for me until May and help me fix this disaster."

Sinaeg snickered. "Fine summary, an' far too brief."

"I will indulge you after sanity prevails. What happened to John? Damon believes him dead, yet our people suffer at his hands."

"He was perfectly faithful for his fifteen years as me viceroy afore ye took the throne. He's so different syne the illness e'en I barely recognize him."

"The Chelevkori are expert form-changers. Is he one?"

"I have na seen him in person, but ye'd ken that better 'n anyone. 'Cept Father." Sinaeg sighed. "After the madness set in, John relieved most o' the palace servers, many o' whom were network agents, an' all yer political staff, except Eugene an' his scribes. Said he needed 'em to keep the state operatin'. Mayhap a language issue."

"Language?" Vixen wondered.

"His troops have trouble wi' Shielin. Some o' their accents are Ostrovan. No' his though, but that part makes sense."

Khael frowned. "How are you still here and not ruling?"

"John's changes were subtle at first, an' I trusted him. His new troops began to arrest folk for minor offenses, or e'en just resistin' arrest. By the time he seized the dock warehouse an' provoked the mariners' strike, he'd filled the jail an' every Watch station wi' hundreds o' prisoners. The riot landed hundreds more in other seized warehouses. I sent him word to fix it, an' he threatened to kill 'em all if I interfered."

Khael tightened his lips in concern. "That is not the John Masterson I knew."

"He has a strange balance of liberties an' terror," Sinaeg mused.

"Long's there's na overt resistance, people 're free to talk or go about their business, wi' his higher fees. Those who file formal complaints are given courtesy an' respect, wi' na retribution so far."

"He left your doors unbarred."

"We treat the injured an' the sick. He needs that—there's many more since he started out. But we're under watch day an' night. His men plague us for services, an' they pay no' dearly enough. Me healers 're no' allowed anywhere near the prisoners. Wi' his restrictions, basic supplies 're harder to procure, an' more expensive than e'er."

"Homeless families have taken meager refuge in the deserted buildings on the slopes." Khael clenched his teeth. Though he felt free to vent with his mother, his anger solved nothing and might drive him to fatal recklessness. He needed more than ever to remain calm, despite all the upsets. "They have little heat or food, and their children starve."

Sinaeg set her lips and nodded curtly. "After the riot I sent out agents to organize a response, but I got word ye were comin' home. I knew ye'd deplore an outright war, so I held back."

"War only hurts everyone." Khael took a deep breath. Kinshuh seemed excessive, even for this inner seething. "Thank you, though. What about Trevor?"

"He's still nominal Commandant o' the Watch, but he's ne'er alone, an' his senior staff's spread throughout the city. The palace's no' safe, either. Desmond sent word there's some kind o' strange doomsday contraption hidden somewhere in the throne room."

"Doomsday contraption?" Vixen echoed, her face curious.

"Ah." Khael sighed. "I sensed a lethal threat a quarter mile outside the city. It is strongest in the palace. Loren showed me an unclear image. I have had no time or proximity to analyze it properly, and I must. The whole city stands at risk, tens of thousands of innocent lives. Vixen and I have three full days, if we are careful, and patient."

"I'll do whatever you need." Vixen's eyes flashed her anger.

"Thank you." Khael's heart warmed, soothing against his burn for justice. Her support meant more than he realized, whether from her obligation to him or the love she tried to hide. "Mother, can you do hair-pieces matched to these colors by Monday night? We can restore our natural looks then for when we confront this false viceroy Tuesday afternoon."

"I'll have wigs made for you." Sinaeg went to fetch a pair of scissors from her vanity. "What's with the delay?"

"Our appointment is three hours after midday."

Vixen swallowed the snack in her mouth. "Is it safe to perform this transformation here?"

"O' course, lassie." Sinaeg returned. "Me house is a secure environment. Khael's hair needs cut so the people 'll readily recognize him, an' that wrinkled leathery skin must go too." She took a moment to look Vixen over. "Ye could use a nicer hair style, mayhap a complete make-over."

Vixen shrugged. "If someone came into my home like we did here, I'd have their head."

Sinaeg smiled. "Feral lass, isn't she?"

"You have no idea." Khael rubbed his chin and chuckled. Even amid the horrors, their familial atmosphere prevailed. "Perhaps we will have more time after we have restored order. May we coordinate through you?"

"O' course. Who needs know besides Grant an' Damon?"

"We require people we can trust in the palace."

"The house guard that's left collaborate as they need, but they're still loyal to us. Desmond did ye proud wi' that 'n." Sinaeg paused and her tone heated up. "Damon was here this morn."

Khael nodded. They would make a nice couple if they all survived. Vixen stared at Sinaeg as if she had also figured it out. She was a bright lass, quite a treasure. The heat in his chest grew.

"He has Paladins in the city already as merchants, therapists, servants an' guards, though many're under watch, too. I expect he'll have all he can get by Tuesday morn. The wait 'll wear on 'em."

"We need maximum support, especially Grant and Damon."

"Grant 'll be hard to miss, but he's no' turned up yet." Sinaeg sighed. "There's profiteers that support the viceroy, an' he has around a thousand men. Ye'll have to expect resistance, even bloodshed."

"Not. In. My. Palace." Khael paused. "Blood never washes out clean. It must be burnt away."

"Then burn the blasted palace down, son. Ye cannot afford to lose o'er that silly rule."

"I would rather not burn anything." Khael bowed his head. She was right. Fog. "We had best leave. If our room is empty too long, it might arouse suspicion."

"Take care, children." Sinaeg laid the hair samples on the vanity. "We'll expect you Monday."

They shared hugs before the couple headed out. The basement seemed empty when Khael and Vixen walked off the stairs. Lyla sat in a fancy chair by the door, sifting through papers. The pair bid her farewell as they headed into the tunnel.

"How are we going to stop this John who isn't John?" Vixen asked once they had passed the first set of cross-passages.

Khael shook his head slowly. "I need more information, especially about that device. I welcome your ideas."

Vixen shrugged. "I don't know enough. Can you use your disciplines?"

"With caution. We must create an opportunity for that to work."

In the alley, the snow had stopped. A layer several thumbs thick covered the next street past the alleys that crisscrossed the whole block. Khael scanned the area for life signs. At Vixen's inquisitive look, he gestured her closer, his mouth next to her ear.

"We must be cautious yet," he whispered. "No patrols nearby, just sleeping drifters. Come here. I will carry you."

Vixen frowned surprise at him, but she seemed happy enough in his arms. He invoked yuso to ensure his feet left no imprint in the snow. Crossing the first street presented no trouble, but halfway through the alleys in the block beyond, his yuso gave out. She walked through the alleys on her own after that. His second exercise consumed as much zhukih just crossing the street. In the next alley he set her down, his breath heavy.

"We must stick to the alleys where we can," he whispered. "I need yuso to cross the avenues without traces, but that costs energy I may yet need."

Part way along the alley in the next block, he stopped. A patrol approached, four men checking the next street for curfew breakers. He wrapped his arms around her and pressed her into the nearest closed doorway set in the alley wall. Her muscles tensed at the shock of his quick move, but she did not resist. The marching boots grew louder, not far away on the street ahead.

A pleasant warmth rose between them in the embrace. In the cold air, her breath caught and sped up. She pressed her chilled face into his neck. Her hands crept around his waist.

Despite the approaching danger, he enjoyed the tickle of her excitement and the embrace. Strange. Would resulting heat between them raise any vapors to reveal their presence?

The hair on his neck stood up at the marching noises, which continued past the alley. Before he could withdraw, she clung to him in a fierce hug. When she finally let go, he drew back and shook his head. He took her hands for a quick squeeze and held one until they finished their silent, trackless way back to their room.

Vixen stopped between their beds, her eyes searching his for direction. They shone, reflecting the desire for him that rippled through her kih. Would she be more comfortable sharing the warmth of his bed, even if they remained fully dressed? His heart raced at the thought.

A chill shivered up his spine. What was he thinking? It took him a long moment to raise kinshuh for his own sake. With a silent, internal sigh, he signed they should get their rest. He retreated to huddle under his blankets, alone.

Fog.

Disappointment fought with relief in her kih. The winter chill swiftly encouraged her to bundle up in her own swath of covers. She had the worst time settling down. Her many elevated energy flows distracted him. He had to force himself to cease focusing on her and concentrate on his security watch. After a long while, her kih smoothed

237

out and her breath became regular.
The itchy, icy burn persisted.

31. Street Fight

As they walked up to the palace grounds the next morning, Khael stopped them at the nearest gate. He had wanted to try and visit the museum, but guards ringed the entire building. Though he itched to observe the viceroy in court, he decided to avoid the temptation for rash action. The mysterious threat in the throne room ceiling still demanded his attention. Better to find a safe way to analyze it.

Vixen took him to a different inn nearby where the food smelled delicious from half a block away. Khael breathed more easily at this change from the Bawdy Babe of last night. As with most taverns, the dining room stood open but nearly empty. He scanned around the inn, noting few guests in the upstairs, most of which lacked any signs of human life.

People in the dining room displayed curiosity about the two strangers. So much for open conversation. Though the lunch pleased him, Vixen's kih radiated severe defensive tension. They ate quickly to preempt the excessive risk of drawing unwanted attention from an overlong stay.

At Khael's suggestion, Vixen walked them through a more residential area of the southwest quarter of the city. Many fair mansions used to populate that section, abundant with large grounds and creative architecture. She would be able to see a spacious, rolling park that used to be famous for its entertainment facilities. It had playgrounds for the young and several sporting areas for adults, even a full practice joust arena. An on-site therapy center provided immediate care and services for anyone injured in the park. He omitted that detail.

Vixen described the venues as they wandered along. Her bright voice and cheerful tone faded. "It's like a fancy ruin here. Where is everyone?"

"The residents either work in shops in the markets or raise their families inside their estates. Those who have servants employ them for domestic operations. Non-residents tend to busy themselves with their own homes and work."

"What about collectors and such?"

"In areas like this, such activities tend to be unsafe. Those who attach themselves to their possessions respond poorly to attempts to deprive them thereof."

Vixen drew her head back. "You sound like one of them."

"I prefer to think of myself as well-educated."

Half a block away from the park Khael directed her to, Vixen stopped.

"The gates are closed and barred," Vixen said.

Khael scanned around the inside of the walled estate. He enhanced his range to cover the entirety of the vast park's many acres.

"I see a few people in what must be the main house," he murmured, then shook his head. "The grounds look worse kept than those of the palace. Of course. Popular entertainment sites like this would counter effective oppression."

Vixen frowned, puzzled. "Wouldn't that make a revolt more likely?"

"To the prince, yes." Khael sighed. "Continue."

The streets bore less traffic toward the outer reaches of the city. Those people's kih radiated depression, hurry, even anxiety, much like the others who moved about. While not as desperate as those eking out survival on the harbor slopes and in the poorer areas, the cloud of gloom weighed on Khael. Waiting until Tuesday to act wrenched at his patience. Kinshuh helped him stave off the combination of this with the irritation his chokkan refused to let up. It might be necessary to keep that active until he prevailed or...

As they strolled along another narrower street where shops and a market used to thrive, the traffic increased to about half that near the palace. Conversation buzzed in low voices, but enough to cheer him somewhat beneath his tight control.

* * *

Vixen pulled Khael to a halt. A short way ahead, a large fugitive in peasant attire ran down the street toward them. Several gray-shirt rangers rushed into the street from an alley to block his path. Another group of gray-shirts chased along behind the fugitive, yelling and cursing for him to stop. Everyone else along the street melted to the sides, catching Khael and Vixen in the crush. They wound up in the front row of the onlookers.

"Someone crossed up the viceroy's men," Vixen muttered into Khael's ear.

He bowed his head with a quiet hiss.

"I hate violence," she said, louder.

The fugitive ran straight into the half dozen rangers in the street ahead of him. His enormous size gave him a clear advantage as he crashed into them. Three went down and stopped moving while a fourth staggered away toward the nearest wall before he collapsed. One of the remaining two yelled something as the fugitive sped up, a staff now in his hands.

Vixen struggled to hold back a cheer for the brave man.

A whole company of uniformed rangers hustled up the street from the opposite direction. Most of these held staves in their hands, but a few in green had drawn swords.

The fugitive barreled right into the new company as if they were nothing more than fleas in his way. His handsome face flashed by Vixen, framed with a heavy beard and mustache connected to his longer brown hair. He knocked down four of the newcomers and hurled a fifth back into the onrushing forces. His dark eyes caught hers for an instant.

Grant? Vixen froze, nausea digging into her stomach. What was he doing here?

Grant disabled two more of the new rangers. They collapsed unconscious like bloody, empty grain sacks. He charged at the ring that now enclosed him. Two rangers tripped him with their staves while a third swung a staff down on his hooded head.

Vixen held her breath, sure the fight was over. Another pair in gray dropped their staves and reached down to haul Grant up. He used them to regain his feet and swung them into each other. Their heads

241

smashed together with a loud, metallic jangle. They also fell, unconscious or worse.

Four rangers with staves moved in, growling. One thrust his staff to jab Grant, but he grabbed the staff and punched the ranger in the head. As that one fell, Grant neatly engaged the other three with the staff. Each of them fell beneath his superior strength and skill, one by one.

The remaining ring of rangers closed in. The first two smashed the staff out of Grant's hands. Another poled him in the abdomen. With a gasp, he grabbed the offending staff. A fourth clubbed his head as two more beat on his back. Grant grunted, loud through his heavy panting.

He turned into the rear threat, his staff cracking one ranger's ribs. Another batted him across the back. The fourth struck his head again, this time so hard the staff broke. Grant's eyes glazed as he fell to his knees. A sustained volley of blows crumpled him into an injured ball.

Were they ever going to stop? Vixen held back a curse.

Finally, one Watchman in green with a sword stepped in. "Enough already. Bind him."

Vixen's face chilled while the gray-shirts manacled Grant's wrists and ankles and locked a metal collar around his neck. Four of the biggest grasped his upper arms and calves and hoisted, cursing him the whole time. Within moments they were all gone.

"'Tis all right, dear," one sympathetic elderly woman told Vixen. "He shouldna've challenged those gray-shirts."

"He may get a fair trial, afore he's cast into one o' those filthy warehouses."

A buzz in Vixen's ears drowned out the dispersing crowd.

"Caroline?" Khael's voice cut through. "Is it safe?"

She faced him with every muscle clenched to control her outrage. "Did you see that?"

"No, sister, I cannot," he said through a slow nod.

Grief overtook her and she froze into his arms, panting out her fury against his shoulder. He held her close until her rigid muscles relaxed again and she straightened her posture. She looked up at his blindfolded face. What if those monsters tortured Grant, or killed him?

"Our task lies ever uneasy upon us," Khael murmured. "It may yield great rewards or harsh penalties. Violence is the most difficult to observe."

"But he was... that was... he—he looked hurt." Vixen wouldn't dare betray Grant by name, but she ached for some reassurance, anything.

"Yes, and he probably knew better." Khael sighed and took her arm. "We must go."

The hum of conversations on the street drifted past Vixen like billowing clouds in the wind, incomprehensible, unimportant. She felt numb, mechanically checking street traffic before leading Khael across. At their inn she almost tripped over the threshold. Khael supported her more than she guided him. Her mind still vague, she sat on her bed facing him over the narrow gap.

"Feel you all right?"

His normal volume startled her. She shook her head and whispered back, "Shouldn't we be whispering, or speaking, ah, with more caution?"

"Thanks." He laid his cloak across his bed. At her frown, he produced a grim smile. "I was uncertain how long your reverie would persist. The inn is empty save the staff cleaning up below."

"I thought you'd gone crazy again. You know who that was, of course. They beat him bloody. Who knows how many bones they broke? How are we going to take care of him in time for him to help us Tuesday?"

"His injuries were superficial, no broken bones. He will heal without assistance. However, his actions were reckless. His loss makes our work more difficult. They will not be kind to him."

"That broken staff must have hurt a lot." Vixen looked at him with rounded eyes. She sighed and her head drooped. "I hope he's all right."

"You care for him." Khael caught her chin and raised her head to

243

face his blindfold.

"He's your best friend, and a fine instructor, when he's not being a tyrant. He's also a terrific fighter, better than what we saw. I'm surprised he went down against only two dozen. He must be up to something. I'm not fool enough to underestimate him."

"Is that the limit of your concern?"

"Yes, of course." She softened her expression and lowered her eyes. "No, not really. He's almost as much a gentleman as you. I... like him. Just don't tell him I said so."

32. Word Wars

The next morning, Khael had Vixen seek a new venue for breakfast that had some potential. Their presence might be less noticeable if they varied their dining choices. Crushing his hope, the usurper's centurion stood across the street where the Palace arc-streets joined. His kih seemed more casual today, and he had a new detector.

"Fair morrow, my friends," he called warmly, crossing through the light traffic toward them.

"Fair morning, Lieutenant." Khael kept his hermit voice steady. "However, we hardly know you."

"But you know you've been followed since our meeting Thursday."

"Yes, and poorly." Vixen stiffened, her bearing frosty, even hostile.

"You found the agents obtrusive, dear lady?"

"I'm not your dear anything, Lieutenant. I find them clumsy."

"I mean no offense. Apparently they were too clumsy. Three of them were found dead last night and one remains missing."

"What a shame." Vixen had a sneer in her tone. "It did seem strange they left us alone after being so obvious."

"I'd like to discuss the matter with you, among others, if you don't mind. Afterward I could give you a tour of the city."

"How would a tour benefit us?" Khael disliked the idea. He had no doubt this Jack hoped to entrap them, most likely for some foul purpose. Any genuine monk from anywhere in the shire would know the city better than this fellow could possibly know it after six months, or less.

"I'm told even the blind can appreciate the sounds and scents of this fair city. In the alternative, I could give your guide a private tour of her own."

Khael grasped Vixen's hand before she could express the angry offense that boiled in her kih. "We seek a quality breakfast."

"I know just the place. Would you accompany me to the Robin Redbreast? We can talk there."

"If you insist." Vixen's icy tone seethed hostility.

Khael squeezed her hand gently and her upset scaled back. With that detector so close, he had to be careful with his disciplines. "We accept, Lieutenant. That diner's reputation precedes it."

"Please call me Jack. This way."

Vixen had little trouble guiding Khael, but he read her true conflict. She despised this enemy agent and wanted to stay as far away from him as possible. Her concerns likely included her theft of Jack's original detector, but she may have been puzzled at Khael's cooperation.

"What subjects wished you to discuss, Lieutenant?"

"Aside from the murdered men and their missing comrade, I was curious about the differences between your philosophy at the hermitage and the mystic, uh, powers."

"Without sufficient familiarity in such subjects, I decline to speculate."

"Then you know nothing of what happened to my men?"

"This is the first we have heard of three murders."

Jack's kih blazed distrust, but he shook it off. "I'll take your word for it, venerable sir. May we discuss the philosophical questions? I can pose examples for your comment."

"I fail to see the use." Khael kept his tone flat.

"Humor me, sir. From what I understand, mystics consider life sacred, but only hold this sanctity inviolate for animals. They appear to suspend this belief only for abomina—,androids, unnatural creatures, humans and other intelligent life. This seems a dilemma to me, even a danger with the more hostile animals. What's your philosophy on this issue?"

"We disdain violence."

After a moment's pause, Jack pressed. "Do you believe in self-defense? If so, how far would you go to defend yourself against stubborn attackers? What about defense of others?"

"Yes, to the point of disability and likewise."

Jack jerked, startled.

"Forgive me, Lieutenant, questions thus compounded tend to confuse issues. This makes answers harder to form or follow."

"Please call me Jack."

"I reserve familiarities for my brethren."

Jack nodded with a grunt. "I'll keep the questions simple. You never use violence?"

"Our primary defense is to avoid conflict. Most stubborn attackers tire out first."

"You wouldn't defend yourselves under any circumstances?"

"Our life's mission is to learn and study, peacefully, to better ourselves."

"You and mystics have that much in common, as I understand it." Jack fingered his lips. "How many members are in your order?"

"We keep no such records. At the hermitage, all are known."

"How many are at the hermitage?"

"It may vary from day to day."

"How many are there today?"

"I could not say. We have been absent since Wednesday."

"How many were there on Wednesday?"

Khael paused. "I doubt we have counted the members for a long time."

"But how do you know when a new member comes in?"

"I fail to see how our philosophy relates to our numbers."

"Just curious." Jack looked around. "Here is the Robin. We can continue at my table."

"You reserved one?" Vixen sounded surprised.

Jack chuckled. "I frequent this place. The service and the food are better than the pal—most places around here, and for a decent price.

They keep the best tables available for us regulars."

The heat and humidity jumped as they went inside. The taproom was about half full, mostly average working men and women, and a few rangers. Jack's kih reeked of smug self-confidence as he led them inside. Catcalls and whistles rang out while they shed their cloaks.

"Hey, Lieutenant, fine looking woman you bring," came a voice from a table to Khael's left..

"Nice catch," another ranger at the same table said with a crude hand gesture.

Jack stopped short, offense at their rude behavior blazing in his kih. "These people are my guests."

"We host her, too, when you done with her."

Raucous laughs emanated from all three men at the table. Khael held his calm against their increasingly crude attitudes. Vixen stood rigid, seething under a thinning varnish of control.

"Yeah. Share and share alike, eh, Lieutenant?"

Jack turned his head toward the source of the discourtesy. "Are you finished?"

The quiet ice in his tone penetrated the air at the table.

"Uh, sure."

"Pay up," Jack said. "Then get out."

"Huh? We not eat yet."

"We protect this place. Not pay."

"Did that sound like a request?" Jack snapped.

Grumbles came from the men as they threw some coins on the table and shambled out the door.

"Forgive those men, they seem to have forgotten their manners." Jack led Khael and a calmer Vixen to a space live with echoes from around the room.

They sat at a corner table, with light pressure from above as if a staircase rose over their heads. Noise from kitchen doors swinging at the other end of the bar accompanied two waiters and one serving matron who moved in and out. Vixen helped Khael sit facing the front door. She took the inside chair to his right, under the stairs.

Jack stood fast. "Interesting. To sit beside the young lady, which I'd like, I must put my back to the door. That I don't do, thus you've placed me at your side, Abbot. A deft maneuver."

"Such plots presume biased intent, sir. Caroline knows I hear better facing the door. She is free to choose her own seat, as are you."

Jack grunted as he sat beside Khael, radiating an unfriendly chill. His hand strayed to the silent detector on his belt. "The strangest coincidence occurred when you left the palace, Abbot. At the time I had a pouch on my belt, a standard issue to palace officers. I noticed mine was gone after you left."

Vixen glared at him. The slight warmth in her kih for his earlier chivalry chilled into renewed antagonism. "That's terrible. I too have lost treasured items now and then. I've never raised the subject to others unless they were friends or family, or suspects."

"How long have you been in the city, Lieutenant?" Khael interrupted the building argument.

"Five months, since August 8." Jack frowned at Vixen. "I was with the first group his excellency needed to fill when half of the palace guards quit."

"Quit?" Vixen harrumphed. "I heard the viceroy dismissed them."

"I am unaware of any such thing," Jack said.

Khael stifled a sardonic guffaw at this latest in a string of lies.

"At least you've kept your armor clean," she said.

"Thank you, miss, but I don't understand."

"Many of your comrades don't seem to find it necessary."

"A knight should be prepared, and always look his best. Unclean armor fails."

The waiter arrived to take their drink preferences and describe the breakfast. When he left, they sat back for a moment to relax. Vixen looked around the room.

Jack focused on her. "I meant no insult, miss. We were discussing philosophy."

Khael cleared his throat. "Perhaps if you tell us yours, Lieutenant."

Jack sat back and fingered his chin. "I follow the knight's creed. We value honor, strength, valor, skill and the challenge of combat. I strive to excel in the Knighthood skills and learn enough from other guilds to appreciate their professions and assist me in mine. I've aligned with my chosen sect and serve their needs. I prosper under their wing."

"Which sect?" Vixen said.

"Does it matter?"

"Doesn't it?"

"It is an ancient, deeply misunderstood sect. We wish to prove our motives and values to the whole world before announcing ourselves."

Hence, Chelevkori. Khael nodded. "What motives and values would those be?"

Jack held his head high. "Pursuit of individual excellence. Service to benefit our sect and all society. We also value scholarly education to further our knowledge, and that of humankind."

"How altruistic." Vixen reeked suspicion. She must have figured out his angle. "If your sect has been so maligned, isn't there any frustration, maybe vengeance, woven into your philosophy?"

"Not at all. We will right history's wrongs by better works, not worse. Look at the viceroy's administration. He has preserved many of the freedoms the prince allowed, even mandated them, often at great sacrifice to his own goals. He diversified the authorities in order to serve the people better and more widely. His regulations ensure the proper evaluation of professional practices, which then assure people the services they buy are worth the price they pay or may charge."

Khael suppressed a snort. "We hear he deformed the state into a complex bureaucracy with fees instituted to profit himself."

"Many feel that way, Abbot, and say so too. They have that privilege, even if they're wrong. I protect those privileges, as well as enforce the laws."

"How do you feel about violence, Lieutenant?" Vixen said.

"As a last resort when negotiation fails, force can be effective to get the right attention or stop a conflict. Violence is a tool, as is any weapon, whether in warfare or assassinations, but only with purpose. Once its purpose is accomplished, there is no further need for it."

Khael leaned forward. "Is not the purpose of violence to injure or destroy life?"

"Self-defense is another purpose, also getting attention. Initiated violence is rarely unavoidable, as you pointed out earlier, Abbot. More than to offer violence, the knight's duty is to make real the threat as a deterrent so alternatives may be considered."

"Interesting. What of magic and it uses?"

Their breakfasts arrived. The waiter dutifully set the dishes around their places. The plates steamed with an aroma that enticed them to suspend the discussion. Between the fine tea and decent food, they dug in with relish.

"I'm no expert on magic," Jack said while they ate. "I've seen devices made of mundane components whose effects others might call magical. I carry one. I've seen clerics perform acts others call magic, but I believe are derived from profound self-control. I am unconvinced magic is a genuine force to be reckoned with."

The endless lies tested Khael's patience. "What does your device do?"

"I am not at liberty to discuss it," Jack muttered. "Sorry I mentioned it."

"Don't you believe your own eyes?" Vixen said. "Surely you've seen events that can't be explained other than as magical."

Jack shook his head. "Not really. I've learned I can't always trust what I think I've seen. In the heat of the moment, we see what we want to see, not what takes place. The only sensible approach is to reflect on the situation and make sense of it once our passions cool."

"Wait." Vixen paused. "Are you saying you don't believe in magic because you can rationalize every unexplained vision once it's passed?"

"No." Jack smiled. "That is not what I meant."

The cascade of dishonesty confused Khael. Jack's lies made no sense, except as a ploy to entice a confession. Vixen shot a brief glance at Khael, but she turned her head down right away. He swallowed his concern over the risky move.

Vixen held her breath. Worry the lieutenant might have caught the slip flowed through her kih. To Khael's relief, Jack's kih showed no reaction. When her face rose toward Jack, her respiration had normalized.

"I've seen a raving lunatic calmed and returned to sanity by the touch of a master," she said at last. "I was uninvolved, an impartial observer at the time. My perception was unclouded by any expectations. I've never needed to rethink what I saw."

"But you don't know what this alleged lunatic was thinking," Jack said. "It could have been an act. High stress often makes people act irrationally until the soothing touch of a calm hand restores their contact with reality."

"If it were an act, the woman was either a secret exhibitionist or had multiple personas," Vixen snapped. "Her behavior after healing was profoundly different from before—shy, embarrassed at her exposure."

This time Khael stopped breathing. What she said practically announced their true identities.

"Either of which supports my suggestion of an unbalanced mental state." Jack frowned with new mistrust. "I recently heard of just such a case, not too far from here. Where did you witness this magical incident?"

"I've seen it happen many times," she said, smooth as silk. "I grew up in Cambridge, near the Enclave. These things happened all the time, though thankfully it's been ages since I've been there."

Khael exhaled slowly, pleased at her snappy recovery.

"You grew up in the Enclave?" Jack sounded surprised.

"Near enough. The abbot's service was my key to escape a miserable future."

"I discovered Caroline's talents during my last visit," Khael said. "That city is a curious mix of civilized barbarism."

"Indeed." Jack's kih shone triumph and delight.

Khael felt the blood drain from his face. *Fog. He knows.*

33. Advantage Taken

Vixen swallowed. This obnoxious lieutenant looked and sounded like he'd won some kind of war.

Almost gloating, Jack continued. "Tell me, when did you happen upon this maid who tries so hard to hide her beauty?"

"It has been a while," Khael said. "How long would you say, sister?"

"I'll never forget, brother." Vixen assumed a dreamy smile, eager to take Jack down a peg. "It was three years, six months and two days ago, on my sixteenth birthday. I tried to snatch his purse, thinking him old and infirm. He caught me in his velvet steel grip and has held me in his influence ever since. For that I am profoundly grateful."

She bowed her head. A tear dripped from her eye to the table.

Jack shuddered. "I feel for you." His voice sounded hollow.

Vixen smothered a snicker as his arrogant bearing melted away. He took them on the promised tour of the city, but his attempts at conversation faltered. Much of their walk occurred in silence. When they finished a small circuit of the top level of the city, he cut the tour short.

"Is there a problem, Lieutenant?" Khael said. "I thought we could visit some of the harbor slope with so excellent a guide. It cannot be midday yet."

"Forgive me, Abbot. The slopes are not safe, and I feel most out of sorts this morning. Maybe the breakfast wasn't quite up to par." Jack sighed. "I learned an important lesson, though, one I'll never forget."

"What might that be, Lieutenant?" Vixen put on a puzzled air to hide her growing delight.

"Never teach your grandfather to fish." Jack made a strained smile. He delivered a curt bow. "I wish you well, sir, miss. I'll see you again Tuesday."

He strode off without waiting for a response.

"What just happened?" Vixen grinned her thrill. "I thought we had a whole day tour."

"He thought he had finessed who we are, but your contrived history confused him." Khael reached for her arm. "Take us to our room. We have much to accomplish before Monday night."

The streets had filled up with people. Normal conversation merged into a rising background buzz that obliterated most details.

"Sister, what occurred on 2787 July 5?"

"Nothing." Vixen snickered. "A year earlier, I registered with the Collectic and my mentor held a small celebration party. I shifted a couple of real experiences around and altered the content."

"Well done."

Vixen felt tingles all over at his praise, even for a lie. Her triumph seemed like a ripe time to press. "What was your deep breath about? Worried?"

"You turned a potentially fatal mistake into a temporary victory. Still, we must be cautious what we say and where. With his suspicions, he and his men will not leave us alone until Tuesday."

"I trust him about as far as I could throw him."

"Let us lunch at our inn, then rest."

When they finally returned to their room, Vixen plopped down to sit on her bed. "What will we do for the rest of the day?"

"Strategy. The effective range of those detectors is around fifty yards. We can go to the palace grounds this evening. There are benches inside the south gates."

"The ones in front?" His nod surprised her. "That'll put us in direct view of the guards."

"It matters not. I can meditate until the curfew. You may sit with me or walk around as you need. I might take a while."

"Meditating?"

"A cover while I disable every detector I can reach. Their function hampers my ability to act, and we need secrecy. I will work as fast as I can."

"But won't those detectors warn the owners?"

"They might, unless we are out of their range or the owners are detached."

That made no sense to Vixen. "How could they be detached?"

"Bathing or sleeping. Many possibilities."

She frowned. "And you can tell what they're doing." Her eyebrows touched her hair, and she made a circle with her lips. Of course, he could.

He smiled. "Get some rest."

Vixen awoke from her nap with a start. Khael gazed down at her, his beautiful dark blue eyes shining affection into hers. She blinked, then frowned. Her head lay pillowed on his lap where he sat cross-legged on the head of her bed.

A dream tried to flee her memory, though it lacked the blind terror of her usual nightmares. In this one, she stood on a hilltop above the ocean, looking down at a crater of rubble, like a city in ruins. A shiny metal object lay in the center of the mess, a tube with a cap at one end and a tail at the other. It had to be important to stand out so clearly, whatever it was.

She sat up and swung her legs over the edge of the bed.

"Welcome back to our semi-private room." He said it quietly enough.

Vixen nodded. People in the inn could hear them, neighbors or eavesdroppers below. "Thanks."

She stretched high toward the ceiling. His eyes lit up in response, but that light cooled, to her dismay. In her last waking memory, he was rubbing her temples to soothe a vicious headache that struck when she lay down to nap.

"What time is it?" She yawned.

"An hour and a quarter before sunset."

"I feel like a wash." She tilted her head toward the washroom. They could talk while the shower made noise. "I won't be too long."

She closed the door and turned the water on. He listened intently as she related her nightmare, but he didn't otherwise react.

"Interesting dream. I will keep it in mind. Now, it will be dark soon. I want to be in place by then. You must be observant."

"What about the detectors close enough to respond when you try it?"

He shrugged. "My eikyo has four times their range. I can disable any device long before it can reveal me. However, if that fails, perhaps you can provide distraction."

Vixen nodded, her eyes dancing all over him. It wouldn't be much, just waiting around while he worked his powers on the unsuspecting enemy. Still, it presented a little adventure. Now their efforts would pay off. She flashed him a wicked smile.

"Are you refreshed yet?"

"I suppose." Something he just said... "How did you find out the ranges?"

"We passed by the Temple of Flamma on Majestic's tour, near clerics practicing spells. Two of his men also had detectors. Majestic was beside us, the others hovered up to eighty yards away. The farthest one failed to respond. The one at fifty yards paced around and its response alternated between active and passive as he crossed that range."

"So, they really aren't attuned to your disciplines?"

"They appear sensitive to any emitted energy. Remember, the Chelevkori hate Loren, and they know little about my disciplines. What makes no sense is that those devices are enchanted."

"They have no integrity." She set her arms akimbo. "I'm ready."

His dark blue eyes stared piercingly into hers. She stared back, unwilling to look away, her soul drowning in his eyes. They filled her vision until all she saw was a pool of dark ocean blue surrounding two pitch black holes. These merged and she fell into the black.

Caught in the vision, she flew at blinding speeds through the black sky, surrounded by a gentle dark blue glow. Faster and faster, she flew, blind to where she went, or what she passed, if anything. She felt invigorated yet apprehensive, surrounded by the loving comfort of this deep-sea color.

"The water ought to be off when we leave," Khael said.

She blinked. The reverie vanished. Fog. "Right."

Back with reality, she shut off the taps. Her muscles tightened as they headed out. This might be their most dangerous gambit so far.

34.   Unnerving

Khael began scanning for the devices when they reached Palace Avenue West. A ranger roamed the area of the grounds nearest their path with one. Seeing no mystics, sorcerers or clerics nearby, Khael smiled under his hood. His eikyo fingers reached inside the device. It began to respond. With an effort, he crossed the dead kih paths before its second pulse.

Curious if there might be a better way, he reviewed how it failed. Could he disable the detection circuit without damaging the indicator? Another came into range from the opposite direction. He stopped walking to focus on it. With a greater effort, he diverted the weaker power path into the inner metal shell. The indicator went out, but the vibrator glowed.

Fog.

He quickly incapacitated the other circuit and held his breath. The bearer's kih flashed surprise and annoyance at the device. The man toyed with it for a moment, then went on his way and ignored it.

Why? Relief overrode Khael's curiosity.

Vixen kept tugging his sleeve, discomfort glaring from her kih. "If you're going to stop, brother, at least let me get us off the street."

"Sure," he slurred.

Another device came into range as she pulled him forward. Within a few seconds, he counted over a dozen. In the closest device, he pushed the correct dead kih power flow into the shell. The indicator died anyway.

He reached toward a group of six and disabled the nearest one. The other five, all within ten yards of that one, responded. His stomach jerked. Two of these bearers paused, possibly uncertain about the pulse, but they continued without further ado. The other three never even slowed down.

Fascinating, and encouraging. All of the carriers so far ignored the alerts. However, he could not afford to rush or get cocky. A single concerned response spelled extreme danger.

"Brother, to find a decent spot for your meditation we really must move," Vixen muttered.

"Patience, sister. Many factors to manage, some new."

Vixen jerked her head up toward his face, curious for signs or a clue. Though he showed none, she emanated more anxiety. She shrugged her shoulders to loosen them and rolled her head once in each direction. That seemed to help her, so he did the same.

"Whenever you're ready, brother."

Khael disabled another close one and tugged Vixen's arm. She guided him through one of the openings in the ivy-laden wall to find a convenient place to sit.

These detectors functioned too slowly to get a fix on him from any short, single exertion. The needle crawled its way toward any unusual zhukih emanation. As soon as the energy discharge ceased, the needle stopped and grounded into the face. The bearers must be aware of this, which explained their indifference to the short alarms he had caused.

Could he move the physical parts inside the devices to cause the same effect? If so, a skilled craftsman who opened such a device to determine why it failed might attribute it to physical damage. The theory seemed worth a test.

Vixen stopped along the outermost path, about ten yards inside the wall. Evergreen trees and shrubs shielded them from casual view. She guided him onto a bench and sat beside him.

"Can we talk yet, brother?" she whispered, her breath warm in his ear.

"Five remain in motion," Khael murmured. "I have disabled several, their bearers indifferent or oblivious. Another dozen or so are at rest, many of whose carriers sleep."

"What are the new factors to manage?"

"When I alter one, others within ten yards respond."

"Be careful." She shivered. "It's getting foggy."

"That benefits us. Alert me if anyone comes this way."

"Your wish is mine."

He flashed her a smile and returned his focus to the last five moving ones. His second effort to activate zarute succeeded, so he probed toward the closest device. The ethereal pincer felt stronger than before, two thick, sharp claws on a firm rope. It stopped short, only thirteen yards out.

After a moment, he realized that his lack of experience limited his range. This was no time to mess around. If any of the devices had been close enough then, his failure would have alerted them. He ground his teeth. Should have considered that before the risky attempt.

When he disabled the next one, the other four responded. The knight with the broken device stopped short. He took it off his belt to examine it, puzzled while he shook and twisted it. The device stayed dead, so he stuffed it back on his belt and appearing angry, continued on his way. The four other carriers converged toward the east side of the main structure of the palace.

Until they separated, he dared not disable them. Too risky. Khael exhaled his frustration.

Vixen shuddered at the sound but kept alert and watchful. He slithered his hand along her lower arm to her hand and gave it a gentle squeeze. Wild excitement stampeded through her kih.

"Are we done?" she whispered, trembling.

He shook his head. Those last four concerned him. The more they converged, the more trouble he had distinguishing them from a growing blur of kih inside.

"There is a large assembly in the museum."

After a few minutes, the mass of kih separated. A few individuals straggled back inside the palace. The rest broke into five groups. One began to sweep the palace from east to west. The other four fanned out through the grounds, each with one detector. As soon as they had separated far enough, Khael reached out to disabled them. His growing experience paid off. These last four efforts all succeeded with no alerts.

One of the groups from the palace spread out toward the south wall, where he and Vixen sat.

"Fog," he muttered.

"What fog?" she whispered anxiously. "Don't say fog. What's going on?"

"Unlike many, the last four bearers had concerns about their detector's alert. Pray their search ends fifty yards from the palace. That leaves us ten."

"Pray? What if it doesn't?"

He held up a finger while he located the twelve immobile ones. The troops continued their advance.

"Let us retreat to a better concealed place."

"Where?" she hissed. "This was the best I could find before the dark and fog."

"Perhaps off the path, in the shrubs."

"Great," she grumbled. "Not just cold but wet, too."

She released his hand and stalked away. Her moves demonstrated marked improvement in her stealth skills and control over her fears. The last thing she would want was to get caught. The guards' search grew too thorough for his comfort. He monitored them closely.

While Vixen looked around, part of his mind took the time to study her kih in detail. Every aspect of it was beautiful, distracting, accelerating his pulse. Her energy contours and their vivid colors transfixed him, far more than her improved physique appealed to his eyes. She moved with the most exciting combination of skill and determination.

For a flash, her kih slipped out of focus and he saw double—one image quite normal, the other a storm of livid internal torment and rage. Astonished, he tore his focus away from the search. Now her kih shone a single, vibrant, whole image about half as bright as his own.

What the fog is that about?

Reluctantly, he dragged his attention back to cripple the last dozen devices in the palace. He scanned the entire building. Apart from the massive search now underway, everything looked normal.

Another amplified sweep after they eluded the search would be wise.

Vixen returned. "This way," she murmured.

They crept a few yards along a path between the dim plant kih. She drew him off to one side through a narrow gap in some higher bushes to a small, clear grassy space barely a yard in diameter.

"Sit down, I'll crouch behind you," she whispered. "Our cloaks can mask us. We can get cozy."

Dismissing the flurries her comment provoked, he dropped to the ground in one smooth move, his staff before him. Vixen shivered. She crouched behind him to nestle his back between her legs. At first she held his shoulders to keep from tumbling backward into the brush. Her balance stabilized, but she held on anyway.

Khael enjoyed the heat of her close, warm cling. His distracted imagination began to stray... He reined it in before it got too far and concentrated on the palace.

She grabbed his shoulders. "Someone's coming."

Khael nodded and looked around, not yet concerned. He checked on the oddity in the throne room, that loop of low-level dead kih. Nothing about which to be concerned.

A fierce hollow of ice spiked in the pit of his stomach. *Nothing about which to be concerned?* That loop contained the threat to him and all life as far as a quarter mile past the city wall. To his frustration, from here the details continued to elude his abilities. Another thorny obstacle to his quest.

A new detector appeared at the edge of his range, on the far side of the palace. By now, the toll of his exercises wore on him. They had to retire so he could rest and renew before the critical store he reserved to keep them safe ran out.

The nearest searchers became noisier. When Vixen pinched his shoulders harder, he winced and choked down a gasp at her sharp grip. Her ears twitched as the guards called to one another. In the dark and fog they sounded much closer than they were. Khael gently pried her painful clutch loose, patting her hands to reassure her.

Time rushed to a standstill. For a silent moment, heat penetrated his cloak where her body pressed against his back and sides. More came through where her small breasts and abdomen warmed his shoulder-blades and spine, less from her legs and hands along his sides and shoulders. For a brief, eternal moment, a heatwave erupted from the center of his being outward through his body to dissipate from his hands, head and feet. His mind whirled.

"Cannot see bloody thing in fog, Davich," one guard complained, loud despite his twelve-yard distance.

"Keep looking for another few minutes, then we go back in," another, probably Davich, said.

"Stupid officers," a third grumbled. "Asinine goose hunt because of idiot box."

"Watch your mouth, soldier," Davich snapped. "You want warehouse detail?"

The conversation stopped, though the sounds of the guards tramping around continued. Vixen held her breath. Excessive strain glowed from a burn in her lungs.

Breathe, he sent her. *Otherwise, you may emit unwanted sound.*

She exhaled carefully. Khael felt the cry she suppressed seethe in her mind. When her breath came evenly, she gave him another, gentler squeeze. He nodded his relief.

After five endless minutes of search, the rangers headed back to the palace. Just before the risk seemed to abate, a lone guard came down a path straight to their former bench. This one took his time to check carefully for intruders. His slow, methodical search brought him within a yard of them. He stopped on the other side of their row of bushes and stood still, listening, watching, turning slowly around in a full circle, his torch held high.

Vixen took long, silent breaths. Khael fervently hoped her breath was not visible in the fog. He felt her joints creak. She inhaled slow and deep and held it.

Khael held his too. He could last for several minutes from simple willpower alone, longer with kinshuh. However, if the hedge and the fog did not hide them, he might need to disable this one.

As a last resort, a leap up to defend them physically might work. That would tumble Vixen over backwards, possibly injure her, and likely make enough noise to attract the other guards' attention. Khael could render the man unconscious without other damage, but only in self-defense. That was a dead give-away. No easy solution surfaced in his whirling storm of unclear ideas. His lungs began to demand more intake.

Would this ever end? Khael began to gather his energy to knock this guard out. Risky, but...

The guard sighed, exasperated. He shook his head and stomped away, muttering angry fragments of words. As he tramped off, Vixen exhaled slowly, then inhaled deeply to catch her breath. Khael let his out, straining his kinshuh. He recovered his own respiration as hers stabilized.

"Are we done yet?" she whispered.

"Almost."

Khael amplified his shikah. His already exotic view of the world shifted into that more bizarre color scheme. All unusual kih flared in stark detail. He made a sweep across his whole field of view, even above and below them to be certain. Nothing extraordinary leapt out at him, just a clearer view of the devices at the extreme edge of his unamplified range.

Wait!

He doubled back to the throne room. His chest seized. The loop looked different now. A series of blotches of some low power substance he could not see before sat distributed along the loop. Not just one loop but two, the second so dim he barely noticed it.

The need for a closer look shrieked into his brain. No, tonight had already fostered too many dangers to proceed. Frustrated and exhausted, he released his shikah extensions. "Let us retire."

Vixen rose smoothly to a full stand and on into a stretch. Her lithe moves helped lift his crushed spirits. The emptiness in his gut ground against his kinshuh.

Khael rose up, the same liquid grace in his movements, his staff in hand. "Most people get cramps from so long a squat. You recovered well."

She shrugged. "I do that all the time. Never bothers me."

"You must be more limber than I realized. Take us back."

He reached out his free hand while he leaned on his staff. She led him out of the grounds in silence.

As they crossed the street, Khael felt a new, vague unease. Another one? It too resembled a chokkan warning, but nothing specific or directed, just incongruous and small. No imminent danger threatened worse than the one in the palace, so he did not mention it. The fog would help.

Vixen slowed as she took him along the street. She seemed to have trouble finding the way back to their inn. Halfway through the third block she stopped.

"What is it?"

"The fog makes it hard to tell where we should be going."

"The next right turn should be ours."

"I thought so, but there was a sign here before."

"Many vendors take theirs inside or home at night."

"Of course. They won't be much use in the dark, or this pea soup, or after curfew."

They slipped through the inn's front door, past the snoring desk clerk and up the stairs. Khael's new unsettled feeling persisted, aggravating the persistent icy prickle that had begun in the forest.

35. Discovered

Khael opened his eyes, filled with unrest. The morning brightened as the sun prepared to come up and dazzle away the pre-dawn fog. His relentless irritation persisted. What were those unrecognizable loops and bulges of dead kih above his throne room? He breathed. They still had time. Vixen and his mother would help—if they could.

The additional vague gnawing that began when they left the palace grounds last night sharpened. Little nips, an angry cat playing with its new-caught mouse, or a starving rat tasting to see if a morsel was worth eating. The problem slithered around his efforts to isolate it. He scowled. What had he overlooked? No new, immediate threat reared its ugly head as yet.

He scanned out to the limit of his range. Many people stirred at this hour. Nothing looked suspicious near the ground. A barb stung his mind as he scanned the air above them. His frown deepened. What did that mean? Nothing worth noticing showed up anywhere within range.

Within range. *Fog.*

Mentally cursing his own negligence, he extended his range. Five hundred sixty yards up, southwest of the inn, a vulture cruised around with a new dead kih device hanging from its neck.

He enhanced his view. A faint cone radiated down from the device. At ground level, it covered several yards around the block where the inn stood. From the side of the device, a thin, different dead kih variant beamed straight toward the palace.

The two emanations differed from those of other types of dead kih he had encountered. These energies glistened in clear but limited, dull colors. The three variants he had learned to recognize were power flow, detection and destruction.

The cone resembled a passive observation field, pale and harmless. He shuddered as he scrutinized the beam. It looked like detection, only in reverse. A form of transmission? Some Ancients' artifacts he had studied exchanged full visual and auditory images with no known range limit. Though never inclined to investigate them before, the principle struck a harmonic chord in his chest.

His heart sank.

These Chelevkori devices bore too many similarities to artifacts. That flaunted their own taboos. The artifacts functioned on a form of self-regenerating kih. Most of the Chelevkori devices he had seen only functioned once, and their power was feeble, even brittle. The detectors seemed less so, but even their energy faded with each use, and they bore traces of sorcery—another taboo.

Signs of desperation?

The surveillance regarding Vixen's explosive pendant, though different, had also escaped his notice. He had checked all around last night, and above. Only after they left the grounds did the sensation begin, but he felt it minor enough to let it go. Then. A growl faded under his kinshuh control, but he yearned to scream.

He looked at Vixen, asleep on her bed, only she had her head up, her upper body supported on her elbows, eyes on him.

"Something wrong, brother?" she said quietly.

"Am I so obvious?" At her nod, his heart leapt into his throat and fell. "The sky may see what the walls hear."

Vixen jerked bolt upright, her eyes wide, horrified. "We're dead."

"Not yet." He put on a cheery face to mask his lost hope. "No doubt we will soon find out."

Vixen stood to stretch her lean frame, a suspicious squint on her face. Khael looked away as she stood up. Her kih gave him enough discomfort. Those views always revealed more than all her past visual expositions, but she grew less inclined to avoid the latter. His kinshuh allowed him a high level of detachment in everyone else. Not her. More and more, he found her body a source of intense curiosity and fierce desire he had to fight off.

She must have felt positively safe with him around, until now. Her footsteps padded across to the washroom, to freshen up for the day, or their doom, whichever lay ahead. Confidence seemed to drain out of her. Her usual bouncy step seemed less springy.

"Be not overlong."

She emerged with an even more depressed face. He closed his eyes without adding shikah. Rather than speak, he went over to her quiet rustles as she selected her garb for the day. It would look the same to a casual observer, plain dress, hose, boots and a cloak. The thick material should hide her figure well enough, lacking the fine royal tailoring of his preferred supplies.

He smelled a hint of salt. "What saddens you so, dear lass?"

The term had previously evoked some pleasure or a hand squeeze. Not this time.

She sniffed. "It's all over. We're finished."

"Perhaps." He put his hands on her shoulders to comfort her. Feeling cloth, he opened his eyes. She had put on her dress. "I know not the thing's acuity, nor how long it has been there, or even what it is. I sensed an oddity last night, but it seemed harmless. I chose to explore it this morning. It may yet be of no consequence. We must adjust our plans according to the response."

She straightened up but still seemed depressed. "You think we could be all right?"

"For the nonce." He forced a smile. "Or it could be terminal."

Her head jerked up. His expression evoked a snicker, but she punched at his stomach. With a subtle twist, he evaded the blow.

"Don't do that." She pulled away from his hands. "I hate it when you get mushy."

His smile relaxed. Sidelining her fears would become more difficult if the opposition reacted as he anticipated. He craved to know more.

The morning quiet hung in the air like a cloud above the streets. Few people were out. Even for a Sunday, the depressed city seemed desolate. Without his sight to appreciate the fine, wholesome architecture above the slopes, the ambiance reminded him of ancient ruins.

They reached the arc split.

"Is it still there?"

He scanned up to locate the device and its bearer. "Yes, but it seems focused on the inn. The mist may be higher or denser than it appears down here."

"What are they going to do with us?"

"Depends on how much they know."

"Let's assume the worst."

"Torture and execution." He smiled. "Perhaps nothing more than arrest pending our hearing."

Her terrified shudder vibrated through her hand on his arm. "I can't," she whispered fiercely. "I'm—I—I'll die in jail!"

All her earlier tremors regarding arrest or jail rushed back to him. That distraction had to go. He stopped and turned her to face him. "Talk to me."

She stood silent for a while, like a soldier at full attention. When she calmed herself, she turned her face up to him. "I've been in jail. Twice.

"The first time I was with my mentor. They arrested him for fraud. I was only eight, so I didn't really understand. Some issue about products he promised to deliver. The Patrols treated me nicely, probably because of my innocence.

"The other time was awful." She choked up as if she would burst into tears.

He pulled her back to his side with a soothing hand. "Continue."

They started to walk again.

"The second time, I'd tried to lift a pouch from someone's belt. I was fifteen and part way through my original initiation. It was practice, just to see if I could do it." She paused.

"Yes?" She had told him she began her initiation at thirteen....

"He caught me and yelled for the Patrols." Her voice shook. "Four rangers responded. They grabbed me roughly, bound my hands behind my back and hooded me."

Khael stopped with a frown. Cambridge City Patrol standard arrest procedures forbid such disrespectful behavior. His father had

270

personally driven that cause home.

"They threw me into the back of a cart and drove for ages. When we stopped, I fell out onto the street. It hurt, but they just laughed and yanked me to my feet. They hauled me into a room in a stone building and jerked off the hood. Then they—"

Her breath caught in her throat and she coughed. "They untied me and forced me to take off all my clothes. The room was dark except for four torches on the wall behind the two men who stayed. I couldn't see their faces at all, but they saw... me.

"I tried to cover myself with my hands and looked around for something clean to sit on. The floor was covered with a putrid scum and there was nowhere to sit. They yelled at me to hold still, with lewd comments about my body. One of them read off a preposterous list of charges: battery, assault, theft, damage to property, injury... nonsense.

"When I tried to protest, they yelled to shut up. One of them came over and put his hands on me. I wanted to break his arms, but I was too scared to move and I shut my eyes. He fondled me roughly, then shoved me down on that slimy floor. I was sure they were going to rape me, but he just laughed and walked back to his partner. They stared at me while I got back up. There were screams coming from somewhere in another room. I was terrified and disgusted with the filth."

Khael said nothing. The first part sounded like a constructed memory, the second one real. Even for a fifteen-year-old that would be extreme, for the Collectic, but... perhaps not as part of a complex, abusive indoctrination process.

"They started talking about awful punishments. I could picture most of them. Amputating my hands, beating me senseless, gang rape, torture with whips and other things I'd never heard of. They joked about females they'd arrested, how they'd end up whores or slaves in therapy centers after jail time, other horrifying abuses. They screamed many questions I didn't know how to answer."

By this time, Vixen shook so much she stopped at a bench they were passing. She grabbed it for support, then sank onto it. Waves of fear and rage undulated through her kih.

271

"Is there more?"

"My mentor finally got me out. He took me home and beat me until I was sore and bruised all over, all the time screaming I was never, ever to practice any skills until my training was over, except in class. He forced me to take a cold bath while he watched with an angry leer. Made my bruises even sorer." She drew in a ragged breath and let out a noisy sigh. "I've been terrified of jail ever since. May be why I learned to hit and run."

Khael waited for her to calm down before he spoke. "The rangers who treated you so were not Cambridge City Patrols, and the place they took you was none of the city jails."

"Wha-at?" Her voice rang confusion. "What do you mean?"

"I have been in Cambridge's jails," he murmured. "Outside the Enclave, they treat everyone with basic respect, even the inebriated or otherwise debilitated. Those who fight back may be restrained, but only while they resist. The Patrols do not mistreat, strip or even search anyone under sixteen without grave cause, and never with such extreme abuse. Furthermore, none of the Patrol offices, city jails or even the prisons are that filthy. My brother, if he knew of such behavior, would hit the roof."

"In that castle? How would he reach it?" The storm in her kih subsided.

Khael snickered. "I meant he would be extremely angry. Have you never heard that idiom?"

"I don't think so. Still, that's no guarantee the jails here aren't that way or worse."

"The prince would never allow it, though with this... who knows? You may have been subjected to a correction for your breach of training rules."

"I... what breach?"

"The guilds prohibit outside practice during formal training classes, unless assigned by the instructor. I imagine whoever trained you arranged a graphic demonstration of what might happen in a less civilized locale than Cambridge. Thought you not to ask of this?"

Vixen paused, her eyes narrowing. "I don't ask terrorists too many questions."

"It may be that your introduction to therapy centers was part of that effort, not solely to keep you from the one here."

Vixen nodded slowly. She seemed less prey to her fear. Khael wanted to smile, but she might not understand his expression.

"Someone's going to pay for that one day." She clenched her fists so hard her knuckles cracked.

"We have discussed revenge. Come. Let us see if any nearby taverns are open."

She stood and took his arm. They headed east into the sunshine breaking through the mist. Her jangled kih settled down as they walked. A block later she hugged his arm for a moment.

Above them, the vulture circled.

"Where is everyone?" Khael muttered as they headed back toward their inn.

They had not found a single place to eat within three miles of the palace while wandering around the southwestern market sections of the city. No one moved around outside the homes and shops they passed, and those inside appeared to be resting.

"At the temples maybe?"

"The temples are all on the east side. We would have passed large numbers of worshipers on their way, and the worship day of Temple Luxean was yesterday."

"Gabe said some of the priests were imprisoned and their temples closed."

"More likely the viceroy imposed rest days on the city to give his own men a chance to relax. The Chelevkori have a history of such practices. It appeases those who work."

Vixen did not react. Three blocks east of the palace, the proprietor of the Robin Redbreast opened its doors to set out a sign.

"Brother, that place Majestic took us yesterday morning just opened."

"I disliked the locale, but this bodes well for better variety farther ahead."

"We've been walking for hours and I'm starving. We'd better find something fast."

A quarter mile farther down the avenue they found another open establishment. When Vixen announced the Lachen-Drachen, Khael nodded. He knew the place, a full-service inn, previously a loyal haven popular with his Paladins.

"Take us there."

Moments later they sat on comfortable padded seats in a quiet, incense-scented dining room. Their corner booth opened toward the door, with the back of their seats high enough for privacy. A waiter brought Vixen something from which she read Khael the breakfast description in a hushed tone that matched her wary posture. Four other people sat in the room, ordinary couples far enough away to diminish Khael's concerns over eavesdropping. No dead kih.

The waiter, a tall, thin lad, returned. He delivered two items that thumped lightly on the table and retrieved his earlier delivery from Vixen. She took a sip of what smelled like a nice, aromatic tea. As the waiter left, a wisp of kih fell out of his pocket and floated its feathery way to the floor. Vixen leaned down to pick it up.

"What is that?"

"Looks like a blank piece of paper." She handed it to him.

"Appearances deceive," he murmured. "It says the room is safe but cannot be guaranteed so for long. This place is under surveillance."

Vixen took the paper back and turned it over. "It's blank."

"The ink is a special one, used at the Center. I can read it."

"Someone from there is here?"

He nodded. "I suspect the server who brings our food will be one."

"He was sort of cute." Vixen groaned. "What am I saying? She'll probably be a voluptuous seductress who drools to fawn all over you. And here I am all darked-out like this." She buried her head in her hands, her elbows on the table.

274

"I see no such things. Recall you are a hermit's student."

She folded her hands on the table and assumed a demure posture, face lowered. He failed to resist a quiet chuckle.

No one except the waiter approached their table and no other messages or papers appeared to give them any further clues. Although they enjoyed an excellent meal and the tea, they finished quite mystified.

Unease at the emptiness in his normal range prompted Khael to extend it. Vixen fished some coins from her purse and set them on the table to pay for the meal. When she reached out to assist Khael up, he grabbed her arm and guided her back down beside him.

"Waiter," he called.

"What is it?" Vixen whispered, instantly alert.

"Majestic leads a company of knights this way from the palace. They will arrive here within a few minutes."

36.   No More Cock-n-Bull

It seemed strange to Khael that all of Majestic's men were knights. Thus far, other than Majestic himself, the only knights Khael had seen were his own Paladins. What did that mean? His mind spun with wild, unfounded hypotheses.

"Shouldn't we get out of here?" Vixen's kih flashed with fear.

He pulled himself together and shook his head from side to side, then nodded. His doubt mixed with accepting her fears. He wondered if his concerned frown was visible through his blindfold?

A shapely feminine kih slipped into their booth. She reached across them to the wall behind Vixen and pulled down on the private lantern mounting bracket. Khael jerked as the booth moved and all the kih outside rotated in a half circle.

"Ye're in extreme danger, Sire," the woman whispered anxiously. "I've reversed the booth so you can exit through the kitchen, but you must get out o' here right away."

The booth jerked to a halt. Where the dining room had been audible before, kitchen noises muffled in through a closed door. The woman reached for both of their nearest arms.

"Come quickly."

She fairly dragged them out of their seats, then let go of them to open the door. They followed her through the kitchen and out a back door.

"Go on. We'll stall 'em long as we can. After that, you're on your own."

"Thanks," Vixen said.

Khael took her arm and hurried her down the alley.

"Where are we going?"

"Away from the palace and the approaching knights. We must double back in two blocks."

Vixen shook her head, nonplussed. "I don't get it. Where does that take us?"

"The Center."

"But they're not expecting us until tomorrow night."

"Resilience is key in their business."

Khael carried his staff as they hastened between the buildings. Several times he felt tempted to drop it, but he held it tight. The vulture circled over the inn. An image of their packs sitting on the beds in their room came to him. He wanted to recover them, but how? Detection or discovery would be equally disastrous options.

They turned north into another back route. He grasped Vixen's arm and stopped.

"What?"

"One moment."

Khael stretched amplified eikyo fingers up to the vulture's device. Despite the few detectors not too far away, the eye in the sky had to go. He crushed all the power flows in the device, clenching his fist at the same time. The cone underneath and the beam to the palace both blinked out.

"The eye is blind."

"We'd better hurry, brother. You probably gave away our destination to anyone monitoring that thing's messages."

Khael jerked the blindfold off his head and stuffed it into a pocket in his robe. He blinked several times to clear his vision while they picked up their trek, feeling cleaner than he had since they left Strattonmoor. Since he no longer needed his elderly stoop, his upright posture and easy stride also gave him a lift. They turned to head west toward the Tap-n-Stot.

Shortly before they reached the next street, he guided her into a side alley. "Arrange your cloak as an extra skirt."

While she did that, he folded his own cloak around her upper torso to simulate a thick coat. All the extra material made her lumpy and plain below her pretty face. With her hood over her head, she looked like a different person.

He reactivated his extended range shikah but kept his eyes open. The peculiar imagery disoriented him and he clasped her hand for her guidance. Every kih overlaid what he saw, even through solid objects. The bright, conflicting dual view hurt his eyes and mind.

They made their way across a bridge over the river. A block and a half before Fourth Way, he drew her into another alley.

"Trouble ahead?" she said. "I didn't see anyone."

"A company of rangers heads from the palace toward the Tap-n-Stot," he murmured. "Fog. We must arrive first or lose our gear."

"Do we really need it?"

"I left my signet in my knapsack."

"Oh my stars. What about Aliotru?"

Khael led her back onto the street toward the next intersection. The odd combination of his visual and kih views and the persistent prickly itch in his mind made it harder to think. The streets were less than half as full as yesterday. They had to do their best to avoid standing out from the few people about. Vixen peered around for signs of pursuit as they went.

"We must release her," he said at last.

"You slowed down."

"The knight company at the Lachen-Drachen dispersed." His voice fell, distant. He stretched his mind to track both distant kih clusters while he also watched where they went. "They seek traces of our passage. The company from the palace has changed direction, but where... Ah, I see."

"I don't." Vixen glared at him. "You want to share it with me?"

He chuckled and focused on their immediate vicinity. "They head for the Center."

"That doesn't bode well once we're done at the tavern."

"We will use extreme caution. The knights may search the Center, which would be better before we get there."

They ducked into the alley parallel to the cul-de-sac of the Tap-n-Stot. He led her to the rear of the inn, skirting many trash barrels and piles of junk scattered around the alley. Two of the larger mounds of rags rose to block their way.

"That's far enough, you two," one of the rag-covered men said, his fist raised.

Vixen started around him. He grabbed her arm. Using this for leverage, she kicked the other square in the face with both feet. The second man fell, stunned. Her actions twisted the first man with her, which opened his back to Khael. He touched the man's head. The bandit stiffened with a gasp and collapsed, unconscious.

"Nice work." Khael studied the failed brigands. No Chelevkori traces, just simple thieves.

"Thanks." Vixen curtsied.

"We must get out of here." He glanced at her. "Return my cloak, please."

She handed him the thick garment. He threw it around his shoulders over his long white hair and pulled up the hood. They stopped behind the inn, where the kitchen door stood open. So did the side courtyard that led to the stables.

"Take off your cloak and hike up your dress," Khael murmured in Vixen's ear. "Open your neckline a little and tousle your hair."

"Now? Really?"

He shook his head. "Your appearance should distract any other observer from thoughts of whom you might be long enough to reach the stable. Walk with a languid sway, saucy."

She hitched the dress up under her belt. Her collar fought her effort to rip it. "Help?"

He seized her top and tore it, more than he intended. His fingers sparked on her bare skin. She jerked and shuddered.

"My apologies."

"That's all right." She narrowed her eyes. "Like what you see?"

Amused, Khael shook his head at the tease. "Tell Aliotru to go home. She will understand."

She flicked her eyebrows up and down, then slipped through the gate to saunter across the yard. Without kinshuh, his last view of her might have incapacitated him, or any man, and ignited envious flames in most women. Of course, without kinshuh he might be balled up in anguish from his non-stop danger thistles all over. He leaned his staff against the fence and strode tall into the kitchen.

"Who're ye an' what're ye doing in here?" one of the cooks inquired as he passed between the counters where they prepared their dishes.

"Be still," Khael snapped, blowing out some of his mental steam. "Have ye na work? Where are the afternoon appetizers? An' tonight's specialties?"

The intimidated cooks gawked meekly while he marched through the kitchen into the dining room. No one dared talk back to him.

The tension returned and Khael's stomach tightened. Free people should not be so easy to overwhelm. Was that why they tolerated this usurper? He strode through the dining room and danced up the back stairs as if he owned the place. None of the diners spoke, though many watched his arrogant passage.

He slipped down the hallway, silent, his eyes closed. Their room was deserted and he saw no detectors inside the inn. Suspicious, he scanned the room a second time. There, a small dead kih crinkle on the washroom door lintel, the only one in the inn. Another eye. Someone had learned or suspected enough to spy on them, where and how.

He gritted his teeth and scanned around. In one of the rooms, a young couple engaged in the early, feverish efforts toward lusty intimacy. They stopped cold when he opened the door.

The girl squeaked her surprise. Khael shut the door and stalked over to them. He threw his cloak on the bed beside them, where most of their own clothes already lay.

"Who—who are you?" The boy turned around to face Khael and hide his naked girlfriend, clutching up his open trousers.

"Perhaps your greatest benefactor." Khael focused his eyes on the lad, but his attention stayed on his own room and every kih from there down to the inn entrance. "I require your assistance for a simple matter."

"We are otherwise... engaged... at the moment," the confused boy stammered. "Get out, sir."

"Oh?" Khael fixed them each with a penetrating stare.

The girl blushed bright red from her bare breasts to the roots of her brown hair. The boy also flushed, his anger on the rise.

Khael raised an eyebrow. "Curious that you use an unlocked, unoccupied rental space rather than your own private rooms for such personal adventure." He let that sink in for a few seconds. "Now, which of you works the rooms?"

The boy dropped his shoulders, his bravado squelched. "I do."

"Here is a key to the third room down the hall. Get dressed and bring me both knapsacks from the beds. Act like this is normal duty and avoid skulking. You will be rewarded."

The boy took the key with squinted eyes. He hitched his belt and retrieved his shirt. "Linda, get dressed. Stranger, I don't know you, but you'd better not touch my girl." In a showy huff, he whirled out of the room.

"Frasier?" Linda wondered quietly.

After Frasier left, Khael looked at Linda, who had not made a move to put any clothes on. Her dress lay wrinkled on the bed and her knee-high hose had slipped to her ankles. She stared at him with a look just shy of outright hunger. His nose twitched at the scent of her arousal, stronger despite the absence of her would-be paramour. He focused on her eyes.

"Is there anything I may do for you, my lord?" she said in a sultry voice. Her blush faded, unlike her smile. She licked her lips. "Anything at all?"

"Can you braid hair?"

Her smile shrank. "Yes."

"Please arrange mine into a pony-tail."

Khael sat beside his cloak, his back to Linda. Frasier's kih reached the room as Khael flexed his skin. The false age wrinkles took close to a minute of the effort to tighten away.

Frasier headed for the washroom and performed some basic clean-up.

Linda slipped off her hose and sat behind Khael, one leg close on either side of his.

"Is there nothing else I can offer you, my lord?" she husked near his ear, rubbing her brazen torso close and hot against his back.

"You owe it to yourself and your Frasier to be consistent. You are too young for me and I am already committed." He needed to throw in the 'too young' despite her obvious maturity.

Only mildly subdued, Linda separated Khael's hair as best she could without a brush and began weaving the three strands into a single braid. She stopped often to untangle his hair, pressing her aroused breasts into his back at the same time.

"Your hair needs to be brushed if I am to do this right, my lord." She rose part way.

"No time. Please do your best without one."

She sat back down. Her head drooped for a moment. In the other room, Frasier's kih hoisted two items off the beds and headed toward the door. Linda tugged Khael's hair into the braid. He smiled as Frasier shouldered the door open at the same time Linda finished her work.

"Here, sir," Frasier set the knapsacks on the floor by the bed. He ogled Linda's naked body with wide eyes, then frowned new anger. "What did you do?"

"Your maid braided my hair at my request." Khael rose.

Frasier thrust Linda's dress at her. She diverted it into her lap. The boy's kih danced with lusty envy, but she gazed her own heat back at him.

The sight of Frasier with the bags when he reentered the room reminded Khael of the padding knights wore for practice. It made them look bulkier, so he adapted the idea for his own new guise. He put on his knapsack, added Vixen's on his chest, and looped both waist straps around his belt. Finally, he retrieved his cloak.

Linda whispered something in Frasier's ear. The couple sat before Khael, their eyes wide.

"Yes?" Khael pulled the cloak over his shoulders and adjusted it to hide the bags.

"I know who you are, Sire," Linda said softly. "I recognize your eyes."

Khael inhaled. She had thrown herself at him and failed. Was this her revenge? "And?"

"Me father will nay like it, Sire," Frasier said glumly. "He's been collaborating with the gray shirts. There's a reward for information about ye."

Khael took a chance and grasped their hands. He sent soothing energy to flow through them. They both grinned and flushed.

"I have a reward too. Here is a crown." He handed Frasier the coin. "I must trust you."

He swept from the room, moving toward the back stairs. Their voices filtered out to his ears.

"Crown! Wow!"

"Frasier Jenney, my hero."

Khael kept his attention on the path ahead while Frasier and Linda resumed their prior activities. He skipped in silence halfway down the stairs, focused solely on his own safety and away from the hot young couple. They could still change their minds once their lusts were satisfied.

At the foot of the stairs, the cook who had objected to his presence in the kitchen argued with the bartender over how to handle intruders.

Khael retreated to the upstairs hall to find another way out. The room on his left, toward the inn's rear yard, contained no people, but the door was latched. He reached his zarute claw through the door. Each use made it easier. By the time the latch fell back into place, he had raised the window and dived out. With a flip in mid-air, he levitated down to a soft landing on the ground, flat on his stomach. The bags threw his balance off enough not to land on his feet, as he had planned.

He rose and stalked around to the gate. Vixen squatted by the fence to the courtyard, cloaked again. She reached up for his hand with a relieved face and continued into his arms for a quick hug. A moment later she grabbed his staff from the fence and his hand.

They dashed toward the mouth of the alley. Two rangers with gray tunics marched in, blocking their path. Khael let go of her hand and casually reached away to pick up a large, full trash barrel from the many that stood along the alley wall. He trudged toward the street with the barrel on his shoulders as if this were his job. Vixen threw her cloak behind her shoulders and took up a liquid sashay.

"You see older man with really long, white hair or young girl in long dress?" the one to their left said, ogling her exposed knees.

"Not recently," she husked. "Who asks?"

"Me either." Khael groaned. "Stand aside, please, or maybe you carry trash?"

The second ranger grunted as the two parted for Khael. He walked right between the gray-shirts into the street. Vixen followed close behind. The men continued down the alley. Khael left the barrel at the street as they proceeded west.

"Your skin looks normal again," Vixen said as they meandered through the crowd. "How did you get so fat?"

"Our knapsacks. I found a cooperative young couple who assisted me."

"I see. Did the girl tear her clothes off and throw herself at you?"

Khael chuckled. "He already had her undressed. I allowed her to braid my hair."

"She did well. Was she cute?"

He shrugged, focused on their path. "Does it matter?"

"The boy couldn't have been happy."

"His father, the innkeeper, is a collaborator, but he fetched our bags at my request. I saw him carry them somewhat like this into the room and adapted the look for me. I gave him a crown, and his lass seemed thrilled to help. I suspect he is quite happy right now."

Vixen frowned and shook her head. "Where to now?"

Khael looked around to verify. "Straight ahead, then two blocks left. There used to be a way in. Let us hope it remains uncompromised."

"Another secret passage? How many are there?"

"Many. I will explain later."

37. Different Tunnel

Vixen gasped when Khael turned them into one of the stores along the street. She wanted a safe place where they wouldn't get caught. A jewelry shop didn't feel right.

"Fair afternoon, milady, milord," the cheerful jeweler burst out. "What can I fetch you today?"

"Gavin, we need to use the back stairs," Khael said.

The jeweler straightened up as if punched. "Me only back stairs go up to me home. Tis private, sir, an' me wife's resting."

"The clouds are in the right configuration."

Gavin peered at him for moment. He recoiled in fright, his face pale. "What're ye doin' here, Sire?" The anxiety in his whisper squeezed Vixen's chest. "His goons just marched by, outside."

"This is urgent." Khael looked more concerned at the delay than what Gavin said.

"O' course, follow me." Gavin seized Khael's sleeve and fairly dragged him behind the counter that faced the door.

Vixen rushed after them through a beaded-glass curtain into a small back room. They passed a meticulously organized desk on the way to a set of heavy drapes. These opened into a second, larger storeroom cluttered with stacks of cartons and boxes of various sizes. Were they supposed to hide in this mess?

"Twas an old pass-phrase, Sire." Gavin released Khael's arm and feverishly bustled around.

"I have been away." Khael folded back his cloak to release the knapsacks from around his waist.

Gavin fussed with supports in the wall shelving and one of the torch rings. He paused with a confused expression before he moved something else.

"What are you doing, sir?" Vixen wondered aloud, puzzled by his flurry. Even a cursory search would uncover any box they hid in or behind.

Gavin stopped and glared at her. "Beg pardon, lass, but who're ye?"

Khael introduced them.

"'Tis Master Jeweler now, Sire." Gavin resumed his peculiar fidgeting. "I have to unlock the passage. I'd hate for you to be caught, meself the more so."

Vixen shook her head, wondering what kind of passage and to where?

Khael nodded. "Congratulations on your mastery, Gavin."

"Ye'll be wantin' those bags off." Gavin hurried to the back. "The tunnel's narrow."

He lifted what looked like a short floor beam, turned it in a half-circle and set it back down. As the jeweler huffed this final exercise, Khael handed Vixen her bag. She almost fell back a step.

"I thought that box was perfect."

"Quite right. Thank you." Khael closed his eyes for a second, fished out the small box from their shrine treasure and put both knapsacks in it.

"Tis open now," Gavin said. "Ye ken the last. Do hurry, Sire, an' best o' luck to you."

A bell rang in the front room of the shop. Vixen and Gavin started.

Khael strode to a crate near the back wall and pushed it down. A slab of floor rotated up to reveal a hidden staircase. "Thank you, Gavin. If we ever need jewelry, we will seek your shop first."

"Dinna mention it, Sire. Just get that moon-brain tyrant an' his hoodlums off our backs." The jeweler hurried through the drape.

Khael led Vixen down the narrow stairs against the wall, hand in hand. When they reached the bottom, he stopped. She wanted to scream, but he stood like a rock. The light waned until it abruptly cut off when the stone ceiling closed. After a series of slides, grinds and clicks, silence fell. Vixen's heart thumped, but Khael's hand in hers muted her dislike of dark enclosures.

"What next?" Her voice echoed a few times. She shuddered.

"Not so loud, please. When there is light we can proceed."

Half an eternity later, a globe on the wall lit up, settling Vixen's nerves. She looked around as her eyes adjusted to the dim light. The room was about three yards square, with a single open door just large enough for one tall person.

Vixen preceded him into a narrow tunnel lined with spider webs along the edges of its many turns. Each section between the corners lit up from the glow of a globe on the ceiling that went out as they passed through. Finally, the passage straightened out for as far as she could see.

"What's with all the turns?" she said.

"The cross-sections are designed to collapse on intruders. They can be triggered by anyone in the passage who knows how or remotely from the Center."

"I feel so-o much more secure now." Her voice shook. She looked up and frowned. "I don't see how. The ceiling looks solid from here."

"This one should. Only the cross-sections are set up so. The whole tunnel is impassable if any one section collapses. Fortunately, they never have."

"Is it safe?"

"I believe it is quite sturdy."

She groaned. "I meant from hostile troops."

"The farther we go the safer."

Vixen shivered. "Where do we wind up this time?"

"This passage ends in my old bedroom. Arianna lives there, last I knew."

"A bedroom?"

"The room was originally a security office. The door has not been used in my lifetime."

The tunnel ended at a solid block wall.

"This is it?" Vixen grumbled.

"Wait."

The globe overhead faded.

"Hey!"

"Relax." He held her shoulders gently while the craggy tunnel went completely black.

The next minute seemed like an hour despite the exciting warmth of his hands. That made the prospect of capture and its attendant horrors less urgent, even in this close blackness. To be near him made her heart pound, at war with the blind wait.

The glowing outline of a short door cracked the wall open. The door swung away from them until it thumped gently against a bumper on the far side wall. Two globes on the other side lit a cleaner, wider and taller corridor.

Though reluctant to leave his soothing grasp, she ducked through the opening. The door closed behind them by itself. This part of the tunnel appeared to have been designed and constructed with more care, though it had similar turns to the smaller one behind.

"How much longer is this, Khael? I thought we were close."

"We started one avenue away from the Center, so we have about a hundred fifty yards to go."

Vixen swallowed. "That's a long block. All with these booby-trapped cross-ways?"

"There is a series in every fifty yards."

"Wonderful." Vixen kept a wary eye on the ceiling as they trudged on. She pitched her next question to sound as innocent as she knew how. "Who's Arianna?"

"My childhood best friend for almost seven years." For the first time, he sounded wistful. "We went everywhere together, did everything, played every game, until I left for my mystic initiation."

Vixen caught her breath at this mention of yet another close female friend. Probably gorgeous. She ground her teeth. "You never, ah, had any, you know...?"

"No. When I returned, she had been a practicing therapist for over two years. She was eager to exercise her skills, as was I with my disciplines. I suppose all initiates are."

I'll bet. Vixen fought down the turmoil inside to keep her voice steady. "But aren't her skills more... intimate than most? With you her best friend and all, she probably had exotic plans for you."

"She had not progressed that far yet, but the Order considers physical intimacy detrimental to our initial development. Arianna wanted to indulge in wild passions. I declined to participate. It took her a while, but our friendship endured. For me, the Saiensu outweighs everything. Also, I find the aspects of her profession of which you disapprove unappealing in a partner."

Vixen nodded slowly. She battled down any show of her unabashed glee though he probably knew already. Her heart danced behind a set face all the way through the next section of the passage.

"Had you no close male friends in your childhood?"

Vixen smiled. "There was one, when I was six. Zasha. He was very cute, with dark hair and dark eyes, but much older than me. The three boys and one girl I recall playing with all had red hair like me. Zasha always said he'd never be trapped in a boring or clerical life; he'd be a knight or a warden someday. When I turned eleven his family moved away or something. I never found out what happened or why."

"Where did you play?"

"It was a big field with lots of grass..." The memory faded.

"In the Enclave?" He sounded suspicious.

"No... it... couldn't have been." She frowned deeper, baffled by the conflict.

Khael kept silent for a few moments. "Were these other redheads friends or your family?"

She stopped, her mind a complete blank. "How strange. I remember their hazel eyes and fiery hair, but no names, or faces, or who they were to me, or where that was."

"Think hard." He faced her, his gentle hands on her shoulders again.

His kind expression encouraged her, but to no avail. Their faces faded to blandness, like unfinished paper dolls, the background gone.

"Nothing." She shook her head. "Why can't I remember?"

Khael rubbed his chin. "Any genuine clues to your true identity seem to be hidden from you, although your experiences may be unaltered."

Vixen's stomach tumbled into nausea. "What does that mean?"

"We must work out that mystery, too."

"You know something." She heard no answer. "Why won't you tell me what you think?"

"I lack sufficient data for more than vague suspicion. At this point, even if you allowed me to help, solving our current predicament must take priority. If we survive, we can tackle that one."

She grimaced and shook her head. Unlike her childhood companions, whoever they were, the pain from his earlier offer throbbed fresh and sharp in her memory.

They rounded one last corner into a square room much like the one at the other end, but clean and dry. As they entered, a chunk of wall swung around from the inside and closed behind them, sealing off the tunnel. A globe on each wall lit the room, which had no visible exit, not even traces of the cracks where the passage had been.

Vixen widened her eyes, amazed at the craftsmanship.

"Have a seat." Khael slithered down to the floor with his usual grace.

She slid down to a cross-legged position near him. "How long do we have to wait?"

"That depends on what Arianna is up to at this moment."

"You said this opens into her bedroom."

"Would you like me to look inside?"

"No, of course not." What a horrifying idea. The last thing she wanted was for him to watch this Arianna's kih and whatever intimate skills she might be practicing at the moment. Her increasingly sore bum on the hard stone floor wore down her resistance. She gritted her teeth. "Would you?"

"Impatient?"

"My bum hurts. I don't like crypts. They're creepy, even clean-ish, dry, well-lit ones like this."

"Let me see what I can see."

She shuddered. "Don't look too hard, please."

He snickered and closed his eyes. A moment later, his face became serious and he raised a finger to his lips. She huddled closer. Any excuse for contact with him was better than none.

"What is it?"

"Arianna is treating an injured patient, and the viceroy's men want to search the Center."

"Will they find us?" Fright pinched her whole body tight.

"Let us hope not. They would have to force their way in, know about or suspect this room and unravel the key."

She frowned. "Isn't it like the one from that alley?"

"No, that entrance is unique. All the others have seven interlocks."

"How many are there? And why?"

"Eight. One of the older ruling families made many enemies. This house was home to one of the competing families—Mother's. It was built for escape from the palace and to disparate parts of the city from here. We may be the first to have used the tunnel in over two centuries."

Vixen slumped as far as her tension would let her. He seemed so unperturbed by any of their recent adventures. With his eyes closed again, he almost appeared to have fallen asleep. To keep from jumping out of her skin, she reached for something to say. "Your mother is Sinaeg Gregory, but isn't she a Stratton or Cambridge?"

"Gregory is her professional name and her mother's family name. She never took my father's name, and Loren declined to allow his name on a therapy center."

"He objects to them too?"

Khael shrugged his shoulders. "He prefers to keep his name out of the public eye." His mien became grim. "Lieutenant Majestic leads the intrusion and he has company. How interesting."

Vixen groaned. She wished her shoulders would relax again, some day.

38. Clean-up

Khael sat up straight and raised his eyebrows, amazed. "Fascinating."

"What?" Vixen yawned.

"The impostor masquerading as my viceroy is a Chelevkori minister, using one of their spells to duplicate John's appearance. He had five centurion bodyguards and three companies of his rangers with him. Majestic also brought his knights. Yet Mother convinced them to leave without a search."

Vixen's eyes widened in surprise. "I thought they were desperate to get to you. And me." She shook her head. "They'll come back, in force. We're dead here."

Khael did not respond. The impostor's easy cooperation sat wrong for him too. Vixen's comment made perfect sense, but not how or why they backed off. They could still overrun the house. The Center no longer qualified as a safe place to hide. Probably the opposite.

Curious, he scanned farther out. "He left behind more armed observers to monitor the Center. They now surround the block from across the streets. We must avoid the doors upstairs."

"What if they decide to raid while we're in there?"

"His men already infest the house, probably frequently. He must count on that... and... so may we." Khael pressed his lips together. "We must dispose of these disguises."

"I'll need a shower or a bath to wash it all off."

"Let me see." He scanned around upstairs for Arianna's kih. "However, we may be here a while."

"Can't you just reach in through the wall and open it?"

Khael looked at her. Had he developed enough strength and skill with zarute to do that? Her unquenchable faith in him soothed his mind more than he realized. "Perhaps."

Vixen lay down and groaned, her head on her arms.

Khael sensed the room to determine the layout of the interlocks. He kanjuh-traced the bars that held the door closed, back through the whole system. It seemed simple enough.

He concentrated to advance to the more powerful zarute and failed. Not the first time. More practice would help. His second effort also failed. *Fog.* With kinshuh refocus, the invisible pincer emerged.

Each maneuver took a separate invocation, a fair amount of time and intense effort. The mechanism would have been trivial with his hands, but this felt like lifting a heavy weight with two individual, ethereal pinkie fingers. After the fourth pull, he had to stop to regain his breath. The parts felt stiff, as if they had never been used. He wiped his forehead with sweaty arms.

Three more hundred-weight pins. Another agonizing bar shift. Worse than lifting weights. Only one left. One more... A square piece of the wall before them swung open and thumped the stone wall.

Vixen squeaked in surprise. She jumped to her feet.

Khael sagged from the strain. His neck and shoulders ached, and he had to unclench his fists. That hurt. Wearily he lumbered to his feet and ducked through the opening. The wall swung shut behind him. He glanced around the room to match the seven parts of the lock with his kanjuh traces. As he reached the first one, Arianna walked in the door.

Vixen gasped. A wave of reluctant admiration and self-inadequacy blasted across the room to Khael. Her face twitched through a rotating cascade of envy and jealousy.

That would not do.

Arianna stalked into the room with her clothes in her hand. When she saw Khael, she jumped, startled. In a flash, she drew a short sword from behind the clothes-stand beside the door and pointed it at them.

Khael put a finger to his lips and frowned. Why was she naked, even here? Surely his mother had arranged to inform her of their presence in the room. All the tunnels were routinely monitored to prevent any surprises. Or was that her intent?

"What're ye doin' here?" Arianna whispered. A furious glare marred her creamy complexion.

"Please close the door," he murmured. "And put some clothes on."

No-one moved. Had she lost her plain sense from the strain of their current situation? After a brief pause, she lifted a robe off the same clothes stand as her scabbard and threw it on. The silky material clung to her skin. At least Vixen's face relaxed at Arianna's covered, less brazen appearance.

"Arianna, you had to know we were here."

Vixen's icy stare made it clear she appreciated his gesture, but she felt unsure of her standing with his old girlfriend in the room.

"I thought ye were in the tunnel, alone," Arianna choked out. "I wasna expecting two inside. An' I was waylaid on me way back from a sick patient."

Khael introduced them.

"I can't stand this." Vixen glared at her and groaned.

"What?" Arianna and Khael asked at the same time.

"Even your voice is perfect."

Arianna frowned at her as if she were daft and turned back to him. "You're no' safe here. The viceroy's men're all o'er us all the time. I just—och, ne'er mind." She shuddered. "E'en the nice ones're difficult, an' they're sparse."

Khael suppressed the image he had flashed upon earlier. She looked fit and trim as always, and his heart leaned elsewhere now. "We need to clean up and at least approximate our normal looks."

"You canna use the house facilities." Arianna frowned and rubbed her chin. "Her ladyship woulda whisked you upstairs if you'd made it here tomorrow night as planned. That'll ne'er work now. You'll have to use me loo here. Twas once yers."

"I recall, but it lacks enough room for two to share."

Vixen's whole being relaxed when he spoke. Her glare softened to another grateful gaze. Much too appealing. He ached to respond. Too much remained at stake, yet another reminder of how difficult he had made his life.

"That a problem?" When neither of them spoke, Arianna gave them a pained look. "Och, come now. Surely you're no' gonna tell me you've ne'er been naked together."

Khael shook his head. "Never mind, we will manage."

Vixen stared at him, her eyes round again. "We will?"

"We must." He smiled, not as wide as he would have liked.

His hair needed washed and cut. If the mansion had been safer, the house spa would have been perfect. Under these circumstances, only the most trusted staff could know of his presence. They might be better off in the stone room outside the secret door.

"I'll do whatever you want," Vixen said.

She needed a hair wash, too. He yearned to delight in that service himself. Not this time. Someday, perhaps. Tonight, she would have to do her own.

"I will wash my hair first, in the loo. Then you can shower." He looked up at Arianna. "Can you cut mine?"

Vixen paled. Arianna started to nod, but she noted the color drain from Vixen's face. Arianna's expression went flat and she shook her head.

"I'd better no'. I'm due back upstairs, so ye'll have to manage that, too." Arianna pursed her lips. "I'll tell Lady Sinaeg an' give you some time. We'll see about fresh clothes, too. Keep the doors latched an' pray na one else wants in."

She stalked out the door. The lock clicked a moment later. Vixen whooshed out a breath of relief.

"Let us wash up." Khael sighed. "I hope she can arrange those clean clothes."

"I need armor, not a clean dress."

"We must make do with what flexibility we have. Unless we're caught, in which case we fight."

She narrowed her eyes in grim pleasure. "I can do that."

Her scintillating green kaleidoscopes shone at him. Beautiful. His heart sped up until he kicked in kinshuh to settle it. Reason restored, he shook his head. Violence would only get in the way.

"Let us hope not." If only it would be that easy....

39. Intimate Discussion

Khael battled with the sink to wash the gray out of his rough-cut hair. He wished he had used the tiny shower instead. Vixen had shortened it with her dagger, but it needed a finer touch. Eventually. When he left the loo, he told Vixen the shower tank was full. She took her knapsack.

While she showered, Khael brushed out his hair. He discovered many gray flecks his wash had missed. When he rolled his eyes shut, his shikah instantly fixated on Vixen's kih. The startling, vivid color pattern, how it flowed together, the shape and form of the whole, still resonated to the core of his soul. For all Arianna's physical aesthetics, her kih held none of the same attraction to him.

Vixen came out of the loo, her fiery hair still wet. She dried it under his unrelenting gaze. The shifting expressions on her face sent thrills through his spine, and he wallowed in the pleasure. Fortunately, his steadfast practice over the last week that gave him enough control to keep a straight face held fast.

"You're staring."

Khael smiled. So much for steadfast practice. "Guilty."

She shivered under his gaze. "Would you like me to trim your hair?"

It took him a moment to catch his breath. "Know you how?"

"As long as it doesn't have to be perfect."

Anything she did for him would be perfect. "Anywhere near my shoulders."

Tiny trimming scissors from the sink cabinet made her cuts take a fair while. Khael closed his eyes and swam in the view of Vixen's kih. Strange flashes of excited activity roamed through her arms and torso at each snip near his neck. They seemed to be spontaneous, yet unconscious. In spite of their potential implications, he enjoyed the shift and play. His chokkan lay silent on this; she as perfectly safe.

Her face twitched from deep concentration. Wild passion swirled and stormed underneath her mask of control. If only there was no need to hold back. Or was it more, perhaps her indoctrination struggling to emerge?

"I like your hair short."

He opened his eyes at the mirror over the sink. Not too poorly done, for an amateur. Her sparkling green eyes danced at his smile.

"I'm thirsty, and hungry." She sounded tired, but even her pout dazzled him.

Khael shut his eyes again. With an effort, he tore his attention to scan farther out than Vixen. Arianna carried something in front of her with both hands on her way back.

He relayed that tidbit and scanned farther out around the block. Many rangers and a few knights surrounded the block. None of them carried any enchanted equipment. That fit the Chelevkori taboos. The three with chronicon swords would be their highest ranked fighters. Two of them had the spell detectors, so he still had to exercise rigorous caution.

The one with a chronicon sword and dagger but no detector looked vaguely familiar. She was the only female among all the usurper's armed personnel. A full Chelevkori minister as advanced as the usurper himself. Could they be siblings? No, her kih differed from his in too many ways. A fury that dwarfed the rage Khael had seen in Vixen flowed through this minister's every move, every breath.

Her kih nagged at him. An itch like those he had felt about Vixen, but far more sinister. He studied her until it dawned on him. This minister reeked advanced expertise in the private Collectic skills exclusive to registered assassins. This woman was more dangerous alone than the usurper and all of his troops combined. Like Vixen, she also possessed extraordinary dexterity and agility, but honed to a peak only a few Master Collectors ever achieved.

She conversed with two rangers in a third-floor room in one of the taller inns across the street. When they left, she climbed through something, a window maybe, and dropped to land in a perfect gymnast's roll, at least six yards down. She rose and walked briskly away, threading through the back alleys toward the palace until she passed out of his range.

A knock on the door made him open his eyes. Arianna slipped in, attired in a conservative outfit more modest than the slinky robe from earlier. She closed the door behind her.

"I brought you some dinner." Her eyes flashed over the two of them as she set the tray on a low table by the far wall from the door. "Ye look much better as a young man, e'en wi' some gray. An' yer lady's also nicer wi' the red hair. Fair job wi' the haircut, too, lass. Now, eat an' drink. I'll no' be staying. There's patients awaiting."

"I need armor," Vixen said.

"Ye'll have to make do wi' what ye're wearing, dearie. I dinna wear armor. Under our present circumstances, I canna haul wardrobe around that ain't me own."

"Thank you, Arianna." Khael smiled before she vanished out the door again. He expected a cold retort from Vixen, but she said nothing.

She wrinkled her nose at the aroma from the tray. Her expression was so cute Khael had to work to maintain his dignity.

"That smells wonderful." She sighed.

"Let us eat. We may not get another chance for a while."

They devoured the small meal with gusto. Her presence so close in the loveseat warmed him from the chill of what he had seen outside and the persistent nagging prickle in his head. Once the food was gone, they relaxed back with their drinks, a fresh wine with flavor and quality not dependent on drugs. Probably a home brew from right here.

"What did you see?" She snickered at his raised eyebrows. "I figured you were surveying the territory. You didn't look happy."

"The Center is surrounded by the usurper's men. A few inside pose as patients, others act as clients." He frowned. "That friend of yours, the female? Was she older than you?"

Vixen sipped her wine, her eyes up toward her frown. "I think so. She tutored me in some areas, even stood up for me...." Her voice trailed off. "There it is again. Every time I try to remember details, they get blurry."

"If you would allow me, I might be able to help."

"No, Khael. I'm not ready for that. Not yet."

A milder upset than before, no fury or pain. His persistent, gentle efforts might yet pay off. The road ahead overflowed with risks, aside from the usurper. Her memory inconsistencies and many reactions led but to one shaky conclusion. She was a Chelevkori assassin, somehow indoctrinated to fall in love with him, and kill him... and to whom he wanted to give his heart.

Khael exhaled. "Perhaps we can relax for a few minutes before the raid begins."

Vixen started. "Raid?" She glared at his smirk. "That wasn't funny."

"We may be safer outside the wall."

"Would you hold me?" She shivered. "It might be our last chance."

"I doubt that." But her eyes shimmered with excess water, so big and round and green. He checked his kinshuh focus. This once. He put his arm around her shoulders. "We must stay alert."

Vixen snuggled in close. "I could get used to this."

If only... "Our desires must wait."

She sighed. "I know. But I do lo—like you, a lot. You changed my life and saved me from a desolate, bitter future."

"I may yet lead you to your death, or worse."

"I trust you." She looked deep into his eyes, her green orbs wide with... what? Something tried to hide in an ocean of powerful positive emotions for him.

Khael wondered if this was a mistake. He delighted in their friendship. Obviously, she did. Her kih vacillated between trust, love, shyness, feeling sheltered, and a frenzied desire to seize him with all her passion. Perhaps if he rescinded...

No.

Until they knew for sure who she really was, their contract protected them both.

"Let us not go there."

"Don't you find me attractive?" she husked. "Most men get aroused when they feel that for a woman."

"I am not most men."

"I know. You're more difficult." She dropped her voice. "Though I like that."

"How knows a maiden like you so much about such things?"

"I wasn't born yesterday. In the Enclave's wilder alleys, people shag each other right outside for anyone to ignore. When I was younger, I didn't know better than to watch. I've seen enough. It looked like more fun than what I heard in those... other places."

Khael blinked. Revulsion turned his stomach. Whether that was real or, much worse, part of her memory corruption, it took vicious contempt to expose innocents to such brutal depravity. "How sad. Children need protection from such experiences." He shook his head. "We have a contract."

"It's your contract. You could change or rescind it."

Khael kept silent, unsure how to respond. The love and trust in her eyes alternated with frustration and lust. He wanted to tell her how crazy she made him feel. How he wanted little more than to wrap her in his arms and unleash all of his passion for her. Take her off to some isolated sanctuary where they could ignore the world and enjoy each other with uninhibited, wild abandon.

No. No, no, no.

He could never take advantage of her that way. To break his word now, even for such an obviously shared passion, would ruin him. Ruin them. She would never know if he could keep his word. Even he might never know. Mystic development depended on absolute integrity, possibly also his chastity until after he acquired the next, crucial discipline.

"We must honor all our agreements with each other in full." He raised her chin when her face fell. "If we cannot keep this first one, how will any others we make succeed?"

"Fog. I hate you, you horrible, wonderful prince." Vixen ground her teeth. "But you're right. I'll just have to be patient."

She kissed his cheek gently, sighed and laid her head on his arm. Snuggling closer into his half embrace, she sneaked her other arm around him.

"Thank you for letting me take the shower," she murmured.

He flexed kinshuh to stave off the heat she incited within him. While he held it active, that and those irritating warnings stayed under control. His control.

"I do hate your Arianna. She's so gorgeous, I feel gawky around her."

"Physical appearance reveals little about the real person."

"She was naked, and beautiful. I wish I looked like that. Didn't you even look at her?"

Khael shrugged. "We are friends, nothing more."

"I couldn't even hold a candle to her."

Khael gazed into her eyes, then drew back. He took a careful, close look at her, let his guard down to appreciate the view. She was quite fetching, not just pretty but really exquisite, from her innermost spark of life all the way out to the skin. Even her inner rage shone with uncanny beauty. Perhaps he was biased from being near her continuously for so long, but in his heart she was far more beautiful than any other woman. Only her mystery stood in the way, and that still intrigued his curiosity beyond reason.

He smiled. "What could possibly concern the sun about holding a candle to a moon?"

She squeezed herself tight around him. Her crushing embrace bordered on painful. He closed his eyes to enjoy the powerful hug.

"That's the sweetest thing you've ever said to me. Thank you."

He savored her feverish embrace for all too short a long while.

"What happens once you're reinstated?" she muffled against his chest.

Fog clouded his brain for a sweet moment of respite. "Assuming all goes well and we survive unscathed, I must dispose of this usurper and his forces, then hold court, probably more than I like. I also wish to prevent any future recurrence. Whatever we cannot finish in the next few days must wait until we return from Cambridge."

"We're going back to Cambridge?" Excited shivers rippled against him.

"Ryan expects the whole family for the Carnival week. He wants our support for his cause."

"Fantastic. I've never been to the Carnival. Who's Ryan?"

"My elder half-brother, the King of Meridium."

* * *

Vixen held her breath. Would he say more, especially about her role in the transition? Uncertain mist rolled in her mind. Half-brother of a king, the king, right beside her. It never really sank in before. What would she do? What would he want from her once he held his throne? Government and the nobility had always been distant. The farther away the better, to avoid as much as possible except as a target. Here it was integral to his life.

She sat up. "I can't imagine where I fit in here, or with you."

"You, my dear friend, fulfill your contract. Earn more of your keep and continue to develop. I will find a place for you on my staff. You may help us disarm traps the impostor has set. If we succeed, tomorrow you can help me create some documents."

"How? I barely know the letters."

"Barek says you read perfectly well, but I am sure you can copy documents."

"You mean forge them?" Her eyebrows leaped toward her hair.

Khael failed to hold back another smile. "I make them official with my seal."

"Oh." Vixen widened her eyes. "I never thought of that."

"Scribes or sorcerers customarily make the copies to look the same, original seals legitimate them. There are no sorcerers here, so this can be a useful legal service for you to perform."

She gleamed. "Great, as long as I can be useful in ways I've imagined."

* * *

Khael sat on the floor beside the larger couch where Vixen slept. She seemed so much more at peace, trusting, though she tossed and turned. This massive change from three weeks ago when they met still amazed him. While he had saved her life several times, she had developed herself along the way. Their disputes had all ended with renewed trust and increased affection.

His heart ached that he could not drop the barrier he had set between them. Not before they laid bare her history and true identity. How could he explain his suspicions without losing her? With a deep breath, he closed his eyes.

Vixen shifted. She felt so right when he held her in his arms. Such a perfect fit, she belonged with him. Forever.

The latch turned and Arianna slipped in the door.

Khael held a finger to his lips.

"Me apologies, but ye maun ken this," she whispered. "We got word of a riot in one o' the prison warehouses. Grant was involved. Probably instigated it. He helped a whole crowd o' prisoners break free. They're running wild o'er the gray-shirts on the harbor." She stopped, too soon.

"But?"

"He's gone missing." She choked up. "He may be dead. We dinna ken."

Tears sprang into her eyes. She put a hand to her mouth and fled the room. The latch clicked—she kept enough presence of mind to lock the door again.

Should he scan for Grant's kih? In any crowd situation, he would only recognize only the most advanced spell-casters or those nearest by. He closed his eyes and prayed for Grant's safe return. They had to proceed without Khael's staunchest ally and best friend. Deep inside, Khael itched for payback.

40. Underground Plans

Khael scanned around the manor, out from the glory of Vixen's kih. The nearest detector was over a hundred yards away. No, there was one upstairs, right next to a chronicon sword. *Fog.* Its owner, a warden, indulged in a massage not two yards away.

The detector's low power ran down as Khael watched. At that rate it would be dead before the owner retrieved it. A quick eikyo flick accelerated its demise.

When he opened his eyes, Vixen had sat up out of her restless sleep, staring at him.

"Grant fomented a break-out from the warehouse where they held him. In the ensuing riot, he disappeared and remains missing."

"He's a big guy; he can take care of himself." She yawned.

"That also means we must proceed without him."

She slouched back into the couch cushions with a morose expression. "How? I'm tired."

Khael frowned, unable to answer. A new chokkan itch made him close his eyes again. He stood, a sudden chill in his chest, and beckoned to Vixen. "We must go back into the tunnel. Rangers approach the Center in numbers I feel imply a search."

"How do we get in there?"

Khael had already begun the complex task of unlocking the door. Each time he closed his eyes, the troops drew nearer. The last two sliders seemed more difficult than he remembered. He felt more than heard a pounding on the front door. Speed would not help, so he gritted his teeth as he opened each catch. The rangers moved into the house upstairs. One last catch...

The wall opened out.

He grasped Vixen's hand and pulled her gently into the stone room. The wall swung closed and he sat down to activate zarute to reset the locks. By the time he started, they had already begun to reverse themselves. Amazed, he observed as the mechanism locked itself.

"Are we safe?" Vixen sounded loud in the small, bare room.

"Yes, and now I know why it was so hard to open the first time. The locks are spring driven to reset once the door is closed." At her glum face, he gave her a puzzled look. "What disturbs you?"

"I didn't sleep well. We're stuck in this hole, together at least, but for how long? I'd like to change into some armor, and there's nowhere comfortable to sit."

Khael's mind raced. He had hoped to gather at least the leaders of his loyals and plan out how to approach the viceroy, and when. That was no longer an option. More than a score of rangers tramped around the mansion. His mother vibrated in the main salon, her kih rampant with fury. Two men searched Arianna's room.

Khael held his breath. If they found him, disaster would follow. Nothing he did in their defense could possibly reduce the risk. The rangers' deaths would be noticed. He lacked experience with his new twist of memory alteration. What if that failed? His lungs ached.

The rangers each bumped into the first lever in the series that would open the door. By some miracle they ignored the twisting hook. As long as they did not come back... He sighed in hope.

"What?"

"Not so loud, please. The search continues, but the room here seems secure."

"I want armor," she grumbled.

He nodded. "The night is young. You may rest if you can."

"On stone? I couldn't get any rest on that nice couch."

"We have blankets."

While she shifted around, Khael extended his scan toward the palace. Whether or not he gathered enough support for his mission, that thing in the palace remained a menace. How to render it harmless? At this distance, the details were still too vague. He returned his focus to the house and a new chill shot up his spine.

The wall door opened in. Sinaeg entered in silence and waited until the door closed.

"What are you doing here?" Khael waved at Vixen's resting form.

"Savin' yer hide, sonny," Sinaeg returned, her voice low and laden with fury. "I arranged for the scum he left behind to take a nap. They'll no' dare report that, an' we have some respite. Here's some armor for yer lass that ought to fit well enough."

Vixen sat up to stretch. Her jaws cracked through a huge yawn.

"There's another twist. The tunnel from here to the palace was compromised at the other end. Someone was mucking around an' there's na way through."

"Perfect." Khael's stomach lurched with his sarcasm. "I had hoped to use it."

"Plan something new," Sinaeg grumbled. "We've about an hour. I dinna want bloodshed inside the Center unless there's na other option, but I winna hesitate. If I'd my way, they'd be dead already."

Khael rolled his eyes. "I wanted to speak to Damon and Trevor, and I must get close enough to the palace to study that thing. Loren knew not its nature, and I suspect the worst."

"The troops upstairs are on four-hour shifts," Sinaeg said. "If I go back now, I may get yer men here on the next one."

"Thanks for the armor." Vixen threw in.

Sinaeg knocked on the wall and it opened for her. After she left, Khael sat down to think.

"Who is Trevor?" Vixen said. "You've mentioned him a few times, but I never heard or asked."

"Trevor Gregory, Commandant of the City Watch, and Mother's uncle."

"Are you going to get any rest?" She leaned back on her blankets. "There's room here. Or have you grown tired of me already?"

Tired of her? As if that were possible. "I must prepare for tomorrow. We have much work and I know not if more rest will help."

"You don't have to rest." She beckoned him with a finger. "I can't."

Khael snickered. "Do you ever stop pushing your limits?"

309

"You sure you won't lie with me?" She curled her finger again.

Saddened to the core, he shook his head. Her defeated look touched his heart and he crawled over to take her hand.

"You may sleep if you wish. I must prepare."

"No, I'll stay up with you. Who knows? Maybe I'll inspire you."

* * *

Khael kept the meeting short. Vixen had helped him plan ahead as well as they could with what little they knew. They also had a welcome, unexpected guest.

"I've heard rumors o' this doomsday device o' the vice—usurper, but all I ken's that it's somewhere in or near the throne room," Desmond said. "Howe'er, there're dozens o' rooms in the palace his men keep locked an' guarded day an' night. They're all spread around the upper floors where some o' the staff offices an' rooms used to be."

"I had not noticed that." Khael narrowed his eyes. "Thank you, Desmond."

"I also must apologize for wrecking the tunnel. Twas that or lose it."

"You did the right thing if it was compromised." Khael took a breath. "Those warehouses are a disgrace. They should be razed."

"Winna that upset the marines?" Sinaeg said.

"Would you reuse such a place?"

"The viceroy's men're combing the streets for Grant, an old hermit, an' a young dark-haired lass," Trevor said. "More o' them surround this block, wi' na gaps."

"They're looking for Grant?" Vixen sighed. "That's a relief."

"All the wall gates are doubled-staffed as o' yesterday," Desmond said. "The usual cordon o' rangers surrounds the palace building. They keep scouring the grounds."

"It sounds as though the usurper is in a panic." Khael mused. "Perhaps we can use this to our advantage. How many Paladins have we?"

"I'd three full battalions outside the city, but only about half came

310

in so far," Damon shook his head. "Our contacts wi' the last dispersed one say they're no' coming back unless ye win."

The betrayal burned Khael's heart. "I thought I had loyal Paladins. Dismiss the others. We have no need for opportunists."

"Some got themselves arrested, too," Damon said. "Is the house guard still in place, son?"

"The men are," Desmond said. "He doesna like us, an' he hated the women, but he doesna ken us all either. I had the ladies take o'er the stables, as more proper women's work. They're itching to fight. He's also been less trusting o' me, so I must be more cautious than e'er."

"I wish I had better news, but I'll need every last Watchman I got to re-take the city from his gray-shirts." Trevor shook his head. "I'm no' entirely sure who's loyal and who's no'."

"Do your best." Khael frowned. What a mess... "We will have to use the tunnels."

"We monitor them full time now," Sinaeg said. "Let's hope they stay clear."

Khael laid out the plan he and Vixen plotted out. It would have stood a better chance of working if he had all the Paladins. His confidence dwindled, but it was too late to change his mind. He would have to improvise at some point anyway. When he finished talking, the others left.

"I'd like to put this armor on."

"I can look away...."

Before he finished speaking, she had unlaced her dress and dropped it to the floor. Her healthier physique inflamed his new-found desire for her. His insides churned as his libido battled his worries over their current situation and mortal peril. She might not need to kill him....

Khael shuddered and took a deep breath. Insufficient. To flatten his internal conflict, he had to flex his kinshuh. As usual, this took more effort than he liked or had enjoyed before meeting this enticing soul. That done, he set aside her seductive charm and the constant

irritation his chokkan continued to grind into him. He turned away from the delightful spectacle she tried to inflict on him.

"This armor is nice, though Olivia's feels better." She paced around the room. "At least these boots fit pretty well."

Khael smiled at her new energy and ravishing looks. "Olivia's will fit you better than any."

Vixen nodded and continued to pace.

"Anxious?"

"Of course. Aren't you?"

"Yes. This plan is too sketchy, we have fewer allies than I anticipated and our time is running out. Everything depends on my ability to analyze and defeat that device, of which I cannot be sure until we are on the grounds and at much higher risk. In a few hours, you may end up my dead cohort, which I wish to prevent, or you will be a member of my official staff. I reek anxiety."

Vixen gulped, but her eyes shone in the dim light. "I'm right beside you, win or lose. I'll do anything I can to help. Even if I hadn't given you my oath, my feel—you couldn't keep me away from something this big."

"Thank you. Let us hope we both survive."

"I won't let them take me." She shivered.

Khael grimaced. He wanted no more deaths on his hands, ever, least of all hers. "We need to use a different exit. This one goes the wrong way."

41. Surprise

Someone shook Vixen's arm to wake her up. From the gentle touch, she thought it was Khael, but no, this person had long sandy hair and silk-shrouded perky breasts.

"Wake up, lass, tis late," Arianna said morosely.

Vixen yawned and sat up. Other than herself and Arianna, the stone room was empty.

"Where's Khael?" Vixen yawned again.

"He left an hour ago to confront that usurping fraudster."

"What?" Vixen scrambled to her feet.

"He tried to wake ye for half an hour afore he left, but ye were dead to the world." Arianna stood and crept through the wall into her room. "I must go."

Vixen searched frantically around her blankets for her armor. It lay by the wall, with her weapons. Furious that he had left her behind, she struggled into the soft, warm leather and yanked on her boots. Her tangled hair could wait.

She grabbed her dagger belts and began to wrap them around her waist when the ground jumped under her feet and knocked her hard to the cold stone floor. A thunderous roar blasted through the door from Arianna's room and the ceiling caved in around her. By a miracle, the heaviest chunks of dirt and stone fell near the center, missing her.

The air filled with so much dust she coughed for far too long before she got in a semi-clean breath. Her heart sank into the hollow of her knotted stomach. Khael must have failed. She shook off the dirt that covered her and shakily climbed to her feet. Holding her cloak over her nose and mouth gave her more respite from the dust, but the chill of what that blast probably meant slowed her responses, her muscles watery and weak. Her jaw refused to clench properly.

Cloudy sunlight shone in through a gaping hole in the ceiling. Gasping in horror, she scrabbled her way up the rubble. She slipped many times before her head poked up out of the ground. Her eyes wide, trembling in every limb, she dragged herself up to stand outside, swaying.

The Center was gone, its gardens shredded. The whole city lay flattened into a rubble-laden crater. A shiny metal tube, like the one from her last nightmare, gleamed visibly near the middle of the wreckage. Devastation stretched as far around as she could see. No palace, no trees, no buildings at all, not even the city wall a few miles away.

No palace. Oh, no. That meant Khael was dead, too. He had left her alone. Forever.

Her heart raced, but her muscles failed and she collapsed. A hammering at her head drummed any sense she had left out of her. She arched her back to cry out, but she couldn't breathe. The stabbing ache in her chest and gut crippled her.

Vixen thrashed upright on her blankets with a scream. Someone scrambled over to her, reached to tear her throat out. She choked in her panic and grabbed at the hand.

"Hush, dear one, there is nothing to fear here."

Her blurry vision eased and she slowly recognized Khael's midnight green vest and pants, one gentle hand on her shoulder, the other in her fist. A soft wail of relief escaped her throat as she leaned into his arms and clung to his solidity. He was alive! The raging torment that tore her apart from the inside seeped out into his arms, his chest, his comforting embrace.

"What is it?" He stroked her silky hair while she breathed into his vest.

"It was awful." Her throat tightened and took away her speech.

"It was only a nightmare, Vixen. How much worse than life could it be?"

What? Her upset abruptly stopped and she snickered. "You're weird."

"Tell me."

She related this one, her voice still trembling.

314

Khael furrowed his eyebrows, deep in thought. "You woke up on time, so you did not oversleep, and I am here." He brushed her silky hair back from her face.

"I don't want to lose you." That slipped out before she could stop it.

"Nor I you. Come, we must rise. Nightmares or not, today we must act."

"Together?" She turned her large eyes at him.

"We work together if at all possible."

Vixen groaned and struggled her way to her feet. She tugged on her trews and hauberk, then her boots. The soft leather seemed a poor choice for armor, but it was thicker and warmer than what Olivia had made her. Not quite the best fit. At least it protected her better than a dress.

She brushed her hair and gazed at Khael. He had shifted back to his meditation position, his eyes closed. If only he'd look at her, join with her now while they still had a chance. Her nightmare had her overwrought he might not survive. The thought of being alone again after so long with him left an ache in her gut she didn't want to face.

A soft clunk heralded the door from the house opening into their room. Arianna hunched over in the open door and beckoned them inside. Vixen hauled up her dagger belts and followed the faster, alert Khael into the room. The scare of her dream faded.

"I've locked down the house for the day," Sinaeg said. "We've na outsiders within. They didna like it, but I dinna give a whit. We're no' serving those scum na more."

Vixen barely heard the words. Her stomach growled about being empty and her focus zeroed in on the platter of food on the tea table.

"Yes, eat." Khael's warm tone sent shivers up her spine. "We cannot stay long."

After Vixen scarfed down the few bites, Sinaeg took them across the mansion basement. In the outer wall of the destination room, a door like the one in Arianna's room hung open to another stone tunnel. Vixen made a face, but she'd expected this much. Khael took her hand

and led her inside.

The tunnel eventually let out in an alley obliquely across the street from the palace. Vixen blinked in the dense fog. If this kept up they might well be invisible. They crept up the alley mouth to the wide avenue. Her heart pounded all the way. She fully expected any second they'd be stopped, caught.

They slipped across the foggy avenue and onto the grounds. Desmond's warning rippled caution through Vixen's mind. For all her feverish efforts, she saw and heard no one near the wall. Khael led her along a circuitous route around the palace through the heavy pines and snowy shrubs. They joined Damon and a few others a small grove of trees across the open, snow-covered greenway from the main entrance. Some stamped their feet, others shuffled around.

"No blades today, staves and batons only," Khael whispered. "When I give the word, take out the cordon of rangers with minimal noise. Once we receive Desmond's readiness signal, we can advance to the doors together. I may be slow, so stay with me."

He fell silent and closed his eyes.

Vixen took a deep, shaky breath. "Are all your men here?" she whispered to Damon.

Damon looked around. He beckoned to another knight behind them. They had a hushed exchange. When he looked back at Vixen, his frown carved deep canyons in his forehead.

"No' certain," he breathed. "Wait an' see."

"Great," Vixen muttered.

Minutes crawled past. Khael shuddered, making her flinch.

"Lord Blackstone?"

Damon looked at her.

"Where are they?"

He just put a finger to his lips.

Vixen squirmed inside. Despite her heightened nerves and energy, she couldn't see or hear anyone else in the area. If it weren't so cold out she'd be sweating, but the cold didn't bother her. Even the uncertain wait wasn't too foul. Khael's silence unnerved her and made her skin crawl.

A Paladin came out of the main palace door between the two gray-shirts who stood guard. While he spoke with the guards, two rangers in the viceroy's gray-shirts marched out of the trees from east of Khael's group and headed up the stairs. The two on the steps nodded quickly. They hurried inside with the Paladin while the new arrivals took their positions.

This same drama played out a few minutes apart at each of the side doors. Minutes later, the Paladin came out again. This time he waved at the group in the trees. Damon returned the gesture.

Several men and women appeared out of the trees to stand behind them. Some wore Paladin uniforms, some gray-shirts and others in scruffy dress, probably disguised so as to get into the court without giving themselves away.

Vixen steeled her frayed nerves. They weren't alone. She turned to Khael. He looked concerned, but he remained immobile.

"Are we ready?" she whispered.

"Desmond gave the door guards a break from the cold," Damon said quietly. "Paladins replaced 'em. With the viceroy's men inside warming up, our mix o' Paladins can take out that cordon when we're ready to move. But the prince has to finish."

She pulled her heavy cloak tighter and waited for a sign from Khael. He stood perfectly still, his monkish coat closed to the breeze, his hood drawn low to obscure his face. What was taking him so long? The area around the palace was too quiet. Something must be wrong.

An eternity later, Khael sighed. "Damn," he whispered.

"What?" Vixen's heart pounded alarm. She clutched her dagger so hard her fist hurt.

"The construct may be an ordinary demolition explosive, but I cannot be certain. There is something hand-sized connected to the circuit, sitting by the throne, probably the trigger right where he can seize it."

"Is it a shiny metal tube with a cap and a tail?" Vixen widened her eyes.

"All I see is the energy in it. In any case, the second wire set looks like a passive power source to detonate it if anyone tampers with the primary."

Vixen swallowed her dry throat. "How much damage can that do?"

"My intuition has never failed me. It will destroy everything up to five hundred yards beyond the city walls."

"But you can disable this thing, right?" Vixen's eyes hurt from the strain.

"I seek a way, and time grows short."

Vixen dropped her shoulders, crushed. "That's not reassuring,"

A chill settled in the pit of her stomach. Khael gave her a tiny, reassuring smile and closed his eyes.

She tore her eyes away from him. To her right, more trees stood where a lazy drift of snow fell through the fog and swirled its way to the white-covered ground. Her ears twitched at the few mild swishes of air, her companions' breath, and the occasional creaking of her joints. Strange that she heard no armor, or mail, or any human sounds.

Khael frowned.

Her nerves shrilled again. What was he doing? How could he save them all? Time dragged on. She ground her teeth at the complete lack of action. His frozen expression told her nothing. If only she could read minds, like him....

A quiet noise from the palace made her start. Desmond stepped out again. He raised his staff once and lowered it.

Vixen peered across the front wall of the palace. No cordon of rangers. In shock, she squinted to check again. Gone. Her gut tightened. Not a single arrow had been fired, but they were all gone. That wasn't right. They must be hiding behind the columns, waiting to ambush Khael.

Khael nodded.

Vixen sucked in a breath. She hadn't realized she'd stopped.

Damon led their small group forward. The Paladins that had appeared from out of the fog followed. They walked toward the palace where it should be warm, or at least warmer than the brisk winter chill out here on the snowy lawn.

Khael dragged. Halfway to the steps, he slowed until he barely took one step at a time. His face shone with sweat. Vixen flexed and released her muscles in desperate hope. His progress came with shorter, slower steps to the foot of the stairs, where he just stopped. His forehead creased in frustration.

Vixen's neck hurt. She hadn't felt this wound up since she met with Khael in the Bar-Jay to return his ring. Her heart plummeted to the churning pit in her stomach.

"What is it?" she murmured. No one answered. She wanted to scream.

Khael's frown deepened and his breath grew ragged. He clenched his fists convulsively.

Fear clawed at her insides. Could she still trust him? An explosion that big would kill them all, probably in extreme, fiery pain. She was right here on the ground, in the blast zone, not floating above or in the safer underground room. He took forever, prolonging the risk, and it wasn't getting any warmer. Anxious, she angled for a better look at his face.

Khael sagged from his bolt-upright posture and opened his eyes. He looked worried for the first time since... well, ever.

"Did it work?" Vixen almost shrieked the question, but it came out a whisper.

To her dismay, he took a deep breath and shook his head.

"No. I cannot reach the device from here."

"What d'we do, Sire?" Damon whispered. "I sent all me extra Paladins to liberate yer mother's place an' the warehouses. If ye canna succeed, we're doomed."

Khael sighed and hung his head. "I see no alternative. I must surrender to this usurper and pray he spares the city. Vixen, you must go to Strattonmoor with Damon."

"What?"

"We're givin' up, Sire?" Damon's face furrowed with frustrated rage.

Khael shrugged, his whole bearing depressed.

"Khael, don't do this." Vixen seized his hands. "Take me with you. I can help, and you promised."

"I cannot risk your life for this." He gave her a bitter smile.

She had to look down to lie to him. "You would break your word?" There had to be another way.... "You're not going in there without me." Her face chilled as the ache of grief forced its way into her blurring eyes. She tried to focus on his face. "I... I love you, Khael."

He closed his eyes to inhale, then opened them. His gaze pierced hers. "Stay with me for a few minutes that I may go in with all my resources. Then you must leave. For my sake and yours."

Vixen shook her head. He released her hands and slithered down to sit still in the snow, his shining eyes closed again. Her hands twisted together over her pounding heart, clinging to every second she could spend with him, even if he wouldn't hold her close. Tears threatened to blast out of her eyes, but she strained them back. If this was their last moment together, he had to know she supported him without reservation, at any cost.

What would he do inside there anyway, besides get killed? She could be his distraction, or maybe actually get to guard him, if only he'd let her. Did she need his permission?

Khael rose to his feet beside her. He caressed her cheek with such tenderness her knees threatened to give way. "Pray for me to whatever deities you hold dear. Pray for all of us."

Vixen whipped out her dagger and set it against his throat. "No, I'm taking you in."

His eyes widened in shock. Was that more fire than the usual peaceful ocean in his dark blue orbs? No matter. This would work better anyway.

"Vixen?"

"What're ye doin', lassie?" Damon demanded, fierce but quiet.

Vixen's idea solidified. "He is my prisoner. Go wait in the trees."

Khael stared at her. Damon reached for her arm, his face a study in puzzlement.

"Back off or he won't make it inside." Vixen snarled to emphasize her point.

Damon scowled at her, his eyes filled with suspicion, but he nodded curtly. The whole contingent headed back to the trees, including Damon.

"Let's go, Your Highness." Vixen grabbed his arm, set the dagger against his side and marched them up to the stairs. "You, guard. Go tell His Excellency I've captured the prince for him."

"Huh?" The Paladin sounded stunned.

His partner gasped.

"Did I stutter?"

42. Showdown

Khael waited on the front porch while the shocked Paladin walked slowly into the palace. His heart ached with every beat, wondering whether she had betrayed him or brilliantly supported him, more concerned about her safety and uncertain if they had any chance of success. He felt no new warning from his chokkan and chose to trust her.

The light snow still swirled its lazy way to the ground. What little wind breezed by kept the porch clear. He inhaled, desperate to enjoy the clean feel of the chill through his airways. Either he had many more such breaths to come, or only a few. Now was the time to appreciate them.

His mind drifted back to the looming threat inside the palace. To his astonishment, the second wiring circuit merely ensured that the device retained enough power to set off the explosion if some but not all of the wires were disconnected from the pouches. All he needed to disarm the behemoth was proximity and enough time to disconnect all fifty leads before the usurper had him executed.

From the base of the steps, his zarute reached as far as the thirteen packets along the front wall of the throne room ceiling. To disarm the remaining thirty-seven parts of this monstrous bomb, he had to get inside. Hopefully his "capture" and some distracting delays with Vixen would give him time to do the rest.

In the most probable worst case, he would die out here on the steps where Vixen would see. This ranked at the bottom of his list of priorities, below any other form or location of his demise. At least his people, his city, and his dear Vixen would probably not get massacred in a monumental explosion. Or the usurper may have planned to commit suicide just to do the maximum damage he possibly could, as seemed more and more likely.

Fog. All and life, or nothing but death. Massive death.

He extended a renewed zarute probe to more of his targets on both sides, as far as he could reach from here. Though easier with repetition, he still had to get a grip on the wire lead and pull it away from the explosive pouch. His zarute grasp seemed to get stronger with each one. Nice. Four more done, only thirty-three still beyond his reach.

While he waited, he scanned his entire range one more time. The cordon of guards lay collapsed around the building with signs of internal affliction, like a disease, or perhaps a poison. Who had the means and influence to arrange to disable so many men so effectively? How many elsewhere suffered from the same effects?

Before he could make a closer analysis, the usurper and a small cluster of knights marched out of the throne room toward the palace doors. Khael opened his eyes as they peeked through a crack between the outer doors, terrified. Next came four crossbows, aimed straight at him. He spread his arms, his gloved hands openly visible.

"So, it is you." The spitting image of John Masterson, Earl of Aistpynt, Viceroy-regent of Shielin, emerged between two of the gray-clad crossbowmen. He stepped just far enough out from the door to take a clear look at Khael.

His kih was nothing like that of Khael's trusted earl, but a full power Chelevkori minister in his guise. How easy it would be to disrupt the flow of this minister's energy and tear away that false form, exposing him before his own men. Of course, they had to know who he was or they would not be here. Waste of zhukih. No.

"You think I'd bring someone else here?" Vixen snapped.

"You were supposed to kill him, stupid girl," the usurper returned.

"You never would have believed me. I figured you'd rather do the job yourself."

Khael bolstered his kinshuh cool over a raging fury with this usurper who had tyrannized his city and threatened to kill tens of thousands of innocents.

The minister stood at least twenty-two yards away from the bomb's trigger. A kih waited inside by the throne for his master's return, most likely with a time limit. Even the most reckless fool would take such a precaution.

323

Patience...

"Actually, yes," the false viceroy admitted. "You guarantee he is no threat?"

Khael clenched his jaw. He had to say this correctly to preserve his integrity. "For the safety of my city and my people, I agree not to resist."

The minister snickered. "I could have you shot right here and now and end this."

"What's your rush?" Vixen's taunt had the desired effect – the minister blanched. "You can take your time, make him suffer. Anyone inside you can humiliate him in front of? Wouldn't that be better?"

The minister squinted at Khael. He took a deep breath before he nodded. "I like that. Maybe you're not so hopeless after all." He raised a hand to the men at his left. "Shackle him securely and bring him inside. At least those miserable criminals in the court will see him humbled before me when he dies."

Two gray-shirt rangers crept forward from behind the knights, as if terrified of what might happen to them. Khael held out his hands. The men reached for them.

"No, you idiots! Behind his back!" The minister waited until they had done his bidding. He straightened up with a cruel smile. "Not just the prisoners. Send out word – in one hour we will have a public assembly right here, on the lawn. We have excellent news for the undeserving scum of this filthy city. Bring him."

He turned and strode back into the building. With Khael shackled, the guards displayed less concern. They shoved him toward the doors.

Vixen followed behind, her kih boiled with rage.

This might just work.

"Have some respect," one of the door Paladins began.

One of the knights shouldered him aside with no shred of manners. "Shut up!"

"Out of way!" snarled another.

The tall, intricately carved, oaken throne room doors stood open,

324

six long yards across the entry corridor from the front door. A sparkle of dust hung loosely in the air. They marched across the muddy, bare marble floor into the throne room. Wet spots littered the dirty aisles. All the carpets were gone and few of the many iron braziers that used to keep the room warm and well-lit stood dark and cold.

The front two rows of seats held shivering prisoners, surrounded by numerous gray-shirts. Like Khael, the prisoners had been manacled. Unlike him, they were strung together by a chain that hung behind the chairs, and none of them had any visible hair. They wore only ragged tunics, not all of them suitable for public display.

A chill shook Khael. Those in the left half of the front row were women, their heads shaven like the men.

Blood coursed in Khael's neck. What unconscionable treatment these people had been forced to endure. How was Grant? Or lived he still? This could not stand. He flexed kinshuh against his mounting anger.

All the art works that used to grace the formerly decorative walls between the many room doors and fancy lamp niches were gone. Damon had reported "stuff" missing from the palace. Khael's stomach twitched, disgruntled at the difficulty of replacement should the originals be lost, or destroyed.

Of course, he had to survive this debacle first. He almost laughed at the irony.

The escort jerked him forward until he stood near the center of the room, a single row of seats away from his throne dais. Khael closed his eyes, in part to shut out the distressing images, and invoked zarute. With enough time, he would finish disarming the bomb and squeeze out a slim chance to save his people and his city before this wicked impostor killed him. He clamped a fierce grip on his trepidation and reached to disconnect the nearest packets.

The usurper strode up the dais stairs to the throne, a buoyant spring in his step. His kih fairly shone his delight. He sat and toyed with something on the left armrest. The four knights with him joined the one who had stayed behind, arrayed around the dais.

"I have an announcement," the usurper crowed. "Your prince has returned, and he has granted me the authority to continue as regent in perpetuity."

Cries of shocked disbelief rang out around the throne room.

"I tell you true, do I not, Prince Stratton?"

One of the gray-shirts holding Khael's pinioned arms yanked his hood back. Gasps surged through the crowd.

Khael's stomach flinched. Twenty-nine charges remained wired-in on the circuit, and the guard's rough interference almost caused that last disconnect to detonate the whole system.

Khael flicked his eyes over the prisoners who would die right here with him if he failed now. "As I said, for the safety of my people and my city, I agree not to resist."

"Yes, that is what you said." The minister burst out laughing. "Like what you see, Highness? Some of these shaven women of yours almost look desirable, even covered in filth as they are."

The sneer seemed to fit a Chelevkori. Khael had never seen such a despicable expression on his loyal earl's face. *Twenty-six to go.*

He exhaled. "I prefer my citizens be granted the dignity they deserve."

"The jailed deserve no dignity. We keep them naked. Can't allow any hidden weapons, they resist less and don't commit other stupidities. They're shaved, too, body hair and all. They liked it, though they pretended not to."

Khael's heart pounded. *Twenty-four.* He clung fast to his kinshuh. A loss of equilibrium here, now, promised an early slaughter.

Vixen snorted. "Is Your Excellency really that threatened?"

The usurper grinned, writhing with glee. "Threatened? This is priceless. We will have to take further action on this."

"Why don't you just let these pathetic wretches go free?" Vixen asked. "We have what we wanted and they're just interference.

Twenty-three.

"Why bother? Come to think of it, I should kill you now." He raised a hand to his bodyguards, who raised their crossbows to aim at

Khael.

"Mercy is the mark of a great leader. You have victory in your grasp, me in chains, and recidivists can always be caught. What harm in letting these rabble go free before you finish your grand exposition?"

Twenty.

The usurper glared at him, but his cruel smile crept back over his face. "Loath though I am to give you anything, I do feel magnanimous today." He gestured to his guards. "The girl is right. Lower your weapons. He is no threat now. You, prisoners, listen up. I hereby grant you amnesty for whatever crimes brought you here today. This one time. Return and I won't be so lenient. Guards, unshackle the prisoners and send them out to wait for my announcement."

Khael bowed his head to mask his relief. Seventeen more and they would all be safe for him to act. If he and Vixen bought enough time with this, and he survived. He closed his eyes to the disorienting double vision that conspired with his shrieking chokkan nettles to slow his every move.

A susurration of grumbling rose between the guards unlocking the prisoners, and the latter muttering about the goings-on before them.

"Quiet," the usurper shouted. "You are free. Be so in silence, lest I change my mind." In the ensuing hush, his snickers replaced some of the noise.

Vixen seemed to be fighting back the urge to leap on this usurper, but her kih held fast, in check.

Khael opened his eyes in slits. To his surprise, this proved less troublesome with so many kih nearby. His non-stop zarute practice reduced the effort to a few seconds for each wire disconnect. Only fourteen more to go, less than a minute...

What little he saw still nauseated him. The floor had not been cleaned in months. Dirt layered on the marble surface tarnished its former beauty. Yet another reason, however petty, for him to triumph here. He continued his zarute work, tiring but crucial.

"Why aren't you gone yet?" The usurper fairly growled his

displeasure.

Eleven. Khael allowed himself a brief scan of the room. Many of the former prisoners now stood along the back wall of the court, pushing off the gray-shirts who shoved at them to get out.

"Why are these criminals still here?" the usurper demanded.

"We want to see what you do to our prince," one man said bitterly. "Your Excellency."

"You can see outside. I have called a city event on lawn. Now get out."

"We demand—"

"You demand?" The usurper snarled. "You don't make demands of me. Get out, damn you!"

Nine. Khael looked up. At last, the double vision no longer bothered and even amused him.

"Is there something to hide, my lord?" Vixen wondered out loud.

Waves of fury washed through the usurper's kih. He seemed ready to throw himself at the crowd, but instead he shook his fist at Khael and Vixen. A shiny metal tube flashed in his hand. "Fine. Let them watch the execution. Leave the rest locked up."

"You fear these helpless, unarmed, naked prisoners?" Vixen sneered.

The usurper drew himself up straight, a haughty look on John's aged face. He shrugged his shoulders. "I fear no one and nothing. Free these miscreants and hurry up."

Seven.

The gray-shirts fought with the chain lock on the women's half-row. After a few curses and some slamming they finally got it open. They took their time with the women, groping them, but a few hasty glances at the usurper encouraged them to speed up.

Five.

"What is the matter with you?" The usurper glared at his own men. "Are you always this incompetent? No wonder I have so much— never mind. Do you all want jail duty?"

"Our apologies, excellency, the locks are old and—"

"Finish the job, or you can join them."

Four.

The last unshackled prisoner shuffled around the outside of the front row of seats. She headed for the rear where the others still stood. Their kih all alternated between rage and misery. Khael could not tell which they hated more, the usurper or his own surrender.

Two.

"It is time," the usurper announced. "Let all watch this execution."

The bodyguards raised their crossbows again.

"What of your public meeting on the lawn?" Vixen waved her hand toward the court doors. "Didn't you promise them a spectacle?"

One. Khael's pulse raced despite his kinshuh. Just a few more seconds...

Impatience glittered in the usurper's eyes. "I changed my mind. The longer he lives, the more delaying tricks he can play. And I don't trust you one stitch."

Zero.

The annoying thistle that had raked Khael's mind since outside the city and increased into stinging, itchy interference with his ability to concentrate dissolved into oblivion. His heart slowed with a new calm. A mirror surface over profound relief unruffled his mind.

He sighed and drew himself up to his full, unbowed height. If only he had not let Vixen send Damon and his Paladins away. Something tickled the back of his mind, but he held his focus tight to vanquish this last hurdle. "I withdraw my offer."

The minister stared back at him with a sneer of incredulous contempt. "You are in chains and about to die."

Two loud clicks and the manacles slid off Khael's wrists and clattered to the floor.

"Am I?" *Lower your weapons!* he stabbed at the usurper's knights. His zhukih reserves shrank.

"You gave word, filthy mystic!"

The bodyguards slackened their aim. Their faces twitched; their confidence crumpled as Khael's thought command battered their minds.

Three sets of doors behind Khael burst open. Damon marched in through the center doors behind Vixen, Desmond on the right aisle and Trevor on the left. Hostile, fully armed female Paladins followed in all three aisles through the clumps of prisoners, who happily made way for them, cheering.

Khael's breast swelled with joy at this pleasant shock. He blinked back grateful tears. "I agreed not to resist for the safety of my people and my city."

"You lied!"

"The safety of my people and my city are now assured. My agreement is complete."

A livid wave chased itself across the usurper's face. "You have lost your mind. Your duplicity just condemned your entire city to death." He held up the shiny metal tube. It matched Vixen's descriptions from her nightmares, right down to the cap at his thumb. "Do you know what this does?"

"Do tell. Tell us all." Khael's heart soared.

The most glorious kih outside his own stepped up beside him and slipped her hand under his arm. His head spun.

The usurper tipped his head to the side. His livid expression decompressed to an evil smile. "So you are the faithless bitch we all knew you were. Excellent. We can all die together." He raised his fist and flipped the cap open.

Khael raised his hand. "Wait, let me guess. That will fire fifty charges implanted in the ceiling, dropping it to crush everyone in this room, including you and all your men. The blast will detonate another seven rooms filled with explosives, which will raze this entire city to a smoldering crater of ruins as far out as five hundred yards beyond the city wall." He paused as the gray-shirts and the prisoners muttered fearful exchanges. "Are you so certain you want to die with me?"

330

"That was always a contingency." The usurper's smile became a grin. "Welcome to my hell."

His five bodyguards lowered their crossbows to their sides, their arms slack and faces pale. They must not have known.

The usurper pressed his thumb into the tube.

Silence fell.

With a howl of confounded rage, the usurper stabbed the plunger again and again.

Unlike the doomsday device, Khael's fiercely confined frustration exploded. A swift read of this twisted Chelevkori mind revealed his identity, and John's stealthy murder. Khael reached eikyo fingers up to the minister and ripped away the energy that fixed the false, assumed form of his earl in place.

"You failed, Versyna Nechetnaya," Khael said coldly. "Surrender. Now."

"Kill him!" raged the melting wax form of an old man becoming younger and taller. His short gray locks lengthened toward his shoulders, a bright, flaming red.

"Excellency?" His bodyguards stared at him in dismayed shock.

"Kill him, damn you!" Versyna snatched the crossbow from his nearest guard and fired at the prince.

Khael winced. A reflexive zarute jab tipped the crossbow up. The bolt sailed over his head. It thudded into one of the doors.

Stand down, he commanded the remaining archers on the dais. Not strong enough...

The closest bodyguard slackened his arms. His crossbow fell with a smack onto the wooden platform. The other three shook off his feeble command, aimed and fired.

Damn.

Khael turned and swept his hands at the bolts, twisting to evade whichever one he could not divert. He slapped the one from his left down to chip the floor. The center bolt also went wide. It flared a slice of bruising inferno across the back of his right hand. The unsteady block failed to save the glorious kih by his side. His breath seized.

Except Vixen was not there.

Where did she...? The third bolt punched through his skin, passing a rib. It slammed into his chest right above his heart.

It hurt less than he expected. William had once taken a crossbow bolt in his left arm. A few seconds after the impact, it scorched like a fire that would never burn out. But this felt more like a soft pinprick, albeit one that bored into the core of his being.

A pulse blew out from his body, a silent mental scream, or perhaps a mere explosive puff of air.

His legs felt watery. Strength drained from his arms. The kih and light around him faded to black. Sound blurred away.

He did not realize he had closed his eyes.

43. Impossible

Chiming sparkles.

A grand symphony of beautiful music bellowed into Khael's deranged semi-consciousness. It should have deafened him. The thunderous sound reverberated throughout his dulled senses, yet nothing entered his ears. They seemed to be missing.

Where are they?

He tried to open his eyes. The brilliant rainbow of sparkles gradually resolved into a magnificent tapestry of shimmering color, similar to his prior visions of Vixen's kih, but brighter, different, more... intense. His limited awareness floated around within the orchestral vision, bursting with a robust life and profound joy he had never experienced. If this was a kih, he loved it with all his heart. Wherever that was.

A disruption flawed the image surrounding him. Some lifeless, alien influence stabbed into it. Around this defect, the kih's physical functions stood motionless. Yet the life-energy itself flowed in patterns, bright and vibrant to whatever fraction of him perceived and moved in this beauty.

It gradually dawned on him that the kih in which he frolicked with such joyous abandon was his own. Except for that alien intrusion, it would have been perfect. But only for him.

The image receded, shrinking away as more kih came into his— not exactly 'view,' more like—awareness. A whole cluster of kih surrounded his. He soared above them all while still rooted at the same base level of… something.

Damon's kih glowed beside his, and Vixen's behind them, her back to his.

So that was where she went. A warm wave of gratitude washed his... heart?

Other kih around his looked familiar. Versyna stood frozen in front of what must have been the throne. The three bodyguards who had fired their crossbows at Khael hung suspended. They seemed to be midway through spine-cracking back handsprings out from the center of the dais toward the floor, eighteen hands below. Desmond stood on one foot to his right, and Trevor to his left, among many other Paladins that had burst in right before... what? A thick gray fog obscured Khael's memory of whatever had happened. The rest of the kih around him also seemed dulled, as if clouded.

Within their pseudo-bodily boundaries, the gleaming kih patterns swirled, like his own. A coruscating ocean of brilliant light surrounded them all, connecting the individual images together.

If Khael had had eyebrows in this dream, he would have raised them in surprise. The rippling, flowing kih patterns never changed position. Not even a hair's breadth.

Time had come to a complete stop.

What kind of bizarre afterlife was this? So detached yet so vital. He had no sensation of his body at all. Nothing but scintillating light and thundering symphony, neither of which stopped.

A slight tickle tugged an extension of his soaring awareness back down into his kih.

A tiny crinkle of energy surrounded the invasive anomaly. His mind frowned, as if that were even possible. He zoomed his focus more closely in on the odd energy surrounding the distortion. Shuri? Not quite as he had applied it to Vixen, or Grant, or anyone else, even Iulianna, or himself.

What means any of this?

The intrusion would consummate its lethal injury as soon as his personal time sense became unstuck from this stasis. Ah, the crossbow bolt stuck in his chest. Healing was impossible in this state. Without shuri already underway when his life flow returned to normal, the bolt would surely kill him. Most likely in slow, intense, blazing agony, like that flash of his father's memory.

A wrinkle in his mind began to glow, burn. The chiming symphony softened and changed key, or something, perhaps less major and more modal. The brilliant blaze of light surrounding the spectacle dimmed. His split awareness commenced a slow merge into the whole.

334

The tentacle that extended to the scene below so he could conceive it better retracted away from his kih back toward his floating awareness.

The whole dream darkened. His awareness faded, slipping away though he tried to cling tight.

No! What to do?

A surge of energy pulsed through him. His disciplines lay prepared, massed at full strength, awaiting his direction.

Ah, of course...

Khael shoved against stiff, growing resistance to infuse the tentacle with shuri, push it back down to his kih. He thrust as hard as he could. The tentacle reluctantly burrowed at the solidifying darkness toward the intrusion. It was harder and farther than he imagined, and it ached from the fire within. Close, so close. The ache rose too high and he feared he could not make the connection.

What had he told Vixen?

"For most injuries, shuri requires proximity, not contact."

A spark bridged the gap.

His ache dissipated, like dust in a powerful wind. The symphony faded to silence. The background light darkened into a more ordinary shikah view. In a sluggish acceleration from minuscule lurches on their gradual way to natural life speed, the kih below him began to shift.

Khael's awareness continued to float above the scene, as if his body resisted his return. His heart refused to beat. One single beat and his aorta would burst under the pressure of the bolt, causing his heart to explode. He raised his mental eyebrows again. Not even shuri had the power necessary to undo that much damage.

Or... did it?

To his utter astonishment, the sublime discipline proceeded. The sluggish process strained his waning patience. All the damage around the intrusion crept toward stability. One cell at a time rearranged itself without blood loss or impaired function.

Was that shuri? Or something else?

Time continued its laggard acceleration. The whole room spilled into a molasses-clogged riot. In this gelatinous choreography, Vixen danced faster than everyone else. Ferocious, unrestrained violence blazed through her kih. She rolled around Damon's back while he kept a steadying grip on Khael's left arm. Damon's grip held Khael's body upright, even though his legs' kih still shone enough fractional stability to resist collapse.

Vixen's kih spun out toward the throne. She slithered down to kick the legs out from under one of Versyna's men, rolling through his collapse into a rise. On her way up, she smashed her fist into another's groin and whirled around him to hammer a third in the temple with the hilt of her enchanted dagger. Her right hand clasped something at her waist, probably another dagger, as she sailed up the stairs to cross her wrists right in front of Versyna's throat, ready to slash it.

A rushing noise invaded Khael's mind.

No blood on my palace floor!

Khael's mind cringed at the force of the exploded thought. He had a rule. Vixen would not be the first to break it. His soaring awareness shot back into his immobile, rooted flesh.

As his shikah resumed its normal state, he realized he had projected his mental scream to everyone in his kinseh range. His heart stood still, lungs waiting to inhale. In an extreme effort of will, his leaden eyes opened with a scary crisp focus on her.

Vixen stood as if she had slammed into a wall. Her daggers creased Versyna's throat, just shy of lacerating the skin on his neck. She whipped her head around, her hair swirling in a slow vortex of captivating flame around her beautiful head. Fabulous green eyes flashed relieved fury at him.

You're alive! "Are... you... in-sane?"

Her slow baritone sounded normal to his aberrant perception, nothing like her usual silken-honey alto. Every action dragged inexorably slowly. The three bodyguards continued to drift their way off the dais. Some invisible, huge fist had slammed into them. It had smashed their crossbows against their chests. Everyone else in the room paused the scuffle to stare at—her words or his telepathic blast?

Through the torpid time crawl, Versyna seized Vixen's wrists and forced them high over her head, twisting her around to face Khael. He strong-armed her hands down until her daggers threatened her own neck.

"Surrender, now, or I cut your slut's throat," Versyna spat out.

Can you take him?

Please, her mind begged through the smirk under her flashing eyes.

Spare his life. To Versyna, he sent, *You can try.*

Versyna's eyes bulged and he sucked in a breath. Vixen smashed the back of her head into his chin. The impact loosened his grip on her hands and she twisted them free. She dropped her daggers and spun her knee up into his groin. Her left hand hammered his throat. He gagged, one limp hand reaching for his neck as the other flopped down. With a speedy calm that amazed Khael, she twirled behind the usurper and seized him in a headlock.

"Try anything, breathe wrong, and I'll snap your wretched, fecal neck," she said.

Relieved at her safe posture, Khael surveyed himself. The wound had sealed itself, waiting to finish healing until he removed the bolt. After a cautious kinesthetic survey, he decided his renewed pulse and continued respiration might no longer kill him. He allowed one heartbeat, then another, neither one too excruciating. Letting his pulse continue, he inhaled a cautious breath.

"Are ye all right, Sire?" Damon muttered into his ear.

Khael expanded his self-survey to the rest of his body. His legs held firm, though filled with water. He flexed his hands, thrilled they still worked. "Yes."

"You really are insane," Vixen crowed, her grip on Versyna unwavering.

"I am mystic."

Subdued chaos pervaded the crowd in the room. The only gray-shirts still standing all held staves, and their shirts had ripped open to reveal green Paladin surcotes underneath. The older prisoners cringed to the wall while the younger ones, men and women alike, pinned

337

down other gray-shirts, pummeling them with vengeful abandon.

"Enough, my people," Khael called. "We prevail."

In the ensuing shuffle, he examined the kih of the fallen rangers. Every one of the gray-shirts except Versyna's five bodyguards, and of course the usurper himself, radiated severe systemic failures. Like the cordon of rangers outside, they had been poisoned.

The sound of a new scuffle filtered in through the doors behind Khael. Without turning, he scanned back to four new rangers wrestling with them a restrained, heavily bruised giant kih. A fifth ranger held a drawn bow with the arrow's head right next to Grant's temple.

"Give up or he dies," the archer growled.

That archer would not hold out long against the poison ravaging his system. Grant deserved to live. A zarutc jab punched the bow back away from Grant's head. The string twanged as the arrow clattered down the hallway. Grant sagged. Khael swung his ethereal fist and slammed all five rangers into the nearest walls.

Grant sighed some kind of curse Khael opted not to decipher. The manacles slid off Grant's wrists as the huge knight collapsed to the floor.

"Paladins, see to my friend. He seems injured."

"I'll recover, thanks." Grant waved a feeble hand from the floor.

Two Paladins rushed over to him.

Versyna gurgled.

"I said—" Vixen tightened her stranglehold.

Khael held up an open palm. "Please. Let him speak."

She narrowed disapproving eyes, but she loosened her grip a touch. The man gagged and coughed in efforts to breathe.

"Impossible," he rasped. "You should be dead, blown to bits. All of us."

"I disarmed your device as we spoke." Khael slowly advanced to the dais. "Your men have been poisoned. Was that also part of your plan?" He took the stairs, one at a time, to the top level, a scant yard from the confined minister. An image of poisonous claws flashed into

Khael's mind. "Your brother tried that. He died from a pulverized ribcage."

"Verkamen?" Grief broke into Versyna's gasps. "You killed my brother?"

"He left me no choice. You can."

"My men shot you, in the heart. The bolt is still there in your chest. You should be dead. And my spell... is gone."

"I took it from you."

Versyna shuddered. "Impossible. No one can do all these things."

Under Vixen's watchful, loving gaze, Khael eased the bolt out of his chest. His energized tissues completed their not entirely painless healing behind its removal. He endured the affliction and held the bolt up before Versyna's incredulous hazel eyes. It shone clean, no trace of blood or flesh.

Khael raised his lips into a tolerant smirk. "What is impossible?"

44. Aftermath

Khael stared down the usurper. Versyna's anger gave way to bitter defeat.

"May I kill this scum now, my prince?" Vixen asked.

"You would kill your own brother?" Versyna asked. "You are lost."

"What brother calls his sister a faithless bitch?" She tightened her grip. "I have no family, certainly not sewage like you. No, wait. That's an insult to sewage."

"Hold him for a moment. Alive, please." Khael beckoned over his shoulder. "Damon, this Chelevkori minister requires special confinement and our tightest security."

"We'll arrange it post-haste, Sire." Damon's gruff rumble sounded more pleased than anything. "Paladins, shackle this... person's hands, feet an' neck, take him to a clean lock-down cell. If he speaks or so much as breathes unevenly, cut off whatever slows him down. If ye must, end him."

Khael sighed. "Use caution, my friends. This man is expert in all the Chelevkori spells of deceit and bodily weaponry."

Four Paladins moved in to relieve Vixen of her burden while ten others rounded up the injured bodyguards from the floor. As they finished hobbling the prisoners, Khael turned to face the noise of marching armored boots approaching the room. A knight in full steel plate armor clattered through the doors, his sword drawn. Ten more knights followed him, all poised to fight. None wore surcotes. Five Paladins assumed positions to block their advance.

"That's far enough," one of the Paladins ordered.

"Stand clear or your prince's 'no blood' rule may fail." The lead knight brandished the sword.

His kih and the sword's chronicon sheen grabbed Khael's attention. "Lieutenant Majestic, put up your sword."

Jack jerked his helmet open. To Khael's surprise, he looked relieved.

"Thank the stars, you live. Yes, I can do that, Your Highness. However, I claim that man as my prisoner." Jack pointed the gleaming weapon at Versyna. "He is bound to answer for sedition and multiple violations of the orders of the Secretariat."

"Fascinating, sir, but you have no authority here to make arrests."

No one moved. The Paladins who blocked Jack's path stood firm, their staves ready to engage the newcomers. Other Paladins around the throne room began a slow advance toward him. Jack nodded, sheathed his sword and raised his hands.

"My apologies, Your Highness, I was not sure you'd be here." Jack turned his head to the side. "Stand down before the prince." As his men sheathed their weapons, he saluted Khael and bowed. "It's centurion, not lieutenant. Our guise as among that traitor's men is no longer necessary."

"Don't trust him." Grant shook a feeble fist at the mystery knights. "He's stinking Chelevkori."

Jack returned Grant's furious glare with aplomb worthy of a diplomat. "I am neither Chelevkori nor do I stink any more than you, sir. I am a certified centurion of the Knighthood, and I will have your respect, regardless of your prejudices or our differences."

"Gentlemen." Khael raised his hand. "We will address this later. This usurper called for a public assembly on the lawn in less than half an hour. I shall hold it. Centurion, we can entertain your claims after that."

Grant nodded his accord.

Jack bowed. "By your command, Sire. I will return then."

"Thank you." As Jack took his men out, Khael faced the Paladins holding Versyna. "Before you take the prisoner away, may I have his weapons?"

One Paladin handed Khael a sheathed sword and dagger. He closed his eyes to check. Both weapons shone with the telltale kih of chronicon.

"You steal my weapons now?" Versyna's dull tone lacked even any pretend authority.

"You will not need them in custody. Your sword will be held for you. However, I believe you owe my collector restitution for your disrespect and violence."

"I don't want any of his junk." Vixen tossed her fiery hair in scornful disdain. "I need to wash my weapons as it is."

"The dagger is chronicon. It is twice as hard as steel, lighter weight, much easier to use and nearly unbreakable. I will not leave you unrewarded for your magnificent performance."

Her eyes wide and shining, Vixen bowed and kissed Khael's hand before she accepted the gift. "How can I refuse you anything, or thank you enough?"

Khael smiled. After all too brief a shared glance, he cleared his throat. "I believe all of Versyna's men, except his five bodyguards, require immediate treatment for poison."

"You would heal my men?" Amazed disbelief rang through Versyna's gruff utterance.

"Mystics revere all life." Khael took in Versyna's shock with a satisfaction that left his heart at ease. "Take these prisoners away." He turned back to the room. "The more men we save, the fewer others will suffer... and the more leverage we have for recompense for their damage.

"Paladins, clear this room. Bring those of the cordon who still live to the museum while I attend the fallen here.

"Desmond, we need a crew of demolitions experts. Post guards on all the locked rooms upstairs but do nothing else with them. Have someone raise the Cambridge banner on the roof.

"Trevor, gather the Watch and round up any surviving gray-shirts.

"Damon, have the grounds battalion prepare for the public and bring in any of Nechetnaya's surviving rangers. Move the dead to the bonfire pits.

"Grant, my dear friend, you require healing and rest. I will send for Mother's best."

Grant nodded, still woozy. Khael winced at the bruises that covered his knight from head to toe. A quick shuri would start his recovery. As everyone else carried out his orders, Khael headed down from the dais to attend to the nearest breathing gray-shirt.

"What can I do?" Vixen's question pierced Khael's tight focus.

"I would have you by my side, if you mind not."

Vixen's eyes shone with her smile. "By your command, my prince."

* * *

Khael stepped out the front door of the palace and took in a deep breath of the fresh morning air. A mild stink thinned as the breeze wafted away the smell of the many dead bodies. Treating the poison turned out to be far simpler and faster than he imagined, but he had only saved two hundred seven of the afflicted men, less than a fourth of their total number. Grant had been easier to treat.

Lyla slipped in during the confusion to coordinate the palace clean-up. She also delivered a message from his mother. Sinaeg had arranged the poison for more than seven hundred of the gray-shirts. The majority lay dead along the harbor, on the slopes, and around the Center.

Khael shook his head. He disapproved, but his mother usually acted as she thought best. "Someone will need to clean up all the bodies."

A short respite gave him time to recover his well-spent zhukih and grieve for the fallen. Now he stood tall, delighted to be alive and whole. The woman by his side might yet turn out to be a fine life-partner, if she did not kill him on the way. Many new questions floated through his mind from what had happened inside, compounding the mystery about this beautiful, vibrant soul.

Vixen practically glowed ecstatic joy at being near him. Underneath his cool, he seethed, unable to hold her, kiss her and more. The sensible fraction of his mind prickled with caution about her background, her history, the plethora of unknowns and paradoxes about her that still implied a risk to his life. In a curious irony, Versyna's defeat may have furthered the Chelevkori plot with her that he suspected, driving her closer to him, giving her more access.

A dozen Paladins surrounded them, fully armed with their usual, sharp weaponry. The house battalion would have to do away with edged weapons to preserve his rule. That would improve all the Paladins' versatility as they rotated through the diverse duties of the five battalions. He winced. Damon needed to discipline the knights who deserted and replace them.

Hundreds of people had gathered on the lawn in response to the usurper's summons. The crowd spilled out across the streets, bringing traffic to a halt. A concern nibbled at him over assassination attempts or the chance of his Paladins engaging in bloodletting. He shook the feeling off. Such depressing portents had no chance of success today,

When he reached the head of the stairs, the crowd began to cheer and applaud. The ruckus raised his high spirits, but it went on too long. He raised his hand and the noise gradually died away.

"Thank you, my people." Khael closed his eyes briefly to choose his words. "I most humbly apologize to you for what has happened here for the last six months. We will have no more regents."

Another round of appreciation made him pause for a several seconds.

"I regret to confirm that your true viceroy, John Masterson, Earl of Aistpynt, is dead. A Minister of the Chelevkori, one Versyna Nechetnaya, has impersonated him since sometime this past July when he was murdered. Accordingly, all members of the Viceroy's Guard, or those in the Skemmelsham Watch who served only the viceroy and since 2790 July 1, are hereby remanded into Paladin and true Watch custody."

A murmur of approval rolled across the lawn.

"I hereby grant unconditional amnesty to all other persons present here or those detained in any jail, warehouse or other prison in this city."

Cheer-filled applause erupted, loudest from those who had just been freed. Khael raised his hand. The noise died down until everyone waited in silence for his next words.

"The Royal Court of Shielin is recessed until we restore normal operations. All laws, rules, regulations, taxes, fees, penalties, fines, or any acts of the regency since this past July 1 are hereby rescinded and void. All monies collected under this system will be refunded in full per official state records."

People jumped up and down, cheered, shouted and stamped. The thunder drowned out any chance of his going on. Khael held himself tall on the stairs above the excited throng. He waved to the crowd while the sounds of fireworks exploding above the roof punched through the racket. That noise would not quiet down enough for further address.

Khael headed back into the throne room and ascended the dais, this time to sit on his throne. He perched on the front edge of the seat, too energized to lean back. Vixen slithered onto his lap, wrapped her arms around him and planted a soft kiss his lips.

Such behavior violated their contract and comprised a total breach of protocol. A prince should insist she desist right away.

Not this time. He enjoyed and returned the gift. The sweetness of her lips on his, the way her tender body perfectly molded into his invigorated him. He broke the kiss before his mind flew into total distraction, but he pulled her into a closer embrace.

"I'm so happy for you," she whispered in his ear.

He pushed her back to find her eyes bright with watery joy. His heart shivered at what he had to do. "Vixen, we cannot do this."

She bowed her head and reluctantly stood beside him. He failed to let go of her one hand that clung to his with firm determination.

The cold, dusty air in the room reminded him of the work left to do or have done. The missing carpets needed to be found or replaced and re-laid once the disgraced floor was clean enough, and the braziers had to be re-lighted. Words to get these tasks underway flowed with ease.

Grant slipped in through a side door, fully equipped and armored. His shaven head stood out starkly, bereft of all the shaggy hair he had complained about. Khael smiled.

A Paladin stuck her head in the door after a short knock. "There's a knight here to see ye, Sire. He says ye offered him some time, one Centurion Jack Majestic, formerly o' the Viceroy's Guard. Should 'na we arrest him?"

"No, let him in."

Three Paladins escorted Jack. He wore a small gold pin on the collar of a brown surcote with ivory sleeves. Colors similar to the ancient formal robes of the Chelevkori...

"Centurion Majestic, come forward."

Jack bowed. "I beg forgiveness of my deception, Sire. My name is Zhak Muzhestov. I come on behalf of the Secretariat of Ostrova to apply for full diplomatic relations with Shielin. I wish I could have told you all this before, but I did not feel it appropriate, and I understand your strategy better now."

"Not Meridium?" At Zhak's nod, Khael tilted his head, curious. "To what end?"

"Our nation wishes to restore our ties with all mankind. The Secretariat feels Your Highness may be least inclined to refuse us. If you accept, in spite of the Hierarch's illegal vendetta against your family, other nations might be persuaded to follow."

"Are the Chelevkori and Secretariat disjoint?"

"Not— entirely, no. Three of the Church's Council of Priests are secretaries, along with six civilians elected from general population. The Hierarch opposes this. Our other two secretary ministers proposed it."

"Don't believe him, Sire." Grant's words drew nods from the Paladins. "Just another sneaky Chelevkori trick."

"We can discuss my allegiances later, Ensign," Zhak said coldly.

"We will discuss this all later." Khael raised his hand at the two knights who bristled at each other. "The court is closed for today, but you may see Lord MacGray this afternoon for such an appointment. You and your men are free until we speak again, though I suggest less formal attire."

"Thank you, Sire. Best fortune to you." Zhak bowed and stalked out of the court.

"He belongs in chains." Grant's eyes glittered under his narrowed lids. "He was usurper's chief executioner from my information."

"No, and he is not." Khael made a curious frown. "Where is Eugene?" He glanced at Grant. "Please ask Desmond to report back here at once."

The towering knight stomped off, stiff but fast. Vixen had been staring at Khael continuously since Grant's comment. Her beautiful green eyes glowed large at Khael. He gazed back. A joyous rush filled his chest. It flagged as their reality set in.

Desmond and Grant returned through the east door right when another disturbance clattered from outside in front. The doors rattled. The same Paladin stuck her head inside.

"Dame Lyla Kincaid and a raft o' two dozen are here to start the clean-up, Sire."

"We will leave this room shortly." Khael stood. "Remind her to stay clear of the guards and any locked rooms and thank her for the prompt response."

The door closed.

"The builders have sent a crew to take out the explosives, Sire," Desmond's voice echoed in the near-empty chamber. "Yet I'm no' truly certain where they are."

"One is strung around the inside edges of the ceiling here, likely inside the upstairs floor. It should be accessible without disturbing any of the locked rooms if they are careful."

"Thank ye, Sire, I'll pass the word to them right away."

"Thank you, Desmond. Please have the house guard keep any persons who come by outside the palace. Only Paladins and known staff can be inside until that is done."

Desmond nodded. "Will that be all, Sire?"

"Where is Lord MacGray?"

"I hear he's across the street supervising his office cleanup. He should be back soon."

Khael nodded. "We must sweep the palace to disarm all remaining traps and verify its safety. As the senior officer who endured the usurper's reign and coordinated our infiltration, I ask you to conduct us around."

"By yer command, Sire." Desmond hesitated.

"Yes?"

"The traps could be extremely dangerous. We've isolated twenty-seven locked rooms in the main building and none in the wings. Many o' the former sit right above the throne room. Also, yer suite on the fifth floor, while wide open, is sealed wi' guards. The earl ne'er stayed there, but one o' his people was in there earlier, an' it too may be fraught with murderous contrivances."

"Excellent work, Desmond." Khael managed a weary smile. "I suspect many of the locked rooms are filled with explosives. Dangerous or not, we are the best qualified for the task."

* * *

"Welcome to the royal suite," Khael said.

Vixen took in the simple elegance of the suite with round eyes. Grant sank into an armchair near the wide main doors. Khael went into his room to wash his face and hands. When he came out, he collapsed on the chair facing Grant, pleasantly relieved. He thought he might finally catch his breath when Vixen took his hand and sighed.

"This is so nice." She stared at him, her eyes still wide. "You really did it."

"You helped."

She hung her head. "I didn't do all that much—"

"You expertly took down three of Versyna's guards and prevented his escape."

"I'd have had more trouble if those other three hadn't back-flipped off the dais for me."

Khael snickered. "I believe I did that. A sort of zarute backlash at being shot. Grant's escort suffered a similar disablement."

Vixen's eyes widened. She seemed quite dazzled with him.

"However, I must admit I have many questions. About you."

Vixen gulped. "When I said I live to serve you, I meant it."

"I trust you. How are you Versyna's sister?"

"I'm not."

Khael tipped his head, puzzled. She seemed to believe what she said, but his chokkan itched as if it were not entirely true. "Could he be the older boy you remember from your childhood?"

Vixen's face went blank. She rolled her eyes from side to side toward the ceiling, as if searching for an answer. When she spoke, her words came slow and halting. "I suppose... I can't see his face anymore."

"We will have to settle that, as soon as you are ready."

"I guess, just not right now, please? I'd like to enjoy your triumph and this setting."

Khael's insides shivered at the potential danger. He craved to trust her more. Not yet. Her clandestine history held too many connections to the Chelevkori. With a resigned sigh, he squeezed her hand. "Would you say this differs from my room at Strattonmoor?"

Vixen chuckled. "Differs? This is a whole new world, like a fairy tale or fantasy epic."

"This is my home."

She gazed around the room again. As she stared into his bedroom, her face slowly shifted from beaming joy to horrified distress. His hand slipped out of her limp fingers.

A knot formed in his chest as her skin paled. "You dislike the décor?"

Vixen shook her head slowly. "What's that room?" She pointed with her new chronicon dagger.

Khael raised his eyebrows in shock. She seemed unaware that she had drawn the weapon. "That is my bedroom."

"And beyond it?"

"A large balcony with a pool. What makes you ask?"

Her beautiful green eyes widened with horror as they finally settled on his. "Khael, your bed is where I killed you in my nightmare."

* * * * *

M. A. Richter

About the Author

M.A. Richter

Even before his long career in software development, he has been a lifelong, avid fan of mythology, science fiction and fantasy works.

As a child, he immersed himself in Edith Hamilton's "Mythology," reading it probably hundreds of times. He also enjoyed C. S. Lewis' "Narnia" series many times until he found his true love of fantasy — "The Lord of the Rings", including "The Hobbit."

While in high school, he ghost wrote what might have become the "Encyclopedia Hobbitannica," if that had not been published first. Isaac Asimov, Robert Heinlein and Frank Herbert are among his favorite SF writers.

When he was introduced to the adventures of fantasy role-playing games with "Empire of the Petal Throne," he became enamored with the idea of creating worlds filled with different life-forms and a wide variety of professional guilds.

He began writing full-length novels in high school, and he considers "Mystic Prince" to be the first of many published novels to come.

Made in the USA
Middletown, DE
03 August 2022

70483018R00210